play*date*

Also by Alex Dahl

The Boy at the Door
The Heart Keeper

playdate

ALEX DAHL

HEAD
ZEUS

First published in the UK in 2020 by Head of Zeus Ltd

9 7 5 3 1 2 4 6 8

A catalogue record for this book is available from
the British Library.

ISBN (HB): 9781789544077
ISBN (XTPB): 9781789544084
ISBN (E): 9781789544022

Typeset by Siliconchips Services Ltd UK

Printed and bound in Great Britain by
CPI Group (UK) Ltd, Croydon CR0 4YY

To Laura, with so much love

'An act of justice closes the book on a misdeed; an act of vengeance writes one of its own.'

—MARILYN VOS SAVANT

I hold you close, so close that it is as though we are one, once again. As though no force in the entire world could ever take you from me. Your fine, long hair brushes against my face and I breathe in its sweet scent; earth and flowers. Your fingertips braid together at the nape of my neck, your skin warm against mine. I bury my face in the damp, hot hollow at your collarbone. I don't know where we are. All I can see is you. And I know that I have to hold on to you, tighter than I've ever held on to anything in my life.

But still. Still, a sliver of space is cracked open between us, bringing a rush of ice-cold air. Still, your tiny fingers are peeled from my neck and you are lifted clean away from me. My eyes are wide open, but they can see nothing but the densest, cruelest darkness. My mouth, too, is wide open – in a scream, but no sound will come. My arms are empty, now, but your warmth lingers on my skin.

And you, my love, are gone.

I wake up. It is still pitch black. You are still gone. I scream.

October 2017

I

Elisa

Sandefjord, 19 October 2017

I've had the day off, cramming all the things I never normally have time for into the afternoon – highlights and a trim, nails, a half-hearted hour at the gym, and I'm almost late for pick-up. First, I got stuck in bad traffic by the E18 motorway exit, and then Lyder decided to throw a fit when I picked him up from nursery, dropping to the floor like a slab of meat, flopping around in my arms and rolling his eyes back as I shoved his limp limbs into his winter suit.

'Stop it,' I hissed, pushing his stockinged feet into his sheepskin boots before grabbing his lunch box, an enormous cardboard artwork and his nursery folder in one hand, my other hand half-dragging my son out the door. 'Come on!'

In the car, Lyder whines about the fact that I haven't brought him a snack.

'Everyone else gets raisins after nursery,' he wails. 'Or carrots. Or biscuits. Carl gets biscuits, the kind with chocolate bits in them, it isn't fair...' I block out his thin voice droning on and on. It's been a long week and I feel the beginnings of a headache at the back of my skull. I press my finger to the spot that hurts, staring at a red light taking forever. Three minutes left until pick-up time. Four minutes before Aud, the sour-faced woman running the after-school club, starts stabbing my phone number with her long acrylic nails.

The light turns green and I drive fast down the last few quiet suburban roads to Korsvik School, making Lyder giggle nervously in the back seat at the squeal of the tires. I pull up in front of the school and hand Lyder my iPhone, his face breaking into a surprised smile. It's 4.29 – I made it.

'I'll be right back,' I say, and hurry across the school yard to the brightly lit red wooden building.

'Mamma!' squeals Lucia and runs towards me. She jumps into my arms and I kiss her soft golden hair. 'You're late.'

'No, I'm right on time, actually.'

'Can I go home with Josephine?'

'Who's Josephine?'

'She's a new girl in my class. Can I? Please?'

'Not today, sweetie. You know we have to arrange playdates ahead of time, it's just easier.'

'Her mom said it's fine. They're waiting, in the cloakroom.'

'Sweetheart…'

'Please, Mamma.' Lucia points through the open doorway to the changing area shared by first- and second-graders.

I sigh and go through with her. A little girl wearing a beautiful pink quilted Moncler jacket and moon boots sits on the bench in the far corner, next to an equally chic-looking mother.

'Hi,' I say, and smile at them both. When the girl smiles back I notice that the left side of her face creases strangely, and then I realize it is a circular, puckered scar cupping her cheek, reaching all the way to her hairline at her temple.

'Hello, I'm Line, Josephine's mother,' says the woman and smiles widely. She is beautiful, the kind of beautiful that has the power to instantly disarm people. Her eyes are wide-set and clear blue, her hair is thick and dark, curling perfectly around her shoulders, and her lips are plump and shiny with nude gloss. She is wearing a khaki version of her daughter's Moncler jacket – cinched at her tiny waist, a white cashmere polo neck, and elegant, knee-high olive-green leather boots.

'Nice to meet you. I'm Elisa. Elisa Blix.' I turn to Lucia. 'We need to hurry, sweets, Lyder is waiting alone in the car.'

'I want to go to Josephine's house!'

'It's absolutely fine with us,' says Line. 'The girls have been asking for a playdate for a while, and we're not doing anything this afternoon.'

'Right,' I say. 'Well, okay, if you're sure.'

'Absolutely sure. Let me give you my number. We live on Asnestoppen, so not far from here.'

'Okay. I'll pick her up around six thirty, if that works?'

'Six thirty is perfect.'

'When did Josephine start? I don't think I've met you before.'

'Pretty new. We moved here from Oslo at the beginning of term.'

'Ah, okay. Liking it so far?'

'Yeah. Josie has settled really well at school and my older son is happy at his senior school, too.'

'Oh, great,' I say, and we smile at each other again. I like her; I could imagine us being friends. There is something calm and centered about her, and I suppose I am quite awe-struck by her seemingly effortless elegance. The girls, too, seem to like each other – as Line and I speak, they do an intricate clapping game I can't remember seeing Lucia do before, then they burst into fits of high-pitched giggles.

'Do you want to call my phone from yours, that way I have your number too?' she says.

'Sorry, I've left my phone in the car with my son. Why don't you just call me, and I'll drop you a text in a sec?'

'Sure.'

'Okay, have fun on your playdate, girls,' I say and give the faux-fur blob on the top of Lucia's hat a little tug.

She laughs and walks away with Line and Josephine, holding Josephine's hand, the two of them skipping in sync, the sound of their squeaky rubber-soled boots reverberating around the empty corridor.

It's just before six when my phone vibrates. It's a picture message from Line, of Josephine and Lucia sitting close together on a huge white sofa in matching pink princess dresses, laughing and cradling a shaggy brown cat. Its paws are crusty with dirt as if just came in from outside, and its eyes are bright yellow and mesmerizing. I am still staring at it when the phone begins to ring in my hand.

'Hello?'

'Mamma?' Lucia's light voice is hiccupy with giggles.

I smile. 'Hey baby,' I say, 'I'm just about to get ready to come get you, okay?'

'Yeah, but Mamma, we were wondering... could we have a sleepover? Please oh please oh please!'

'Oh.' Lucia has never slept at a friend's house before, though at seven, some of the girls in the class have started sleeping over. I know my daughter isn't a particularly anxious child, but she doesn't know Josephine that well, and I've never even been to their house.

'Mamma, please! It's Friday!'

'I know. Just... you don't have any of your stuff with you. And you've not been on a sleepover before.'

'Yeah I have! With Julie!'

'Yes, but she's your cousin. I don't know.'

'It's so fun here! Mamma, please! Here, talk to Josephine's mom.' The phone goes quiet for a moment, then Line's voice fills my ear.

'Hi there, Elisa. What a fun girl you have! The two of them are having such a good time.'

'Yes,' I say, 'Lucia sounded very happy.'

'So, you gathered the girls have been asking for a sleepover. What do you think? It is totally fine with me. My husband is in New York for work and doesn't get back until tomorrow and Josephine is generally easier to deal with when she has a buddy around, so I don't mind in the slightest.'

'Oh. Okay. Yes, well, it's just that Lucia hasn't slept at a friend's house before.'

'Right. Well, I mean, we could try, and if she feels like going home, I could just give you guys a call and you could collect her?'

'Yes. Yes, I suppose that would work. Okay, so I will

7

need to pop round with her stuff. You know, toothbrush, pajamas, teddy, of course.'

'Sure.'

Fredrik walks through the door so red in the face from the fierce wind it looks like he's been slapped.

'Hi,' he says, pecking me on the cheek. 'Where are the kids?'

'Lyder is zonked out in front of *The Lego Movie* upstairs and Lucia is at a classmate's house. She's been asked to sleep over, actually.'

'Oh, right.'

'That's okay, I suppose?'

'Yeah, I don't see why not. We can put Lyder to bed early and get some us-time.' He winks at me and runs a light hand across my bottom before grabbing a bottle of Mexican beer from the fridge, snapping its cap off and taking a long glug from it, his Adam's apple rising and falling in his throat.

'Yes, it actually works quite well. My flight tomorrow is at nine, so you could just have a slow morning with Lyder and then go get Lucia sometime before lunch.'

'Yeah, okay. What time do you think you'll be back?'

'I land at five thirty.'

'Was it Milan?'

'No, Rome.'

'Lucky you.'

'Well, it's not like I'll see anything other than the airport, honey.'

'And blue skies.'

'True. There is that.' I smile at my husband and go into

the hallway to pull my boots on. I am driving, but I still put on a woolen hat – though it is only October, winter seems to have come fast on icy winds from the east.

'Hi,' says Line, 'come on in.'

I step into a large, immaculately tidy hallway with a vaulted ceiling and expensive-looking spotlights. When I take my boots off, my feet are immediately warmed by underfloor heating. I hear children laughing upstairs, and when we go up into a huge open living space, Lucia and Josephine are doing cartwheels, still in princess dresses, stopping only to heave for breath through peals of laughter.

'Wow, what a beautiful house you have,' I say. It's all sleek modernity, with unbroken white surfaces, quite the contrast to our home, which is full of family photographs, boxes of toys, kids' drawings tacked onto walls. This is clearly the kind of family who can answer an unexpected house call without worrying about piles of shoes in the hallway, towering dishes in the sink, overflowing laundry bins in the bathroom, half-eaten jam sandwiches abandoned on windowsills. Unlike us.

The house is built at the very top of a rocky hill, above Asnes beach on the Vesterøya peninsula, with no immediate neighbors. One wall is entirely glass, looking out onto the rugged coastline dotted with patches of forest and a moody ocean rolling out far below us, its frothy crests occasionally visible in the sweeping lights from the lighthouse across the bay.

'Thank you,' says Line. 'We're really happy with it. I think I saw half the houses in Sandefjord before we finally bought this one.' She laughs and so do I. 'Do you want a tea? Or a glass of wine?'

'I have to get back to my son before he goes to bed around seven thirty,' I say. 'I promised him a bedtime story.'

Line smiles, and I am struck again by how beautiful she is.

'Sure. Just a quick one then?'

I nod and she returns after a moment with two glasses of champagne. 'It is Friday, after all.' We could definitely be friends. I follow the crawl of a droplet of condensation down the outside of the glass, then raise it towards Line in a little toast.

'Maman,' says Josephine, '*regarde*!'

Line claps as Josephine does a wobbly double-cartwheel, then collapses onto the carpet.

'You speak French?'

'Yeah, sometimes. Josephine used to go to the French school in Oslo. We figured another language is always an advantage.'

I feel suddenly dull and painfully average next to this glamorous woman and her sophisticated daughter. 'I see. And, yes, you're absolutely right, such an advantage.'

'What about you guys? Are you from around here? It is a really nice place to live, isn't it?'

'It *is* nice. Quiet, I guess, but still central. I'm from Lillehammer originally, and my husband is from Sandefjord, so we chose to live here as he works in Tønsberg and I work out of Torp Airport. It takes me less than twenty minutes to get home from there.'

'Ah. So what do you do?'

'I'm a flight attendant. For Nordic Wings.'

Line's eyes light up. 'Oh wow. That must be a fun career.

I always had a vision of myself as a flight attendant when I was much younger. Sometimes I wish I'd pursued it.'

'It can be fun. But it gets less and less glamorous, put it that way. I used to work long-haul, for Qatar, before the kids. That was probably more like the vision most people have of the job.'

Line smiles and takes another sip of her champagne.

'Then, when we had the kids, I started working for Scandinavian Airlines, but commuting to Oslo Airport got pretty exhausting – two hours' drive each way was just too much – so I started with Nordic Wings three years ago. It's been great for this region, to have a new low-cost airline connecting us to lots of European destinations, but it's hardly glamorous. Anyway. What about you – are you working?'

'Yes, I am a make-up artist. For TV, but I work freelance.'

'Now, that sounds like fun. Do you get to meet anyone famous?'

'Nah. I do mostly newsreaders.'

'Right.'

'It's easy to combine with the kids, though. You know – flexible. I only take jobs when I can see they'll work around whatever the kids have on, as well as my husband's schedule. He travels a lot for work.'

'What does your husband do?' I try to imagine the husband – he must be quite the guy to attract someone like Line.

'He, uh… He's a banker. He works with investment stuff for a… a French bank. Paribas.'

I smile and nod – Line sounds just like me when people ask me what Fredrik does – *Uh, something to do with financial law in, umm, a law firm.* We speak for another couple of minutes about the girls and how well they get on, and I give Line Fredrik's phone number so they can make arrangements for pick-up tomorrow.

I stand up and walk over to where Lucia and Josephine are playing the clapping game again.

'Mamma has to go home now, sweetie,' I say, but Lucia barely glances up. 'Sure you want to sleep over?' She nods, not going to break the chant.

'My name is funky lady,
Lady funky, what you got?
One, two, three, clap!
One, two, three,
One clap, two clap, triple clap!'

'If you need to speak to me, just call, okay?'
Lucia nods again.

'I've brought you your stuff. Minky Mouse is in the bag, too.'

She smiles and steps into my arms in a close hug. Her forehead and neck are sweaty from the exertion of the cartwheeling, and I kiss her hot red cheek. 'I love you.'

'Love you, too,' says Lucia.

'Let's play twins again,' shouts Josephine, grabbing Lucia by the arm.

'Yeah! Let's!'

'Lucia is my twin!'

I smile, first at the girls, then at Line. Looking at them with their arms wrapped around each other, grinning widely, each exposing several missing teeth, they could well be twins, except for Josephine's thick chestnut hair and Lucia's fine blonde hair. They have quite similar brown eyes and full lips.

'Have fun, little twinnies,' I say and go back downstairs, trailed by Line. She gives me a little wave as I step into the cold darkness outside. I stand a moment outside the house looking up at thin drifts of clouds being pulled across the sky by the brisk wind. Tomorrow will be bumpy.

2

Elisa

20 October

We're almost an hour delayed when we push back from the gate, but the pilots are confident we'll recover the time with the strong tail wind. I close all the galley lockers and run through the check-list, then speak to the passengers as we taxi away from the terminal. Gloomy clouds churn above us: another grey and windy day.

'Welcome on board this Nordic Wings flight to Rome Fiumicino. Please pay attention to the security information playing on the screens above you. We wish you a pleasant flight with Nordic Wings.'

I close my eyes briefly as the plane is lined up ready on the runway, then the pilot urges the throttle and we shoot down the tarmac. The plane takes off, trembling through the low clouds, then settles into a smooth glide as we surface into the bright blues above them. I lean back in the jump seat and smile at a baby perched on its father's knee in the second row. The baby waves at me with a chubby fist and I wave back. I wonder how Lucia is getting on at her sleepover. I texted Line just before I had to put my phone on flight mode, to say Fredrik was free to pick her up whenever suits them best, and to just get in touch with him directly.

As we continue to climb, I make some small talk with the trainee flight attendant sitting on the jump seat next to me. Her name is Charlotte, and in less than five minutes I learn that she is from a small town in Northern Norway, that she is really, really into manga and likes to dress as her favorite character, a pink-haired schoolgirl called Taya. She also tells me that she has just moved in with her boyfriend, but that he's a bit of a man-child.

I'm pleased when the signal sounds and get up, motioning for Charlotte to do the same. I run through the check-lists on auto-pilot: bathroom check, coffee, oven started, trolley checked. I love that no two days are the same on my job, and yet all the routines are reassuringly repetitive.

By the time we begin to approach Rome and I sit back down in the jump seat, I realize that I'm feeling so tired I could actually fall asleep, slumping against the constraints of my three-point belt. I guess many people have it like this. I've read that it's a result of the stresses of modern life, especially for women. Work, children, relationships. We just don't get any breaks.

It doesn't have to be more complicated than that – those things are enough to make anyone feel exhausted from time to time. I close my eyes and listen to the clunk of the landing gear extending. One of our most senior pilots is flying us in today and he touches down so smoothly I'm not immediately sure whether we have actually landed. I smile at the passengers, and watch the terminal buildings come into view, shining softly in brilliant sunlight. My husband was right – lucky me.

It's not until all the passengers have been wished a very '*buongiorno*' and ushered off the plane that I get five seconds to myself. It's just gone two o'clock and I grab a sandwich from the kiosk by the gate and sit down in the crew room by the departure gate. I flick my phone from flight mode to roaming and call Fredrik.

'*Ciao, bello*,' I say when he picks up. I work hard, these days, at keeping up the banter between us. Marriages grow stone cold easier than one might think, and I don't want it to happen to ours – we've come too far.

'Hey there, how's Rome?'

'Gorgeous, I'm sure. I've literally got fifteen minutes before I need to go back on and prep for the return. How did Lucia's sleepover go?'

'She's not back yet. I spoke to the mom this morning, they've gone to the pool.'

'Oh, right. When are you going to pick her up?'

'She said she'd drop her back home around three.'

'Okay, cool. And Lyder?'

'My parents came and took him to the Reptile Museum in Larvik.'

'Lucky kids. And what's Daddy up to this afternoon while I slave away?'

'Isn't that pretty obvious? Flat out on the sofa with *Game of Thrones*. Duh.'

My husband chuckles before we hang up, and an image of him this morning flits into my mind. He was still sleeping when I slipped from the bed at six, but I paused a moment at the door, watching him in the shaft of light from the hallway. He was on his front and naked, facing me, his eyelids quivering. His buttocks were pale and he still had a clear tan line from our trip to Tenerife two weeks ago.

I remember last night's sex, how he propped me up against the headboard, how hard he tugged my hair, how excited his short, hot breath felt in my ear as he came. I feel myself blushing and turn my thoughts to my groaning stomach – I haven't even had breakfast. I bite into my sandwich and close my eyes as I chew sundried tomatoes and plump fresh mozzarella. When I finish, it's time to get back on the plane. I brush some crumbs off my navy uniform skirt, then glance at my phone again. I decide to message Line. It is so kind of her to take the girls swimming on top of a sleepover.

> Hi there, hope all is well with you guys. Thank you so much for taking L to the pool! We'd love to have Josephine over soon, too. Perhaps next week? All best, Elisa x

Back on the plane I prepare the cabin with the rest of the crew. The captain tells us we are going to be at least half an hour late pushing back as we arrived late and missed our slot. While I love my job, I get so tired of delays, especially because it means cranky passengers, and funnily enough, an asshole tends to turn into a mega asshole in the air. Still, I should be home by seven, and I'm looking forward to our Saturday night family ritual of watching a talent show, a big bowl of candy on the table and the kids sleepily snuggling against me and Fredrik. We're lucky. So lucky. How did I deserve all of that?

I call the gate and tell them to let the passengers through the jet way. There's an almost instant rumble of wheelie bags and stomping feet, and I focus on placing my best flight attendant smile back on my face. My phone vibrates in my pocket and I quickly pull it out so I can put it on flight mode, then away. I glance at the time, 3.47, then the message, from Fredrik.

> btw did you hear anything from Josephine's mom? She said she'd drop her back by 3 and they aren't here yet. I need to go get Lyder soon...

I take a deep breath. Seriously. What is it with men? I'm in Rome, on a plane, at work, *and* having to deal with playdate logistics back home. It's always the same story. I'll be at Copenhagen airport, rushing to grab a quick snack before getting back on the plane and I'll get a message from my husband saying 'I'm not going to make pick-up and could I please find someone to help out?' Or I'll be boarding a flight to Madrid and Fredrik messages me to ask 'Where's Lyder's gym bag and what does it even look like?'

The flight is just over half-full – seventy-two adults and seven under-twelves. I sit back down next to Charlotte and avoid the usual small talk as the plane pulls back and begins to taxi. I'm feeling a little distracted, no doubt due to Fredrik's dubious organizational skills. But... but what if something is wrong? An accident at the pool? A car crash? Or someone taken ill – an allergy perhaps? Lucia once had a small reaction to sesame seeds, I didn't think to mention that to Line, maybe she's given her a sesame-something and my child has had an anaphylactic reaction and Line's phone battery is flat so she can't even get in touch?

Stop it, I say to myself. *Stop.* Still, my heart is thudding heavily in my chest and I wish I could just check my phone one last time before takeoff, but it's locked in the crew locker. The plane picks up speed and it clunks noisily against the tarmac lights on the runway before lifting off. I squirm in my seat and fix my gaze at a point just above the overhead luggage compartments, focusing on deep, even breaths.

The pilots give us the clearance signal and I stand up to start the coffee, before running through the after takeoff check-list. My breathing feels shallow and strange. I've struggled with anxiety for many years now, but this time it's particularly bad and I have to hold on to the side of the drinks trolley to regain control of myself. I run through my breathing exercises over and over but I can feel my face grow red and am certain my colleagues and the passengers can tell something is wrong.

'Are you okay?' asks Charlotte.

'Yeah. Yeah, sorry, just a little bit of vertigo. It happens sometimes. After years in the air.'

She nods but looks concerned.

The passengers' seat belt sign is switched off, and immediately people start unbuckling their seat belts and moving down the aisle towards us.

Come on, I say to myself. *Get it together.* I wish I could have a drink, but that's obviously not an option. I managed to wean myself off diazepam last year, after a long and devoted love affair with sedatives, though now I wish I hadn't.

I smile, answer questions, serve coffee, smile some more,

ALEX DAHL

all the while trying to keep my focus on the cool metal of
the trolley beneath my fingertips. *You can do this*, I tell
myself, again and again. But I'm not sure I can. My thoughts
race wildly, and it feels like the plane is flying faster than it
should. I imagine it dropping through the clouds, lurching
uncontrollably, then smashing to the ground, disintegrating
in a blur of flames and smoke. It's like the sensation of speed
is tearing at me, ripping my skin off.

I lock myself in the bathroom for a long while and hold
my own gaze in the mirror. 'It's okay,' I whisper, but tears
spill down my cheeks, drawing charcoal lines of mascara.
It is only when Charlotte knocks on the door, at first softly,
then insistently, that I manage to regain some control of
myself. I reapply my mascara, then step back into the bright
cabin, the familiar whoosh of the engines momentarily
calming, and I smile with a confidence I don't feel.

We land at Torp just after six thirty. By the time all the
passengers have disembarked and I've finished the check-
lists, I am so tired I can barely think straight. Fredrik and I
shared a bottle of wine last night after Lyder went to bed,
and all the sex meant we didn't get to sleep until past 1 a.m.
I just want to go home and collapse onto the sofa. I grab
my stuff and switch flight mode off. I'm walking through
the jet way when my phone picks up a signal. Immediately
it begins to twitch and chime in my hand. Six missed calls
from Fredrik and five unread WhatsApp messages. My eyes
automatically go first to the most recent, sent four minutes
ago, and my blood runs cold.

Have you landed? Hurry through. I'm at arrivals, waiting
for you. Hurry, Elisa.

20

3

Elisa

Fredrik's face is crumpled, pale, perplexed, frightened. I race towards him, the clack of my court shoes reverberating around the arrivals area of Torp Airport. I sense people's alarmed glances; it isn't normal to suddenly run without reason.

'What is it?' I manage. 'Why are you here? Where are the kids?'

'I... I can't find Lucia.'

'What do you mean you can't find her?'

'The mom didn't bring her back at three, like we arranged.'

'What? Why? Why did she say they were late?'

We rush through the revolving doors into a windy drizzle before dashing across the road to the short-stay car park.

'I've been calling and messaging her on the number you gave me, but it just goes straight to voicemail.'

'Shit, I must have given you the wrong number.'

We stop for a brief moment at the parking lot's payment machine, catching our breaths, searching each other's eyes.

Yes, that must be it. Wrong number. I pull my phone out. No new messages or missed calls. I don't get it – even if I gave Fredrik the wrong number, Line has mine. Why hasn't she called if she's going to be four fucking hours delayed dropping my kid back?

'Wait, you said she called you this morning about the pool. So you must have her number.'

Fredrik retrieves his credit card from the machine and we half run across the rain-lashed parking lot. A jet taking off directly above us drowns out his reply.

'What?' I shout.

'I said she called from a private number.'

'What?'

We get in the car and stare at each other in the hushed, cold space.

'I didn't really think about it at the time… But I guess that's a little… weird.'

'What the fuck? Fredrik, what the actual fuck? Why didn't you tell me that when I called you from Rome?'

'I didn't think about it. I… There wasn't anything weird about the conversation, so I guess I didn't really react.'

We wait in line to exit the parking lot, both of us staring straight ahead at the cars in front of us, spewing coils of smoke into the cold air, desperately trying to think of a reason, any reason, why Line hasn't been in touch.

'Look,' I say, in an attempt to calm myself down more than anything, 'I'm sure there is a good explanation for this. She must have lost the phone. Or… Or maybe her kid got sick or something. Maybe she sent a message that the girls are just playing at their house or whatever, and we didn't receive the message for whatever reason.'

'They aren't at the house. Asnestoppen 25, right?'

'Yes. How do you know they're not there?'

'I drove there. Twice. I went to the pool too. They weren't in the cafeteria and I couldn't see them in the main pool or the kiddie pool either.'

'Was there a car in the driveway, at the house?'

'No.'

'Here, take a left here. We need to go there right now.'

Fredrik glances at me, then indicates and takes the second exit at the large roundabout with a fountain at its center. We pass the ferries and boats in Sandefjord's harbor, then the empty sea-front restaurants, now closed down for the winter.

'Honey,' he says, 'I think we need to call the police.'

'What? No. No, it's a misunderstanding. It has to be. Come on, it's Sandefjord. Safest place on earth. I mean, she can't... Nothing bad has happened, I know it's just a crazy misunderstanding.'

Fredrik drives fast towards Vesterøya. Not fast enough. My breathing is shallow and I've dug my nails into the palms of my hands. Every conceivable worst-case scenario rushes at me, and I clamp my eyes shut and though I haven't prayed in so many years, I begin to silently pray. *Please, please, please, not Lucia. Not Lucia. Let this be one of those fucking awful –* 'Oh remember that time when we really thought something terrible had happened and it all turned out to be the silliest of misunderstandings.'

Fredrik hardly slows down and the car lurches off the main road and onto the coastal road leading to Asnes. Seawater floods the road and we speed through the deep puddles, sending tall volleys of water onto the pavements.

I press my hand against the hammering pulse on my neck. This is real. It's 7.19 and I can't think of a single good reason why Lucia hasn't been brought back or why Line isn't communicating.

'Wait, you're right, of course you're right. We need to call the police. Jesus.' I unlock my phone and begin to stab at the screen but my fingers are shaking so hard and I can't stop the tears from falling.

'Hold on. We're here,' whispers Fredrik, urging the car up the final, steep slope up to the huge house, before pulling into the driveway. 'Look – the lights are on. They were off before. And there's a car. They must have come back. Thank God.'

A black Nissan Leaf is charging in the open garage. I rush from the car to the front door. A fierce wind jostles up the steep hillside, enveloping us like a small tornado. I pound at the solid oak door as hard as I can and press the doorbell at the same time. There's a faint sound from within, a steady hum – a vacuum cleaner nudged against the skirting boards?

I need Lucia. Now. I need my girl. I need to press my nose into her wispy, golden hair, I need to feel her thin arms close around my neck. I can't help myself: 'Lucia!' I scream at the top of my lungs. The faint noise from within stops, and we hear light footsteps approaching. The door opens.

4

Elisa

At the door is a very short Asian woman. Her hair is pulled into a severe bun and in her hand is a silver cordless vacuum cleaner.

'Hello,' I say, hysteria edging into my voice. 'Is my daughter here? Lucia? She's Josephine's friend.'

Blank stare.

I step forward and look past her into the brightly lit hallway for a sign of Line or the girls. 'Do you speak Norwegian?'

The woman nods. 'Nobody here,' she says in a heavy accent. 'Changeover.'

'Changeover? What do you mean?' asks Fredrik.

'I do the changeovers. For Airbnb. New people coming Monday.'

'I'm sorry, I don't understand, you have to help us!'

The woman looks weary now, her knuckles tightening on the half-opened door.

'Look. My daughter is with the people who live here. The owners of this house. Line and... you know. Line and her husband. She's playing with their little girl. Josephine. I need to know where they are.'

The woman looks genuinely confused. 'Nobody lives here. This house is owned by a man who lives in Stockholm. He uses it for Airbnb. I'm sorry I can't help you.'

I turn my gaze from her to Fredrik and his face begins to blur and melt away with the onset of desperate, frightened tears.

'We need to come inside,' says Fredrik.

'No,' says the woman, and begins to push the door shut. 'Nobody here.'

'Open the fucking door,' shouts Fredrik but it is shut firmly in our faces.

I sink to my knees, sobbing uncontrollably now. 'Call the police,' I whisper.

The walls are stark white, and the floor is a light grey concrete, pockmarked with darker splotches. Fredrik and I sit close together at the center of a long table, and across from us sit two police officers. One is a man in his thirties, a good-looking guy who seems to be of South American origin. He has kind eyes, and smooth brown skin, and as I speak, hiccupping and crying, stopping to take short, strained breaths, he nods gently. The other is an older woman, a stern-looking blonde who surprises me by reaching across the table and squeezing my hand as I blurt out everything I can remember in the lead-up to this impossible moment. Fredrik looks stunned, his ashen face contorted into a grimace of sheer disbelief.

The policeman slides a series of photographs across the

table. They are of various women – white, black, Asian, old, young, plain and more distinctive-looking. I shake my head; none of them are of Line.

'Are you sure?'

I nod again. I'd know her anywhere.

'Did she mention her husband by name at all?'

'No. She only said he was in New York. And that he's French. No, maybe she didn't say he's French. She said he's a banker who works for Paribas.'

The policeman writes 'Paribas' on the notepad in front of him. 'Did she mention any other place or name?'

'No. Wait. Yes, she said she had a son as well as the daughter. "My son has settled well at his senior school", she said. But she didn't mention a name or the name of the school. And she said that the girl used to go to the French school in Oslo. She spoke French to her mother at one point.'

'And that could have just been a lie,' says Fredrik. 'Every single thing she said could just be a straight-up lie.'

A cold panic spreads out in my insides at the thought of this. We believe what we are told, accepting what others say as truth, countless times every day. But should we?

There is a knock at the door and another policeman appears.

'We've managed to get in touch with the secretary at the school. Josephine wasn't yet formally registered at Korsvik School.'

'What do you mean?' I ask. 'Line said they'd arrived at the beginning of term. It's already mid-October. How could she not be registered?'

'It would seem that isn't true. Josephine only arrived on Wednesday and was just signed in for three trial days.'

Fredrik and I exchange another glance. My heart is beating too hard; I feel faint. I also feel strangely cool-headed and alert, as if every cell in my brain has been sharpened. I need her back. I need to stay calm to get my baby back. But all I want is to scream, and I can't help unleashing an anguished sob.

'I don't understand – she must have provided a passport, a birth certificate, something…?'

'It would seem she gave a social security number, which hadn't yet been checked by the school. We've checked it now, and unfortunately it isn't a real number. She told the secretary she'd bring in the passport on Monday.'

'What about the house? If she rented through Airbnb, she would have been registered. We've used Airbnb before – they make you verify your profile and you have to use a credit card—'

'We're working on establishing what credit card was used, as well as the IP address the booking came from.'

'And her phone?'

'We believe she's discarded it, but are working on recovering it right now.'

'Wait,' says Fredrik. 'So if she took our daughter and left last night shortly after my wife went home, she will have had, what, almost twenty-four hours? They could be anywhere by now?'

The policeman nods gravely. 'I can assure you that we will find Lucia. We *will* find her. This kind of thing very rarely happens in Norway. And almost all children that go missing are recovered alive within forty-eight hours. We're putting a lot of resources into this case. We've decided to appeal very broadly across all the media channels in the hope that key witnesses will step forward.'

'But… But what if they kill her in the meantime? This is my baby!'

'Mrs Blix, it would be impossible not to have such thoughts in your situation. But let me assure you that we will work around the clock with all the resources we have available to locate your daughter.' It is the woman, Kristine Hermansen, who's talking. 'The psychologists will speak with you next. It is of extreme importance that you take care of yourselves over the next few days. For Lucia, okay? Be strong for her. She is out there and we are absolutely certain she is alive. She will need you more than ever when we get to her. And we *will* get to her. Do you understand?'

Fredrik and I exchange another glance. It physically hurts to look into his haunted eyes.

'After you've spoken to the psychologists, we hope you'll feel able to participate in a press conference. We seem to get the best results when the parents appeal directly to the public. Tomorrow we'll need to take you back to Asnestoppen to see if anything of Lucia's has been left behind at the house. Our technical team is already there, but unfortunately the cleaner got there before them.'

'Why are you so certain she's alive?' I whisper.

'Because, statistically speaking, no matter what the motive for this crime is, Lucia is worth a lot more alive than dead. Children are very rarely killed in a kidnap situation, regardless of what the sensationalist media might have you believe. The fact that she was taken by a woman is also relevant – women are, quite frankly, much less likely to be involved in a murder plot.'

'Please,' I say, into the wall of bright flashing lights. 'Please just let her go. We will do anything. Anything.' My voice is strangely calm, as if it's been pre-recorded. I remember seeing other mothers – people like me, now – on television, in another life. In that life I had no idea what it is like to stand here, to say these words. To beg. I'd turn away from their desperate eyes, from the photograph of their child clutched in a white-knuckled hand, from their painful, impossible fear. How could anyone live even for a second without knowing where their child is, I'd wonder. I still can't answer that. I can't think straight.

'You seemed like a truly lovely, kind woman,' I continue, speaking as if directly to Line, making my voice clear and soft. 'I felt like we could have been friends. I don't understand what the reason for this could be. But I want to say this to you – please, please don't harm Lucia. I beg you. From one mother to another, please do not harm my child. If you come forward now, the consequences of this will be so much smaller than if you don't. We can all go back to our lives. We won't hate you, we will spend our lives in gratitude. Lucia needs to be with us. Please, please end this now.'

I step back off the podium and catch Fredrik's eye. Tears are streaming down his face and he gives me a light nod. The policewoman, Kristine Hermansen, places a hand on my shoulder and leads me away from the press and their cameras and their cacophony of shouted questions, into a small room with a red sofa and two blue arm chairs. I sink into the sofa and close my eyes, the ghosts of flashing lights still blinking on my retina. After a long while the noise in my head stops and the lights fade and all that is left is a numb, quiet darkness. This is my life now.

5

Elisa

We sit in the car outside our home looking at its modest but sweet façade. It's a good set-up we have here, and now it is over. No matter what happens, the ordinary family life we have led has been destroyed forever. I can't bear to turn my head even an inch, nor meet my husband's eyes. How will we manage this night here, without her?

We walk slowly to the door, like sleepwalkers, and Fredrik fumbles with the lock. We stand entirely still in the hushed, dark silence of the hallway cluttered with shoes. Everything seems the same as usual, but nothing is. I force myself to imagine that this is just like all the other times when both kids have gone to Fredrik's parents for a sleepover, like they often do. We liked it when they were gone. We'd look forward to them not being here.

I dig my nails into my palms as hard as I can and unleash a flood of tears. Fredrik puts his arms around me but I can't tell if he is holding me up or using me to support himself from collapsing. We cling to each other, sobbing, for a very long time.

'We should get some sleep,' whispers Fredrik. 'The police will be here in less than six hours.'

'How?'

Fredrik pulls the little box of sleeping pills given to him by the police doctor from his pocket and rattles the box softly.

We are picked up by Gaute Svendsen, the nice South American police officer, and Kristine Hermansen in a plain blue BMW police car and driven out to Asnes. Passing the MIX ice-cream kiosk on the corner, I feel a sharp wrench in my gut at the memory of Lucia and Lyder sitting outside on the wooden bench slurping blue slush after a boat trip last summer, precious little faces beaming. I force my eyes away from the empty bench and let them rest on my hands, held tightly clasped in my lap, and don't look up again until the car comes to a stop.

The house on Asnestoppen is not like I remember it. It's impersonal, stark, empty. Was it like this before? No. There were candles burning and a cozy, if somewhat sleek atmosphere. It looked like someone lived there; a very stylish home, but a home nonetheless. I can't quite put my finger on what it is that's different now except that it feels like a blank canvas. I hold Fredrik's hand tight as we follow two police officers and a technician in a forensic suit upstairs. We've each been handed a pair of gloves and our shoes are covered by blue plastic covers.

'Anything at all,' says Gaute Svendsen, 'even the smallest detail or item that you recognize as Lucia's, could prove crucial.' He points to the bronze kitchen island, on top of which several items are displayed. 'These are some of the things the technicians have recovered which may or may not belong to your daughter.' There is a pink hair slide, a green child's toothbrush with a dinosaur head cover, a little notebook, a set of plastic toy keys and a black wool sock.

I point to the toothbrush. 'That's hers,' I say, my voice emerging as a whisper.

'That's good,' says one of the technicians, a petite bird-like woman with a frizzy black perm, reminiscent of a nest. 'We will be running DNA tests on it, and a toothbrush should give us a lot to work with.'

'Why will you be running DNA tests?' My heart is beating so fast, I have to place a hand on the cool metal surface of the kitchen island.

'Because as the investigation advances, we will be able to identify potential forensic matches with your daughter.'

'What, like if you find a... a body?' asks Fredrik.

Gaute Svendsen and the technician exchange a quick glance.

'If, for example, we recover a car we suspect has been used to transport Lucia, we can ascertain whether or not she has been in the car.' A heavy silence ensues, before Gaute indicates again to the few pitiful objects laid out in front of us. 'Nothing else that belongs to her?' he asks.

'No.'

'We also found this upstairs,' says another technician, a young woman with a dyed pink fringe emerging from a plastic hair cap, holding a small metal box. She hands it to me and inside is Minky Mouse.

I close my eyes and bring the tatty toy mouse with her knitted pink tutu to my face, drawing the unmistakable scent of my child deep into me.

'Jesus,' says Fredrik.

I sink to my knees, clutching Minky, Lucia's most prized possession, knowing she would never have parted from her unless by force. I keep my eyes tightly shut, conjuring the last few moments I saw her in my mind.

'Honey,' says Fredrik, gently trying to pull me back up, but I keep my eyes shut because she's there, in my mind, doing cartwheels and laughing, entirely happy and trusting in what she perceived to be a safe environment. I failed her. All those nights when she was little and I sat at her bedside, whispering into her ear that I would protect her, no matter what. That she would be my whole world. That life would be exciting and fun and good. But I failed.

'Come on, honey,' Fredrik says again, and this time I stand up.

'I'm going to kill that woman with my bare hands,' I say.

It's nearly 9 p.m. by the time we leave the police station. No news, no nothing, no Lucia. All that remains is the vast black hole she has left behind.

'Fred, can you stop by your parents'? I want to bring Lyder home.'

'They said he could stay for as long as we need him to, honey, don't you think it's a good idea to—'

'I need my son, Fredrik,' I say, and he realizes that there is no point in trying to talk me out of this, and turns right towards his parents' bungalow, ten minutes' drive away, in Bugården.

'Where's Lula?' asks Lyder as soon as the door opens, looking past me into the dark night, his little face pinched and anxious.

'We don't know, darling,' I say, dropping to my knees and pulling my son close. Though he doesn't usually, he lets me hold him for a long while.

'Has somebody killed her?'

'No, of course not,' whispers Fredrik, emotion thick in his voice.

'They said it on the TV.' I glance past my son into the house, and pick out the tinny sound of television voices.

'It's not true,' I say, gently stroking my son's soft, longish hair back from his forehead. Lyder keeps staring at the closed door behind me as I kick my shoes off, as if his sister might have been left outside in the cold night, alone.

'Can you make them turn that off?' I say, to Fredrik.

We sit for a while in my in-laws' over-furnished living room as Fredrik recounts the most recent developments. Vigdis wrings her hands and shakes her head mournfully. Lyder listens in from where he's sitting beside the train set that he's laid out on the carpet, Percy the engine held suspended in mid-air.

'I just don't understand,' Vigdis keeps saying.

Karl nods furiously, his red face redder than I've ever seen it, but he doesn't speak.

We drive home in silence. I don't turn around; I'm pretending in my head that both of my children are in the back seat. My mind is racing wildly, and I have to use all of my self-control to keep it off the worst scenarios. But I can't fight them all off. A still, dark lake appears in my mind, its surface a vast mirror reflecting the sliver of a brilliant new moon, and far below it – my beloved daughter. Next I see an unremarkable hillside somewhere, a place only animals ever roam. A small patch of earth has been upturned and carefully rearranged, and there, deep beneath the soil – my beloved daughter. I see a drooping, old wooden cabin in the pine forests, far from any neighbors, the kind of place where the silence is so heavy it becomes a sound itself, and there, locked away in a cold, timber-walled room – my beloved daughter.

My palms are slick, my mind is churning. All I can do is say her name over and over in my head like I do every moment of every day. *Lucia*: 'light', 'pure light', 'love'. I think of the others, the children whose faces we all know, the ones who disappeared and never returned, the ones whose parents launched appeal after appeal – will my child go down in history as one of them?

I force myself back to the present moment, to being in this car with my husband and son, and let my eyes rest on Fredrik's tired face, lit ghoulishly by the orange streetlights. He pulls up in front of the house and the three of us sit a long moment in the dark silence of the car. It feels impossible to go into the house and continue our lives without her when she's out there somewhere, alone.

I'm walking up the shingle path to the front door when Lyder, who has rushed ahead of us, shouts, 'Mummy, Daddy! Look – a letter!' In his hands, he's holding a plain white envelope addressed to the 'Blix Family'.

6

Selma

Selma picks Medusa up off the windowsill of her tiny Oslo apartment and carries her over to the bed, which fills the entire sleeping alcove. She draws the white gauze curtains to the alcove shut, giving the bed the dreamy feel of a cozy four-poster, and lies back. The shaggy forest cat purrs loudly as Selma runs her hand down her back, pausing to scratch the hollow at the beginning of her tail, before starting over again, from the base of her skull. Medusa was a kitten when Selma first saw her, mewling loudly on the ground-floor balcony of her father's apartment in Drammen. After that, she used to turn up every day and stare at Selma through the window as she chewed her breakfast and read the morning paper before school.

'Don't let her in,' her father would say, 'or we'll never be rid of her.' But Selma did let her in, and, eight years later, even her father has grown fond of Medusa. Whenever he calls Selma, he always enquires about the cat first. 'How's my favorite girl?' he'll ask, chuckling. 'And how are you?'

Selma can hear the phone vibrating loudly on the kitchen

table. For two days, she's been chatting to a guy called Victor on Tinder, but he's getting pushy about meeting. It must be him. *It's always the same story*, she thinks. She likes the look of someone and swipes left. A chat starts and at first they seem so unique and interesting. But after a day or two they run out of things to say. So why would she meet up with them? She kisses the top of Medusa's head, and Medusa, realizing that Selma is about to withdraw her full attention, dramatically flips over on her back, tugging at the air with her paws; she knows she's irresistible like that. Selma scratches her soft belly, then gets up.

She has a missed call and several messages from Olav, her boss.

> Sorry it's late. Have you seen the news? Little girl gone missing. Can you come back in? I need you to cover this.

*

It's past 5 a.m. when Selma gets up from her chair and stretches her legs. She'd hoped to get home for a couple of hours' sleep before the next press conference at nine, but there's no chance of that – her apartment is up in the St Hanshaugen district, a good twenty-five minutes' walk from the Dagsposten offices. The case is everywhere; stuff like this never happens in Norway. She's been up all night, reading through every single bit of information from the police and other news sources; she needs to be one step ahead of the other journalists.

'You okay, Eriksen?' asks Olav, holding out an open packet of Oreos to her.

39

She takes one and nods. 'Yeah. Just… Just it doesn't make any sense.'

'Tell me about it.'

'I mean, I don't think I have ever come across an abduction case like this. A woman, just taking off with a kid spending the night with her own kid…'

'If the other girl even was hers. We don't know that for a fact.'

'True.'

'It looks like a professional job to me,' says Olav. 'There don't seem to be any real leads. I'd guess the woman and child were paid, and that a network's behind it.'

'Maybe. Just, it seems so elaborate, you know? The hired house, the whole posing at the school. If it is a network kind of abduction, it seems very targeted. Like they were after Lucia Blix specifically, not just any old kid. Would have been easier to snatch someone off the street.'

'Would it, though?'

'Olav. This is Norway. Kids aged six or seven quite often walk to and from school on their own. Little kids play out on the streets unsupervised, especially in a quiet town like Sandefjord. I can't imagine it would be that hard to kidnap a child in this country.'

'I suppose you're right,' says Olav, scratching the fuzz on his jaw. He's been trying to grow a beard for months now but can't seem to get past pale ginger down.

Selma imagines he must be thinking of his own kid; he has a son of a similar age to Lucia Blix.

'They just seem so normal – Fredrik and Elisa Blix. But you know what they say, with missing kids it's almost always something to do with the family. JonBenét Ramsey,

Madeleine McCann... The theories always seem to return to the parents, don't they? For all we know, it could be a financial thing – they could be in trouble and somehow staged this.'

'Oh come on, Selma, you seriously think it's to do with the parents? Like you said yourself, they seem completely normal.'

'I don't know. I'm just saying that at this stage we know nothing. Nothing at all.'

'I'm heading off. Gotta catch an hour or two. I'll see you at the conference at nine.'

Olav disappears down the hallway and Selma is the only person left at the office. The newspaper's regular nightshift guy works remotely from Houston; he can monitor the press agency feeds just as easily from the US and rarely does anything so urgent happen in Norway that the editorial team has to pull an all-nighter.

Selma picks absent-mindedly at a cuticle until it bleeds. She puts her finger in her mouth and stares hard at the screen. It is a still from the public appeal Elisa Blix made at the first press conference. She is a tall and thin woman with attractive, even features. Her hair is light brown and swept up into a messy ponytail. Selma guesses she's around thirty-five. She presses 'Play' and watches the video again, though she has already watched it countless times. Elisa's anguished face leaps to life and the camera zooms in on her deep brown eyes, swimming with tears. 'Please,' she says, 'please don't harm Lucia.' She pronounces it 'Lou-see-yah', not like the Italian 'Luchee-ah', and Selma wonders how an ordinary mother in Sandefjord came to choose such an unusual name for her child. *Lou, see ya.*

Selma clicks on the next video, a narrative of the events as they appear at this stage, set to a series of pictures of Lucia, released by her family.

'She is about to turn eight years old but is short for her age,' says the man's voice. 'She is not used to being away from her family and is likely highly agitated. Lucia has no birthmarks or discerning features other than a scar that runs through her left eyebrow, and members of the public are encouraged to remember that her appearance may have attempted to be changed. Lucia Blix disappeared from a detached house in the Asnes area of Vesterøya in Sandefjord sometime between 7 p.m. on 19 October and 4 p.m. on 20 October. She was staying with a child believed to be called Josephine and a woman claiming to be her mother, who called herself Line. The police have so far been unsuccessful in establishing the true identities of the woman and child and are treating the case as a high-priority abduction case. The woman is believed to be in her mid to late thirties and is of a slim build. She is approximately 5ft 8 and has dark brown hair and blue eyes. The other child is of a similar height and build to Lucia Blix, and believed to be between six and eight years of age. She has a noticeable curved scar on her cheek, at least two prominent teeth missing and long, chestnut-brown hair—'

Selma pauses the video and opens Facebook on her phone. There's only one match for Elisa Blix. Her profile is set to private, but Selma can see her cover photo and her profile picture. She clicks on the profile picture. It is a photo of Elisa posing at the door of an airplane in a navy uniform. The picture is dated 2011 and on the aircraft's wing it says 'SAS'. She's wearing a becoming shade of red lipstick and a wide smile. Selma sees that she is an attractive woman, someone whose appearance might spark jealousy or perhaps infatuation. She writes 'beautiful' on the notepad in front of her, then 'professional job?' and 'elaborate planning'. The picture has 141 likes. Popular lady. Selma clicks on the comments. One is from her husband, Fredrik – 'Babe!' The rest are standard fawning friend comments like 'You get more and more beautiful', and 'Wowzers, Mrs Blix'.

Selma clicks on the cover photo, which seems to have been taken last Christmas and shows the nuclear Blix family gathered in front of a Christmas tree. To the left, in a green velvet armchair sits Fredrik, a carefree smile on his unremarkable face. Could he be capable of bad things? Selma commits every part of his face to memory, looking for anything remotely out of the ordinary, but she doesn't find anything. Next to him in an identical chair sits Elisa. Her hair is loose and blown out in glossy waves. She is wearing a black sequined dress and the same red lipstick. Her eyes are enhanced by a dramatic flick of black eyeliner. The children are sitting cross-legged on the floor in front of their parents, each holding a large square present and grinning widely. Elisa's hand rests on the little boy's shoulder – Lyder is his name. Lucia and Lyder. Fredrik and Elisa. A handsome family. Normal, it would seem. Almost comically average. Middle class, 2.0 kids. Why them?

Selma zooms in on Lucia Blix's face. She's a cute kid, no doubt about that. Perhaps even unusually cute. She has a healthy glow to her skin, soulful brown eyes and thick, dark eyebrows that contrast with her light blonde hair. Selma can just about make out the scar that runs through Lucia's left eyebrow and wonders how she got it. She stares at the child's face for a long while, imagining all the possible scenarios in her head. Captivity, death, abuse... Something tightens in her stomach. How could anyone set out to hurt a small child? How afraid little Lucia Blix must be in this exact moment, separated from her loving family. Selma zooms back out and takes in the family as a whole: mother, father, brother and sister. She can't imagine what it must be like to have a family like theirs. But Selma knows better than most people how much it hurts to be suddenly torn apart from your loving mother. She stares at Lucia – she's exactly the same age as Selma herself was when her life as she'd known it ended.

7

Elisa

In the room at Oslo police headquarters are three investigators, one of whom I recognize from the media as Oslo's police chief, Hans Gundersen. We've been briefed that several more people are watching us via video link – our local officers in Sandefjord, others at Kripos, the national agency for the investigation of serious crimes, plus various as yet nameless men and women from other branches of the police system. We're met with deeply sympathetic but solemn expressions, and there's also an alertness about them; they're all observing us, and they don't mind us knowing it.

'Police headquarters in Oslo need you to come in for a more in-depth assessment of the threat level to your family before Lucia's abduction,' Kristine Hermansen said when she called last night. So here we are. We've been told we are likely to be here all day, and perhaps well into the evening. Fredrik and I will be speaking to the police together and separately, like on the first night but in much greater detail.

I feel a prickling sensation up and down the length of

my spine, as though my nerves were tiny live creatures biting me. It would be impossible not to be nervous in this situation, even for the most innocent person in the world.

I put all my effort into maintaining some kind of composure as I sink into the surprisingly comfortable chair across from the interrogators, who fix me with observant eyes and carefully honed expressions of utmost empathy. I think of the mothers and fathers of other abduction victims, how many of them were vilified and hounded and suspected of foul play, and how the press was only too ready to crucify them with the barest scraps for proof. I swallow hard, mentally bracing myself for the possibility of speculative front pages: 'Elisa Blix, Murderer?' 'Lucia Blix, Sold on the Dark Web by Evil Mother?' 'The Blix Case: Suspicion Mounts Against Parents in Baffling Abduction Case.'

'Mr Blix, Mrs Blix, thank you for coming up for this. I trust you were comfortable in the car?' Gundersen says.

Fredrik nods. The police sent a chauffeured car for the ninety-minute drive here from Sandefjord and on some deep level this made me uncomfortable, like they want to keep tabs on us and are watching our every move. They're welcome to watch me every day for the rest of my days if it means I can have Lucia back, but it's a strange feeling to be the object of such intense scrutiny.

'What's happening with the ransom note?' asks Fredrik.

'It is currently undergoing a full screening and analysis by the forensic team. We are hoping to secure DNA from the note,' says Gundersen.

'It just doesn't make any sense,' I say. 'They ask us to await further instructions or they'll hurt her, and then there's just… nothing. Silence.' I swallow hard at a painful lump in my throat.

'It is by no means certain it has actually come from the perpetrators. Unfortunately with a case like this, there can be unstable people watching who try to get involved in a bid for attention.'

'But, I mean, it sounds crystal clear to me,' I say, the anguish of reading the terrible words washing over me all over again.

We have Lucia. She is safe and taken care of. We will be bringing a financial claim and if it isn't met, we will kill her.

'We are keeping all avenues open, but I can assure you the note is central to our efforts at this time.'

'Jesus,' says Fredrik.

'Yes. This case is unusual in so many ways. A kidnap like this is unprecedented here in Norway, particularly with regard to the meticulous planning that enabled the abductors to take Lucia. Most other kidnaps involving children have been clumsy crimes of passion by desperate family members, or crimes of opportunity. In both cases, the perpetrators generally leave substantial clues and forensic material behind, making it relatively easy for us to close in on them in what we call the most critical window, the first forty-eight hours after abduction. In the case of Lucia, we unfortunately have very little to work with.'

Hans Gundersen pauses for a long while, letting his eyes travel from me to Fredrik and back. I nod, painfully aware that it has already been over twice that since I held my girl in my arms.

'What seems obvious here is that someone was after your daughter specifically.'

I nod again, but tears are already blurring my vision.

'It is crucial that you share with us any ideas you might have as to why that might be,' says the man sitting across from us and to the left, an older officer with sparse reddish blonde hair carefully arranged in a fruitless attempt to cover his glistening skull. 'We need to establish whether you might in some way have come into contact with a criminal network or persons associated with such networks, or whether you could have involuntarily uncovered some information which might make you a danger to someone.'

'Look,' says Fredrik, his voice soft and dejected. 'My wife and I are pretty much the most average small-town couple you can imagine. We're every statistic – two kids, mortgage, full-time jobs, busy days, a few friends, all of whom we've known for years.'

Something about the way Fredrik describes us makes me suddenly, irrationally angry. Is that all we are?

'Yes, well, as you know, we've started looking into your immediate circle of family, friends and acquaintances, and there hasn't been anything to suggest any motives for involvement, so we are urging you now to think very carefully about more peripheral or random encounters. Most significantly, whether you have been the subject of any kind of abuse or threats, whether online or in real life.'

Fredrik and I exchange a glance. Could he have stumbled across something potentially dangerous? My husband, whom I've known since the summer I turned seventeen, whose idea of risk-taking behavior is overtaking in the middle lane, and whose main interests are craft beer, *Game of Thrones* and the occasional mountain hike? Impossible. And yet, we are all more than the sum total of what we show others, even our spouse and children. There are vast unseen spaces inside us that could be filled with anything at all.

'Mrs Blix, since you created your Instagram account, you have shared 742 images of one or both of your children. Your account is public, which means anyone can access these images. We are currently trying to establish whether there are patterns to the 'likes' received, particularly those for images of Lucia, and whether anyone unconnected to you has taken a particular interest in your profile. Is there anything you could add to assist us in this?'

'No, I don't think so. Just, of course, I wish I hadn't shared all those pictures of her. Them. I just didn't think...'

'Mrs Blix, our role is most certainly not to pass judgment. We are merely looking into your social media activity as one of many possible areas where you could have initially come into contact with Lucia's abductor.'

Tears rush down my face and drip onto my navy wool sweater. 'Should I make the profile private now?'

'No, leave it public. We will continue to monitor activity on your account, looking for patterns.'

I nod.

'We'll take a half-hour break. Down the corridor to your right is a cafeteria; you'll be able to grab a coffee or a snack there.'

After the break, I am taken into another, smaller room – alone. I am made aware of the video link again, that there are others watching. The police officers are Hans Gundersen, Haakon Kjeller and a small, squat female officer whose name I don't catch. I recognise Kjeller as the officer with red hair. For a very long time, they fire questions at me, some so close together I barely have time to think; I've watched enough police procedurals to know that this is exactly the point.

'Tell us about your experiences with jealousy,' says the woman, watching me with small, black eyes that remind me of my mother.

'Jealousy? Uh, not many.'

'Did you have any known enemies when you were younger?'

'No.'

'In school, for example.'

I don't understand how it is worthwhile spending time going over my friendship dramas in high school. Monica Røyert and Hege Evensen might have been bitches, but I doubt they'd steal an eyeliner from me, let alone my child.

'Not really,' I say. 'My parents were strict when I was at school. They were Jehovah's Witnesses. I didn't participate much in the social side of things.'

Strict is an understatement. I want the police to stop asking about my early life, it still makes me feel uncomfortable.

'I see. What about at work? Any threatening passengers?' asks Gundersen.

'Well, yes. In my job, you do meet the occasional loony.'

'Loony?'

'You know – weird people. Like, I've had male passengers try to feel me up while I'm serving them, for example. I've been sworn at and threatened when I've refused people more alcohol. That kind of thing.'

The woman nods, as though these scenarios are common in her job, too.

'Has anyone you've come into contact with through your job tried to establish contact outside of work? Adding you on social media, for example, or otherwise attempting to access your personal information?'

'No, I don't think so,' I say.

'Have you had any marital indiscretions?'

'No,' I say, and find my voice suddenly weak.

What do they mean by marital indiscretions? Secrets between husband and wife? There are *always* secrets between husband and wife.

'Have you engaged in communication with anyone other than your husband which could be interpreted as suggestive or sexual?'

'No.' *Yes.*

'Why did you and Fredrik seek out marital counseling on two separate occasions, in 2008 and again in 2013?'

'Because having children almost broke our relationship, like so many others, I imagine.' *Because I fell in love*, I think to myself. I could tell them this, but I don't, because it would only make everything even worse.

'Are you close with your family?' asks Kjeller.

'Yes, reasonably close,' I say. I picture my loving father, who was the single good thing about my life in Lillehammer, but then I can't stop myself from shivering slightly at the thought of my stern, dismissive mother, the silent house I grew up in, the endless door-to-door visits. A more truthful answer would be *hell, no*. My child has gone missing, and still, my own mother has not been in touch.

8

Elisa

There is another break, and Fredrik and I are left for a while in a waiting room. Here too there are cameras and I can't help but wonder if someone is watching our every move.

Fredrik looks bewildered, like he knows he's supposed to be somewhere but can't think where.

'You okay?' I ask.

'No,' he says. 'We need to speak, Elisa.' His voice is weak and hoarse, as though he's been shouting at the top of his lungs.

'Okay,' I say. I want to know what he has to say, but at the same time, I fear his words. He has the power to wound me.

He glances up at me, and when I see the expression in his eyes I have to look away. When I finally bring my gaze back, his eyes are red-rimmed, wild, unfamiliar.

'What's going on, Fredrik?' I ask. 'Did you find the questioning tough? I mean, I did too, even though—'

'Elisa,' he says, cutting me short. He snorts and shakes

his head, as though a second conversation is going on inside there. 'Stop. Okay?'

'Okay. Tell me.' I reach across the low plastic table between us and place my hand on top of his, but he instantly recoils, as though my touch has seared him.

'This is about three years ago.'

'Three years ago?'

'Yes. The summer of 2014.'

I try to remember what happened the summer of 2014.

I was unraveling at the seams. I was torn to pieces by grief. Much like now. Although back then, on the surface, things would have looked calm. Harmonious.

'What about it?'

'I've done something, Elisa. Something bad.'

My heart lurches in my chest and I stare at my husband hard. Could Fredrik, my placid, ordinary husband, really have done something bad, something which has come back to haunt us and taken everything? But Fredrik has never done anything bad. I was always the black sheep. Growing up, my parents called me exactly that, shaking their heads, at first with amusement, and later, with disappointment and shock and ultimately condemnation as I became a wild teenager. A very wild teenager. In marriage it's been the same – the black sheep is me. Isn't it?

'What have you done, Fredrik?' My voice is calm and controlled, a contrast to the chaos in my mind and heart.

'I had a thing with someone...'

'A thing.'

'Yes.' He won't look at me now.

I almost laugh out loud at his nerve, and feel a crazy compulsion to tell him the things I keep filed away deep inside me, and we could sit here together watching our life burn to cinders. For a minute I am struck still by a wild fury. The desire for revenge is a breathtaking punch in the stomach. I could get it by telling him that I have only ever loved one man and it sure as hell isn't him. But I don't. Instead, I'm surprised to find that I'm crying. I never imagined Fredrik would do anything to hurt me.

'I'm sorry,' he says, and now it is him reaching across the table, trying to comfort me. I snatch my hand away and wipe at my tears, but they keep coming and I'm angry with myself for losing my composure. The thought that something Fredrik has done could have cost us our daughter is unbearable.

'Why are you even telling me this now? Did you tell the police?'

'Yes. Well, I had to. After what they asked about revenge, and whether anyone has ever threatened us.'

'Wait, so you had what you call "a thing" with someone and now you think it could be linked to Lucia? Why would you even think that?'

'Because she threatened me. She said she'd ruin my life, Elisa.'

He begins to cry, huge throaty sobs that fill the little room, and I want to scream and sob and lash out at him for having possibly brought someone dangerous into our lives.

'Do you... think it could be her? What did the police say?'

Fredrik shrugs miserably. 'It never occurred to me until now. We never even met in person—'

'You never even *met*?' If I wasn't so worked up, I'd laugh. Fredrik's big confession and they didn't even meet! I'm hugely relieved, of course. But I'm not going to let him off the hook yet.

He shakes his head and continues to look painfully embarrassed.

'It was just an ongoing flirty conversation on Messenger. I've never heard of a single case where a child is taken by a scorned ex-flirt before. Not one.'

'Me neither.'

'So it just didn't occur to me.'

'Why did it end – this "thing"?'

'I didn't want to meet her in real life. And she got mad. Really mad.'

'Why didn't you meet with her?'

'Because I love you.'

At this, I laugh incredulously, though I know that it's true. Fredrik does love me, deeply, and with an intensity that feels both safe and stifling.

'When you say she got really mad, what do you mean exactly?'

'I told her I would never jeopardize my family and she turned... you know... nasty. Then she abruptly stopped contacting me and I just wanted to forget the whole mess.' He looks up at me, his eyes pleading, bloodshot, swimming with tears. 'I felt terrible, Elisa. I really did. Still do.'

'Jesus, Fredrik!' I stare at him, seeing him in a different way for the first time in years. 'She sounds like a random weirdo for sure. But not a child-snatcher. And you didn't even do anything with her.'

'I don't know... The whole thing was so weird. But it was years ago, and I'd almost managed to forget about it until the investigators began to ask those questions.'

'So what happens now?'

'I've given the police the log-in details to all my social media accounts. They think they'll be able to recover the conversation even though I looked for it a while back and the whole conversation was gone and so was her profile.'

'What was her name?'

'She called herself Karoline Meister. I've googled her name but nothing comes up.'

My fury has given way to the usual mild frustration with my husband. Here he is, tearfully confessing to a 'thing with someone', insinuating it could be connected to our child's disappearance, when actually all he's done is engage in a bit of a chat with a strange-sounding woman.

'Fredrik? Elisa? Will you come back through – we've managed to recover the conversation you referred to.' As I sit back down, Hans Gundersen shoots me a strange look that I realize is pity. This makes me furious again, and I focus on not letting my feelings show, swallowing hard and making my face blank and unreadable.

'Fredrik, do you consent to the conversation between yourself and Karoline Meister being viewed by Elisa?' asks Gundersen.

'Uh, yes.' Fredrik's voice is low and his cheeks burn red.

'Elisa, are you sure you are comfortable with being present as we run through this? I will say, some of the material is very personal and inflammatory.' I nod. It's a Facebook chat from years ago that went nowhere. How bad can it be?

9

Elisa

I'm surprised by the sheer volume of the chat projected up on the screen. No wonder Fredrik wasn't too keen on divulging his 'little thing'. From June through August 2014 they'd chatted almost daily, sometimes for several hours.

Haakon Kjeller points the remote control at the screen, starting to scroll through the early conversations.

Karoline Meister: Hi there, hope you don't mind me saying hello. Your profile is really interesting.

...

Karoline Meister: Yes, I realize you're married – beautiful family. Friendship only ;)!

Fredrik Blix: Wow, love your new profile pic!

...

FB: What a coincidence, I love mountain hiking, too!

…

KM: You must work out a lot ;-)

Eye roll. If this wasn't so embarrassing, I might have laughed out loud. Fredrik squirms in his seat, his face a deep red. Then, as I keep reading, I begin to understand why Fredrik made a big deal out of this 'thing' – he's crossed more than a few boundaries, and I wonder if it would almost have been preferable if he'd just gone and slept with someone. I can feel the eyes of the police officers on me, watching my reactions carefully, and I will my face to be still and unreadable.

17 June 2014

Fredrik Blix: Hey there…

Karoline Meister: Hey you ;) What are you up to today?

FB: Just holding the fort at home. My wife's in Cyprus all weekend.

KM: Woah. How come?

FB: Girls' trip. Again.

KM: Does she go away a lot?

FB: Yeah. She's away for work a lot, though she's just changed jobs so hopefully she won't have as many hotel nights in the future.

KM: That must be hard on you. And the kids.

FB: Yeah.

22 June 2014

KM: Just came back from a 10k run. Phew.

FB: Haha, Cool. Me too, actually!

KM: Nice. So, would you say you're a sporty man?

FB: Definitely. Working out is really important to me.

KM: Me too. Does your wife go running with you?

FB: Nah. She hates everything that gets her pulse going.

KM: Everything? ;)

FB: Haha.

3 July 2014

FB: Hi, you there?

KM: Yeah.

FB: Missed talking to you yesterday…

KM: Yeah?

FB: Yeah.

KM: I was on a date, actually.

FB: Hm.

KM: Hm, says Mr Married.

FB: Touché.

KM: Don't you want to know how my date went?

FB: Nope.

KM: Gonna tell you anyway. It was boring. I sat there, wishing he was you…

FB: Be careful what you wish for…

KM: I know what I wish for.

FB: So, are you going to see the guy again?

KM: Nope.

FB: ??

KM: I'm holding out for a handsome lawyer in Sandefjord who makes me feel like I am standing on top of a mountain, a fresh breeze of air sweeping across my face, actually.

17 July 2014

KM: Home alone?

FB: Yep. E's working late. Kids at my parents'.

KM: Wanna Facetime?

FB: Okay…

(incoming video call 1:42:07)

18 July 2014

FB: Just a quick hello to say that last night was amazing. You're beautiful.

KM: Out of 10?

FB: 11

KM: I win.

19 July 2014

(incoming video call 2:03:44)

21 July 2014

(outgoing video call 0:49:30)

22 July 2014

(outgoing video call 0:17:22)

24 July 2014

KM: Hey you. I missed you last night. So used to our clandestine calls by now.

FB: Haha, yeah. Me too. Sorry.

KM: What happened?

FB: She came home earlier than I'd thought she would. We had a bit of a tense evening, actually.

KM: …

FB: Nothing crazy. Just the usual. You know, disagreeing over who should be doing what at home, that kind of thing.

KM: Sounds riveting. Where is she tonight?

FB: Out with her girlfriends in Oslo. She's staying over.

KM: How do you feel about that?

FB: Okay I guess. Nice to have the house to myself.

KM: Does she go out a lot?

FB: More than a lot of people with a four-year-old and a two-year-old, I'd imagine.

KM: If I was your wife, I'd spend my entire life snuggled up to you on the sofa…

FB: Haha. Said no one ever.

KM: Seriously, I would! I hope you don't mind me saying this – I just feel like you sometimes get the short end of the stick.

FB: Do you mind if we change the subject? Been a long day.

KM: Of course. Wanna play a game?

FB: Go on.

KM: It's called the Karoline is Going to Video Call You and Take Her Clothes Off Game.

(incoming call 01:20:52)

29 July 2014

KM: Hey, did you get a chance to think about possible dates we could meet up?

FB: Um, the next few weeks don't look too great... We are leaving tomorrow for a week and then E is working back to back the week after, and the kids' nursery's closed that week. Thought I might take them down to my parents' cabin in Kragerø.

KM: Sounds idyllic.

FB: Baby, don't.

KM: Don't what?

FB: Be like that. You know I want to meet you.

KM: Where are you guys going again? Tomorrow?

FB: Nice.

KM: Nice.

FB: Haha.

I remember that summer holiday. Fredrik was short-tempered and constantly on his phone, the kids cried, whinged and fought non-stop, I drank glass after glass of rosé, starting after breakfast and only stopping in the early evening when I'd pass out on the sofa when the kids finally went to bed.

KM: Will you do me a favor?

FB: Okay.

KM: Every time you fuck her, think of me.

FB: Done.

1 August 2014

KM: Hey

KM: Hello?

KM: The pics of your kids in the pool are so cute. Lucia looks just like you!

KM: Um. Hello?

2 August 2014

FB: Look, don't take this the wrong way, but I'd rather we just talk about you & me and stuff.

KM: As opposed to what?

FB: My family.

KM: We hardly ever talk about your family?

FB: It feels like you ask about them a lot.

KM: I'm just curious about them, I guess. I love kids and yours are so beautiful.

FB: Thank you.

KM: The picture E posted of L&L on the beach with the kites was just so sweet.

FB: Where did you see that?

KM: On her Instagram.

FB: Why were you on her Instagram?

KM: Why wouldn't I be? Great feed.

FB: Karoline, I'm sorry, that's a little weird.

KM: We met once, your wife and I.

FB: ??

KM: You know, back in the day. In Lillehammer.

FB: What were you doing in Lillehammer?

KM: I'm from there.

FB: Okay, this is getting really weird. You told me you're from Tromsø.

KM: And you told me we were going to meet in person weeks ago. Over and over you said it.

FB: What does that have to do with anything?

KM: People lie.

FB: Hey. You're freaking me out.

(outgoing call 0:00:00)

7 August 2014

KM: Hi there. Just sent your wife a friend request.

FB: Hey Karoline, seriously, wtf? I don't understand what's going on.

KM: No. You really don't.

FB: Wtf? Trying to call you, pick up!

KM: No.

FB: Karoline, what's going on?

KM: I've fucking had enough of you, that's what's going on. Go back to your perfect family and enjoy it while you can.

FB: Karoline!

KM: Enjoy your little life while you still have it. You're going to be so fucking sorry for this, asshole.

'Oh my God,' I whisper.

The police officers all look at the table, a gesture of privacy, perhaps, as Fredrik and I stare at each other.

'I'm so sorry. Elisa, I don't know what I was thinking... I'm so—'

'Fuck you, Fredrik.'

10

Elisa

It's past 11 p.m. when the chauffeured car meanders through the hushed, deserted streets of Sandefjord. I can't look at Fredrik, but his presence next to me in the back seat is like a giant bleeding wound. I'm not actually that mad at him, not anymore. But I am hurt. I'm especially hurt that he divulged so many personal things about me as a wife and mother to this random stranger on the internet. I do my best.

The police were interested in Fredrik's confession, though they didn't seem terribly alarmed by it. 'This is most likely a bored housewife or a disturbed and harmless individual,' said Hans Gundersen, shaking Fredrik's hand, then mine, surprisingly gently, as we left. 'But don't worry, not a single stone will be left unturned in this investigation.'

Another storm has pummeled Sandefjord today, leaving flooded pavements by the harborside and broken twigs and branches in Hvaltorvet square, blown across from the park. There isn't a single person out tonight; everyone is huddled inside their safe, beautiful houses with their safe, beautiful families. I realize I don't care that much about Fredrik's confession – I care about getting my daughter back and rebuilding my family. That's the only thing that matters to me. I want to run from door to door, inspecting every house, loft, basement and garage, screaming my daughter's name at the top of my lungs until I find her. I *have* to find her.

Could it be that she is still here, in little Sandefjord, the place I perceived as the safest place imaginable? Could it be that here, too, killers and kidnappers live under the radar, people who look and act just like everyone else, quietly biding their time, carefully selecting their victims? How hard would it really be to hand over a little girl to someone like that who would then keep her locked in a basement? Most Norwegian houses have raised basements containing either independent little apartments for au-pairs or tenants or simply lots of storage space. Who on earth would know if Lucia was being held in such a basement?

The car turns onto the winding road which leads to our house at the end of the cul-de-sac. I try to work up the mental strength to face another night in that empty house, but my thoughts are churning with images of Lucia held in any one of Sandefjord's thousands of basements and with the questions the police bombarded us with throughout the afternoon, questions that got more and more intense until I couldn't be entirely sure of the truth.

Who, why, where, what, why, why, why?

At home, we stand a long while in the kitchen in the dark, Fredrik taking his asthma medication, me just wringing my hands under the too-hot water – the pain feels good.

'Do you think you can forgive me?' asks Fredrik, finally. I don't answer him.

Another loaded silence fills the air and I wonder if this is how it will be from now on: secrets and half-truths crowding the spaces between us. Fredrik looks as though he might burst into tears again. I turn away, back to the running water, feeling a strong desire to just be alone and digest it all.

'So,' says Fredrik and I tense up, waiting for him to continue, but he doesn't.

'So what?' I say eventually, when I can't reasonably just keep standing here, scalding my hands.

'Did you tell the police anything I don't know about?'

'Like what?'

'Like. You know. Karoline Meister.'

'What are you asking, Fredrik? Whether I've been indiscreet, too?'

'Yes.'

I leave him waiting for a long moment. I could open my mouth and tell him some secrets of my own, but the difference between my secrets and his is that mine wouldn't make a sliver of difference to Lucia's case.

'No, Fredrik. Look. I'm exhausted. Broken.'

'It was pretty intense.'

'Yes, it was. I feel like I've been put through a paper shredder.'

'Yep, that just about sums it up.' He remains very still. 'It makes you wonder, doesn't it,' he says, keeping his eyes on mine, 'whether past choices, and people we've come into contact with, even randomly, might suddenly bring something new to the investigation.'

'Yeah.'

'Which is why it is so incredibly important that we tell the whole truth. Every single little thing might make a difference.'

'Absolutely.'

'So you told them absolutely everything?' His eyes are cool now.

'Fredrik...'

'Is it that unreasonable for me to ask? Really?'

'Yes, it is. Really fucking unreasonable. Considering...'

'Okay. I'm sorry. It's just that, over the years, there have been times I've felt you were so far away I didn't know if you'd come back to me.'

'You don't have anything to worry about.' This is true. Now.

He nods, then turns away from me and I see how tired and afraid he is, like me. He's just a desperate parent who needs his child back. Like me. 'Come here,' I whisper, and he pulls me into his arms like I wanted him to.

'I'm so sorry, Elisa,' he says after a while. 'Today was just so intense.'

We break apart, and lean back against the kitchen counter. I rest my head on his shoulder and he touches his head softly against mine.

'I blame myself, you know. I can't believe I could have been so stupid as to post hundreds of pictures of the kids like that.'

'So many people do, though. I guess I didn't really think about it, either.'

'Yes, but you kept your social media private.'

'Yes, by chance. You mustn't blame yourself, Elisa. This is nobody's fault.'

'But I do.'

'I don't, for what it's worth. I love you, and we *will* get through this, no matter what.'

'What do you mean, "no matter what"? There's only one possible outcome here. We have to get her back – alive.'

Fredrik nods, but he doesn't look entirely convinced.

'I think they might be right about it having something to do with social media, that someone random has seen my posts and become obsessed with her. She is, objectively speaking, an especially beautiful child – everyone's been saying that – and if that's the case, she's more likely to be alive, right? They'll be able to trace her by analyzing the traffic to my account. They'll—'

'Elisa. Stop. Please. Let's go up, get some rest. All we can do is wait.'

'You go up, then. I'm going to go through all my social media accounts one more time; maybe I'll see something the police have missed.'

Fredrik sighs, then gets up and goes upstairs. I go over to the sofa and open my Instagram, scrolling through post after post of my beautiful daughter and son, 742 of them, available for every single psycho child-snatcher out there to see. My eyes are twitching and burning with exhaustion and all the shed tears, but I won't stop until I have read every single comment, until I have looked at every last person who's liked an image of my children.

II

Selma

It's two days before Halloween and most of the shopfronts on Oslo's upscale Bogstadveien are decked out with garish displays: skeletons hanging from wires, ghouls with empty eye sockets and evil smiles, porcelain pumpkins and jack-o'-lanterns, hairy spiders clinging to plastic webs, dolls with cracked faces, chocolates wrapped in eyeball foil. Selma stops absentmindedly in front of a hardware shop for a long moment, waiting for the light at the pedestrian crossing to turn green. Some creepy dolls have been placed inside the large gleaming stainless-steel pots, and a cartoonish witch sits atop a purple Le Creuset casserole dish. On a shelf, a huge chef's knife has been plunged into a real pumpkin, with scarlet pomegranate seeds spilling from the 'wound'. Selma crosses the street and continues towards downtown, bracing herself against the brisk wind, drawing in the autumn air, closing her hand hard around a ball of tissue in her jacket pocket.

Her phone starts vibrating and she pulls it out, squinting at its screen in the sunlight as she reaches the House of

Literature and the edge of the royal palace's park. It's a message from Olav.

Morning. The police have just announced an unscheduled press conference at 11. Blix case.

Selma half runs through the park, simultaneously scrolling through the newsfeeds of *Dagsposten*'s competitors, *VG* and *Dagbladet*. 'Breakthrough in the Blix case?' asks a *VG* headline, though when Selma clicks on it she realizes it doesn't say anything new, rather only speculates about what will be announced at the unexpected press conference. Her right flank begins to hurt, and she slows down at the end of the park, grateful for the chance to catch her breath at the red light. Could it be that they have a breakthrough in the Blix case? It's now ten days since Lucia was taken and the circumstances of her abduction have only seemed more and more bizarre with every passing day.

'She's either dead by now or she's been hidden so well she'll never be found,' Olav said yesterday, staring intently at the blown-up picture of the little girl on Selma's screen, as though she might suddenly come to life and reveal her whereabouts. It was genius, really, Selma thought, nodding at her boss's words. The playdate. Buying all that time before anyone realized she'd been taken. She could be anywhere by now, anywhere at all. Or she could indeed be dead.

Selma stops at Deli de Luca on Karl Johan, as she does every morning, even when she's in a hurry, like she is now.

'The usual?' asks the girl behind the counter.

Selma smiles and nods.

She walks the last few hundred meters to the office,

drawing in the delicious aroma of the double caramel spiced latte. It is her one and only luxury most days – it has to be at sixty-two kroner, but Selma knows she's likely to be at work well into the night, like she has been every night since 20 October, when Norway suddenly had one of Europe's most baffling abduction cases on its hands. She nods to her colleagues Kai-Marius and Lisbeth before sliding into her chair in the little pod they share by the floor-to-ceiling windows, her cheeks stinging from the icy wind.

Olav saunters over as Selma waits for her computer to start up. 'Hi there,' he says, leaning against the flimsy partition wall that separates her pod from the rest of the open-plan office and placing a chocolate-chip cookie on her desk, like he does every morning.

'Hi.' She smiles at him then turns to the flurry of emails ticking into her inbox.

'So, shall we walk over there at around ten thirty?'

'Sure.'

'What do you think they've got?'

'Well, I imagine it must be some kind of breakthrough,' says Selma. 'Maybe the kidnappers have made another demand? Or they've got a DNA match?'

'Yeah, that's what I was thinking.'

'It just seems so odd,' says Selma, 'for this to be a ransom case when Lucia Blix is obviously from such an average background. The kidnappers are clearly professionals, so why didn't they target a kid from a loaded family, if it's money they're after? It makes no sense.'

'No' – Olav rubs at a raised red patch on his cheek – 'it doesn't.'

'I'm going to write a bullet-point list of the case, right now.'

'You do that every day, Selma.'

'We're missing something.'

'That's a job for the police.'

'It's a job for the hungriest reporter in town.'

Olav laughs and walks away.

Selma glances at Kai-Marius and Lisbeth, who are huddled together and watching a YouTube video of Ariana Grande doing an impersonation of Christina Aguilera, then plugs in her headphones, opens her long and carefully organized 'Blix Case' document and highlights the Swedish points in bold.

- The **mobile phone,** a Samsung Galaxy S7, used by 'Line' when she contacted Elisa on 19 October, was found in some shrubbery by the roadside just south of **Strömstad,** across the border in **Sweden.** It was most likely thrown from a **moving vehicle** and the SIM card and phone are currently undergoing analysis.

- The house at Asnestoppen 25 in Sandefjord was rented through Airbnb on 15 October, by a woman named Kathrine Sæther. This profile has been revealed as fake, using a **stolen driver's license** and the hacked Facebook account of a woman of the same name for verification. The house was rented for a week for 9450 kroner and paid for with a Mastercard registered to a **Heiki Vilkainen,** a **Swedish citizen** of Finnish origin. Vilkainen is unaccounted for and on **Interpol's list for wanted individuals.**

ALEX DAHL

'You ready?'

Olav's voice cuts into Selma's highly concentrated state and it takes her a moment to recall where they are going. The press conference. She nods and gets up, shivering slightly in the warm editorial office at the thought of stepping outside into that cold wind.

'We can confirm that we have made an arrest in the Lucia Blix abduction case. A twenty-one-year-old man from Oppegård was apprehended yesterday afternoon and has been formally charged with perverting the investigation and falsifying case material. He has confessed to writing the ransom note of 21 October and delivering it to Fredrik and Elisa Blix. His confession is supported by our forensic findings. He is, however, not currently suspected of being involved in Lucia Blix's abduction.'

Police chief Hans Gundersen speaks in a low, monotonous voice, but he is a man of natural authority. He is broad-shouldered and has the physique of an aging military man, thinks Selma.

The room explodes in a cacophony of shouted questions and flashing cameras.

'Is the suspect connected to Fredrik and Elisa Blix?'

'We don't believe he is.'

'Does the man have previous convictions?'

'I am unable to say at present.'

'Does he have an alibi for the 19th and 20th of October?'

'Yes, he does.'

'What is his motive for sending the letter?'

'We have not yet established a motive.'

Selma and Olav look at each other. Another dead end. Some weirdo who wanted attention and went to the lengths of crafting a threatening letter to the parents of an abducted child – sometimes Selma finds it almost impossible in her job to believe that humans are inherently good.

'Let's get out of here,' she says, eyeing the exit through the throng of journalists.

'Yep. It's pretty clear they don't have anything else new.'

They walk back to the office at speed and Selma almost has to jog to keep up with her very tall, lanky boss. Olav Hammel is the kind of guy who does a fifteen-kilometer forest run before work, or at least that's the impression Selma has. His thick dark hair and deep dimples make him look boyish, though he must be well into his forties. Selma herself is more of a Netflix and takeaways kind of girl.

'You know, I don't know what it is – call it gut feeling or intuition or whatever – but I feel as though they're looking in the wrong places,' she says.

Olav stops walking and looks at her. 'What do you mean, Eriksen?'

'I'm not really sure,' she says, letting her eyes rest for a moment on a plane flying low above them, rocking visibly in the fierce wind. 'It's just a feeling I have. That the answer is simpler than it seems, but the investigation is heading in the wrong direction.'

'Well, I've learned not to mess with your intuition, Selma.' Olav starts walking again, though slowly now, a thoughtful look on his face. 'Why don't you just go with whatever hunch you have and see what you come up with?'

Selma nods. 'I'm going to really focus on the parents,' she says. 'Look deep.'

Olav grunts his approval and Selma turns her face into the wind jostling through the gap between two tall buildings; it claws at her hair, slicking it back like a jet of water. For a moment she closes her eyes, allowing herself to be taken over by the feeling that's become familiar to her over the years, the sense that she's detaching from the outside world and getting sucked deep inside herself, held there as if within an impenetrable cocoon.

It's close to midnight and Selma is the last person left in the office, by several hours. Olav sent a message a couple of hours ago: 'Go home, Eriksen. It's bedtime!'

She isn't tired, not really. She might close her eyes for an hour or so on the sofa in the meeting room, but she's not going to go home. Not when she's like this – when she's managed to step into that zone where it feels as though her attention and insights have been sharpened to lethal incisiveness. It is in this zone that Selma is sometimes able to see the connections and inconsistencies missed or overlooked by others. Hyperactive, scatterbrained, classic ADHD – Selma has been labeled with all of that. But the upside of her kind of neuro-wiring is the extreme singular focus that she brings into play when she turns her attention to something she is really interested in; that and her ability to remember vast amounts of small details. Concentrating on dull tasks can be tricky unless she takes her meds, but if she's really taken with something, she can devote herself to it so completely that it's as if she's tapping into a secret sense. She discovered her talent and love for writing in high school, and she's ploughed every last bit of energy and focus into that ever since. As a journalist, the way her brain works finally became useful – applauded, even. She looks around the empty editorial office. She deserves to be here, but who would have thought that back in school?

She returns to her screen, which is filled by Elisa Blix's Facebook cover photo, the one from Christmas. The perfect family. She stares at Elisa's features, at the wide, red-lipped smile that doesn't seem to quite reach her eyes – or maybe Selma is imagining that.

'Who are you?' she whispers. 'Why *you*?'

12

Lucia

19 October 2017

Josephine and I turn the lights off and sit in the tent. I wish I had a tent in my room too. She holds the torch and I turn the pages. I read out loud – I'm better at reading because she says the same word many times in a row. We laugh because it's a funny book about a dog that lives in a family with lots of children who all love him so he gets taken for so many walks his legs get tired.

'When do we have to go to bed?' I ask.

'Mamma will let us stay up late because it's a special occasion.'

My mamma said I can call her when I want if I want to go home. I won't, at least not now. Now is nice. But I might when we have to go to sleep, if I feel scared. Minky is here in the tent with us too, and Josephine's cuddle toy, a pink stuffed pig called Troof.

We finish the book and Josephine holds the torch underneath her chin so her face gets spooky and I laugh and then I say, 'Josephine, stop.'

'Just call me Josie.'

We leave the tent and decide to do some drawing, so Josie looks through lots of drawers for pencils, but they're empty. My drawers are full of junk and my mamma always says I have to sort them out or else. She finds the pencils in her bag and then we sit close together on the warm wooden floor and start. I draw the dog from the book. He's hiding from one of the family children behind a sofa, his long black tail showing.

'Where's your daddy?' I ask.

'He's gone,' says Josie.

'Oh,' I say.

Josie's breath and my breath are the same speed and every time she breathes out I feel it on my arm, like a little wind. Josie's drawing a girl swimming from a beach.

'When is he coming back?' I ask.

Josie looks at me and shrugs, but she doesn't answer. She's sad. I know that because her mouth is pressed shut. I'd be sad too, if my daddy was gone. I think about my daddy – he likes to tickle my belly and call me his little ragdoll. I feel sad because right now he and my mamma and Lyder are in my house, maybe watching something funny on TV and eating cheese puffs, but I'm here. I swallow hard three times and draw the dog's ears carefully. They are long and floppy.

When Josie speaks, I'd forgotten that I'd asked her a question.

'I never see my daddy.'

I open my mouth to say 'Oh' again, but just then Josie's mamma comes into the room and says, 'Hey, girls! Oh, are you okay? You look a bit... Did you have a tiff? Anyway, put your smiles back on and come with me. I have a surprise for you.'

13

Lucia

My mamma says I'm too big to be carried, but Josie's mamma doesn't think that, because she picks me up in the night and carries me. I say, 'What's happening?' and she says, 'We're going on a trip,' and I say, 'I want to go home,' and she says, 'We *are* going home.'

It's dark in the house, so I don't see the man until we're right next to him. He's standing at the top of the stairs and he has a black hat on and a black scarf wrapped all the way up his face so I can only see his nose and eyes.

Josie's mamma hands me to the man and he says, 'I thought you said you'd knocked them out.'

'I did,' says Josie's mamma, and then the man makes a loud noise, like my daddy does if I get out of bed too many times at bedtime.

He carries me fast down the stairs and I shout 'No!', but the man looks at me and his eyes are big and angry, so I stop. The front door is open and the man carries me fast through it, making his eyes even bigger and pressing his finger to his lips. It's raining and everything is wet and shining and I want to scream but I can't and my mouth is open and little drops of water fall into it.

14

Lucia

I'm in a box in the ground, like dead people. Or maybe the box isn't in the ground yet, because it's moving in a strange way, like it's sliding fast down a hill. My eyes are open, but I can't see anything. I open my mouth to scream, but there's no sound, only a squawk like from a bird that's fallen out of its nest onto the road and is waiting to get run over. I try to touch something, but my arms feel heavy and they flop back down.

'Hello?' I whisper, even though I know I'm on my own. My eyes begin to cry. Why haven't Mamma and Pappa come for me yet? What if they never come? How can I get out of the box? And what if I do get out and the bad man is standing on the outside? Or what if I don't escape and the box is thrown into the sea and water comes in slowly, drowning me?

There's a strange sound. Like an engine. Could the box be in a plane, flying me far away? Or maybe I'm not inside a box at all but the boot of a car? I stroke the hard surface I'm lying on with my fingertips and it's cool and smooth.

Not metal, not wood, more like tough plastic. My fingers move further along and the bottom of the box goes up in a smooth curve, then across in a low ceiling. It's like I'm a baby bird inside an egg, but I don't think baby birds feel afraid inside their eggs.

Mamma always tells me that I'm strong and that I can do anything. *My baby girl is stronger than she looks*, she'll say, and she'll laugh, her eyes creasing in the way I love, and she'll pinch my arm muscles. I clamp my eyes shut and try to see Mamma in my mind. And there she is – squatting down beside me, wearing her navy uniform, looking at me with her brown eyes that are just like mine. My mamma is Big Me and I'm Little Her.

I try to think what Mamma would say if she could speak to me inside the box. *Be strong, baby girl, be strong until I can hold you in my arms again.* I repeat it in my head, over and over. *Be strong, be strong, be strong, be strong.*

I must have fallen asleep because I don't know how much time has passed when the top of the box is suddenly lifted off, making my eyes hurt when the light comes in.

The bad man reaches for me.

'Shhh,' he says, pressing his pointing finger to his lips. 'I'm not going to hurt you, okay? Just please shut up.' His eyes aren't angry but soft, like Daddy's eyes when we play games and he realizes I'm screaming for real and it isn't funny anymore.

The man scoops me up like a sack of potatoes, puts me over his shoulder and starts walking. I look past him and realize I must have been shut inside the ski box on the roof of the car that's parked behind us. We're indoors in a large garage like the ones at Mamma's airport where they keep the small planes when they're not flying.

He carries me to a van with no windows and puts me down on the metal floor inside the back. I look up. There's a half-open sliding panel right above me. 'Are you okay to climb up?' the man says, nodding for me to open it all the way.

There's a kind of bedroom in the roof of the van. I put a foot into a little cubby hole on the wall and pull myself up. Now I can see into the sleeping space and up there are Josie's mamma and Josie, asleep, holding Kimmi the cat.

Josie's mamma opens her eyes and smiles at me. 'Hi, sweetie,' she whispers and reaches out to try to stroke my hair.

I start to cry again, but I'm not sure if I'm happy or even more sad to see them. I lie down beside Josie and her mamma, burying my hands in Kimmi's fluffy coat.

The man pokes his head and shoulders up into the sleeping space. 'Ready to go?' he says, and Josie's mamma nods.

'Where are we going?' I whisper.

'Home, sweet girl,' says Josie's mamma. 'Sleep now.'

Home... 'I need Minky,' I say, but no one gives her to me, even though I've had her since the day I was born and can't manage without her.

'This will make her sleep,' says the man, and the mamma presses a tissue to my nose and I want to scream, but I can't.

I wake up again and I'm still in the van bedroom next to Josie and I try to make her wake up but she doesn't.

'Hello?' I say. 'Hello, hello, hello...?'

It's dark and the van is moving, but it feels more like a boat rocking than a van driving. I crawl forward and slide the panel to the side to look down into the back of the van and it's dark but not totally dark and there's no one down there.

I try to wake Josie again, but she won't wake up and I can't tell if she's dead. One time I saw a dead dog. We went on a trip to a country where it's so hot that sometimes dogs die and in that country people's dogs don't always live inside the houses.

I try to wake Josie for a long time and when I shake her shoulders she makes a strange sound, so she can't be dead.

I don't know how it happened because I didn't want to sleep more, but I must have fallen asleep because when I wake up again Josie is gone.

I look down into the van and it's moving, but like driving now. It's still dark outside. Josie's mamma looks up and sees me. She says, 'Oh hi, sweet girl.' She looks like Snow White, only old. Or maybe like her stepmother. I hide in the corner. I cry a lot. After a long while, the mamma comes and says we're going to the bathroom. I don't want to come down, but I have to. I have to pee very badly.

The van has stopped in an empty parking lot in the woods. There's a hut with writing on the door and a picture of a lady under it, but I don't know what the letters mean.

When I've been to the toilet, the mamma grabs hold of my elbow and says, 'Come with me.'

'No,' I say, and I try to wrench my elbow loose, but she's very strong and I can feel her nails digging into my skin. 'I want my mamma and I want Minky.'

I look over at the van and I can see Josie in the front

seat. The man has a baseball hat on and he's standing outside smoking. My daddy doesn't smoke because it rots your heart.

'Come on,' says the mamma, and I don't come, but she makes me by pulling my arm.

I can hear cars driving fast nearby, but I can't see them through the trees, so they can't see me. The mamma walks me away from the toilet hut, gripping my elbow still, and away from the van, and we stand underneath an orange tree that drips onto us from its wet leaves.

'Look,' she says, 'you need to listen to me. There's something you need to know. We've rescued you. Those people, they weren't your family. Not really. They were pretending. You were taken by them when you were little.'

'No!' I say, and the mamma keeps talking, but I start screaming it – 'No! No! No!' – and then the man comes running towards us and the next thing I know is I'm in the van bedroom again and screaming 'No!' again and again, but no one comes.

Josie sings in the dark. I close my eyes, but I know not to cry because the man will hurt me. He promised. 'If you scream or cry or try anything at all, I'll fuck you up and that's a promise,' he said when he put me into the box.

I'm glad I'm not in the box anymore but in the van with Josie. It's moving fast and it's almost nice to be up here in the little space. At least I can't see the man.

I roll over so I face Josie. 'Can you help me?' I whisper.

Josie shakes her head slowly and keeps singing.

I grab the bag of peanuts and shake a few into my hand.

'Please eat something,' said Josie's mamma earlier, 'or I'll worry about you.'

'I will never eat anything you give me,' I said, but I can't help it now. They're salty and crunchy and delicious. I don't know why my mamma never let me have any, even though I asked her many times.

I wonder if my mamma is on a plane now. If she looks out the window, maybe she'll see a road and maybe it's the road I'm on and maybe she'll even see this van.

'My mamma and pappa are going to find you and you'll go to prison,' I said to Josie's mamma, and I know that's true because taking other people's children isn't allowed. And it is true that my mamma and pappa are going to find me, because me and Lyder are the two best things that ever happened to them.

But Josie's mamma said, 'Oh, sweet girl, don't waste your precious thoughts on them. They're not even going to look for you.'

15

Lucia

When I wake up, the van has stopped. It's still dark, but the sky is starting to get light at the edges. Josie and her mamma are sleeping. I crawl to the front of the van's bedroom so I can look down into the driver's seat but no one is there. Maybe we've stopped so the man can pee and if I hurry down now I could run away before he gets back and maybe I could find some kind people who could help me and then it would all be okay again.

I slide down into the front seat and stop to listen. We are stopped at a gas station and I can see a brightly lit kiosk with a lady behind the counter from here. I can get there, it's just a quick dash across to the kiosk. I try the door, trying to be quiet so Josie's mamma doesn't wake up. It's locked. I try the other door, and this one's open. I creep outside and move quietly around the side of the car. All I have to do now is run as fast as I can into the kiosk. The lady will help me then, she has to. I come round the side of the car to the other side but there's the man, holding the fuel pump. I turn and begin to run, I can still make it, but he's faster than me and stronger, too.

'Hey,' he hisses and drops the fuel pump. 'Come here, you little shit.' He picks me up and I try to kick him, but he pins me to him and holds both my arms and my legs at the same time. He pushes me back into the van and jumps in, driving off fast.

'Get back up there or I'll break every fucking bone in your body,' he screams and I scramble back into the bedroom in the roof. Josie's mamma is awake now and she grabs me at the back of my neck.

'And then he'll kill you,' she whispers. Then she places her handkerchief over my nose and mouth and when I breathe in there's that weird smell again.

I wake from the van stopping.

'Come,' says Josie's mamma, and her face looks tired and pale. We climb back down and I realize that we're inside a garage. It's so narrow that the van door pushes against the wall when Josie's mamma opens it.

Josie comes down from the space in the roof behind me and we all go inside the house.

'Where are we?' I ask, but no one answers.

We're put in front of a television and Josie's mamma finds a cartoon for us to watch, but it's in a strange language. She gives us a bag of Haribo sweets and then she and the man go into the kitchen and shut the door, but we can still hear them. The mamma laughs, but the man sounds angry. After a while she comes out with a plate of pizza, and I eat it, even though I said I'd never eat anything they gave me. The sky is totally light now and that's strange because to me it feels like the evening and I'm not used to eating pizza for breakfast.

We watch cartoons for a long time. Josie turns to me and her face is pale like a ghost in the light from the TV. 'Do you want to play the clapping game with me?' she asks.

'No,' I say. I'm afraid. My arm hurts from where the man grabbed me. I don't want to be here with Josie and the strange adults. All I want is to go home, but if I even begin to think about home, like the patch of peeling paint on our door, or the yellow roses on the windowsill or my room which is too messy but cozy too, then my eyes begin to cry. Why haven't Mamma and Pappa come for me yet?

They'll never even look for you.

'What about Funky Lady?'

'No.' I never want to play with Josie again.

'Don't cry,' she whispers.

'I want to go home.'

Josie nods and returns to the screen. We sit watching for a while, tears falling down my face. When the mamma comes back into the room, I manage to stop crying, but only because I'm so afraid of what the man will do if I don't. He said he will break every fucking bone in my body.

'Come with me,' she says.

I stand up. My legs tremble.

We go upstairs and I sit on the closed toilet seat next to the bath tub while Josie's mamma rubs a strange shampoo into my head. 'Don't touch it,' she says.

She takes me back downstairs and I watch more TV with Josie, the shampoo stinging my head. It smells bad, like maybe gasoline. It itches and I have to scratch it even if the mamma said don't touch, but when I bring my finger away from my head it's dark brown. I wipe it on the sofa.

After a long time, Josie's mamma washes the shampoo out of my hair. 'Look,' she says and hands me a mirror.

My hair is dark brown like Josie's. I stare at myself and for a moment I almost want to laugh because it's so strange. The mamma brushes my hair, carefully getting rid of tangles. She strokes my head as she goes along and when she's finished she bends down and looks at me.

'You really are special,' she says.

I look away.

The doorbell rings and the voices of the mamma and the man in the kitchen go quiet. Then the mamma comes into the room where we're watching TV. 'Quick,' she whispers, grabbing me by the arm, but I pull it free. I'll do what she says, but she can't grab me like that.

I hear another woman's voice from the kitchen, shouting in a strange language, and the man shouts back. We rush up the stairs, and in a very small bedroom Josie and I have to lie next to each other on a very small bed with a thin duvet thrown over us. Josie's mamma leaves us and after a moment we can hear her voice, too. We can't make out the words, but the adults are shouting and one of the ladies cries really loudly at one point. We hear a loud bang and then the man shouts even louder than all the other crying and shouting. Then for a long time there is talking but no shouting.

Josie and I hold hands under the duvet. Then we peel the

top of it down slowly, slowly. There's nobody in the room and the house is quiet except for a calm voice now and again.

'Come on,' whispers Josie.

'We can't,' I say. 'Your mamma said to not move no matter what.'

'Yeah, but that was ages ago and she's forgotten we're still up here and I'm hungry.'

'Me too,' I whisper.

We creep quietly down the stairs and from the landing we can see into the kitchen. It's empty, but the door to the living room where we watched TV is shut and we can hear voices from in there.

'I think it's just Mamma and Mikko,' says Josie, too loud, and I press my finger to my lips to make her be quiet.

On the kitchen counter is a bag of peanuts and a packet of Oreos. We move fast, like thieves, and my hand is reaching for the cookies when the door opens and a woman I've never seen before stands in front of us. She has black, choppy hair and black writing on her neck. At first she looks so confused you'd think someone had hit her on the back of the head. Then she realizes that Josie and I are just little kids, so she smiles, because most people smile when they meet little girls for the first time. But then her face changes, and maybe the cookies were hers because she looks very angry or maybe sad.

'What's your name?' she whispers, looking straight at me, but Josie and I start to run and the lady tries to grab me, shouting, 'Hey! Hey you! Come back here, little girl! What's your name?'

Josie and I run as fast as we can upstairs and pull the

duvet back over our heads. This time, the shouting is even louder, and there's some screaming and loud bangs too. We hold hands under the duvet again. Josie cries because she thinks the man has killed her mamma. We must have fallen asleep because when I wake it's dark outside and Josie's gone. The house is silent but then I hear a sound – heavy boots stomping up the stairs.

16

Elisa

I hear his voice long before I'm able to extricate myself from the hazy clutches of medicated sleep. Something is in my hand: my phone, still. I open my eyes, but I can't immediately identify my surroundings. White and beige striped curtains, rectangular shards of light scattered across the ceiling by a futuristic chandelier, piles of *Lego* magazines on a low table in front of me; this is my living room and I'm on the sofa. It's light outside. My husband is talking.

'Lucia,' I whisper, my tongue thick with the aftereffects of the sleeping pills. This is the first time I've slept properly since they took my baby. 'Lucia! Has something happened?' I try to sit up and search Fredrik's wild, bloodshot eyes.

'There's been a sighting! She was caught on CCTV on the morning of the 20th. They've only just uncovered the footage. In Sweden. She was with a man. We need to head down to the police station. Hans Gundersen and Haakon Kjeller are on their way down from Oslo.'

I rush around the house getting ready while Fredrik fills me in.

'It was taken at a Shell gas station near Karlskrona on the south coast. About eight hours' drive from here. There's a ferry that runs from there to Poland. The police believe she may have been taken across on that.'

'What about the woman – was she with them? And Josephine?'

'No. Lucia appears to have been on her own with the man.'

My nails sink into the pale flesh of my palms. Who is the man, what has he done to my girl and why does he want her? She is seven years old and unaccounted for in the presence of a strange man. A seemingly normal mother has handed her over to this man, who could be taking her anywhere. But why?

'Why?' I scream, and I can't stop screeching it, over and over, rushing from room to room like a wild animal. I pick up the heavy blue vase Fredrik's mother gave us for a wedding anniversary and throw it across the living room. It shatters against the wall, leaving a dent in the wood paneling. I stand staring at it and this snaps me out of my desperation. I begin to pick up the shards, but Fredrik stops me and holds me so close I can't move.

'God help us,' I say, into the warm crook of his neck.

He pulls back slightly. 'What?' he says, body alert.

I say nothing else, just focus on syncing my breath to his.

There is no mistaking her, though the images are grainy and taken from above. Lucia is pictured trying to run across the concourse from a white van towards the twenty-four-hour gas station. In the second image, the man, who was refueling, drops the fuel pump from his right hand and grabs Lucia with his left hand. In the third, he is seen holding her tight like a baby, his left hand sliding the door of the van back open. Lucia is wearing her navy pajama bottoms with white stars, and a fluffy red sweater I've never seen before. The man is wearing a baseball cap, but from the way he tilts his head it appears he is bald underneath it. He's heavily built and has the short, thick neck of a boxer. A man that big could crush Lucia in his hands like a porcelain doll.

'We're running the plates across the system at the moment,' says Gaute Svendsen. 'And we're running the images through a facial recognition system.'

'What about the woman?' I ask. 'Line?'

'There haven't been any confirmed sightings of her yet. We're now working on the assumption that she was used only in the initial stage of the abduction and is no longer with Lucia. She's most likely known to the police if that is the case. She would have been recruited on the street or through criminal acquaintances, so when we're done here we're going to take you through to the database to look at a long list of previous convicts that fit the profile.'

17

Marcus

He stands at the window, looking out. It's just a normal window, though it doesn't open from the inside. His room is pleasant but sparse, like a room at a Premier Inn on the outskirts of a commuter town, the kind of place he sometimes used to crash for one night after meetings before flying out again the next morning. He has his own no-frills bathroom with wall-mounted soap dispensers that are refilled weekly, and a mini fridge under his desk where he likes to keep a couple of Fantas and some chocolate from the tuck shop.

His room looks out at a solid wall of rain-lashed pines. Who needs fences with nature like this, he sometimes wonders, though of course the fences are there, beyond the trees, where he can't see them. It's true what they say: Norwegian prisons seek to evoke repentance by measures other than barbed wire, floodlights and concrete. Here, the guards, who call themselves guides, knock if they need him, and they pretend that Marcus can choose whether or not to unlock the door to his cell, which is always referred to as his 'room'. He addresses the guides by their first names and they treat him more or less how a junior employee could expect to be treated in a company.

A storm is moving in, heavy rainclouds blackening the sky above the forest, vicious winds flattening the tops of the trees. The prison nestles in forested hills that fringe the town and that further north swell into snow-capped mountains. Most of the rooms face directly onto the forest, but the canteen offers panoramic views of the valley, as though to purposefully show the inmates the freedom they're missing and should be striving for.

And yet, Marcus doesn't miss the outside world the way he might have once imagined he would. He doesn't constantly think about the restrictions, nor does he pine for the life he used to lead. When you've lost everything, what is there to miss? The one thing he does find himself craving is the feeling of tearing through a summer field in the dewy purple light of morning. That he could still have, outside. Everything else is lost.

On the way back to his room after breakfast, Marcus stops at the news stand. All four major national newspapers are running the same photograph on their front pages. A little girl, angelic-looking with a sweet gap-toothed smile and soulful brown puppy eyes.

'Abducted!'; 'Snatched!'; 'The Playdate Tragedy!'; 'Lucia (7) MISSING!' read the headlines. Marcus grabs the closest newspaper, *VG*, and flicks to the second page, a sickening feeling spreading out in his gut.

The shocking abduction of Lucia Blix (7) in Sandefjord has sparked an international manhunt for the perpetrators, believed to be connected to a notorious Eastern European trafficking network.

He drops his gaze from the newspaper to the stripy moss-green carpet of the inmates' recreation room, his heartbeat suddenly loud and fast in his ears, his hands shaking violently. Feeling the attention of one of the guides on him, he is careful to walk slowly over to a seating area, where he continues reading.

Lucia Blix was taken by a woman posing as a mother with a child of a similar age on Friday 19 October. A major breakthrough in the case came recently when it was discovered that Lucia was captured on CCTV early on the morning of Saturday 20 October near Karlskrona, Sweden, in the company of a man identified today as notorious criminal Mikulasz (Mikko) Vrcesk Eilaanen of Ruisa, Estonia.

Eilaanen has previously served time both in Finland and Sweden for crimes connected to the so-called Vicodius network, which is known for its involvement in numerous international offenses, including trafficking, drug dealing, sexual abuse, assaults and murder.

Marcus forces his eyes away from the shocking article, and from the shy smile of the tragic little girl, to another picture on the opposite page, of the girl's mother, Elisa Blix. The picture seems to have been taken at a press conference:

she is clutching a photo of the child, her tear-lashed face contorted into a grimace of absolute horror. He moves his gaze to the last picture, a posed family portrait: mother and father, son and daughter. He stares at each face in turn, familiar and unfamiliar at the same time, before closing the newspaper, his hands trembling uncontrollably.

18

Elisa

Every day is the same as the last. And every day passes so slowly, like we're suspended inside a bubble where time simply doesn't exist. I don't sleep much at all. I lie in bed counting out the minutes of the night. In the morning, I don't gently stroke Fredrik awake, the way I sometimes used to, letting my hand travel slowly across the familiar landscapes of his skin. I just get up and sit at the kitchen table drinking black coffee, staring at the darkness outside. I wake Lyder, feed him, try to listen to his uninterrupted chatter, then I drive him to nursery, slowly, because it has rained heavily all week and the roads are slick with icy water, and because my hands shake. I don't walk him into the building like I used to, before. Instead, I pull up right in front of the gate and make my son, my sweet little five-year-old boy, walk to the door by himself while I watch from the car. He doesn't seem to mind this, but even if he did, he'd have no choice – I can't bear the questions, the gentle squeezes on my arm, the rounded, tear-brimmed eyes staring at me. I feel them anyway, even through my cocoon space: the stares of the other parents dropping their kids off.

By the time I get back home, Fredrik has gone to work. He had a week off and we agreed at the end of it that it would perhaps be best for everyone that he went back to the office. Every day, I sit on the sofa staring at the black TV screen or the bare trees outside, or the news on my phone, the seconds trickling past impossibly slowly, until eleven o'clock when the police call. It is always Gaute Svendsen who rings. Today, it's almost ten past eleven when he calls, and the ten minutes I'm left waiting are like a long, painful life.

'Hi, Elisa, it's Gaute.'

'Any news?' I ask this before even saying hello, though I know that they would have called me already, eleven or not, if there were any news at all.

'We're still trying to establish whether there might be any CCTV evidence of Line. It seems impossible that she should have evaded every camera. We're looking at airports and ferry ports and gas stations in the days leading up to 19 October as we believe she only arrived in the area on the Tuesday, as you know. Unfortunately, unless there's an incident within forty-eight hours, these tapes are generally taped over. Also, it's problematic that we have absolutely no leads as to where she came from.'

'Okay,' I say. I just want to put the phone down so Gaute can spend his time looking for Lucia, not updating me on non-existent progress.

'How are you holding up?' He always asks this, though I imagine the answer must be pretty obvious.

'Fredrik went back to work on Monday. I... What am I supposed to do?'

'I don't think there's anything you can do but wait. I can't imagine how hard that waiting must be, Elisa. Just know that we are putting everything we can into finding Lucia.'

I lie on the sofa, just staring at the last few orange leaves clinging to the black, rain-lashed branches outside.

After a long while, I get up and stand by the window. The rain has let up but the street is wet and covered in rotting, trampled leaves. The little square windows of the other houses on our road are dark: everyone is at work. I wish I was up high, in an airplane or at the very least in a tall building, then there'd be a chance that I could be looking at wherever Lucia is now, without knowing it. The police believe she's in Poland or further east, where the network they think is holding my child operates.

I'm not sure I believe it. I feel her, close. It's the one thing that gives me some comfort – as though in her absence a new channel of communication has been established between my child and myself. I can actually feel her. For that reason, I know that she's alive. And for that reason, I can hardly sleep; I need to be feeling for her every minute to know that she is still out there. If I go to sleep I risk waking up and not feeling her at all, and I would know then that she has been taken forever. Of course, I do occasionally pass out, falling into a brief doze on the sofa, or losing count of the minutes deep in the night when Fredrik sleeps fitfully beside me, or closing my eyes for a moment too long when I read Lyder his bedtime story.

I move away from the window and walk into the kitchen.

It's a mess and I could use this waiting time to clean it up. It would give me something to do, a few minutes filled. I pick up a sponge and stare at it. It's cold and wet. My throat constricts and I know I should let myself cry. But I don't. I put the sponge down and wipe my hand on my jeans. I stand still, expecting tears to come, but they don't. Instead, my throat feels tighter and tighter and I have to bend forward to draw a breath of air. For so many years, I've suffered from anxiety. I've spent so many nights awake, frozen by the terrors in my own mind; so many days barely functioning or cushioned by diazepam. I've had moments when I would have done anything to escape the sheer hell of being me, and this makes me want to both scream and laugh out loud, because all of that was merely a dress rehearsal for what I am living through now.

I have done bad things – I can't escape that fact. I've hurt people. I've made choices incompatible with being a decent person. Perhaps I deserve bad things in return. But my child does not.

I am slow, sluggish, separated from the churn of the world, but on the inside I'm on fire. I'm in a suspended state of blind, black panic, a cruel filter through which everything must be experienced, so that even the most mundane of tasks, like wringing out a sponge, seems an impossible undertaking. I am held as if underwater in an iron grip, snatching the smallest bubbles of air, tearing at the cold darkness surrounding me.

I get in the car, like I sometimes do, and drive around the neighborhood as if I'm looking for someone, which is of course precisely what I am doing. My foot feels heavy on the gas pedal. I drive slowly down our road, keeping my eyes on the brown, wet tarmac, avoiding the decorations I know are there in all the windows: skeletons strung from curtain rails, electric skull tea lights, clumsily carved pumpkin faces. This evening, all the lights will be lit, the sound of children's rhymes and laughter will fill the street, and our doorstep will be busy with little ghosts and wide-eyed vampires clutching plastic buckets full of sugar. In Lucia's room, on the back of her door, hangs a new costume, a pretty pink and green dress torn to shreds and splattered with fake blood. It came with a white lace-veiled hat with a plastic knife handle protruding from the middle as if the child wearing it has been stabbed right through the head.

The rest of the day drags on. I take a diazepam to combat the flashes of pure panic and the desperation and terror of the last twelve days. Now is not the time for sobriety.

I collect Lyder and place him in front of the TV screen with a bowl of macaroni, peas and ketchup. It's just after four o'clock and it's getting dark; Fredrik will be arriving home soon. I will open several party-size bags of Haribo candy and empty them into the bowl that's shaped like a giant claw, picked out by Lucia from Nille's homeware department the day before she was taken. I will help Lyder into his mummy costume. I will splash cold water on my face and take another diazepam. I will stand at the door with Fredrik and Lyder, waiting for the doorbell to ring – this area is so full of families with children that there's little point sitting down in between the groups of trick-or-treaters. I will obsessively run my hand across my back pocket where my phone is, ringtone always set to loud, imagining the moment when it finally rings unexpectedly and Gaute Svendsen's booming, excited voice fills my ear and he says the words I need to hear: *We've found her – she's here! Lucia's been found! Hurry! Hurry!*

Lyder reluctantly steps into his mummy costume. Fredrik drinks a beer, then another, straight down, standing at the kitchen counter, scrolling through his phone. I take a diazepam, and a third of a Klonopin too. My arms feel so numb and leaden I can't tear open the candy bags and have to use scissors. We wait for the doorbell-ringing to begin, drifting aimlessly from room to room. But it doesn't. Nobody comes because everybody knows what's happened to the Blix family. Fury burns white hot in my stomach. Lyder starts to eat the candy and neither Fredrik nor I stop him.

'Come on,' I say, bundling my little mummy boy into his down jacket. I can tell he doesn't want to go outside – he, too, is struggling with how different and broken everything is, but he lets me lead him by the hand without protest. We walk down the shingle path and onto the main road. There are many families out: moms and dads chaperoning sugar-crazed kids. I turn back towards our house and see Fredrik standing with his back to the window, probably still drinking and scrolling. Lyder and I start walking behind a group of children and their parents. Suddenly I catch sight of a little girl with long blonde hair holding the hand of a heavyset man and I stop in my tracks. Lyder tugs at my arm and says something but I can't move even a centimeter. I'm rooted to the spot and all I can see is the girl, getting smaller and smaller, merging with the night, led away by the man. I scream.

19

Selma

Selma's eyes hurt after so many unbroken hours in front of the screen at work. She lies back on her bed, stroking Medusa and looking up at the unblemished grey ceiling. She could head over to the boxing club or go for a quick run – it's a particularly cold evening for October, but she could do with the fresh air.

She gets up and stands a while at the window, looking down onto Ullevålsveien and St Hanshaugen Park behind it. The sidewalks are unusually busy, and Selma remembers that it's Halloween. Tiny ghouls and witches rush around shrieking and laughing, swinging bucketloads of sweets, held back from the crawling traffic by mothers and fathers with blinking devil horns and half-heartedly painted faces. When she was a child, Halloween wasn't yet celebrated in Norway; it wasn't until her late teens that she started seeing jack-o'-lanterns and kids trick-or-treating. She's glad it wasn't a thing when she was little; after losing her mother, she became preoccupied with death and for years she had nightmares about skeletons and ghosts. At night in her dreams, a bleeding, sinewy, skeletal hand would emerge from the ground, or from a book or a wall, throttling her, and she'd wake, thrashing and shrieking, held tight by her father. She's in no doubt that she would have had panic attacks if people dressed as monsters from the underworld had rung the doorbell every Halloween.

The doorbell rings, and from the long-drawn-out buzz Selma can tell that it's a child pressing it. She ignores it and returns to her thoughts. Lucia Blix has been missing for twelve days now and, statistically speaking, the chance of finding her decreases drastically as each day goes by. By now she'll most likely have reached her intended destination, wherever that is, and her abductors will simply need to make sure she remains concealed. Because they had such a long head start before anyone knew she'd been taken, they're so much less likely to get caught.

Selma's been working on the Blix case all day. She sat poring over Google Earth, following the road from the rental house in Sandefjord to where 'Line's' phone was found near Strömstad just across the Swedish border, to the Shell gas station near Karlskrona where Lucia was captured on CCTV. The abductors had clearly taken her across to Sweden on one of the car ferries from Sandefjord to Strömstad and then headed south towards Karlskrona on the E20 motorway. The police are combing through the passenger lists for relevant ferries from Sandefjord, and from Karlskrona to Poland in the hours and days after Lucia was presumed to have gone missing, to try and establish any links to previously known offenders or persons connected to Mikko Eilaanen and his contacts.

Police are urgently appealing for Mikko Eilaanen's

estranged girlfriend and mother of his six-year-old son, Silwia Truja of Riga, Latvia, to come forward for questioning. Sources close to Ms Truja say she hasn't been seen in several weeks but that she has no contact with Eilaanen. Their son is in state care and has been for several years. Eilaanen was released from prison in December 2016 after serving eighteen months for GBH.

Selma studies the picture of Silwia Truja published by police. She's much younger than Eilaanen, still in her mid-twenties, and is posing in front of a rundown apartment building, presumably her home, crossing heavily tattooed arms in front of her chest, her dyed jet-black hair pulled sternly back from her face and gathered in a frizzy bun at the top of her head. Elisa Blix has been shown photos of Truja and insists she's not the person to whom she handed over Lucia on the playdate.

The doorbell rings again and again, several short, insistent bursts this time, and Selma swears under her breath. Medusa stands by the door, arching her back, hissing, readying herself for an intruder. Selma walks over to her and picks her slinky body off the floor, holding her close and planting a kiss on the top of her head. She lifts up the doorbell receiver and the video function starts up. A dark-haired little girl stands alone on the doorstep, staring straight into the camera. She's around five years old and is dressed in a green dinosaur costume, a stegosaurus hood framing her little face and completing the unusual outfit. Something moves at the side of the frame and Selma can make out the shadow of an adult standing nearby.

'Trick or treat?' the girl whispers, her expression grave and nervous.

'Sorry,' says Selma, 'I don't have any candy.'

'Okay,' says the little girl.

Selma replaces the receiver in its cradle and stands a moment looking at it, disturbed and distracted by the child. Again she thinks of Lucia Blix, not much older than this girl. She closes her eyes, and now it is Lucia she sees, dressed in dirty clothes, lying face up in the back of an empty van, her expression dejected and serious, listening to the rise and fall of her abductors' voices drifting through the thin metal wall of the driver's cabin. When the van goes over a pothole, Lucia is jostled and shaken on the bare floor. She cries silently. She throws up repeatedly in the corner of the van and when it lurches, her vomit flows towards her, making her cower in one corner, by the double-door. There is a tiny window high up, but it's too dirty to look through, even if she were able to reach it.

Selma puts Medusa back down on the floor and slips into her running shoes as if on autopilot. She remains in a dreamy, detached state as she takes the stairs down the four flights to street level and begins to run as soon as she's outside. She crosses the street between two cars waiting on a red light, and across the road in the oncoming lane behind the lights stands a white van like the one she saw in her mind, blowing exhaust into the crisp October air. She stares at it, and at the two men in the front, both looking out the windows, one of them tapping out a rhythm on the wheel. These two men, or any men like them, could be carrying a little girl in the back. She begins to run faster when she reaches the park on the other side of the busy road, trying to root herself in the present with each slap of her foot on the paving stones. Still, the vision of Lucia stays with her.

Selma's been having vivid visions, like the one of Lucia Blix in the back of a van, ever since she was a young child. Sometimes all it takes is meeting a stranger's eye and then it's as though a separate dimension opens through which she sees that person's life in intense detail. She doesn't know if her visions are ever accurate or just a byproduct of an exceptionally active imagination, but she's concluded that it doesn't matter – they still contribute to her rich inner life, and they sometimes lead directly to her being able to guess at connections she wouldn't otherwise have arrived at.

At times, real or not, these visions have brought Selma great comfort. There's a photograph of her mother as a young girl, likely in her early teens, and sometimes, if Selma stares at it intently enough, she is able to build the entire scene around the moment the photo was taken. The picture is in the matte, sepia colors of the sixties, and her mother is sitting at the kitchen table on a wooden bench. In front of her on the table is a plate of food. On the occasions when Selma is able to fully immerse herself in the picture, the food on the plate goes from a virtually indistinguishable dish to a fragrant, steaming *lapskaus*; delicious slices of *vossakorv* sausage floating in the broth of the stew, the potatoes slightly overcooked and crumbling. Selma can feel the spoon her mother is holding in her own hand, its cool, smooth silver snug in the crook of her thumb. She can run her hand across the waxy red-and-white checked tablecloth and angle her head to look out the window, onto snow-covered fields, dark pines crowding together on a little hillock at the edge of the field. Selma can also look the other way, to where her mother's aunt Bodil stands at the stove, stirring the *lapskaus*, humming to herself, her apron straining across her broad back.

Sometimes, after staying inside one of these imagined scenes for a long while, Selma feels depleted and strange, as though she has used up a large amount of mental energy to construct such detailed images of a moment in time. She is overwhelmed by that same sudden tiredness now, after running less than five minutes, and she has to stop to regain her breath. She looks up at the night sky, glowing russet at the edges from Oslo's artificial lights, then at a tall oak tree, the last of its leaves on the ground around it, like a discarded dress, leaving a smooth naked body underneath.

She tries to root herself in the moment, reestablishing a slow, even breathing pattern, but she can't rid herself of the image of the little girl being flung from side to side in the back of a fast-moving van.

Back at home, Selma stands a long while under the powerful water jet in the shower, rinsing herself of the mental images that bombarded her on her run. She needs to clear her thoughts and maintain focus on the facts at hand. *You're not going to find anything new in this case simply by imagining stuff*, she tells herself and returns to her notes.

- **20 October** – at 06.08 a.m. Lucia Blix is caught on CCTV with a man, now identified as Mikko Eilaanen, an Estonian citizen, at a Shell gas station 20 km west of Karlskrona in south Sweden. The white modified Renault van, registration LY78 NJ8, was reported stolen from a building site in Andebu on 15 October and has not been recovered.

- **Heiki Vilkainen,** whose card was used to pay for the Airbnb in Asnestoppen, served a sentence for aggravated assault at Fosie Prison in Malmö, Sweden from 2000 to 2005.
- **Mikko Eilaanen** served a sentence for drug-related offenses in the same prison between 1999 and 2001, and again between 2003 and 2007. Eilaanen also served two separate nine-month sentences in 1996 and 1997 for assault and drug offenses in Viru Prison in Estonia.
- Thug, working for someone? Who? Connection to Fredrik and Elisa Blix? (Unlikely.) Connections to Vicodius network (likely/established?), possible motive – trafficking. But why *her*???
- No further sightings of Lucia Blix or Mikko Eilaanen have been made.
- Where is Vilkainen?

20

Elisa

In the morning a bright sun has replaced the milky fog of last night, but its sharp rays do nothing to soothe my mood – I feel even emptier. I think about how it felt to be held tight by Fredrik, but even though there wasn't a single space between his body and mine, the distance between us is so vast he seemed light years away. I wish I was going to work today; it would at least give me something to pin my thoughts to, somewhere to rest my hands.

I get up from the sofa and make a peppermint tea. I turn the teabag around and around in the mug, feeling almost hypnotized by the swirling movement, when I realize that my phone is ringing upstairs. I usually keep it on me, but I must have left it beside the sink in the bathroom. I take the stairs two at a time, but still, it stops ringing before I get to the upstairs landing. It immediately starts up again and my heart is hurtling around in my chest now, my blood rushing, and when I finally reach it my hands shake so hard I knock it to the floor, cracking the top of the screen into a fine web of glass shards.

It's a private number, meaning the police are calling.

'Hello?'

'Elisa? It's Gaute here.'

'What is it? Have you found her?'

There's a slight hesitation on the other end and for a moment I'm convinced Gaute Svendsen is going to tell me they've found her. Dead. But then I remember that if she was found dead, they definitely wouldn't let me know by phone – there'd be a knock at the door.

'We haven't found her. But there are some developments. We've had a tipoff from a member of the public. Someone spotted the van not far from where the CCTV image of Lucia with Eilaanen was captured in south Sweden. Do you want to come here and I'll run through all the details and what happens next?'

Gaute ushers me into his office and offers me coffee. I shake my head. I feel as though I am itching inside and I just want him to tell me what's going on. Fredrik is in Bergen for work today and I feel angry with him for not being here, even though that isn't rational. I think I am angry with him, deep down, for returning to work. How does he even manage to perform his minute routines? Walking over to the coffee machine, smiling at someone, blinking in the bright overhead lights, writing an email, scrutinizing a case file. How?

'Kalle Josefsson, a local farmer, was out in his field with his twelve-year-old son, August, on the morning of 20 October,' begins Gaute. 'Josefsson runs a poultry farm ten kilometers from the Shell station and they were testing a drone that the boy had received for his birthday. They flew it towards the edge of the land they own, where it borders another farm, some state-owned forest and a few private properties at the top of a track. It would seem Kalle only realized that they'd captured the van with the Norwegian plates when he looked back through the images and remembered the police appeal. The police down there are waiting for a search warrant as we speak.'

'A search warrant for where?'

'Kalle and August's picture shows the van pulling into the driveway of a private property. The place is called Mölleryd.' Gaute opens an envelope on the table in front of him and slides two photographs across to me. They are slightly blurred and taken from a distance, but in the first one I can clearly make out the white van, noticeable by its narrow and tall body, turning off a road onto a track. In the second image, the van can be seen again, from further away, with a little yellow house in the background. Next to the house is a dark shape that I can't immediately make out.

Gaute seems to have followed my gaze. 'Another car in the driveway,' he says.

I swallow hard, taking in the nondescript yellow house, so like other modest Swedish houses I've seen on our many drives to Sweden. Like so many Norwegian families, we make several trips a year across the border to buy meat and alcohol at significantly discounted prices.

'Do you... do you think she could be being held there?'

'It's a real possibility. If she isn't still there, we might at least find clues that could lead us to her current whereabouts.'

I'm about to open my mouth to speak again when Gaute motions for me to wait a moment and pulls a vibrating mobile phone from his pocket.

'Okay,' he says. Then, 'Uh huh. Okay. Yep.' He hangs up and places the mobile phone back in his pocket.

'That was the team over in Sweden. They are on their way over to Mölleryd now and intend to do a full search of the house and grounds. We should hear back from them within an hour.' I nod, but inside I'm crumbling.

'Why don't you try your husband again? Perhaps he could wrap up whatever he's doing and head back here sooner rather than later.'

'I... Shouldn't we maybe go there or something? To that place? In Sweden, I mean. In case she's there. She'll need me—'

'Elisa, we know very little at this stage. All we know at the moment is that the van she was photographed next to arrived at that house later. Chances are she's no longer being held there.'

There is a long uncomfortable silence between us, and I'm certain we are both thinking the same thing. *What if she died there?*

Fredrik comes rushing into the room, beads of rainwater studding his suit jacket and more scattering from his hair as he runs a hand nervously through it. I've been by myself for a long time, panic rising and falling in me like giant swells on a black ocean. Gaute asked if I'd like to go and sit with the police psychiatrist, but I felt like I needed to be by myself, to gather all my strength.

Fredrik holds me close. I press my face into the familiar curve of his neck, drawing his scent deep into my lungs – Dior, rainwater, faint eucalyptus.

'I do this thing,' I whisper, my voice hoarse after all the crying last night. 'I place all the memories and experiences that could hurt me into this imaginary box. And I never open it.'

He stiffens momentarily in my embrace. 'I do that too,' he says softly. 'I think everyone does.'

'How are we supposed to… just… keep going right now? I have chest pains. Like my heart is beating too slow and then too fast,' I say.

'This is the most extreme situation we will ever experience.'

I nod and keep my eyes squeezed shut. 'How do you feel?' I ask.

His eyes brim with tears. 'Like you, I think.'

It's as though I'm entirely losing control of my mind and all the images I need to shut out hurl themselves at me, each one worse than the last. A little girl, covered in blood. A man looking down at her, face blank. A blood-curdling scream cutting through the dark night. A little girl, broken, her short, twisted legs splaying strangely outwards. Open eyes that will never see again. Fingers already blue at the tips, crusted with blood.

'No,' I whisper, but I know now that I can't shut the deluge of horrific images out anymore. 'No, no, no!'

'Elisa,' says Fredrik, very gently, and I feel his hands touch gently upon my shoulder.

I recoil and stay bent forward, my fingers pressing into my eyes as if to make sure they stay firmly shut.

'No!'

'Stay with me, Elisa. It's just a panic attack. Breathe…'

'I…' I begin to speak, and it's as though I've lost all hold over myself and simply cannot stop myself from telling Fredrik the impossible things, all of them, all of the things I've been keeping inside of me, but just then Gaute opens the door and I don't know whose face is more disturbing, his or mine.

'Elisa...' he begins.

I can tell it's bad news; he won't quite look at us – rather, he looks in our direction, fixing his gaze on a spot on the wall behind us.

'The team have searched the house.'

I begin to cry, and my voice echoes around the little room. Gaute Svendsen is still talking, but I can't quite grasp his words. I catch him exchanging a worried glance with Fredrik and I make an effort to somehow pull myself back together and stabilize my breath. There was something about the moment when I opened my mouth to speak, the exact moment Gaute opened the door. I was about to release it all. Everything. Maybe deep down I believe that if I do, I will get Lucia back. And when I heard the door go, I believed for a split second that Gaute was going to burst in, shouting the news that our little girl has been found, that she's weak but completely unharmed and ready to come home.

'... a body.'

I just catch the last two words of Gaute's sentence and I stare at him.

'What? Say that again?'

'I said... the team in Sweden have uncovered what they believe to be human remains at the house in Mölleryd. A body.'

21

Selma

She is getting ready to leave, tidying her desk and closing her laptop. Kai-Marius and Lisbeth left several hours ago and it was already dark then. A couple of the juniors are still here, as well as the tech guy, Hasse, who always works until eleven, when the night supervisor arrives. Olav is still in his office and Selma glances at him through the glass wall as he turns slowly round and round on his chair, bright yellow headphones trailing from his ears. His mouth is moving and Selma can tell that he's on the phone. She waits for him to do another full turn so she can give him a quick wave on her way out, but when he does face her again, his expression has changed. He looks troubled, no, shocked, and stands up, indicating urgently for Selma to come to his office.

She hurries through the empty rows and he walks towards her, removing the headphones from his ears.

'Hey,' he says. 'Glad I caught you. The police have just announced an extraordinary press conference. In fifteen minutes, at the Plaza. Blix case.'

Selma's heart begins to pound hard in her chest and for a moment she feels woozy and untethered. She tries to bring herself back to the moment, and to her boss standing in front of her.

'Have... have they found her?' If it was good news, wouldn't his expression be elated and overjoyed? For two weeks now the entire country has held its breath and prayed for the child. But... his face. Another vision worms its way into Selma's consciousness, and this time, too, it's as clear and harsh as a slap in the face. The girl, bludgeoned and still, eyes open and unseeing, half-wrapped in a stiff blue tarpaulin and left in a ditch off a dirt track, deep in a pine forest...

'No,' she whispers, just as Olav says, 'My police contact wouldn't say. Just that they have found a body. In Sweden.'

'No,' she says again. And then, 'Jesus.'

'We need to hurry,' says Olav.

They don't speak in the taxi, and it takes less than five minutes to get to the Plaza Hotel behind the central station. Selma leans her head against the window, her whole body tense and pumping with adrenaline. The poor, poor girl. She uses all her energy to stave off the images of the murdered child, and the effort leaves her trembling. Olav shoots her a worried glance as they pull up in front of the tall building, and then they are out of the car and hurrying through the Plaza's lobby to the press room at the far end of the ground floor. When they step inside, it's already crowded, even though it is almost 10 p.m. and the press conference was announced less than an hour ago.

The police chief, Hans Gundersen, steps onto the podium. He is unreadable and serious, and a stubborn blonde curl sticks up from the side of his head even though he has clearly tried to smooth it down with thick wax. A light grey stubble shadows his jaw and he blinks several times in the bright lights of the auditorium.

'We have called this press conference to address a major new breakthrough in the Lucia Blix abduction case. A body has been found.'

The room explodes into a cacophony of sound, a kind of collective, anguished groan. They're all seeing her now, imagines Selma, dead and discarded, aged seven.

'While we are unable to confirm the identity of the deceased at this point, we can confirm that it is *not* the body of Lucia Blix.'

Again, a kind of collective exclamation fills the room: surprise, relief, confusion.

'The body was discovered this afternoon at around 3 p.m. at an address in Mölleryd, Sweden, that is of significant interest to the investigation. The van next to which Lucia Blix was captured on CCTV on the morning of 20 October has been recovered at the same address. The body is that of an adult female. She was found buried in the garden of a private property owned by the wife of a man currently serving a long prison sentence at Fosie Prison in Malmö. Both Heiki Vilkainen and Mikko Eilaanen have previously served time at the same prison. Lucia Blix is still unaccounted for.'

Hans Gundersen pauses for a long moment, letting this news sink in. The journalists start shouting questions, but Gundersen silences them with a hand.

'Yes – TV 2?' he says, and Arne Theissen from TV 2 News clears his throat loudly before speaking into his microphone.

'Can you confirm whether the deceased is believed to have been murdered?'

'I'm unable to say anything about the cause of death at this point, but like I said, the woman was found concealed and buried in the grounds of a private property. Yes, *Aftenposten*?'

'For how long is the woman believed to have been dead?'

'This is currently subject to investigation.'

'Has any trace of Lucia Blix been uncovered at the property?'

'I am unable to say at present. Yes, *VG*?'

'Is the deceased believed to be the same woman who abducted Lucia Blix?'

'I am unable to say at present, but police are actively pursuing all lines of inquiry. We are working on the assumption that the child was held for a period of time at the property in Mölleryd before being transported onwards to another location in a different vehicle.'

'Are police still working on the assumption that Lucia Blix is being held by a trafficking network?'

'Yes. Due to the established connection between the identified prime suspect, Mikko Eilaanen, to known trafficking networks in central and Eastern Europe, we believe it is highly likely that Lucia Blix is being held by one of these cells, having been kidnapped to order for reasons still unestablished. Yes, *Dagsposten*?' He gestures at Olav and Selma, standing towards the back of the room.

'Have the police uncovered signs of a struggle or violence at the address in Mölleryd?'

'I am unable to say at present. The property is currently

undergoing a full investigation by Swedish forensic teams. Yes, *Bergens Tidende*?'

'What happens next?'

'The discovery of a body is, as always in this kind of investigation, a game changer. This case remains our highest priority and every effort is being made to recover Lucia Blix safely.'

Back outside, Olav and Selma are both quiet and lost in thought. They walk across the pedestrian bridge to the central bus terminal, then along deserted Schweigaardsgate towards Oslo Cathedral and the T-bane station at Jernbanetorget.

'I really thought they'd found her dead,' says Olav, shaking his head back and forth, his voice soft.

Selma nods and opens her mouth to answer, but no words will come. To her horror, she realizes she's crying; big tears flow fast from her eyes, dropping off her nose and chin faster than she can wipe them away with her sleeve.

'Hey,' says Olav, stopping, tugging gently at her arm, making her stop too.

She shakes her head half-heartedly, but still no words will come, and she lets herself be hugged lightly by her boss.

'It's okay,' he says. 'It's been intense. Why don't you take tomorrow off and spend it just, you know, reconnecting and gathering your thoughts?'

'No,' she says, forcefully. 'I'm fine.'

'Selma, look, I know how you feel. We've all put so much into the Blix case, and tonight was a real shock. But it's important to take care of yourself and maintain a professional distance, no matter how much you care. You know that.'

'I am keeping a professional distance,' she says, but even as she speaks the words, she knows they aren't true.

'Take tomorrow off. That's an order. And on Thursday why don't we focus on some of the other important cases we're working on?'

'Olav, I told you, I'm fine. Totally fine. I'm just... tired. And you're right, tonight was a shock. I think I'm just relieved it wasn't Lucia they found...'

Olav nods, unconvinced, then waves to hail a passing taxi. 'We'll share it,' he says, and with a wink adds, 'On *Dagsposten*.'

'I was going to walk,' she says, eying the empty streets, suddenly craving the fast walk uphill, past Oslo Cathedral and Deichman Library, alongside the ancient cemetery of Vår Frelser, then the last bit up Ullevålsveien to her street, Schwensens gate, her feet and her mind in overdrive. 'Bye,' she adds, waving at Olav through the window of the cab as it drives off.

A very light drizzle starts to fall as she passes the imposing statue of Christian IV in the middle of Stortorvet square, and she rubs hard at her arms through her too-thin anorak. Glasmagasinet department store has gone into full Christmas mode; ornate seasonal decorations, baubles and tinsel fill the display windows. She walks fast, trying to order her thoughts, but they bombard her, making her head spin. She forces her mind to the moment the woman's body was discovered in Mölleryd. She sees the police officer's dawning realization as the grisly discovery was made. She sees a sniffer dog, a smallish, squat spaniel, tearing at the cool grey earth, whimpering and sniffing, then barking. The police officer, perhaps a young man in his twenties with a spray of acne on his neck and mellow, water-colored eyes, would have rushed over to the dog. The young man would have stood to the side, stroking a downy patch on the side of his cheek, watching as the forensic team uncovered what was unmistakably the remains of a human – a woman, bit by bit.

The police hypothesis that Lucia has been kidnapped by a trafficking network will be strengthened by the discovery; the woman, 'Line', employed merely to instill trust in Lucia and her mother, then murdered when she was no longer needed. But where is 'Line's' child, or the child that posed as her child, the little girl referred to as Josephine?

As Selma places her key in the apartment lock, her mind is once again filled with the gruesome image of the little girl, gone forever, tossed like trash alongside a remote forest track. Though the image is not real and Lucia Blix most likely is still alive and being held somewhere, Selma is haunted and overwhelmed by it. She stumbles into the apartment and for the second time that evening succumbs to a powerful onslaught of tears.

22

Elisa

I play around with a parallel narrative. In it, I'd say *no*, that afternoon in the vestibule at Korsvik School, firmly and non-negotiably, when two little girls ask for a playdate. *Not today, sweetie,* I'd say. *No,* I'd have to repeat. *Lucia, no. Drop it now, okay?* I wouldn't be talked around. I would bundle a sulking girl into the back seat, and I'd spend the five-minute drive home irritated by the kids' squabbles. *Shhh,* I'd have said. *Or else.* In this parallel universe I do not know what it's like to realize that your child has been taken from you. I don't know how it feels to stare at the closed door of her bedroom, acutely aware that the room is empty and dark behind it, her favorite toys and teddies lined up along the windowsill where she left them. I don't know what it is like to wake morning after morning, realizing that no nightmare could be worse than your life. I will never know. I wonder if she knew that yesterday was her birthday. I wonder if she was alive to turn eight.

In this parallel world, I do not know what it is like to stand in front of a room full of journalists and their hungry cameras, blinded by lights and sheer fear, begging for Lucia's life. I won't ever know. In it, I just live my life the way that I'd finally come to see it: as a magical life, with my husband, my daughter, my son. It's a life that feels mostly like Tuesdays: neutral, unexciting, predictable. The kind of life that's almost mythical and miraculous in its simplicity; a life that can't be bettered, or at least not in any truly significant way – my past taught me that, at least.

That life didn't always seem magical to me. In fact, I'd hated it, stumbling through each long day filled with resentment and frustration, counting down to the moment I could lie down in the dark, drunk, relieved the day was over. And I came so very close to destroying it.

By the time Lucia was taken, I had learned the hard way that the life I had was precious and that I needed to hold on to it by any means. And still, she was taken from me, grabbed from the center of our family as if by a hand reaching up from the underworld.

Lyder has gone to my in-laws' for the afternoon, and it's just Fredrik and me at dinner. I've made spicy Spanish tomato soup, but I've added too much chili and Fredrik eats slowly, stopping constantly to drink water but saying nothing. I can't be bothered to apologize, though the food is practically inedible.

'I was wondering if we could talk about something,' I say. Now is as good a time as any – I've been trying to find a moment to speak about what's haunting me.

'Sure,' he says, smiling at me across the table, eyes bloodshot and rimmed by deep blue circles.

'You know Karoline Meister...'

'Yes,' says Fredrik, his eyes dropping to his soup, his voice hesitant.

'I feel like they aren't really pursuing that—'

'Elisa, they have. You heard them – random loony on the internet.'

'Yes, but—'

'At least we've finally had some breakthroughs – we know more than we did a week ago.'

'Yes, but like what, really?'

'Like the fact that she was taken by a network.'

'Yes, most likely, but—'

'But what? It would be insane to waste police resources on some crazy woman on Facebook when we know for a fact that Lucia was taken by a criminal network.'

'I just worry that there could be others... you know, people from the past who could hate us and that that's why she's been taken.'

'What do you mean?'

'Look, you know that situation with Karoline Meister, well, I've had something too. A very long time ago. A thing...'

'Elisa, stop right now.'

'No, Fredrik, you need to hear—'

'I don't want to hear about some flirt that happened years ago. Leave it be. Please. I'm begging you, Elisa. Please let's just bury these insignificant, stupid missteps in the past and focus on finding Lucia.'

'Yes, but what if it's somehow related—'

Fredrik silences me by placing his hand down very firmly on the table, and though it's not quite a slam, it's an unusual thing for my gentle husband to do.

ALEX DAHL

'I'm sorry,' he says.

'I'm sorry, too.'

We fall into silence, me picking at a leftover crust of toast, Fredrik intently working his way through the revolting soup, not stopping until his spoon scrapes against the bowl and every last drop is gone.

23

Lucia

The man is wearing a big jacket and the heavy boots I heard on the stairs. On the side of his face is a red-brown smudge and I think it's blood.

'Let's go,' he says.

'Where's Josie?' I ask, but the man shakes his head. It means he won't tell me.

His voice is scratchy, and his eyes are red – it's what happens when you shout a lot.

All the lights are off in the house and we go downstairs slowly. I look around for Josie and her mamma but can't see anyone.

Outside, it's very cold and the moon looks like a sparkling lump of ice thrown high into the sky.

'Over here,' whispers the man and points at a blue car that's exactly like my grandpa's car. He lights a cigarette, and his stinky white smoke clouds the black air.

I have to lie down on the back seat, and the man covers me with a scratchy light blue blanket, pulling it up all the way to my chin. Then he gets in the front seat and then the car starts moving. I want to scream because even if it was terrible to be with Josie and her mamma and the man, it's much worse to be with just the man. I'm too afraid to make any noise, but my eyes can't help crying. In the end I just close my eyes very tight and listen to the car sounds and pretend this is my grandpa's car and it's him who's driving me and that we're going home.

It's light and the man is standing outside the car, watching something on his phone and smoking. He must sense me looking at him – he turns and sees that I'm awake. His smiles at me, giving me a little wave with the hand holding the cigarette. Then he gets back in the car. We're in a forest, by the side of a small gravel road.

'Do you need the bathroom?' he asks.

I do, but I don't answer him.

'You can go here, no one will come, and I'll turn around.'

I really have to pee, so I get out of the car. I look back at him, but he's staring down at his phone. The road we're on is up high and there's a long, steep, rocky slope down through the forest to my right. I could run, now. Or I could run back the way we came – he wouldn't be able to turn the car around very fast on such a narrow road. I glance at him again, but he hasn't moved and he isn't looking at me. My legs are shaking and the air is very cold. Where would I run to? There's nobody here. Even if he didn't catch me, I'd be lost in these woods. Besides he probably would catch me, I remember how fast he was the last time I tried. 'And then he'll kill you,' Josie's mamma said.

I pull my tights down and pee behind the car. When I

stand back up, the man's hard eyes are on me in the mirror, making sure I don't even think about trying anything funny. I get back in the car.

'You don't have to be scared,' says the man. 'You can sit up for a while, but when I tell you to lie back down, you listen, okay?'

I nod, and he hands me a Coke and a stick wrapped in foil, then starts the engine. My stomach groans when I unwrap it and see a long baguette with ham and cheese.

'Where is Josie?' I ask when I've finished.

'You'll see her soon,' he says.

'And my mamma?'

'Her too.'

I drink the Coke and look out at the tall, dark trees. They're enormous Christmas trees and there are so many of them, it must be a very big forest. We stay on the road for a very long time, maybe many hours. We don't pass any other cars, and the man doesn't seem worried about this.

'Where are we?' I ask.

He looks at me in the mirror.

'Arden.'

'Is that a country?' I ask.

'Kind of. It's a huge forest that covers lots of countries. The bit we're in now is in Belgium.'

Two deer cross the road. After a while the road begins to drop and the trees get shorter. At the bottom of a valley we cross a stone bridge and I see rushing brown water underneath it.

'You know, I have a son,' says the man. 'He's about your age. Cool kid.'

'Where is he?' I ask.

'They, uh, won't let me see him.'

'Who?'

'Child protection services.'

'Why not?'

'Because I went to prison,' he says.

I nod and look at his big hands holding the steering wheel. They are covered in tattoos, even the fingers.

'Why did you go to prison?' I ask.

'You don't want to know,' he says, but I do. I stare out the window for a while, and the car drives up another long hill. When we reach the top, I can see a house in the valley far below, in the distance, smoke coming from its chimney.

'You need to lie down,' says the man.

I've been away for many days now. First the ski box. Then the van with the bedroom that was on a boat. Then the yellow house. After a day and a night there, with the TV and the shouting and Josie, the man took me away by myself. We drove for a very long time, all day and maybe all night. For three or maybe four days now, me and the man have been staying in another house. I never saw it from the outside because I was asleep when we got here, and when I woke up again, I was inside the house. I imagine it as the little house in the valley I saw from the car, the one with smoke drifting up above Arden's big trees like purple ribbons.

All the walls are slanted and made of wood like at my grandma and grandpa's house. The room I wake up in is on the top floor and there's a little attic window that can't be opened. There's a bathroom with a shower but no shower curtain on the same floor and you can only get up here by ladder. I don't cry or scream because I will be killed if I do, the man said. He's here somewhere in the house, I can hear him and other men, too, their voices booming up to the attic.

The first day I stood by the attic window all day. It's tiny, the same size as my face, and it looks out on a forest. All I could see was trees, trees, trees. I stood there all day until it got dark and the trees looked like thousands of people lined up, but even though I waved and knocked on the window, nobody came.

At the end of the second day, when it was dark, the man came up the ladder. He said, 'Sorry.' I didn't look at him. He left a bag from McDonald's by the ladder and then he climbed back down. I didn't want to eat it because the man must be the baddest man in the world, but I could smell the cheeseburgers and the fries, it filled the whole room, and in the end I ate it all. Over by the mattress underneath the window, someone had left a plastic bag with coloring books and pencils and lots of bags of candy. There was Gott & Blandat, Bilar, and salty licorice, my little brother's favorite. I wished he could have seen all those sweets and, even more than that, I wished he was there with me. No, I wished that I was at home with him and we were watching NRK Super and eating all the candy. I cried a lot in the night, but very quietly, so I wouldn't be killed.

The third night I woke up and there was a man in the room, a new man. He had curly red hair and he wore white shorts and a white vest. He stood close to the bed, watching me, and he was laughing, but his laugh sounded like a dog barking: 'Woof, woof, owww.'

I started to scream but stopped because I was so afraid. I heard running and it was the other man, the man who took me from Josie's house.

'What the fuck! What the fuck! Get the fuck away from her, you fucking pig!' he shouted. He shoved the red-haired man very hard and he fell backwards towards the ladder, and then he scrambled down it.

'I'm sorry,' said the other man again, sitting down beside me, and his eyes weren't scary then. 'Do you need anything?'

'I need Minky Mouse,' I said, my throat closing as I spoke Minky's name.

'What's that?' he asked and I explained that she's my soft toy and I'm not so good without her, and he said, 'But I bought you a new soft toy.' I nodded, but tears fell from my eyes. He didn't kill me even though I cried, but he patted my head very gently with his big hand and said, 'I'm sorry,' again.

Now the man has gone back downstairs and I'm sitting on the mattress eating my way through the rest of the candy, even though it's the middle of the night. I can hear men's voices, sometimes loud and sometimes soft, as if they're arguing. I wonder what will happen if there's a big fight, with knives or guns maybe, and the red-haired man or one of the other men kill the man who brought me here. Then no one will know I'm here except the very bad man who laughs like a barking dog.

I blink hard to stop myself from falling asleep and get up to look out at the outline of the trees, their tips jagged and black in the moonlight, like mountains. Suddenly, the big tooth at the back of my mouth falls out! I've been wiggling it for a few days and now it's come out, stuck in the Gott &

Blandat wine gum I was chewing. I pick it out of the sweet and hold it up against the light from the moon coming in through the window. It's all bloody and it's huge, with a long root on the end of it. My mouth is filling with blood. It's disgusting and I spit lots of times, tears streaming down my face. I'm wishing so hard for Mamma's arms to be hugging me, her hands smoothing down my hair, the sound of a proper kiss loud next to my ear. If I was at home, Mamma would fetch a glass of water and I would drop the tooth into it, watching it sink slowly through the water like a little white pebble. In the morning there'd be a twenty-kroner coin in its place.

Now, there is no Mamma and no water glass, just a half-drunk plastic bottle of Coke the man brought me. I drop my tooth into the black liquid and watch it settle in one of the rounded grooves at the bottom of the bottle. I cry and cry and cry, stopping only to run my tongue across the bloody hole where my tooth was.

When I wake up, I'm in the boot of a car.

24

Marcus

Through all his years at Tollebu Prison he's been accepting of his sentence, and he's found some peace in that. It has also helped that he's always been a man who finds meaning in books, in nature and in his own thoughts. As part of the rehabilitation measures for the non-violent prisoners, he's allowed to work at the timber yard in the valley two days a week, Tuesdays and Fridays. Together with three other men from Tollebu and two guides in plainclothes, Marcus grinds and then sands long lengths of wood which then go to Riva, the furniture factory in Hamar. The money he earns is spent on Fanta, chocolates and newspapers from the prison shop. He is also a member of Tollebu's chess club and volunteers one afternoon a week at the little prison library.

Ever since he first read about the kidnap of Lucia Blix, a dark cloud has forced itself into Marcus's monotonous life. He has struggled to sleep, tossing and turning at night, haunted by terrible imaginings of the poor girl. During the day, his head feels murky and drab, like he can't quite grasp a thought; Lucia Blix is perpetually on his mind, like a backdrop all other thoughts must rest upon. The inmates have spoken at length about the case, and a current of fury courses through the prison whenever it's brought up. They may have dealt drugs, messed up a few guys, carried weapons or stolen some cars, but taking an innocent seven-year-old from her parents is a whole different ballgame and wouldn't they all like to get their hands on the likes of Mikko Eilaanen and his chums.

Marcus suspects that many people in Norway have been similarly affected by the young girl's plight. A case like this is unprecedented in this safe, trusting country that places so much value on allowing children their freedom.

As Marcus walks to breakfast his heart sinks to see the Blix case dominating the newspaper headlines yet again, the little girl's beautiful face plastered across the front pages. He steps out from the stream of men moving down the corridor towards the canteen and picks up a copy of *Dagsposten*. Its headline reads: 'Woman at Mölleryd Identified as Silwia Truja!'

He flicks to the second page and scans the article.

Is the Investigation Turning Into a Murder Inquiry?

By Selma Eriksen

Police chief Hans Gundersen brought forth new information in the abduction case yesterday afternoon, revealing that the identity of the woman discovered at Mölleryd has been established as Ms Silwia Truja, the woman investigated as the initial abductor in the case.

Marcus flicks to the next page, where there's a picture of Elisa Blix getting into a police car, mouth set in a stern line, eyes covered by black sunglasses. '"It's Not the Same Woman," Insists Elisa Blix,' reads the headline.

Marcus closes the paper and goes straight back to his room. He lies down on the bed with his shoes on, thinking. The images in his mind are of the little girl's mother. Elisa. He feels a need to get in touch with her that is so strong, it's physical. It would be wrong. Terribly wrong. Impossible, too.

There's a soft knock at the door. He considers not answering but knows that's not an option.

'Hi, Pål,' he says, opening it to reveal one of the newer guides standing outside.

'Hey, Marcus. Uh, I noticed you didn't come to breakfast and wondered if you are okay?'

'I'm not feeling well, actually.'

'Oh, right. Are you okay to go to work?'

Marcus has forgotten it's a Tuesday. It's almost time to be bussed down to the timber yard. He looks forward to Tuesdays and Fridays – the manual work, the camaraderie between the men, the perceived equality between prisoner and free man, if only for a few hours.

'I think I need to stay here today. Upset stomach.'

'Okay. I'll pop back with the sickness paperwork for you to sign.'

Marcus nods, gives Pål a brief smile, then gently closes the door. He stands still for several long moments, wondering what to do next. Then he sits down at his desk, finds a blank sheet of paper, and begins to write.

25

Lucia

The car isn't moving and I wait and wait and cry a little bit. I tap very softly on the ceiling, which must be the door of the boot, but nothing happens. I tap the rhythm of Funky Lady, saying the words in my head, and still nothing happens. I feel like falling asleep again, when suddenly the boot opens a crack.

'Hi there,' says the man. 'Sorry about the boot. You can come out now.'

It's dark outside and the car is parked in a big parking lot with no other cars. The moon is high and there's a strange darkness behind the parking lot, but then I realize that it's a high mountain and the parking lot is at its foot. The top of the mountain is white and next to it is another mountain. There's a river somewhere near, below us – I can hear it.

The man hands me a cardboard box that reads 'Burger King'. I open it and inside is a huge burger, the kind adults get.

'Thank you,' I say and the man nods and lights a cigarette.

'We're almost there,' he says.

'Home?'

He nods and I look around again. It does look like Norway again, with the snowy mountains. But Sandefjord doesn't have any mountains, it has rocky cliffs and nice beaches and forests with lots of blueberries. There are forests here too, so maybe we'll just drive through them and then we'll see the sea and Sandefjord.

'Okay, let's go.' The man opens the door to the back seat. 'Lie down or you get in the boot,' he says.

'How much further is it to go home?'

'A few hours.'

I lie down and stare at the ceiling. At first I feel sick because the car is turning a lot. Then, it begins to drive faster and faster and the road isn't bumpy anymore – we must have left the forest. For many hours I just lie here, staring at patterns in the fabric padding the inside of the car. I try not to think about my mamma and my pappa and my little brother because I don't believe the man when he says he is taking me home, but then I think about them anyway and it makes me so sad I have to hold my breath so I don't start to scream. I also try not to think about the red-haired man with the barking laugh who stood by my bed. Instead, I say the names of all the children in my class in my head. *Leah, Nazanin, Ella, Sofia, Olivia, Mathilde, Ylva, Mille-Theodora, Konstanse, Josie...* I'm about to start on the boys, but I begin to feel sleepy again – it's strange how tired I am even though I've been lying down for so long.

I wake with a start and it still feels like the middle of the night. It's raining hard and noisily. The car has stopped. I sit up but there's no one in the car. I can make out the blurry shape of a house right in front of the car, but it looks different from any house I've seen before. All the lights are on and there are leaves covering the whole front wall as if it was made from plants. The windows have little doors and there are two sets of chimneys. The enormous double-door is a nice purple and so wide you could drive a car through it. Then, while I'm staring at it, it opens.

26

Elisa

More days, more nothing. I spend most of my time alone, praying, which is something I'd never thought I would ever do. And yet I find myself turning to the prayers that were drilled into me throughout my childhood. 'Please... Please...' I whisper, staring up at a bleak sky, clasping my hands tight, and for the first time in my life, prayer brings me a sliver of comfort. Deep down, I'm afraid of God and the idea that such a force of divine justice might exist. What if my parents were right and the fires of hell blaze eternally for those who don't live by *His* word?

I think about my father. I miss him. So much. One of the things that made my childhood experiences with religion so difficult was reconciling my kind and gentle father with the words he'd speak – of damnation, of judgment, of the unquestionable importance of a devout life. My father was an intelligent man who believed in the inherent goodness of humans and their necessary subordination to God. I grew to resent that God, because he'd always choose Him over me. Maybe that isn't true, but it's how it felt. Could I recover some of that faith that was drilled into me in my early life? 'Dear God,' I try again. 'Please...' But the silence is deafening.

Other times, for comfort, I draw, though I'm no good. I sketch images of Lucia cartwheeling, her face always animated, with carefully colored-in red cheeks. I write letters, which I feed to the flames in the wood-burning oven. Some I write to my father, apologizing for what happened between us. Others I write to my mother, who would tear my letters to shreds were she ever to receive them. I wonder if she knows about any of the things that have happened to me. Whether she cares. I want to write to Lucia, but every time I try, it's as if I freeze; my heart starts pounding and my hands shake. I'm not ready yet.

Today is blustery and almost dark throughout the day. I sit by the window, cradling one mug of tea after another, watching the raindrops dent the surface of a big puddle on the street outside. It's easy to lose track of time like this, lost in my own mind. I allow my daughter to come to me, dancing through time. I let myself hold her close, lingering on the way her fine hair feels brushing against my cheek. Hours pass like this, and I only snap out of my reverie at the sound of an engine. I open my eyes and watch the red and yellow post van maneuver down the flooded street.

In the letterbox are three bills and a thick cream envelope addressed to me, my name and address printed on a plain white sticker. It was posted in Lillehammer and for a moment I wonder whether it could be from my mother. It isn't.

★

It's dark outside by the time I stop crying, though it's only just four o'clock. I crush the letter in my hand. I smooth it back out. I crush it again, and place it into the fireplace, then hold a match to it and watch it burst into flames. My thoughts roam from Lucia to Fredrik to the letter, to my father, to my mother.

A while ago, I told Fredrik that my mother and siblings still haven't been in touch. He said, 'We've been over this so many times, Elisa. You know what it's like when you leave the church.'

'Yes, but they're my family,' I said.

'Not anymore.'

Maybe it's the letter, maybe it's the effect of having allowed all these thoughts of my family and the religion I left back into my mind, but I decide to stop waiting for my mother to forgive me. I decide to take matters into my own hands.

I stand up and glance around the room for my phone. It's over on the kitchen counter, dark and silent. I pick it up and dial the number that remains the same as when I was a young girl. She picks up on the first ring, as though she'd been sitting on the little stool in the hallway waiting for my call.

'Hello, Mother,' I say. A sharp intake of breath, followed by a long, exaggerated sigh.

'Elisa.'

'I...' I haven't planned this, and at the sound of her curt, cold voice, the whole disastrous state of our relationship crashes back down over me. I consider putting the phone back down, but am surprised by an onset of stinging tears. I guess we're always children with our mothers. 'I wanted to speak with you,' I say, and realize that this is true. *I wanted you to have been in touch*, I could add. *I wanted you to care. To choose me, for once.*

'And why is that?'

'You must have heard… About Lucia.'

'Yes, well, I can't say I was surprised.'

'What do you mean?'

'How can you be surprised that this has happened after what you did to your father?'

'How can you even say that? I loved my father.'

My mother snorts loudly. 'You killed him, and you know it. You might not have believed in the power of God before, but I imagine you do now. You deserve this.'

'Mother,' I whisper, my voice thick and almost inaudible through the sobs I can no longer control, but the line has gone dead.

27

Lucia

Maybe it's the noise of a car door slamming that wakes me. I look around. It's light and I'm in a big, airy room. There are two very tall windows with no curtains and I get out of the bed and walk across the room to the closest one. The floor is made of wood and is cool beneath my feet. I'm wearing a thin white nightdress that I haven't seen before.

I look out of the window at a milky sky. I see white hilly fields and a forest, its trees yellow and bright orange and some almost bluey-green. Beyond the fields are some white pointy clouds, or at least that's what I think at first, but then I realize they are huge mountains with snow on their tops.

I remember last night now; eating the burger in the parking lot with the river nearby, its sound like thunder, the man's smoke going up my nose while I ate. 'We're going home,' he said. I knew he was a liar.

I look down and see Josie's mamma sitting in the driver's seat of the car that brought me here. It's parked in front of another house that's very big but has no windows. Its roof is made from brown metal and it has huge red doors, opened wide. Josie's mamma drives the car slowly into the house, its wheels spinning in thick mud.

There's a large courtyard between the house I'm inside and the house Josie's mamma drove the car into. There's another building too – it has only one floor but it's very long, with many dark windows. Like the house I'm inside, it also has plants covering it. There are lots of puddles in the courtyard, some so big they're like little lakes, and I remember the rainstorm last night. I also remember seeing Josie's mamma again for the first time, standing in the enormous open door like a witch in a nightmare. The man carried me up the stairs in the dark. I wonder where he is now. He was nice to me even if he's been to prison. He knows the way home; could he take me there?

Then I remember that I heard the man and Josie's mamma talking in the night, and when they were finished the man drove away in a small white car. I got up and watched from the window.

Josie's mamma didn't want him to go – I was on the landing, listening. I can move around in this house if I want to, it's not like the attic house in Arden where I had to stay locked away because there were dangerous people there.

'It isn't safe for you,' Josie's mamma said to the man. 'Stay here until it all dies down.'

'This won't ever die down, goddammit, Jacqueline!' the man said.

'Please don't go,' said Josie's mamma, but then the door slammed and the man drove off down a long driveway and into the thick woods.

My windows have little purple doors that I can shut

to make the room totally dark. I think this is a farm. I've been to a farm before, but that farm was different because it was at the edge of a town and I could see houses in the distance and chimneys blowing smoke from factories. Here, I can see nothing but big sky, fields, mountains. And Josie's mamma, coming back out from the windowless house. She looks different now. She isn't wearing make-up. And her hair is a different color – it was almost black before, but now it's light brown with yellow streaks. She is crossing the courtyard and looks up at the house and sees me standing here. Her face, which was angry or maybe sad, becomes smiley. She waves at me, but I take a step back and stand beside the window so I can't be seen from outside.

I hear her steps on the stairs. I stare at the door, which looks like it was made from a knobby tree trunk. The house is completely quiet. Then the door opens.

'Hey, sweet girl,' says the mamma, 'how about I fix you something to eat? You must be starving.'

I make myself look her in the eyes. 'No.'

'You can't hide up here forever,' she says.

'I'm not hiding,' I say, 'and I'm not staying here forever. I'm going home.'

Josie's mamma is standing in the middle of the room and I run past her and through the door. I can hear her laughing as I run down the corridor. There's a huge wooden staircase that goes all the way around a big open space, like in movies. I rush down it, and downstairs there are many rooms one after the other, but I pull open the main door and run outside into the courtyard.

It's very cold and I'm not wearing socks or shoes or anything, only the nightdress, but I don't care, I have to find someone to help me. I scream 'Mamma!' as loud as I can, then I scream 'Help!', but I can't see anyone at all. I turn around to see if Josie's mamma is coming to catch me, but the door is wide open and empty. I don't know where Josie is either, but I don't care, I just want to get out of here. I run through the gap between the house with the black car inside and the long, low house to the side of it, and come to a metal fence with a strange round door. I've seen one before – it's to stop cows because they can't go through it, but people can.

I hurry through it and then I run up a long hill towards where the forest begins. The mushy mud makes my bare feet slip. I'm halfway there when I see that there are two big cows in the field, chewing and looking at me, so I run even faster. There are sharp stones underneath the mud and grass, and they slice my skin open. I fall three times but get back up again and keep running. When I reach the first trees I turn back and look. I can see the houses but no people. Thick smoke puffs from a chimney on the biggest of the houses, the one I was inside. From here it looks like a fairytale house with the purple window-doors and the thick leaves covering the whole house. I have to get away from here. I can't see any other houses, just fields and trees and mountains. It's nothing like at home in Sandefjord, where one house looks into the garden of the next, and where you can almost always see the sea. The mountains are even higher than they looked from the window and maybe they're the same mountains I went to with Mamma and Pappa, where me and Lyder learned to ski in the kids' club.

I step into the forest. The trees are taller and thicker than they looked from the house and it's quite dark. I'm so cold.

My eyes begin to cry even though I don't want them to. How can I find someone to help me when there's nobody here? I walk a bit, but I'm too cold and my feet hurt so much and when I look down I see that they're bleeding from lots of places and this makes me cry more and all I can hear is myself crying, but then I hear something else too and I stop for a moment and it gets louder and louder. It's a voice shouting my name, but in a happy voice, almost like a song. 'Lucia! Lucia! Lucia! Where are you, sweet girl?'

I have to get away. If I don't get away from her, I'll never see my mamma and pappa and Lyder again. But this is all my fault to begin with. It's my own fault that I'm here. My whole life, I wanted a sister. My brother is stupid sometimes. He only talks about Lego and farts and dinosaurs and he doesn't like it when Pappa tickles me on the sofa because he gets jealous so he hits me even if it isn't allowed to hit, and when we drive in the car he makes engine noises all the time even if we're going really far, like to Grandpa's cabin. So I wanted a sister. I wanted a sister so bad I even prayed for one. On my birthday Lyder peed into the bathtub so he would get Mamma and Pappa to look at him instead of me even though it was *my* birthday, and I screamed at him that I hated him and that I wished he'd never been born and that all I wanted was another family. My mamma grabbed my arm and said, 'Hey, don't you ever say that,' and, 'Be careful what you wish for, you drama queen.'

'Lucia!' calls Josie's mamma and her voice is louder now. Closer. 'You've got this all wrong, sweetie. Come here so we can talk.'

I move very quietly over to a tree with low-hanging branches. I pull myself up onto the lowest branch, like it's one of the climbing frames at my school. I step onto a higher branch, but it isn't strong enough and it snaps off loudly and I fall down onto the bottom branch and I grab hold of it but it's bendy and I can hear it groan. If I can hear it, then probably so can Josie's mamma. I grab another branch and pull myself onto it, then another and another. I sit entirely still, trying to figure out where the voice is coming from. It's really close now. My whole body shivers. I press my face close to the thin trunk, letting it rub against my cheek. My eyes are still crying because now that I am sitting still my feet hurt so much and I won't look down at them because if they are full of blood I might scream.

'Lucia!' calls Josie's mamma, and she must be almost right underneath me, though I can't see her; it's a Christmas tree kind of tree and the branches are thick and prickly and very dark green. I hold my breath and count silently in my head. When I get to thirty-six, I hear twigs snapping and Josie's mamma must be walking away. But it isn't twigs, it's the branch I'm sitting on. It suddenly breaks right off, dropping me down onto the one underneath it, and I scramble to grab hold of something and climb higher, but there isn't anything, and I slam to the ground, scratching myself badly on other branches on the way down.

I can't breathe and when I open my mouth to scream, nothing happens and I can't move because I landed on my leg and it hurts so much. I lie still and look up at the white sky high above the black and green branches. Josie's mamma might not have heard me fall. She might go back to the house and I can try to get up and find help.

'There you are,' says a voice. 'You know, if I didn't know better, I'd say you were playing dead.' Josie's mamma is standing over me now, laughing a little, but then she notices that I'm hurt and her face becomes worried. She sits down on the ground next to me, and says, 'Oh no, darling, what have you done? Oh, sweet girl, Maman is going to fix you.'

My eyes start to cry again and Josie's mamma wipes the tears from my face and then I notice that her eyes have changed – they are brown like mine now. I want to ask her how come, but I also want to not speak to her.

'You aren't my mamma,' I say.

She picks me up very gently and wraps me in a fuzzy pink shawl that smells nice, like sea and flowers, and she carries me slowly back out through the forest, towards the fields and the mountains and the farm in the hollow.

'Yes, I am,' she says.

28

Jacqueline

The weight of the child in her arms as she crosses the field is just right – familiar and heavy but not too heavy. The girl is genuinely hurting and the cuts on her bare feet bleed onto Jacqueline's beige overcoat. She cradles Lucia like a much younger child; she's not struggling anymore. Jacqueline's sneakers are slick with mud and by the time she reaches the cattle gate, her legs hurt with the strain.

The front door is wide open and she rushes the last few steps across the courtyard. Inside the farmhouse, Josie stands watching from the top of the staircase. Lucia's sudden hoarse cries echo around the vaulted entrance hall. 'Mamma!' she screams, over and over, her voice breaking like glass shattering on stone.

Jacqueline repositions her so that she is flung over her shoulder like a baby, and blood drips onto the coarse stone floor from one of the wounds on her feet. She takes the stairs slowly, rubbing the girl's back as she goes, and her screams turn guttural, then gravelly, then whispered. In the bathroom, she places the child gently on the closed toilet seat and runs a bath in the deep, ancient tub. At first, Lucia won't get in, and when she finally does, she starts up again, wailing and sobbing. The water must hurt her cuts – blood seeps from them into the water in pink, cloudy bursts. Jacqueline very gently runs a sponge across Lucia's jutting shoulder blades, around the deep hollows of her collarbone, down the small of her back. When she is finished, she hauls her from the water like a big glinting fish and towels her off tenderly. Her little face has gone from tortured and anguished to wan and unreadable.

Very carefully, she sits the child back down on the closed toilet lid and takes her feet in her hands, rubbing antiseptic ointment into them in slow circles. Most of the bleeding has stopped now, except for one cut that's particularly deep. She wraps a gauze bandage around that foot, giving the back of Lucia's calf a little squeeze when she is finished.

She can't believe the little girl is really here and that they have actually managed to bring her here. For the past couple of days, Jacqueline has felt giddy with excitement. At Mölleryd, when Mikko's ex-girlfriend showed up unexpectedly, she'd feared it was game over, that it would all go to hell, but now she realizes that the woman's appearance there was a gift from heaven. They did what they had to, and it turns out to have been a stroke of genius. 'Mölleryd Body Likely the Female Abductor', read VG's main headline this morning. She read it standing ankle-deep in mud at the very edge of one of the fields belonging to Le Tachoué, where it's occasionally possible to pick up a 4G mobile signal. She laughed into the cold wind rushing down from the mountainside behind her. Could it really be that she was free?

She picks the child up off the toilet seat and carries her across the hallway to her bedroom. In the weeks before Jacqueline and Josie traveled to Norway to bring Lucia home, she spent a lot of time on the child's room. She removed most of its previous contents to a smaller bedroom towards the back of the house, the one that overlooks the meadows and the forest beyond. She replaced the toddler's bed with a beautiful carved wooden bed, perfect for a big girl like Lucia. She bought new clothes for both Josie and Lucia: pristine white linen smocks and soft cotton tights and T-shirts with nostalgic prints, two sets of everything. Jacqueline likes children to look like children and not like small, commercialized teenagers. She agonized over making the room just right, because she knew that coming here would be very difficult for Lucia; of course it would.

'I spent a lot of time making this room nice for you before we brought you home,' she says, placing Lucia on the bed, taking extra care not to graze her injured feet. 'This used to be my bedroom. And before that it was my grandfather's, your great-grandfather's. It was him who built this house. I wanted you to have the room with the best views of the Pyrenees. When you feel better, I'll point out all the highest mountains to you. We have all the time in the world now.'

Lucia turns towards the wall and sheds more tears onto the crisp white bedsheets.

'I got you some new stuff. It's all in your closet. It's really nice stuff, sweetie. I hope you'll feel like taking a look later.'

'When can I go home?' asks Lucia.

'Look, you and I need to talk—'

'No! I just want to go home!'

'I understand how hard this is. And how confused you

must be. You must think I'm a terrible person and that your life is over. But, sweetheart, that couldn't be further from the truth.'

Jacqueline sits down on the bed next to Lucia and leans in closer, but Lucia presses her body against the wall.

'Are you ready to hear the truth?' she whispers, straight into Lucia's damp pink ear.

Lucia strains away from her, but Jacqueline puts her hand firmly on her shoulder, makes her turn back around and holds her firmly in place. 'You need to hear the truth, because in all your life, nobody ever told you the truth.'

29

Marcus

Every morning he goes to sit in the prison chapel's hushed, unfussy space for fifteen minutes, focusing on simply breathing from his stomach, slowly in and out. The chaplain doesn't attempt to engage him in conversation today; he just nods when Marcus enters before returning to his tasks. Marcus wonders if, were the chaplain to find out what he did, he would still be able to look him in the eye and tell him that Jesus loves him anyway.

Since he's been at Tollebu, Marcus has become interested in his own mind and its processes. He reads psychology books and practices mindfulness, letting himself be entirely still inside a moment. He reflects on forgiveness and vengeance, and how, in his case, both are fundamentally impossible. He's unsettled by the case of the missing child and can't shake the thought that one bad thing leads to another, and then another, and another still. One eyelid begins to twitch and he makes himself focus on the plain wooden cross above the plain wooden altar. If Jesus could hang on the cross to absolve humanity of sin, could there be forgiveness for him? *No*, thinks Marcus. *For me – never, especially now.*

To calm his racing heart, Marcus lets his mind go to one of his favorite places. In his other life, he used to travel frequently, all over the world, and he used to love that moment shortly after takeoff on a cloudy day when the plane emerged into the brilliant blue above the clouds. It brought him comfort, to think that the sun was always shining, whether he could see it or not. He'd lean his head against the plastic window, taking in the cloud formations far below, knowing that those exact patterns and peaks and colors would never again be repeated in all of time. He'd feel overcome by a kind of yearning, a sensation of being close to something bigger than anything else. He tries to summon that same feeling now – the feeling of being held entirely by a world so impossibly beautiful.

30

Lucia

'Memory is a strange thing,' says Josie's mamma. 'You don't remember me because you can't. So many things are lost, for all of us, in our minds. That doesn't mean they didn't happen. Do you remember lying flat on your back in your baby stroller? No? And yet, you did. For months and months you lay there and I smiled down at you and you smiled back. You don't remember those smiles now, but I do. Do you remember the first thing you ever ate? The first time you stood up and fell back down? The way you and Josie used to like to sit in the bay window and wave at Daddy going off to work? See, sweet girl, your mind can't remember those things, but they all happened, all of that and so much more. I will help you to remember who you are. I will teach you who to be, now.'

She strokes my hair softly and I want to swat her hand away, but it feels good to be touched, so I let her, for a moment.

'The lady you lived with took you from me. Maybe she

didn't mean to. Maybe she wasn't all bad. But what she did was very, very bad. What she did was the worst thing one person can do to another. To take someone's child, Lulu – it can never be forgiven. Never. Not ever.'

'It's not true!'

'It is true.'

'No! My mamma is my mamma and you're a bad lady and soon you're going to be in prison!'

'My darling, I understand that you are angry and confused. Everyone has lied to you, your entire life. But I swear, Lucia, I will never tell you lies. Never.'

'I want to go home!'

'Look at me, *mon amour*. Look at me. Sometimes the heart remembers when the mind does not. With time, your heart will remember, and your mind will understand that you belong here, with me and Josie.'

I'm so confused and scared and I squash my hands over my ears and try to put my head under the pillow, but I can still hear her.

'I know this is a lot to take in. But we have all the time in the world now. No one will ever find you here or take you away from me again.'

I scream and scream, but she keeps talking.

'Shhh, sweet girl. Stop screaming. No, stop it, you need to settle down or I will have to make you go to sleep. Shhh, that's right. Shhh, just breathe. I don't expect you to understand right away.'

She places her hand over my heart, hard, pushing me into the bed. She is closing her eyes but tears are running down her face and I don't want them to drip down onto me. My heart is beating very fast against her hand and she keeps saying, 'Shhh, sweet girl, close your eyes and let your heart remember.'

I try to scream more but my voice is used up so I grunt like the animals in the woods.

31

Elisa

I know things now, things I could never have imagined I would ever come to know. I know that the body will keep going and going and going, breathing and doing its daily businesses, and resting, even, in spite of the heart thinking it isn't possible. It's been more than two months now. For every day that passes, we are less likely to ever see Lucia again. It's the elephant in the room, the vast abyss between Fredrik and me, the painful, unavoidable truth. I'm not stupid, I've read the statistics. Gaute Svendsen at least has the decency to recognize this. He still calls every day at eleven. He still hasn't brought any news. None. She is gone.

I know now that there are people out there capable of doing evil things to other people and perhaps getting away with it. I know this better than most people. A twenty-one-year-old man from Oppegård had the idea of writing a ransom note to a family whose daughter had just been taken from them. Why? Who would do such a thing? Once in police custody, he said it was a joke. They let him go, saying he was unlikely to become a repeat offender. A woman posed as a fellow mother at my child's school. She sat with me, told me little snippets from a fabricated life, and looked me in the eyes, all the while knowing that she would take my daughter from me. Why? It is all I ever think about – *why?* My own mother believes I deserve this living hell.

A man, who, judging by what the police have managed to uncover, had a rough start in life as an orphan in Tallinn and grew up to become a drug dealer and gang member well known to the authorities in several Eastern European countries, helped to transport a child of seven across country borders to an unknown destination and destiny, only to disappear without a trace.

Why? Why would someone do such things? And yet I know better than most people that most of us are capable of terrible things.

I think a lot about the woman who called herself Line. I wish she really was dead and decomposing in the cold earth next to that wretched house in Mölleryd, her beautiful face turning sunken and waxy, then rotten, then unrecognizable. The police insist that the woman found in the ground there must be the same woman who took Lucia, but I know in my heart she isn't. I refuse to believe that the woman I spoke to and spent time with was actually an Estonian criminal and drug addict just pretending to be a middle-class Norwegian mother. Her accent was flawless, and there was nothing about her demeanor that made me suspect for a single second that the polished house and sweet child weren't hers. Their faces weren't even similar, regardless of how good at disguising herself she might have been. 'You'd be surprised,' Gaute Svendsen said to me, shaking his head curtly. 'They can be unbelievably cunning and sophisticated.'

Besides, what about the little girl? I believe the little girl she referred to as 'Josephine' was that woman's own child and not merely a decoy. She seemed like a normal little girl. A girl who was confident and secure, well taken care of. Mothered. But how could she be if her mother was a child-snatcher with connections to the kinds of networks responsible for taking Lucia? The partially decomposed body of Silwia Truja was found by police tracker dogs, buried in the garden. If the girl really was just a prop, she could have suffered the same fate in a different location, but I refuse to think about that because if there's one little girl dead in the ground, then most likely there are two.

In the weeks after they found the body, Fredrik and I were quietly and cautiously optimistic. Now that there'd been one breakthrough, surely another had to be right around the corner?

But the days dragged past. One after the other. And today is 23 December and we're facing Christmas without Lucia. The baby I wanted with every cell in my body, whom I carried in my womb, transfixed by the wonder of it all, whom I gave birth to and breastfed and swaddled and held and loved – so fiercely – is gone. She's alive – I have to believe that, I will always believe that, and I can feel her still, though for every day that passes, the connection I sense between us feels increasingly fragile.

I spend my days lost in the dark recesses of my mind, turning that *why?* over and over and over. There are people in this world – millions of them, in fact – who believe that we get what we deserve, that the world is governed by a cosmic law of karma, as inescapable as it is true. These beliefs aren't that far removed from what my mother holds to be true. You do something bad, and that thing will generate negative energy which will come back to find you, albeit in a different shape or form. Is losing Lucia karmic retribution for the bad things I have done? Though the thought tears me to pieces it also makes sense on some gruesome level. I know it will consume me until nothing remains, nothing but a bitter, dangerous core.

Downstairs, Lyder is watching a Spider-Man cartoon. His face is wan and pale in the flickering light from the TV. It's late, almost bedtime. Fredrik has gone to his parents' house to help them extend the table for tomorrow's festivities. Growing up, my family never celebrated Christmas, and neither did Fredrik's. Since leaving the church and becoming grandparents, his parents have started to embrace the tradition, and it's been one of my favorite things about parenting – introducing such a beautiful tradition to my children. Fredrik's two older sisters and their families will also be there with us tomorrow. We will eat roasted pork belly with hard, glazed crackling and listen to the sounds of the children playing with their new toys in the next room, but all I'll be able to hear is the silence of the one child missing. We will try to follow the conversations around the table, and we will graciously accept the heartfelt wishes that Lucia be found soon. We will breathe and blink and talk and walk, we'll unwrap presents and raise our glasses and drive home and unlock the door to the empty house, and we'll lie awake all night beside each other, seeing different incarnations of Lucia in our minds.

'Come on,' I say to Lyder. 'Let's do the tree.'

'We have to wait for Daddy!'

'No, I think it would be nice to surprise him.'

Lyder slides reluctantly off the sofa and follows me over to the terrace door. The big Christmas tree is out there, leaning against the side of the house, acclimatizing.

'It's ready to come inside, now,' I say. 'Why don't you help me?'

Lyder holds the door and I grab the trunk about halfway up the tree. Its pine needles sting my palm and I drag it through the door, a sprinkle of needles and snow landing on the floor. When I've placed it into its stand, helped by Lyder, I hand him the familiar baubles we've collected over the years, one by one. He is unusually quiet and seems to take the task of hanging the glass ornaments on the tree very seriously.

'Is Lucia never coming home?' he asks, keeping his eyes on a high branch, where he is attempting to place a knitted Santa Claus figure by standing on a chair, me supporting the bony small of his back as he stretches.

'I don't know, darling,' I say. It's the first time I've said this. My son has asked this question many, many times since 19 October, and I have always told him that of course his sister is coming home. Soon, I've always said. *Soon.*

'What color is Lucia's hair?'

'Oh... Don't you remember?' I ask, my voice emerging in a weak whisper.

'No... Was it yellow?'

'Yeah, kind of. Blonde. Almost gold.' I can feel that soft, golden hair beneath my fingertips in this moment, like she's here and I'm stroking her hair – I just can't see her.

'I think she's dead.' Lyder speaks in the casual way children do, but his words strike me with such force, I can't move even a centimeter. I force myself to slowly remove my hand from his back. I lock my eyes on a purple glittery reindeer decoration sitting in its box, little black dot eyes staring back.

'Please don't say that,' I whisper. I take several deep breaths, reminding myself that it was just a careless comment, not a statement of fact. Children say the most awful and strange things sometimes. I will myself out of my shocked state and stroke the back of Lyder's head gently.

He turns to look at me. His face has changed without me noticing. It's thinner, like he's only just now shrugged off the last of toddlerhood. His eyebrows have darkened, and his hair, which was almost as light as Lucia's in the summer, is now chocolate brown with golden streaks. He is nothing like her, and exactly like her at the same time; although their features are entirely different, the ghost of her is there in his expression, and in his deep brown eyes. As I so often have, I look for something of Fredrik in him. In Lucia, it was there in the twinkle of her eye, the sweet, slightly crooked smile and the fine, silky blonde hair.

With Lyder it is different. As he grows older, shrugging off his bland, chubby babyhood, and his features sharpen, all I can see is *him*.

My love.

My hand, which was holding a beautiful jade bauble out to Lyder, begins to tremble and the bauble drops to the floor and shatters, spraying a vivid splash of glitter and glass across the parquet.

32

Selma

'Merry Christmas,' says Alf, her father, and ushers Selma inside, taking her cabin-sized suitcase from her hand.

She kisses his hot, red cheek and kicks off her UGG boots before unzipping her down jacket and releasing Medusa onto the floor from her travel basket. The cat looks around before huddling against Selma's legs. She picks the cat up and follows her father through to the open-plan sitting room with the kitchen at the far end. He has laid the table for three, like he always does. A plump Christmas tree with red and gold plastic baubles from the supermarket stands to the side of the balcony door. Selma pulls some presents from her handbag and puts them alongside the ones that are already under the tree. Medusa studies the tree carefully, as though she can't compute that her humans have brought it into the house. Then she goes and sits by the balcony door, staring out at the snow and the dark night. Selma wonders if she remembers being a little kitten on the other side of this door, looking in.

Her father hands her a glass of Prosecco and they stand

smiling at each other for a long moment, neither knowing where to begin their conversation.

'So,' he says, before taking a big gulp from his glass, 'did you have any trouble getting here?'

'No. It was fine, really. Less than an hour from door to door. I got caught in a bit of traffic coming through Asker and Lier, but otherwise the drive was pretty smooth.'

'I thought you might have come while it was still light,' he says, and Selma feels a pang of guilt at the thought of him here alone, waiting for her, pottering about his little apartment, listening to Drammen's many church bells ushering in Christmas.

'It's still only four, Dad. And I'm all yours until Thursday.'

'Good,' he says, refilling her still almost full glass, then his own, before turning up the soft flute music playing from the television. 'I'm glad you're home.'

They sink into the deep beige leather sofa that has always stood facing the TV. When she was a child she used to do front flips on it when her parents weren't looking and she still remembers how, once, her mother caught her at it and stood watching her with a stern expression, then couldn't help but burst out laughing. She runs her hand up the soft leather behind her back. Her mother's back must have pressed against it so many times; might it still hold something of her – a gentle slouch or impression?

'How's work going?' says her father, jolting her from her thoughts.

'Yeah, great,' she says, then reconsiders. It's her father, after all. They're close. 'Actually, it's not that great. I don't know, I just feel like I've really stagnated recently. There are more and more cuts – just the other day, they let Kai-Marius go. He'd only been there a couple of months less than me. Made me feel like I might be next, you know?'

'They wouldn't let you go, would they?'

'I never used to think so. Olav has always seemed really happy with me, but you know what they say, you're only as good as your last article. And this autumn I literally put everything into the kidnap case, Lucia Blix, but... nothing. We didn't get anywhere with it at all. It's like she just vanished. And people want news, new angles, exclusives and all that, and there just hasn't been a thing.'

Her father nods thoughtfully. He, like everyone else in Norway, must have his own theories about what happened to the little girl. 'You know, with cases like that, it seems to me that they're either solved pretty much straight away or never. Like Therese, for example.' His gaze moves away from the TV screen, on which a long line of dancers dressed like candy canes are twirling and leaping to Tchaikovsky, and out through the window to the myriad glimmering lights of Drammen. He's referring to Therese Johannessen, the nine-year-old who disappeared without a trace less than ten minutes' walk from this apartment a few years before Selma was born. Everyone in Norway, and especially in Drammen, knows the images: the little girl's mischievous, gap-toothed smile, the mop of dark hair, the grey block of flats dominating the hillside in the suburb of Fjell, where she lived, the grass-lined concrete pathway where she was last seen, skipping on her way home. Therese, like Lucia, dominated the national headlines for months after her disappearance, and is still occasionally featured now, so many years later. Will that be Lucia's fate, too – will she become a fading photograph, a child frozen in time, always innocent and smiling, forever gone?

'What do you think happened to her?' asks Selma, watching her father's broad, open face.

'Therese?'

'No, Lucia Blix.'

'Aren't they fairly certain she was taken by that Eastern European network?'

'It seems like she was, yes. But the question remains – why? Why her?'

'It just doesn't bear thinking about. What they might do to a little girl like that, what she must have experienced. It almost makes you hope they just killed her straight away. Any other fate could be worse than death. Much worse.'

'I'm totally certain she's alive,' says Selma. 'And that's what makes this case hard to give up on, even though Olav won't let me spend much time on it any more. I'm convinced she's alive and that someone somewhere knows something. People don't actually disappear without a trace. It's just that the traces are well hidden.'

'Yes,' says Alf, stroking his silvery beard. 'I guess it must be really hard to accept that a case most likely won't be solved when you've been working so intensely on it.'

Selma nods and finds to her annoyance that her eyes are stinging with tears.

'She was only seven,' she says after a long moment. 'Seven. I know how it feels to be separated from your mother at that age… I really thought I could help her somehow. That I'd see patterns that other people can't, that a revelation would suddenly appear to me. I know it sounds ridiculous when I put it like that, but it's true – I believed it. There's something that doesn't add up, Dad. Something strange, but I just can't quite put my finger to it.'

'Selma, it isn't your job to solve the case. It's your job to report on the progress of the people whose job that is.'

'I know that! But you know how I see and *feel* things and connections that other people often can't or won't see. You *know* that. But this time I just can't seem to come up with anything that could shed new light on it. Nothing.'

Her father knows her well enough not to bother with any meaningless phrases intended to make her feel better about the Blix case. Instead, he tops up her now empty glass and they sit in silence for a long while, lost in separate thoughts, watching the dancers on TV. Eventually Selma feels the tension and stress of the last two months beginning to melt away. She is relieved and comforted to be here, in her childhood home, with her father and Medusa, about to celebrate Christmas, her father's legendary *pinnekjøtt* steaming on the stove, the mutton bones filling the apartment with their deliciously distinctive salty smell.

They take their time with the meal, stopping occasionally to raise a shot glass of aquavit before knocking it back and erupting into laughter. After the last of the *pinnekjøtt* bones have been sucked dry, Alf lifts his wine glass.

'To Ingrid,' he says, looking solemnly at the empty space set for his wife at the head of the table.

Selma imagines all the other homes missing a loved one tonight. She raises her glass and swallows hard before taking a sip. Losing her mother when she was seven changed something in her, she is well aware of that. But at least she knows where her mother is; she is comforted by the notion that Ingrid's physical being has fused back into the earth, that elements of her have become parts of other living beings. She visits her grave in the summer and sits by her headstone, reading books and looking across the gentle downward slope of the graveyard to the wide, sluggish river further down. Imagine not knowing where she was. What must it be like to go day after day, year after year, having no idea where the person you loved most was?

Her thoughts return to Lucia Blix. Where is she tonight, on Christmas Eve? Selma can bring the child's features to mind easily enough – she's spent hours staring at her beautiful, haunting face, but when she tries to imagine her where she is in this exact moment, her mind draws a blank. She can picture Lucia's family, though, stumbling through their first Christmas without their daughter. How they'll probably be putting on a show of normalcy for the sake of the younger brother; how, in spite of everything, they'll have to smile, and eat, and talk. They'll watch their little boy tearing open his presents, they'll help him slot batteries into toys, and they'll watch him play with them, Fredrik and Elisa Blix avoiding each other's eyes – Selma can picture them clearly in her mind.

It is deep in the night when she gets out of bed and stands a while at the window. A waxing gibbous moon, still generous with light, hangs high above Drammen. Selma turns back from the window and sits down in the middle of the floor, the parquet cool against her bare thighs. Medusa watches her from the foot of the bed, her jade eyes narrowed and glinting in the moonlight. Selma closes her eyes. And there she is – her mother. Ingrid. It's as though Selma's fractured and elusive memories merge with the mother she knows mostly from photographs to produce a real, three-dimensional woman in her mind. In this moment, Selma can fully reconstruct her mother. She can move in and around the image of Ingrid, excavating long-forgotten moments, the sound of her voice, the touch of her slim hand on her own brow. She stays like this for a long time, feeling her mother become separated from the murk of less important memories, like a bone unearthed and gleaming.

Selma watches herself being held close by her mother. Ingrid has long light brown hair. Had. It fell out, in clumps – Selma remembers the horror of it coming loose in her hand from her mother's skull. But now, in this moment, Ingrid still has her long hair. She wears an expression of pure joy on her face, and her eyes are firmly shut. Selma's expression is different: anguished and apprehensive, like she can sense the rot already eating her mother from the inside.

As she sits there observing her young self with her mother, something shifts in Selma. She has a strong sense that she knows something but can't quite grasp the knowledge. She glances around the room briefly – it's still her quiet childhood bedroom, it's still Drammen outside, and the cat is still motionless and suspicious on the bed. She closes her eyes again, half-expecting the vision of herself with her mother to be gone, to have slipped back into the opaque river of fractured memories that runs through all of us, but it remains crystal clear, except that now her own young face has been replaced by that of Lucia Blix. Lucia's distinctive dark eyebrows are drawn together, her brown eyes are cast downwards, her full lips are puckered in a frown. She's being held by a woman in the way a mother would embrace her own child, but the woman is not Elisa Blix. Selma uses all her energy to try to bring the woman's face into focus, but she remains a blurred stranger.

When Selma reopens her eyes, it's as though all of the excess energy that usually courses through her has suddenly run dry. She stumbles unsteadily back to her bed and falls into a deep, dreamless sleep.

33

Marcus

It's strange, spending Christmas with other people. After all these years, he still can't quite get used to it. He finds the inmates' excitement about the festive season moving. Tollebu offers various craft workshops for prisoners to make cards and simple presents out of scrap pieces of wood and fabric, and these are always oversubscribed within hours of being advertised on the noticeboard in November.

Before, in his other life, he used to spend Christmas alone in his apartment in Frogner. There was nothing sad about that; he used to enjoy the quiet, reflective days, and he'd put up a little tree by the fireplace, drink some fine whiskeys and sit looking out at the lights of Oslo through his panoramic windows. That had changed when he fell in love. He'd wanted to be with *her* over the holidays, cooking for her, making love for hours in the middle of the day, watching her breathtaking smile spread across her face when she opened her presents. He got it, then, why other people got so excited about Christmas. He'd wanted a baby with her, too – a little person to pass traditions on to, a new soul to guide.

He stays a long while in his bed after waking up, staring at the unbroken white of the ceiling. He tries to imagine the kind of Christmas he might have been celebrating today if those things had happened for him. Would they still be happy together? Would they raise their glasses in a champagne toast, laughing as they watched their kid unwrap presents, soft hymns playing in the background, snow falling outside? There might have been more children by now, little boys and girls whose faces would be a wonderful blend of his features and hers. Instead, he is here, in Tollebu Prison, about to celebrate his sixth Christmas behind bars.

He dresses quickly and goes to the chapel before breakfast. The chaplain looks up, surprised to see him there at this time, and it occurs to Marcus that the chapel might be closed in preparation for the various services happening later in the day.

But the chaplain nods towards the empty pews and Marcus sits down near the front. 'I was hoping we could talk about forgiveness,' he says.

34

Lucia

When I wake up, Maman is sitting by my bed, like every day.

'*Bonjour*,' she says. It means 'Good day'. Every day she helps me remember my French and every day I do remember more and more words.

'*Bonjour*,' I say.

'Bad night, huh?' she says, and I remember how I screamed many times in the night. I wet the bed, too. I run my hand across the plastic sheet underneath my bottom. I remember standing by the side of the bed, shivering and naked, the floor very cold under my feet, while Maman changed the sheets. 'My poor lamb,' she said, and then she helped me into a clean nightdress and back into the bed. Maman never gets angry.

'A bad night, but today will be a good day,' she says. 'It's Christmas.'

This doesn't make me happy. It makes me very sad. Maman sees this. She puts her hand above my heart, where she has stitched my real name on the nightdress, like she's done on Josie's, like we are hard to tell apart and she can only know who is who by reading the names on our chests. We're not, because we're not that kind of twins. We're the kind that look a bit alike but not the same.

'Come on,' she says, but I don't want to come with her. I want to go home.

'I want to go home,' I whisper.

Maman is good at pretending like this is okay to say, but it isn't, and I can tell.

In the woods me and Josie choose a tree. It's very tall and a little bit wonky on one side, like someone pulled off half the branches, but we don't care and Maman cuts it down with an axe. We help her haul it onto the sled and then Josie and I sit close together holding the tree so it doesn't fall off down the long hill to our house. Our house has a name. It's called Ferme du Tachoué. It's called that because at the bottom of the garden there's a little river with the same name. I like this name. Ta-choué. Ta-chou-ay. Sometimes I say the word over and over in my mind until it feels very strange and it makes me feel calm. And I like the house. But I still want to go home. Many people have two homes. Maman says that it's okay to miss the other home, but that this is my real home. I know that's true now because I have seen all the pictures – the pictures of me and Josie when we were babies, and pictures of me when I was quite small, sitting on the steps outside feeding my goat Samba a carrot stick.

Back in the house, Josie and I sit and draw for a while at the kitchen table. Maman has made a fire and soon we'll have soup. Then, tonight, we will do the big party, says Maman. We are going to leave the farm and drive in a car, for the first time. It's going to be fun, but I shouldn't think for a single second to try anything funny because if I do then The Lady and The Man and The Little Boy will be killed, for sure, Maman said.

We are going to the church where I was christened, and where Maman was christened, and her *maman* too. She's my real grandmother, but she lives in Paris and doesn't want to be a grandmother because she isn't a nice person. We're going to eat lobster before we go there and I can stay up all night if I want.

'Lulu-Rose,' says Maman, 'would you like to make a beautiful drawing for The Lady and The Other Family?'

I don't know how to answer this. Maman has told me The Truth every day since I came here. At first I didn't believe her at all and I screamed a lot. I still want to go home more than anything in the world, at least most of the time, but I know now that Maman only ever tells The Truth. Maybe it would be nice to make a drawing for The Other Family. I think about my bedroom at home, and all my things and my brother – no, The Little Boy – and the playground in between the houses where I used to play, and the way my m— The Lady used to sing to me before bedtime. If she was away on a plane, I listened to her recorded on Daddy's phone. The song was called '*Kjære Gud*', 'Dear God', and it was about God protecting all children. My m— The Lady used to sing it to me even though she doesn't believe in any gods because when she was little herself she loved that song. I can't remember all the words when I try and I wish I could have that recorded song now.

'Hey,' says Maman. 'Hey.' She sits down beside me and strokes my hair. 'You don't have to.'

'I want to,' I say.

She nods and gets up. She goes into the library, where there are thousands of books collected by Maman's parents and grandparents. There is also an old black-wood-and-gold chest where she keeps the best paper, special-occasion paper. She comes back with a sheet of it. It's thick and smooth, with a line of real gold around the sides.

'You said they wouldn't look for me,' I say. 'Or miss me.'

'I'm afraid that's true,' she says. 'They could never love you the way a real family does, Lulu-Rose. The way I do. But *you* miss them. And that's okay. So if you think it would be nice to send them a pretty drawing, then we'll do that. Just don't expect anything back from them, okay?'

I nod and begin to draw.

35

Jacqueline

She ushers the two little girls towards the wide-open Gothic doors with their distinctive pointed arches. The rumble of the river, forceful after a week of heavy rain, all but drowns out the voices of the congregation gathered on the steps waiting to enter. People smile at them, moving back to allow the young children to pass. Jacqueline recognizes some of them and wonders whether they might recognize her too. Inside the church, the sound of the river is like distant thunder, but there is otherwise a reverent, hushed silence. Hundreds of lighted candles bathe the vaulted space in an eerie, soft glow. She steers the girls towards an empty pew near the back.

An old woman walking up the aisle glances at Jacqueline and the girls, then does a double-take and bends down to kiss her on both cheeks. '*Joyeux Noël*,' she says.

Jacqueline vaguely remembers her as one of her mother's old friends. Madame Bouchard, her name is. She recalls playing with her sons as a child, at a large farm overlooking a lush, empty valley, not unlike Le Tachoué. '*Joyeux Noël*,' she replies.

'How beautiful your daughters are. What is your name, *petite fille?*' Madame Bouchard hovers in front of Josie, whose little face shimmers in the glow from the candles on the intricate carved wooden mezzanine above them.

'Josiane.'

'*Et toi?*' Madame Bouchard turns her gaze on Lucia. '*Comment tu t'appelles?*'

Jacqueline remains completely still, suspended in the long moment, her hand resting on Lulu-Rose's knee. She gives it the smallest squeeze. How could she have risked everything, for this? And so soon. It's too soon, far too soon. She can't know for sure that the child won't suddenly stand up and start screaming, the entire congregation turning towards them, intrigued.

Realization might dawn if the child begins to speak in a foreign language. Someone might put two and two together and recognize her from a picture glimpsed in an online news article and then forgotten. Still, Jacqueline feels cautiously optimistic, and a little festive, for the first time in many years. The constant worry that she might be unmasked is starting to ease. She finds herself enjoying this new life in small bursts untainted by fear. She keeps a keen eye on the investigation, and nothing at all has come up to suggest a link between herself and the missing child. But why would it? Besides, the woman who took that poor child was found dead in the ground. She closes her eyes at the thought of that woman's last moments of life.

She glances around. The people present who know of her also know that she married a foreigner and had twins and that she only occasionally returns to this remote, very quiet corner of France where she grew up. They'd seen them with their own eyes on several occasions, though it was a while ago now, the beautiful little girls with pretty smock dresses and long chestnut hair. People here – honest, simple village people – would be able to vouch for Jacqueline and her family, no doubt about that. Some might have heard that she's now a widow – poor woman, so young. They might have spoken of the tragedy, waiting in line at the butcher's or the newsagents', shaking their heads sadly. *No wonder she wanted to come home, poor woman.*

'*Je m'appelle Lulu-Rose*,' says the child, her voice entirely clear and unwavering.

The old lady touches each girl gently on the forehead and says '*Magnifique!*' before joining her own family, who are waiting for her further up the aisle.

Jacqueline is flooded with relief and a love for her girls so pure that it could take her breath away. The church bells ring out midnight and as Lulu-Rose and Josie look around in wonder with tired eyes, Jacqueline remembers the sheer magic she'd felt, coming here with her own parents as a child, for midnight Mass on Christmas Eve. It's why she's brought the girls tonight, even though it's risky.

The service starts and Jacqueline closes her eyes, letting herself be carried along on the hum of voices singing the old, familiar hymns, and draws the warm, spiced air deep into her lungs. It was the right thing to do, to come here with her girls. Home.

In the car home, Josie falls asleep almost immediately, slumping sideways into the middle seat. Lucia, precious, sweet, incredible Lucia, now Lulu-Rose, stares out the window as Saint-Girons peters out into the drab retail area at its southern fringes. They pass the Carrefour hypermarket, its empty parking lot glinting with rainwater that has hardened into a film of ice, then a police station, a car dealership and a cemetery. Jacqueline catches Lulu-Rose's eye in the mirror and smiles at her, but the little girl immediately looks away, into the dark night.

Because of the ice, Jacqueline has to drive slowly, and for a long while they just sit in silence, absorbed in their own thoughts. The last time Lulu-Rose rode in a car, she was still Lucia Blix, brought from Sandefjord to an isolated rural corner of Ariège in the French Pyrenees by Mikko Eilaanen. Now she is Lulu-Rose Olve Thibault, daughter of Jacqueline, twin sister of Josiane, a sleepy eight-year-old heading home. Her loving mother steers the car through the silent night – up, up, into the foothills of the Pyrenees, off the main road, onto first one dirt track, then another, and then a third, carefully navigating the hairpin bends as the foothills steepen into mountainsides, until finally she pulls up in front of their huge ancient Ariègeoise farmhouse.

Both of the girls are asleep now. Jacqueline carries Josie into the house first, pushing the unlocked door open, breathing in the smell of home, taking the stairs slowly as the child shifts in her arms. She goes back for Lulu-Rose and buries her face in her silky hair as she carries her carefully up to bed. She stands for a moment at the foot of the bed, watching the little girl settling deeper into sleep, mouth slipping open, eyes shuttling back and forth beneath thick dark lashes. She hadn't entirely expected to feel this intense love for the girl. She'd thought it would take more time, perhaps months, or years, even, for the little girl to fuse into her family and fill the gaping hole. As it turned out, she was an almost instant fit. From the moment Jacqueline laid eyes on Lucia Blix in the messy cloakroom at Korsvik School, the second time she'd ever seen her, she knew, right down to her bones, that her instinct had been right.

There you are. And you're mine.

36

Selma

A couple of days after Christmas, Selma messaged Olav asking him to call her about the Blix case as she'd had some new thoughts. He texted back the following day saying, 'Unless you know where the kid is, it'll have to wait until the new year.' The message was accompanied by a close-up photo of a huge beer with the slopes of Kitzbühel visible in the background. So Selma has had to wait until today, a clear and very cold January morning, to tell him about the vague intuition of hers that has now hardened into total conviction.

'Close the door,' Olav says when she knocks lightly on the glass wall of his office cubicle. And that's when she knows. His next words are as strange and blurry as if he were speaking underwater. He is sorry, so sorry. Digitalization, reduced reach. No reflection on ability.

'I've tried to find a way around this,' he says at last, still not quite able to meet Selma's eye. She stares at him, her whole body tense; she is incandescent with rage. 'But, as you know, our policy is last in, first out.'

She feels herself nodding and forces herself to stop; she wouldn't want Olav to think for a single second that there is anything right about this.

'You know that I am *meant* to do this,' she says, her voice clear and loud. 'To be a journalist.' She has always prided herself on her extreme self-control, especially in pressurized situations. Whenever adrenaline rushes through her, she instantly becomes calm and clear-headed.

'Nobody knows that better than me. You're good, so very good already, and still so young. You're remarkable, and you know it. And here's the thing. This… this could be the making of you.'

Selma laughs incredulously; she is not going to stand here and be told by Olav Hammel that being let go from the only job she has ever wanted, a job she is damned good at, is anything other than a big fucking mistake.

'Tell me the truth,' she says, and Olav manages to meet her eye for just a moment. She can imagine how she must appear, standing across from him in the little glass box of an office, door awkwardly slid shut. Her long hair, the exact same dark blonde as her mother's, fans out around her shoulders, a little frizzy on top from so many weeks of hat-wearing. Her eyes are blazing and to be avoided, judging by Olav's reaction. Her fingernails are digging into the soft pink flesh of her palms, though he won't be able to see that from where he's standing. 'Tell me. Is this to do with the Blix case?'

He sighs heavily and sinks into his chair, swiveling it back and forth a couple of times, the way he used to when she first came to work here.

'No, Selma, it isn't. Absolutely not. I've told you – we've

been affected by digitalization, just like everyone else has. So many reporters have been forced to go freelance. Which, by the way, can be great. I think it would suit you really well. And I'd appreciate it if any future articles were to land on my desk first.'

Selma laughs again in disbelief. 'I thought we were friends.'

'We *are* friends.'

'I don't think so.'

'Selma, look, this is really difficult for me.'

'You think it's harder for you than for me? Thanks a bunch, Olav. Come on.'

'You know that's not what I meant.'

'I just want the truth.'

'And I've told you: last in, first out. It has to be like that. Though... if you're really serious about this and you can take a bit of advice from an old friend, I'd suggest casting your net a bit wider in the future. You are whip-smart and one hell of a journalist, Selma, but most national papers value versatility and the ability to move between stories. Things can get a little... one-track sometimes. That's all.'

'There's a difference between one-track and thorough, Olav.' Selma spins round to head out into the open-plan office and sees Lisbeth staring fixedly in their direction, mouth open. 'Bye then,' she says, softer now. She places a hand on the door handle and turns back around to face him. She can tell by his expression that he meant what he said, about being her friend.

'Out of interest, what did you want to tell me about the Blix case? A new idea?' he asks, as an afterthought.

'You'll read it in my article. I'm going to break that whole case wide open, you wait and see. I'll send it to you. But it's not going to be cheap, Olav.'

She slides the glass door open and continues to her desk in silence, ignoring Lisbeth's meek, curious presence beside her. She puts her jacket on and zips it slowly all the way up to her chin, taking strange pleasure in having the eyes of all her colleagues on her. Then she walks out, deliberately slowly, her head held high.

April 2019

Fifteen Months Later

37

Elisa

I had to insist in the end. I even got my GP to write a medical note to my bosses saying I would benefit from returning to work and that my personal trauma is unlikely to affect my performance in any way.

I drive to the airport myself and park in the outdoor staff parking area at the far end of Torp, bordering thawing fields. It's 5.30 a.m. and completely dark. Spring hasn't arrived yet; shavings of light snow fall as I walk towards the terminal building. I draw in a deep breath of air – the cold doesn't bother me. But soon, the snow will melt and plump little flowers will push their heads through the black earth, vibrant green leaves will sprout from thin branches, the sun will begin to warm, the patches of snow on Sandefjord's surrounding hills will melt away, the world will buzz with the intoxicating arrival of spring, the world will turn and turn and turn, without her.

By now, Lucia is nine and a half years old and I haven't held her in my arms for eighteen months. I am like those mothers we've all seen on the news: pale, thin, aged overnight. Every day and every night, I am haunted by the CCTV image of my child, held by that man at a roadside service station, shoved into a white van. Despite a massive search operation across the European continent for Eilaanen's whereabouts, it is as though he vanished into thin air after that October morning in Southern Sweden. The police have raided several more addresses, in Riga, in Malmö, in Mölleryd, in Kraków, and even as far south as Sicily and east as Minsk. Several sightings of Eilaanen have been reported in Poland, Latvia and Lithuania.

And still, nothing. All the leads they find just peter out into nothingness.

Stepping into the staff lounge, today feels briefly like any other day – like *before*. Back when I'd go to work and look forward to the long day ahead, and, even more, to coming home at the end of it. Back when my life was like a shimmering airtight bubble floating safely through space, sealing all the darkness out. Can I be that woman again or is she lost forever?

'Ladies and gentlemen, we are very pleased to welcome you on board this Nordic Wings flight to Barcelona-El Prat. Please pay close attention to the security information on the overhead screens. The captain will be back with more information when we reach cruising altitude.' It's Trude Jensen, a colleague I've known for over a decade, who makes the announcement. We used to fly together for Qatar and, by coincidence, we both started at Nordic Wings around the same time.

She replaces the microphone in the cradle and gives me a reassuring smile. 'I am so glad you're back,' she says.

'Me too,' I say. 'It's been a long time.'

I lean back against the jump seat and look out at the near full cabin. It's 7.51 a.m. and we are pushing back right on time. I must have done this thousands of times, but right now it feels like the first time. What if my phone rings with news of Lucia while we're in the air?

'You know how much I have prayed for your family.'

I nod and turn away a little. I catch the eye of a handsome younger man in the front row and give him a smile, though I can feel my heartrate starting to pick up and my hands growing slick with sweat.

'I just can't believe they never found her,' adds Trude, as though this is something one could say to someone like me.

'Yet,' I say.

'What?' Trude inches closer to compensate for the groan of the engines.

'Yet. They haven't found her *yet*.'

She looks at me, her eyes wide and sad, as though I'm the only person who doesn't realize that they haven't found her yet because she's gone forever.

'Of course,' she says softly. She reaches out to touch my hand, which I've been holding in my lap, but I see her doing it and move my hand to smooth down my hair before she gets a chance.

The pilot pushes the throttle to maximum, the jet trembles and the engines roar as we hurtle down the runway. I focus on my breath and clear my mind. As the plane soars into the sky, the empty desperation of the last eighteen months briefly falls away and for a few short moments I am no longer broken, anxious and tense. I'm like the plane; nimble and strong and free.

It will only be a matter of seconds before this little pocket of peace disintegrates and I am returned to my default state of being, my inside landscape like a war zone: barren, numb, ravaged. But for this single moment in time, I am just gliding through air.

The thing I haven't prepared for is that several of the passengers recognize me.

'Anything else?' I ask a white-haired lady in 9A and hand her the Americano she ordered.

'No, thank you, dear,' she replies, her eyes wide and brimming with tears. I can tell she'd like to say something, but she wisely realizes that there is nothing at all she could say.

Trude and I work our way down the cabin but soon have to return to the jump seat and secure the trolley because of turbulence. A middle-aged woman in 12 F is so frightened by the turbulence that she begins to cry and tries to stand up. I mouth for her to sit down but she doesn't listen and, in the end, Trude moves slowly down towards her, holding on to the backs of seats – the turbulence is at one point so bad the three-point seat belt chafes painfully against my chest. I close my eyes and again have the sensation of never having sat here or done this job before. Trude and I spend the next half hour strapped in next to each other, awkwardly avoiding conversation and smiling at any nervous-looking passengers.

With less than forty minutes to go before landing, the

pilots manage to find a calmer altitude and we finish the service, then start to collect the trash. A man towards the back of the plane has a whole row to himself and has fallen asleep with his mouth dropped wide open, his tray table still down, full of meal cartons, a coffee cup and two beers. Funny how the general norms of alcohol consumption in the morning don't seem to count in the air for most people. I step into the middle seat and quietly begin to retrieve the trash when I glance out the window.

We are flying over brown and grey-green fields that thicken into forest-clad hills and then white-capped mountains in the distance – the Pyrenees. We must be somewhere in the south-west of France. I stare at the picturesque landscape far below us, and what strikes me about it is that while I can make out a few houses and farmsteads, every settlement seems really far from the next, a few nestled entirely isolated against the crest of a hill or deep in the woods. I feel a terrible cold anxiety at the thought of this. How many millions of places like this exist in the world, places where it would be easy to conceal a stolen child, even one of the world's most high-profile missing children, with no immediate neighbors to even notice her presence?

I just can't believe they never found her.

A teardrop slips from my eye onto the crumpled beer can and paper serviette I'm holding. I quickly wipe my eye with my other hand before turning away from the window.

At the beginning, I could feel her continued presence so strongly. I held on to that feeling for months and months, but it's gone now. Now when I think about Lucia, which is all the time, it's like looking into a vast empty space inside me. I can no longer quite bring her into three dimensions;

even when I look intently at photos of her, as I do every night, she remains an image. At the beginning, it was as though she leaped off the photo paper, and in my mind I could hear and see her talking and moving and laughing and crying. But not anymore.

I take several deep breaths and try to chase away these thoughts. I've learned to control where my mind goes and which images I allow. I've had to. Whenever my mind inches too close to pictures so gruesome they would tear me apart, I consciously imagine them as being held inside a sealed white box. They are there, I must carry them, but I don't have to open the box.

I try to do this now, by placing Mikko Eilaanen and the fact that he was the last person seen with my child inside the box, because if I open it and look at the various possible scenarios, I will literally go mad. And as Gaute Svendsen said on that first night, I can't go mad, because Lucia will need me when they find her. *When they find her.*

I quickly glance back at the rolling fields, foothills and majestic mountains before making my way slowly back up towards the galley. I run through the check-lists, each task second nature after so many years on the job. And still, a thought won't leave me: how many places like the one we just flew over exist across Europe and beyond? Lucia could be anywhere. Anywhere, and with anyone.

38

Jacqueline

She walks around the periphery of the forest, holding Josie by the hand, staring into the dark mass of trees, ready to spot the slightest movement. The child's hand is warm and soft, but Jacqueline is getting increasingly cold, both with fear and because the sun is receding into the dip between two distant peaks, burning pink, then orange and then blood red. She screams for Lulu-Rose so loud her throat hurts, and Josie screams for her too, until her voice breaks and runs dry. What if she has fallen from a tree and cracked her head open and is lying stunned and alone somewhere, maroon blood flowing from her skull into the ground seething with squirming insects and new plants throbbing with life, tall trees rising up all around her like the walls of a tomb? What if she chose to hide behind one of the enormous tree carcasses by the river, torn from the earth by the winter storms, and she slipped and tumbled into the icy, wild water and didn't manage to get back out, carried flailing, then still, downstream?

Or what if she wasn't really playing the hiding game at

all but was simply biding her time before running as fast as she could down, down, across the river via the stone bridge, through the fields, across the road and down to the scattered stone houses of the hamlet, where she hammered on doors until someone opened up and she could shout, 'Help me! Help me, please!'

Jacqueline's breathing is becoming labored, air pushed to the smallest pockets of her lungs, panic burning black behind her eyes. Josie can tell she's agitated and the little hand grows limp in hers, but Jacqueline keeps dragging her along, sliding her gaze very slowly across the mountain ridge, across the rolling brown-green fields, over the unbroken expanse of sky, to the vast forests that look like black hairs on a hillside chin, as though Lulu-Rose could be anywhere at all. She isn't worried that anyone might hear her screams; there's nobody here, not for miles and miles.

If you try to run, the first person to find you will be me. Always.

If you try to scream, the only person who will hear you is me. Always.

'Maybe we should get someone to help us,' says Josie, her dark eyes dilated and almost black in the last light of the lowering sun, her words floating up into the trees like air bubbles. A plane streaks past high above them, heading south.

'Help us?' Jacqueline hisses, bringing her face close to Josie's, spitting out the words as though they'd scratched her tongue.

Josie recoils.

'Help us!' She laughs now – a cruel, cold laugh. 'Nobody

can help us, don't you get it? We have to find her, no matter what.'

They're on the crest of a hill overlooking the empty, shadowed valley and a brisk wind surges past them. She pulls her hand free from Josie's and rubs hard at her upper arms. Then she starts walking again, faster now, dragging the little girl along, and they slip into the gloomy woods.

Twigs snap, little animals scurry into hollow trunks or down burrows, the wind scrambles the leaves high above them, and water trickles somewhere deeper inside the forest. Though the sky is still a pink and purple slash up above the treetops, it's almost completely dark down amid the crowd of trunks. She draws Josie close, then opens the torch on her iPhone and shines its light around them and upwards. A bird takes off with a shrill cry and Jacqueline has the sudden eerie sensation of being watched. A cold, wretched dread washes over her; is this how it's going to end, after everything that's happened? Could Lulu-Rose really have run away and alerted someone, speaking the words that aren't even true anymore – *I don't belong here, help me, I want to go home?*

A rustling sound makes them turn around. Lulu-Rose is standing very still, almost indistinguishable from the trees.

Jacqueline lowers the torchbeam and rushes towards her. When she pulls her into her arms, Lulu-Rose is trembling with cold. She peels off her jacket and bundles it around the little girl's thin body.

'I'm sorry,' Lulu-Rose whispers. 'I'm so sorry, Maman.'

Désolée, *Maman.*

Maman.

They walk down the hill towards the farmhouse together,

a little-girl hand in each of Jacqueline's. At home lamb and baby potatoes roast in the oven. After dinner there will be board games in front of the library fireplace. A sleepy cat will cuddle up close to her sleepy little girls. She will carry them up the stairs to their beds one at a time, then she'll sit with them, smoothing their long strands of brown hair, kissing their smooth, cool foreheads.

They can make out the shape of Le Tachoué now, big like a ship, held by miles of rolling fields as empty as an ocean. Lulu-Rose has warmed up a little and skips lightly as they go, as if she's never had a worry in the world, as if she's never been someone else's, as if she hasn't just spent several hours in the woods on her own, watching the sky turn from cool cobalt to inky and sprayed with stars.

In the night, when the children have been asleep for many hours, Jacqueline lies awake, listening to the distant lament of a fox. The frightening moments of the afternoon keep coming back to her: her fear, the cooling afternoon, the heavy silence of the woods, the missing girl. Had she reacted the way she did because it reminded her of the very beginning, eighteen months ago, when Lulu-Rose fled into the forest, fell out of the tree and tore up her feet, and Jacqueline carried her home, gently bathed her and told her that she had been taken from her as a much younger child? Lulu-Rose had gone into deep shock after that, crying every day and running away constantly, either up the hill to the forest or down to the river. She refused to speak even a single word to Josie, and sometimes refused to leave her room for several days. Jacqueline had waited it out and eventually, like she'd hoped she would, Lulu-Rose began to come around. It started slowly.

In the afternoons, Jacqueline would often bake bread with Josie. Lulu-Rose started to appear in the doorway to the kitchen, at first as a shadow, always making sure to stay just out of sight, and then, after a while, she would come and sit at the kitchen table, watching. One day she walked determinedly into the room, washed her hands under the tap, then gently lifted the plump white dough from underneath its damp rising cloth and started to knead it the way she'd seen Josie do it.

Their trip to Saint-Girons for midnight Mass that first Christmas Eve was another turning point. Soon after, the girls began to play hide-and-seek together. Inside the house at first, and then, as winter mellowed into spring and then summer, they played in the garden, in the fields, down by the river, and up in the forest. When Lulu-Rose had been at Le Tachoué for a few months, she started to return to being the happy child she'd appeared to be in Norway. Happier, even, thought Jacqueline. Here, the little girl was free of the endless rush of family life with two working parents in a busy town. Jacqueline was always around, always willing to join in the girls' games, always ready to soothe and kiss away a small injury. Besides, how could someone like Elisa Blix be a good mother?

That first winter, in the mornings, after driving Josie to school, Jacqueline would sit with Lulu-Rose in the library, teaching her French. For four hours every day, the little girl would be taught intensively by Jacqueline herself, and Lulu-Rose clearly had an ear for languages; by summer she was proficient in oral French, to the point where she and Josie began to speak it together spontaneously. The lessons also helped forge a real bond between Lulu-Rose and Jacqueline.

At the beginning, Jacqueline couldn't be sure whether Lulu-Rose actually believed her when she told her about the past and about how bringing her here had been the only right thing to do. After a while, she started to ask a lot of questions, and the two of them sometimes spent hours poring over old photographs in beautiful soft leather albums when Josiane was at school. 'Is that me?' Lulu-Rose would say, pointing to a round-faced baby with long black eyelashes and little rosebud lips stretched in a sweet smile. Jacqueline would nod, stroking Lulu-Rose's hair, and sometimes she'd have to lean in and kiss the top of her head so the girl wouldn't notice the glint of tears in her eyes. She'd watch Lulu-Rose turn the pages of the album, thinking about how that little hand had once been held every day by someone else.

They had both needed some convincing of this new life, but, considering the circumstances, that was surely entirely normal.

There had been the matter of the name. For very obvious reasons, she couldn't keep calling her 'Lucia'. To use only 'Rose', the name on her birth certificate, also seemed wrong. So 'Lulu-Rose' was a compromise. As it turned out, the name suited her: sassy but delicate, playful and original.

Before she'd brought her to Le Tachoué, Jacqueline had had occasional doubts. She would pore over the numerous photos of the little girl on Instagram and Facebook, uploaded by Elisa Blix for the world to see. She committed every last detail of the child's face to memory, trying to overwrite the face she'd known. *Could I love you?* she'd wonder. *Yes*, she would tell herself, her heart aching. But it wasn't truly until Lulu-Rose came home that Jacqueline knew that she'd been right.

Eighteen months on, Lucia is fully integrated in school and the dust has settled at Le Tachoué. Jacqueline often lies awake at night, like now, thinking about how, finally, order has been restored and she once again has everything. Still, sometimes, in these dark pockets of the night, she feels a niggling murmur somewhere inside, like an itch. What more could she want? She can't turn back time; second best is as good as she can expect. Perhaps a man in her life would bring new happiness, but Jacqueline can't bear the thought of someone holding her close or gently running his fingertips across her skin. How could she ever think of love or sex and not instantly be reminded of her husband?

She sits up slowly, willing the memories away. She has a strategy for moments like this: she consciously focuses her mind on the landscape around Le Tachoué, the one thing that never fails to calm her. She dangles her feet over the side of the high bed until they find the sheepskin slippers on the floor. She crosses the room and opens the window, then unhooks the metal clasp of the shutters. The fox is still wailing and its shrill barks fill the room. Though the days have been pleasantly warm in the last week, the temperature still drops below freezing at night, and she can make out the shimmer of frost on the moonlit fields. The distant silhouettes of the mountains glow faintly with snow. She looks down the rolling hillsides below Le Tachoué towards the forests of Lucasso, which have been in the Thibault family since the seventeenth century and where you could walk for several days without coming upon another settlement. Years ago, the government wanted to lay a section of the new district road connecting the Ariège to the south coast through those woods, but Jacqueline's grandfather refused to sell the land. 'This forest belongs to itself,' he said. 'My job is merely to look after it.'

The world, and life itself, have at last become beautiful to her again. For years she thought that would never happen. Seven years, it took.

She leaves the shutters and window open and returns to bed, drawing her duvet up to her chin against the cool air. She thinks of the afternoon, of how Josie came hurtling into the kitchen saying they'd been playing hide-and-seek at the top of the garden and that she couldn't find Lulu-Rose after almost an hour of searching. It's not the first time Lulu-Rose has chosen to stay hidden long past the point when it's no longer funny. Jacqueline wonders whether this is her one small rebellion, a subconscious mutiny, her only way of exerting some control. It is with thoughts of Lulu-Rose that Jacqueline finally falls asleep, a faint breeze from the Pyrénes Ariègeoises whispering across her face.

39

Selma

It's the first warm day of the year, over eighteen degrees at ten in the morning, but Selma doesn't know it; she is still curled up underneath her duvet in deep sleep, her mouth open, Medusa snuggled into the warm space between her chest and her arm. The doorbell rings, first once, then again, but it isn't until the third attempt that Selma stirs. She tries to open her eyes, but they stick together and she has to rub at them hard. It was past 3 a.m. when she made it to bed, the images from *Call of Duty* lingering in her mind for a long while before she was able to sleep. She hasn't left the house for two days, or perhaps it's three. She couldn't say which day of the week it is, but it hardly matters.

The doorbell rings again, but just after the sound dies away she hears the jingle of keys and then the smooth click as one is inserted in the lock.

She hops out of bed, scrambling to pull her hoodie and a pair of sweatpants on; she's slept in only her underwear.

'Pappa!' she says, as her father enters her apartment, a

tired and hesitant expression on his face. 'You can't just come in without asking!'

'Selma, why don't you check your phone? I've messaged you three times, called you twice and repeatedly rung the doorbell. What was I supposed to do? I didn't know if you were okay.'

'Of course I'm okay,' she says, still annoyed but filling the kettle anyway. 'Why wouldn't I be? I just went to bed late, that's all.'

'Selma.'

Her father tries to catch her eye, but she avoids looking at him, letting her gaze travel across the open-plan studio apartment instead. Medusa is on the windowsill now, looking out at the bright blue sky. Clothes have gathered on the backs of all the chairs, flung there after yet another long night of gaming before Selma stumbled to bed. Peppes Pizza boxes tower next to the overflowing recycling bin. A potted basil plant has wilted to a brown, shriveled skeleton next to a mushy dark brown banana on the kitchen counter. She reaches for the box of Twining's Earl Grey her father brought last time he came, but it's empty. She shrugs and searches defiantly through the empty cupboard above the sink.

'Selma, this needs to stop. Now.'

'What does? Me just living my life and you not liking it?'

'No. You barricading yourself in and refusing to engage with anything.'

'That's not what I'm doing.'

'Isn't it?'

'No.'

A heavy silence hangs between them and Selma briefly

recalls how they used to laugh so easily together. That feels like a long time ago now. But then again, so does everything.

'Did you go to your therapy appointment on Wednesday?'

'Yes.'

'Selma...'

'Okay, fine. No, I didn't. I don't need a shrink.'

'Are you taking your meds?'

'Yes... Okay, fine. No, I'm not. And do you know why? Because fundamentally I just don't agree with having to take drugs in order to conform to the world's expectations of me, do you get that?'

'What expectations are you talking about, Selma? We're not talking about expectations. We're talking about being able to function. This...' Alf gestures with his hand at the sorry state of Selma's apartment. 'This isn't functioning, and you know it. Look... I know the last sixteen months or so have been really hard on you. I just wish there was a way for you to re-engage with the stuff you used to care about.'

'Like what?'

'Like boxing.'

Selma snorts out loud at the idea of returning to the gym. The only workout she gets these days is the virtual kind. Her once impressive muscles have softened, and she is now rail-thin. She doesn't miss the exhilaration of a workout, not at all – she's quite content in her own company, whiling away the days with her beloved cat and the videogames, pushing away any independent thoughts and images until she is bleary with tiredness in the early hours.

'And work.'

'Work? What are you talking about?'

'Don't you think it's time to start getting serious about work again, Selma?'

'Are you actually for real?'

'Selma, everyone experiences a setback sometimes. When I was young and just starting out, I was—'

'A setback!' Her voice is suddenly shrill. 'A setback! I was fucking fired, Dad!'

'Yes. Yes, you were. And you need to get over it, is what I'm saying. I know how disappointed you were. And how hard you worked at that job. But, sweetheart, it isn't at all like you to let yourself be defeated like this. You're a fighter.'

'No, I'm not. I'm tired of fighting, don't you get it?' She has to turn away so her father doesn't see the tears that have sprung to her eyes. She fumbles with an old jar of Nescafé, blinking desperately, but the tears continue to fall onto the wooden worktop.

'I think you should persist with the freelancing, Selma. It'll take time to get established again, sure, but it'll suit you, being your own boss. And you'll never get fired again.'

Alf winks at her, and though she would usually have found his comment funny, she certainly doesn't now, and she stares at him.

'No.'

The freelance life didn't work out like Selma had intended. She just never managed to get started, and increasingly she retreated into herself. In the first few weeks after Olav let her go, it was as though a black cloud had descended on her life, rendering her unable to participate in anything. She hardly ate or slept but spent her days and nights either pacing around the apartment or scouring the internet for updates on the Blix case. She wanted, so badly, to be the journalist who landed the big breakthrough scoop on that case. And most of all she wanted a happy ending for the little girl. But as she was dragged further and further into the bleak clutches of depression, she stopped caring. Even when the case occasionally grabbed the headlines again, she couldn't be bothered to read the articles properly, just scanning them before moving on to something else.

'How about you come and stay with me for a few days?' Alf says.

'No,' she says. But then she thinks about her old room, and how good it would feel to just be at home, listening to the distant murmur of her father's radio from downstairs, running her hands across her mother's old perfume bottles in the bathroom, sitting in the window with her legs drawn up, watching the lights of Drammen in the dark. Besides, she knows she's only a day or two away from having her electricity cut off, she hasn't paid a single bill in months, and then what would she do? 'Okay,' she says, and lets her father draw her into a slightly awkward hug.

In the car, she holds Medusa close and leans against the window. Her whole body feels leaden and weak. She barely remembers what it was like to feel strong and light, throbbing with energy, the way she used to, before everything went to hell.

40

Lucia

I open my eyes, but it's still dark. Maman is sitting on my bed, making it dip, and her warm hand is on my cheek, stroking it, like every morning.

'*Bonjour*,' she whispers.

I stretch out the way my cat does and Maman laughs a little. '*Bonjour*,' I say.

'Come on, sweet girl,' she says, and I get out of bed and slide my feet into the soft, warm slippers underneath it.

I take her hand and together we cross the landing and push open the door to my sister's room. Josie is still asleep, and I can hear her breath going in and out. Maman sits down on one side of the bed and I sit on the other, so my sister is in between us.

'*Bonjour*,' says Maman and strokes Josiane's cheek gently.

Josie opens her eyes a crack then closes them again. After a while of Maman stroking her cheek, she gets up too, and the three of us go downstairs.

Every morning it's exactly the same. Maman walks down the stairs first, holding a lantern with a real candle inside it, making the stone walls glow like we've painted them with gold. It isn't because we don't have normal lights, we do, but because it makes mornings special. Behind Maman, Josie and I walk down together, wearing our nightdresses with our names stitched on them. My name's in purple and Josie's is in pink. We walk through the dining room and the sitting room and the library to the kitchen with the fireplace that's so big that Josie and I can stand inside it, all with only the light from Maman's lantern. It's lucky that I am safer here than anywhere else in the whole world, otherwise I might be afraid of what could be in the shadows. But I'm safe here, only here. The cat comes with us, rubbing her fur against our ankles.

We sit down at the long wooden kitchen table covered by a red-and-white wax cloth that doesn't get dirty even if you spill stuff on it. Maman puts the lantern down in the fireplace and lights lots more candles while Josie and I do our special jobs. Her job is to put the eggcups and plates in the right place with the knife to the right and the spoon above. My job is to pour the apple juice to the second line in each glass. When Maman has finished lighting the candles she takes the bread she has made out of the oven. It's quite knotty, and it has dusty bits from where she rolled it in the flour, but it smells really good. She breaks it into three pieces and puts a piece on my plate and one on Josie's. She sits down opposite me and Josie and holds Kimmi on her lap, twirling her ears slowly with her fingers. Cats like that, so Kimmi purrs.

Maman smiles and her eyes shine in the light from the candles. She puts Kimmi down on the stone floor and then she stands up to get the boiled eggs. We eat without talking, like we always do. The bread is warm and soft, and the yummy salty butter on it is from the cows in the field. The eggs are from the chickens behind the barn.

When we finish eating, the sky is starting to go pink and orange.

'Off you go,' says Maman, handing us a big paper bag of corn, spinach and brown pellets.

Me and Josie run to the back door and grab our blue wool coats. We take our slippers off and put our muddy wellies on, then we go out into the cold air. We cross the courtyard, holding hands. Feeding the chickens is our job. We like it even though they sometimes rush around and peck at our wellies. Today they are chattering loudly when we open the hatches and they hurry out from their houses. We throw whole handfuls of corn and spinach at them, then we scatter the pellets around, and they go crazy, making me and Josie laugh. Sometimes we laugh so much together that our stomachs hurt.

Back at the house, Maman has changed into her day clothes. Today she is wearing a dark blue silky blouse and a pair of thick trousers in the same color. The trousers shine a bit, like the tiniest stones have been sewn into them. Her hair is tied back and coiled in a tight bun at the top of her head. I want her to do mine exactly the same. Not even a little bit of hair has fallen out of her bun and she looks like a ballerina. Or... a flight attendant.

For a moment I see The Lady very clearly in my head. She is standing in the corner of the kitchen in my house – no, in *that* house – over by the refrigerator, closing the zip on her little suitcase. Her uniform was the same color blue as Maman's clothes, but on the shoulders it had two gold stripes and a wing I used to run my fingers over when she scooped me up to hug me goodbye. The Lady was always leaving me. But she was also always coming back. I liked it when she came straight from the airport to get me from school – the other kids thought she was cool, and Mille-Theodora once said she wished *her* mother could fly planes.

I feel strange. Like something is in my throat when I swallow. A pebble, a lump of ice, a too big piece of carrot. I cough to make it go away, but after the cough comes a squeak, like from Kimmi when we step on her tail by mistake.

'Hey, sweet girl, are you okay?' Maman is looking at me from where she's standing over by the window in the kitchen, pulling Josie's hair back with a comb.

I try to answer, but the pebble is in the way and her face is blurred now. Maman's face becomes a stranger who becomes another stranger and it is like ten faces flashing in front of me and then she becomes The Lady. I want to scream and make her go away, but I don't. Instead, I blink and Maman's face becomes clear again. It's sad or angry or worried.

'Hey,' she says and drops Josie's hair just as she was about to do the hair tie, so it flops back around her shoulders. 'Hey.'

Maman sits at my feet and puts her warm hands around my waist. 'My sweet angel, are you having bad thoughts? Dangerous ones?'

I nod.

She leans in and kisses me softly in the middle of my forehead. It feels good.

'It takes time,' she whispers in my ear. 'But we have all the time in the world now.'

She ties the hair tie tight on the top of Josie's head, then walks back over to me. She begins to run the comb very gently through my hair, over and over, and I close my eyes because it's a nice feeling. 'Like yours,' I whisper.

'Always, my sweet girl,' says Maman and she twists my hair higher and higher until it's ready to be coiled around itself like a cinnamon bun.

'Come on, *mon amour*. It's time for school.'

41

Elisa

We still do Friday nights like we used to, but the new normal is Fredrik, me and Lyder. We have tacos like every other family in Norway, then we settle in front of a movie with a big bowl of popcorn and sometimes candy, too. Tonight, the movie is about some animated chipmunks on a cruise ship, and Lyder has fallen asleep. Fredrik and I keep pretending to watch the film, because what else would we do? The silences between us are louder than the conversations we have at this point. Every time we talk, it seems to lead to disquiet, blame, and an even wider space between us.

I become aware of a change in the atmosphere and glance at Fredrik. He has paused the chipmunk movie and is looking at me intently. 'What?' I say.

'What's the matter, baby?'

'Nothing.' Everything. Obviously.

'You're crying.'

He's right, my face is wet with tears. 'Oh.'

He reaches across to stroke my arm, but Lyder is awkwardly slumped between us.

'Talk to me, Elisa.'

'Well,' I begin, letting my mind run free with all the possible things I could say to my husband. I decide on something that's been bothering me for a very long time now. 'Sometimes I can't help but think that this is what I deserve, you know?' I look at the familiar room around me, at the TV screen, at the empty space next to Lyder where Lucia should be, little mouth chomping popcorn.

'*This?*'

'You know. This situation. Lucia being gone.'

'Why on earth would you deserve such a thing?'

'I just can't help but feel that it's some kind of punishment.'

'Punishment for what?' I can tell by Fredrik's tone that he's getting impatient with me.

'For sinning, or—'

'*Sinning?*'

'God punishes sinners.' My words swell in the air between us, and Fredrik seems to struggle for something to say. We never speak of God or religious belief in our house; our upbringings have made that impossible.

'We don't believe in that kind of God, Elisa,' he says softly. 'And besides, even if we did, how could we possibly deserve... this. Okay?'

'But what if I've done something in the past that's brought this down on us, like karma, or—'

'Honey, please. We've come too far for this. Way too far.

Please.' He turns back to the TV screen and presses 'Play', bringing the chipmunks back to life.

Lyder stirs and suddenly sits upright, blinking comically, then continues watching the movie as though he hasn't just slept for half an hour. Fredrik and I disappear back into our distant, separate worlds.

42

Jacqueline

They've started to go on frequent excursions. Jacqueline knows, now, that she can trust Lulu-Rose when they go places, that the child won't suddenly cry or scream, alerting strangers and begging for help in a foreign language. Lulu-Rose speaks French, and while she's not yet quite at native level, neither is Josiane, having spent most of her early years in Norway. Both girls occasionally stumble, but Lulu-Rose is now at the level where she can pass for a French girl most of the time. Sometimes Jacqueline will be scrubbing the kitchen surfaces or stirring something on the stove and will overhear her speaking unselfconsciously to Kimmi in French. It makes her stop and smile, and when Lulu-Rose realizes she's being watched and looks up, she too smiles – a wry, self-conscious smile – and Jacqueline's heart aches in her chest.

Jacqueline glances in the rearview at the girls, both of them sitting up very straight, staring out of the window at the vibrant green pastures and the sweep of blue sky. They're grinning widely, and occasionally they look at each other and burst out laughing. Jacqueline grins too at the memory of their stunned expressions when she sat down opposite them at breakfast earlier and said, 'So, what do you say we get a puppy?'

She drives slowly down the narrow winding lanes to the hamlet, then left towards Rivèrenert. The road is bumpy and crisscrossed with muddy tractor tracks. The girls giggle in the back seat. Jacqueline feels light and happy.

'You're going to need to come up with a name,' she says, and they immediately start to shout out their ideas.

'Toffee!' says Josiane.

'Willy,' says Lulu-Rose.

At the last sharp turn before the main district road to Saint-Girons, Jacqueline looks up at the lush, rolling foothills that hide Le Tachoué from view. When her mother was a child, this road had not yet been constructed and everyone had to use mules to reach the valley and transport goods. She pictures her mother as a young girl in her grandfather's wooden cart, being pulled slowly by mules up to the ancient farm.

She saw the notice about the puppies taped to a lamppost in the parking lot of Josiane and Lulu-Rose's school and thought: why not? In spite of everything that's happened in Jacqueline's life in the past few years, her objectives have always been to be the best mother and to keep the girls happy. A puppy will make them even happier. It will also be a reward of sorts for Lulu-Rose, whose behavior continues to get better by the day. She isn't running away or hiding in the woods as often, or wetting the bed, or crying uncontrollably for hours, like she did a year and a half ago. She seems settled and happy, like she's never been anyone else.

Occasionally Jacqueline leaves the girls at Le Tachoué for a few hours in the afternoon and drives to Saint-Gaudens or Lannemezan or Foix – places where she is known to no one. She always parks on a residential street on the outskirts and walks until she finds an internet café. There, she orders a black coffee and spends an hour scrolling through everything she can find about the most recent developments in the Lucia Blix case. She studies the desperate, baffled faces of the police and the Blix family. Her plan has worked even beyond her wildest dreams – the police believe Silwia Truja took Lucia, and she is dead. There's no reason to believe they will ever come looking for Jacqueline Thibault. Eighteen months later and they still have nothing: nothing at all to link her to Lucia Blix. Eventually, the media will stop talking about the Blix case altogether, because that's how these things work. And Lucia Blix will never be found, because she no longer exists.

The girls sing loudly in the back seat on the road from Saint-Girons to Salies-du-Salat, and she can't help but laugh at the sound of them. It really is a beautiful day, and she keeps glancing in the rearview mirror at the still white peaks of the Pyrenees receding behind them. These are the mountains they look across at from Le Tachoué and to Jacqueline the sight of them is as much a sight of home as the farmhouse itself. She slows down as they approach the sweet little town of Salies-du-Salat, known for its impressive spa. She's brought the girls here a couple of times before, including last month for the annual tarot festival, for which Lulu-Rose and Josiane dressed as witches. It turned out the festival was for adults, so they bought some baguettes and trekked up to the haunting ruins of Notre-Dame-de-la-Pitié, where the children had hours of fun riding broomsticks made from branches torn from the trees in the recent storms, their gleeful cackles echoing into the valley.

She pulls off the D117 and onto a smaller road and the girls fall silent, staring at the houses, trying to guess which one is the puppies' home. It turns out to be a charming modern house built in the old style with a huge terrace facing the Pyrenees. When they get out of the car, the sound of barking starts up from inside and a man opens the door, holding a chunky, squirming puppy underneath his arm. He sets it down on the ground and it ambles towards Lulu-Rose and Josiane, who have dropped to their knees on the muddy ground and are cooing hysterically. It is white and impossibly fluffy, like a live stuffed bear. Jacqueline laughs and so does the man, and she finds herself unable to take her eyes off him. He holds out his hand and she presses it limply instead of shaking it the way she usually would, taken aback by the powerful current that passes between them.

'Hello, I'm Antoine,' he says, still holding her hand and laughing as though Jacqueline has said something amusing, even though she hasn't even spoken yet. 'Thank you for coming. The puppies are excited to meet you.'

Inside the house are another two puppies, and their mother Safina, who watches carefully as Lulu-Rose and Josiane play with her little ones.

'This one!' says Josiane, holding one up, letting it lick her entire face.

'No, this one,' says Lulu-Rose, tickling the belly of another puppy.

'Coffee?' says Antoine, raising an eyebrow and smiling.

'Sure. Looks like we'll be here a while.'

She watches him as he prepares the coffee with a fancy espresso machine. What is it about this man that she is so drawn to? From behind, his long, muscular back resembles Nicolai's, and there is also something about the way he moves – slowly and deliberately, as though he's never known stress or hurry, and perhaps he hasn't. It is possible to lead a very calm life here, in this part of France, if that is what one is after. Maybe he is childless and works from home, spending his breaks sipping macchiatos and looking across rolling fields to the Massif du Mont Noir. She imagines he might have views of Marimanha, the distinctly pyramid-shaped peak across the Spanish border. She glances around his kitchen for clues as to who lives here or signs of a wife and children.

'Are you from here?' she asks, taking the coffee he hands her and savoring the strong, bitter smell that fills her nostrils as she leans against the wooden worktop that runs down one entire wall of the kitchen.

'Born and bred,' he says, his eyes resting on her longer than necessary.

She smiles and nods.

'What about you?'

'My mother was born here. Over near Rivèrenert, on an old farm in the hills. My father was Norwegian.'

'Ah. Unusual. Explains the Scandinavian blonde hair. So where did you grow up?'

She laughs – the hair is hardly natural – over the past eighteen months, she has been progressively lightening it.

'We lived here until I was seven, when my grandfather died, then we moved to Norway. My mother lives in Paris now.'

'And you've moved back here permanently?'

Jacqueline nods and takes another sip of the coffee. 'My husband passed away a few years ago,' she says, dropping her voice and glancing in the direction of the girls, who are busy and oblivious with the puppies in the adjoining room. She is surprised at herself, for saying the words out loud. But she wants Antoine to know that she is on her own and that he can look at her like that. Like she is something wonderful. 'I realized that I wanted the girls to grow up here.'

'I'm sorry to hear that. I understand you wanting to come home after something like that. Especially with the children.'

'Yes.' She doesn't embellish; she learned long ago that with men it's a good idea to let them drive the conversation and come to her, rather than show any kind of obvious interest.

They stand a while watching the girls play with the dogs, smiling at each other occasionally, not in the polite way strangers might, but warmly, like friends.

'Yeah, I left this place for several years myself,' continues Antoine after a while, like she knew he would. 'I traveled around a lot. Lived in Toulouse for six years. Los Angeles for one. Then my father died and all I wanted was to come home. I've been here ever since, except for occasional work trips. If I had children, I couldn't imagine them growing up anywhere else either.'

He gazes out through the floor-to-ceiling windows that open onto the terrace and give an uninterrupted view of the unblemished countryside and the Pyrenees beyond.

She has the impression that he said 'if I had children' to let her know that he does not.

'What do you do for work?'

'I'm a writer. Or rather, I wanted to be. I do content stuff, mostly from home.'

She smiles again, and this time she makes sure to narrow her eyes a little and turn her body slightly towards him. Ninety per cent of communication is non-verbal – she knows this, too.

'What about yourself?' he asks.

'I'm a make-up artist. I'm not working at the moment. I decided to take some time out to be there for the girls after... after my husband passed away. Insurance meant that I could do that.'

Antoine nods thoughtfully. 'It must be hard, to be by yourself with them.'

'It's okay now,' she says. 'It's been a long time.'

He smiles at her, a wide, genuine smile, and she feels naked when he looks at her, in spite of her smart clothes and perfect make-up.

'We'd better get going soon,' she says, breaking the electric moment. 'I'm sure the girls will have decided on a favorite little fluffball by now.' She's pleased by the flash of disappointment in Antoine's eyes. She turns away, and in the next room she squats down on the floor in between the girls.

'We want the girl,' says Josiane, pointing to one of the puppies. 'That one.'

Jacqueline reaches out to run her hand across the dog's back, but the puppy flips over and holds her front paws tight against her chest, waiting for a belly tickle. Jacqueline laughs and obliges.

'Good choice,' says Antoine. 'Don't tell the others,' he

says, mock-whispering, 'but she's my favorite too. What do you want to call her?'

'Boulette!' shouts Lulu-Rose and both girls collapse in fits of giggles. Of course they want to name the puppy 'Meatball'.

'Your daughters are hilarious,' he says and winks at her.

Another charged moment passes between them and Jacqueline finds herself looking at his hands as he strokes Boulette, picturing those hands caressing her own skin. 'Aren't they!'

'So, Boulette will need another jab and an anti-worming treatment. She'll be ready to go home with you early next week. If you want, I can drop her round. Over near Rivèrenert, did you say?'

It's late when she gets the girls to sleep. They insisted on a sleepover, building a makeshift bed with blankets and pillows in the tent in Josiane's room, and they eventually fall asleep in there after hours of excited chatter about Boulette, their newly long legs poking out from the tent flap. Jacqueline checks on them on her way to bed and stands a moment looking at their protruding bare feet, white and impossibly fragile in the cool light of the moon. Four little feet, just the way it was meant to be.

She remembers the first ultrasound of her pregnancy, when four little feet appeared beneath the sonographer's wand, wriggling the smallest of toes, treading water, kicking. 'How will we manage?' she whispered, turning to Nico, who was staring at the grainy screen, transfixed. Then he laughed and squeezed her hand.

She falls asleep quickly for once, jostled into unconsciousness by swirling thoughts dragging her one way and then another, like small but strong waves. Her last conscious thoughts are of the moments she spent in the kitchen with Antoine, how there was something so intensely familiar about him and at the same time so seductively new, like a house you just know is meant to be your home. He is there tonight, in her dreams, looking at her as though she is something wonderful.

43

Lucia

Boulette is coming home today! Me and Josie sang all the way to school because we are so excited. Maman says Boulette has to sleep in her crate in the kitchen so she doesn't get too spoiled, but me and Josie have a plan. We're going to wake up in the night and take Boulette upstairs to the tent in Josie's room and let her sleep between us like a real teddy.

The teacher says, '*Écoute*, Lulu-Rose,' but I can't focus because I'm so excited. I look over at Josie, but she is bending over her book, writing carefully. I want her to look at me so we can laugh. The teacher, Maîtresse Millau, had to move Josie to over by the door and me over to the window in the front, because otherwise we whisper too much. Now I have to sit next to Gabin Chameau, who fidgets all the time. Even Gabin is writing in his exercise book, so I keep trying to write what Maîtresse has asked us to – seven sentences about what I think *liberté*, *égalité* and *fraternité* mean.

I look around again and this time Josie is looking around too and when we look at each other we giggle quietly. I hold both my hands up against my chest like paws and she sticks her tongue out and pants, and this is so funny I laugh loudly and Gabin notices and laughs too, but then Maîtresse slams her fat hand down hard on her desk and puts her finger to her lips. Her eyes are bulgy and big behind her round glasses and sometimes at home me and Josie make fun of her, walking around slowly in circles and tut-tutting.

When Maman first found me and brought me home to Le Tachoué, I wasn't allowed in school. Every morning after we'd finished feeding the chickens, Maman drove Josie to school. Le Tachoué is far from the school, which is in Saint-Girons, because we are far from everything and it used to take one hundred minutes before Maman came back, sometimes more. I timed it on the little egg that counts time like Maman taught me because she knew I got worried to be there alone even though Le Tachoué is the safest place in the world.

'Can I come with you?' I'd ask every time, but Maman always shook her head sadly. 'No, my darling,' she'd say. 'Not yet.'

I'd try to read a story in my room, but I couldn't make out all the words then, even though Maman was teaching me every day. Instead, I'd look at the pictures and I'd look at the timer. Sometimes I'd get up and stand by the window again. The mountains, which were grey with a bit of white when I first came here, turned all white, and then the snow began to melt again and it was summer and that was when I started to understand more. Josiane and I played every day in the forests and the fields and Maman would leave us a basket with baguettes, boiled eggs and ham on the big rock where the forest comes up to our river, and we didn't go back home until it was nearly dark, laughing all the way. I loved it then, but sometimes in the night I cried because I was so sad, too.

Now the mountains are black and white and grey. The white patches glow pink in the sun and I have to shield my eyes when I open the curtains in the morning. It's spring again and the fields are bright green, and we can play in the forest again. The forest, which I thought was scary when I came here, actually isn't scary at all, and most days Josie and I play there before it gets dark. We find treasures there and we bring them back so Maman can help us make them into crafts. One wall in my room is completely full of things we've made from the forest. My favorite is a picture made from twigs that we glued together then spray-painted gold in the courtyard behind the barn.

In the beginning I was afraid of everything. I was afraid of the man, and Maman, and the house, and the animals, and even Josie. All I wanted was to go back to The Other People, but that's a long time ago now. Sometimes it's like I see their faces when I'm looking at someone else, like one of the children in my class. Gabin's face becomes the face of The Little Boy in The Other Family. Lyder. When I thought he was my brother I didn't like him because he always tried to take my things and sometimes he hit me and told lies. But now I don't have a brother anymore I sometimes think about how funny he could be and how he made me laugh by doing really silly things, like pushing Coco Pops into his nostrils. Gabin does things like that too, and maybe that's why I'm his friend even when the other children think he's weird.

In the night-time, if I can't sleep, which is often, I say

the names of the children in my old class out loud. I don't know why. I want to remember them, but I can't remember all their faces now. Mille-Theodora, Konstanse, Olivia, Ella, Max, Hans-Christian – no, Jens-Christian – Ylva… Before I've remembered all of them, the names of the children in my class now come into my head instead. Gabin, Carel, Sophie, Jean-François, Raphaël, Enzo, Lila, Josiane, Noémie…

'*Alors*,' says Maîtresse and I notice that she is standing right next to my desk. She picks up my writing book and sees that I've only written one of the seven sentences. It is: 'Liberty means you can do what you want.' She reads it aloud but in a mean voice and some of the girls look at each other and laugh. Maîtresse moves on to Gabin and he hasn't finished either. His handwriting is so crooked that Maîtresse makes a big show of not being able to read what it says at all.

'You two,' she says, 'come with me.'

In an empty classroom Gabin and I have to write '*Je suis trop grand pour faire des bêtises*' fifty times each while the other children play outside. We can hear them laughing and screeching through the open window. I don't care because Gabin is funny and the whole time we're writing he pulls crazy faces like his face is made out of plastic, and he sings the sentence in strange voices:

'I'm too big for nonsense.
I'm too big for nonsense.
I'm too big for nonsense.'

*

'Drive faster!' we shout, and Maman pushes her foot down on the pedal a bit harder so the car goes faster, but still the drive home takes so, so long. By the time we get to the track that leads to another track that leads to a muddy driveway that leads to Le Tachoué, me and Josiane have started chanting 'Boulette! Boulette! Boulette!' and Maman can't help laughing.

When we park in front of the house, a little white car is there and the man who owns Boulette's mummy, Safina, is standing there, holding Boulette in his arms.

Much later, when I wake in the night, Josie is sitting on my bed, smiling and pressing her finger to her mouth. We open the creaky door in the way that stops it from creaking, lifting it up a bit by the handle, then we sneak across the landing and listen.

The house is quiet. I picture Boulette in her crate, small and afraid, whimpering like a baby that's made to sleep alone in the kitchen.

We hold hands down the stairs and across the hallway, because it's big and dark and frightening at night. In the library we stop and listen again and this time we do hear something. It's a soft sound, not quite crying, and it's coming from the sitting room, not the kitchen. Maman must have put Boulette's crate in there. It's the warmest room in our house.

We move closer and see a soft glow from the door, which is half open. The sounds are louder, and now we can tell that it's actually voices, and Maman laughing. We creep up to the door and peer in, and Maman is on the sofa with the man who owns Boulette's mummy. She is sitting across him and her sweater is off and Josie pulls hard on my hand and we run back down the long hallway to the library, where we stop and look at each other and cover our mouths as we giggle. Maybe Boulette heard us because there's a little puppy cry from somewhere. We sneak back towards the kitchen, turning right after the library instead of left into the sitting room, and there she is in her crate. Josie scoops her up in her arms and we rush back upstairs as quietly as we can.

In the tent, Josie and I giggle at Maman making kissy noises with the man. It's weird. But the man is nice.

'He can come and live here with Boulette's mummy and daddy and they can have puppies every year,' I whisper and Josie nods sleepily.

We hold Boulette between us, running our fingers through her soft fluffy fur, and there is nowhere I would rather be in the whole world.

It's Sunday and I wake up early, with the sun. Josie and Boulette are still asleep. We've had her two weeks now and she's getting fatter and even cuter every day. The house is quiet, and I go and stand in the window.

I decide to go and see Samba. I put on my farm suit, which is like a waterproof onepiece that's so tough you can slide down a muddy, pebbly hill in it and it won't get broken – I've done that.

I let myself into the barn and breathe in the sweet and strong smell. Samba begins to bleat because she knows it's me and she loves me. I open the latch and she tumbles out, making her funny laughing sounds, and I laugh too, hugging her close, but she scrambles out of my arms because she wants me to run about with her.

240

I put her on the rope and we go outside, across the courtyard and down the path that leads to the garden. The sun is making the sky pink and red and purple. In the garden behind the house, Samba and I play chase. She likes it when I run after her, but most of the time I win because she stops to chew the leaves off the bushes. She can't help it – leaves are like candy to a goat.

After a while, I sit down on the grass, but I get cold as soon as I stop moving. Samba skips around me, waiting for her treat, and I get the carrot out of my pocket and giggle as she pulls the whole thing into her little pink mouth. She doesn't want to go back in her enclosure and it takes me a while to get her in there – I have to tie the rope around her neck and yank it hard to get her to move. She sits on her hind legs and stares at me with her blue eyes. In the end, she comes, but only after a really long time – goats are very stubborn.

I go back towards the house. Maybe Josie and Boulette will be awake now, and Maman too, and the house will be filled with the smell of coffee and we'll sit down for breakfast together. I cross the courtyard, jumping through a couple of deep puddles from the rainstorms, but just then I hear the crunch of tires. I stop and stare, because we never get visitors, except for Antoine. It's a black car, but it's not Antoine coming to visit Maman. It's the man from before.

44

Jacqueline

'Maman! Maman!' Lulu-Rose is shaking her awake, little fists frantically pummeling her, hysteria edging into her voice. 'He's back! The man is back!'

Jacqueline sits up fast and looks around the room, still dim with the soft grey light of early morning. She's alone; it's the first night this week that Antoine hasn't slept over.

'What…?'

'The man. Mikko. He's here!'

Jacqueline leaps from the bed and rushes to the window. It's true, he really is there, leaning against a car she's never seen before, smoking a cigarette, shielding his eyes from the sharp sun that's just rising above the mountains across the valley.

'*Putain*,' she whispers, her mind crowding with thoughts. *Just breathe*, she tells herself. She'd known this could happen someday. It suddenly seems ridiculous that it wouldn't. Why would anything ever just go to plan so she could live happily ever after?

'Stay here,' she says to Lulu-Rose, before pulling her

close in a quick hug. 'Go to Josie and play in the tent for a bit, okay?'

'Please don't let the man take me away,' the child says, her soulful brown eyes brimming with tears.

Over my dead body, thinks Jacqueline, fearing that might turn out to be the case. *No.* She hasn't got this far only to have Mikko Eilaanen come back and take it all away from her.

'Nobody will ever take you away,' she says, before rushing down the stairs and pushing the massive main door open.

Mikko smiles as she appears, as though he's a welcome visitor, as though they're old friends. His face is scratched and his skin is greyish – he looks like he's been sleeping rough. 'Ah, the lady of the manor,' he says, chuckling.

The downy hair at the back of her neck prickles and rises at the sight of him. 'Mikko.'

'Long time, no see.'

'What do you want?'

At this he chuckles again, but harder now, and it leads to a cough, which makes him wince and press a hand to his side. 'Well, a cup of coffee would be nice. Long drive.'

She shows him through the long series of interconnecting rooms leading to the big farmhouse kitchen – library, sitting room, dining room – disturbed at the thought of this man's eyes roaming around her beloved Le Tachoué and her ancestors' possessions. In the kitchen, she places the kettle on the stove and turns around to face him. Mikko is half-slumped across the table, exhaustion carved into his face, his right hand pressed to his side.

'I... I think I might need you to help me, actually.'

'Help you?'

'I'm a little injured.' He removes his hand from inside his sweater and it comes back red and slick with blood.

'Jesus, Mikko, what the hell...?'

'That fucking asshole Batz stabbed me. And Vilkainen's dead.'

'Dead? What the hell...? And... Batz? Have you been back to Belgium?'

'Yeah. Had no choice. I was in Sicily, but I ran out of cash and the police were closing in on me.'

So that's why he's back here. 'Why are you here, Mikko?'

'Can you please just help me clean this up a little? It's not deep, but it feels like it might be getting infected.'

She leads him into the library and over to the chaise longue by the window and carefully folds back his filthy woolen sweater, moist with cold, sticky blood. He has a clumsily bandaged wound on the side of his stomach. Blood oozes through the bandage and when she peels it back she sees that the gash is vivid red with the start of an infection. It's a wide slash, but it doesn't look deep.

'What the fuck, Mikko,' she hisses. 'You can't just show up here like this. I'm not your fucking wife.'

'Yes, well, you owe me.'

'*I* owe *you?*'

'And you know it.'

Jacqueline's knees tremble as she takes the stairs – with fury and with fear. She shouldn't have let him leave the first time, when he brought Lulu-Rose home. She'd tried to stop him from going – she was all too aware that the only way she could ever be safe in this life was if only one person knew the truth about what happened to Lucia Blix: her.

She rummages through the wicker basket beneath the

bathroom sink and finds gauze bandages, hydrogen peroxide and antibiotic ointment. She looks at herself in the mirror, holding her own cool gaze for a long while, telling herself that she will come out on top in this situation. She has survived so much, and all she needs to do now is stay calm and maintain focus on what is really important – her simple but beautiful life at Le Tachoué with Josiane and Lulu-Rose.

'You okay?' she asks as she settles back down on the little stool next to where Mikko is reclining.

'It hurts.'

She nods and very gently runs a cotton ball soaked in hydrogen peroxide around the periphery of the stab wound. Mikko winces, his bottom lip protruding like a stubborn little boy's.

'Tell me about Sicily,' she says, keeping her voice steady and gentle.

'I went there to take the heat off. The Blix case blew up big time, didn't it? Batz and the guys have been doing a lot of business down there for years. As long as you pay, the police leave you entirely alone. Corrupt as fuck.'

'What kind of business?'

'Migrant stuff.'

'Migrant stuff?'

'Getting people from A to B. People without papers.'

'Ah.'

'It's fucked up, what's going on down there. At first it was stuff like, you know, taking a bunch of guys up the coast at night, that kind of thing. High risk. The way I like it.'

She runs another cotton ball across the wound, pressing it into the fiery red tissue, making him gasp with pain. She enjoys this little moment causing him some pain.

'But then, as time passed, I saw some seriously fucked-up shit. Once, off the coast of Marettimo, we came across a tiny upturned boat with a mother and her baby clinging to it. She'd lost her other three children in the waves. Three, Jacqueline.'

'Jesus.'

'Yeah. So we started going out more and pulling people out of the water, and there was always someone needing help. But there were also lots of nights I didn't go out there, didn't rescue anyone, when I was drinking in a skanky bar in Agrigento...'

She gives him a sad little smile and presses the new gauze bandage gently into place. 'I think you need to get this stitched.'

'Can't, though.'

'We'll have to look at it again tonight.'

He makes as though to get up, but Jacqueline stops him with a hand on his shoulder. 'Stay there.'

She returns after a moment with a steaming mug of black coffee and his face lights up. *Nobody has ever taken care of this man*, she thinks, and for a brief moment she feels a pinch of empathy for him, this big, crude thug who makes his living transporting people from country to country in the dead of night.

'Why are you here, Mikko?' she asks, her voice still calm, but firm.

'I want more money, Jacqueline.'

'Impossible. I don't have any.'

'Then you find it.'

'And how am I supposed to do that? We had a deal! You can't just turn up here asking for more.'

'Look at this place – I'm sure you've got a few bucks stuffed in a mattress somewhere. You find it or I take that little kid for another ride. I can think of more than one buyer who'll pay more for her than you did. Much more.'

Jacqueline's heart hammers so hard, she worries Mikko can hear it, but she forces herself not to rise to his threats. 'How much?'

'Fifty grand now. And another fifty next year.'

He could hold her hostage forever, turning up at Le Tachoué every time he runs out of money or falls out with his dangerous friends.

'Okay,' she says, releasing a long, shuddering sigh. 'Fine. But I need you to be gone by tomorrow.'

45

Lucia

I can hear Josie's stomach growling. We've been in the tent, drawing, for a very long time. The voices from downstairs are muffled one minute and shouty the next. I draw a family of fish leaping through a stream, their fish faces smiley. There's a knock on the door, then Maman enters.

'*Salut, les filles,*' she says, smiling at me and Josie when we stick our heads out through the tent flap.

'*Salut,* Maman,' we say.

'Listen, I know you're worried about Mikko coming back here, but it's going to be okay. Hey, don't cry, Lulu-Rose.' Maman reaches out and wipes a tear off my chin before I even realize that my eyes have begun to cry.

'He... he said he was going to take me away again.'

'He's not.'

'He said.'

'I'm sorry you heard that. I've spoken with him, and we've agreed he's just going to stay here for one day, okay? He's not feeling very well, but as soon as he's better, he'll go.'

'No, Maman,' says Josie, 'he's a baddie.'

'He's not really a baddie,' I whisper, 'but I don't want to go anywhere with him.'

'Look, you're not going anywhere. I'm going to fix this. I need you girls to help me, okay?' Maman has dropped her voice to a whisper. 'Get ready, we're going to go out in a little while. I know an amazing ice-cream shop in Saint-Lizier.'

'Ice cream!' says Josie, clapping her hands. I try to picture a big chocolate ice cream with sauce and sprinkles, but all I can see is the man.

In the car, Maman doesn't say anything. Her knuckles are white on the steering wheel because she's holding it so hard. I suddenly remember how The Lady used to drive, stopping and starting a lot, sometimes swearing, joking that she was 'better with airplanes'. Josie keeps looking at me and I can tell she's afraid. There's something about Maman's face that's wrong; it's pinched and scared, like she's just bitten into a rotten apple. She pretends like everything is normal. I take Josiane's hand in mine and we both squeeze every now and again as we drive through the fresh snow into the valley. It is almost summer and all the snow melted and then it snowed again and Maman said '*Merde!*'.

In Saint-Girons we wait in the car while Maman takes money out of the bank, first at Carrefour, then at Caisse d'Epargne behind our school, then at Société Générale. We read the signs out loud, and Josie makes me laugh by pronouncing everything as if she's reading Norwegian. There's nobody around on the streets because it's early Sunday morning. Maman gets back in the car, her face red with cold, her eyes sad, though she smiles at me and Josie.

'Time for ice cream!' she says. 'The whole point of this excursion.'

'What is the man doing at Le Tachoué?' asks Josie.

'He's sleeping,' says Maman. 'He needed some rest. Listen, girls, this is what we're going to do: we're going to be really, really nice to him for one day, okay? Just one. Then he'll be gone by tomorrow. I promise.'

'Promise?'

'I promise.'

We drive on to Saint-Lizier, but when we get there the ice-cream shop is closed. We get out of the car and press our noses to the window, trying to see the delicious ice creams in the plastic boxes behind the counter.

'I'm sorry,' says Maman, and she looks so sad, I think she might cry. 'I know another place we can try.'

We drive again, through empty grey streets where the snow has turned to slush. There's a gas station at the edge of the town, with flashing neon signs. Inside, there's a freezer with a choice of Magnum Classic or Magnum Almond.

'Fabulous,' says Maman. 'Choose which ones you want, girls.'

She goes around the little shop and finds some things she needs, and in the end she buys quite a few things, so the young man behind the counter has to come and help her put it all in the car. Josie and I bite into the delicious hard chocolate shell and watch him load some cans of gasoline, a long piece of rope and a metal wrench into the car.

At home, the man shows me and Josie how to make a little chicken from twigs and cotton wool. He gives us Belgian chocolate from his jacket pockets and says, 'The Belgians suck at most things, but, oh man, can they make chocolate.'

He tells stories about when he was young and traveled around the Baltic Sea on a big sailing boat for naughty boys who got kicked out of school. He drinks wine and stares at Maman when we have dinner – a whole roasted goose from a farm nearby. Maman and the man drink more wine and Maman laughs almost every time the man speaks. I'm glad they're friends again. I was so afraid this morning.

When it's time for bed, Maman helps the man to sit down in front of the fireplace in the library, Kimmi on his lap and more wine in his hand, and then she takes us up to bed.

'We want a sleepover in the tent!' says Josie.

'Okay,' says Maman. 'But, listen, I need you to stay up here no matter what, okay?'

'Okay.'

'No matter what. Do you understand?'

We nod.

'Goodnight, my sweethearts. I love you so.'

I'm almost asleep when Josie says, 'Lulu-Rose, wake up!'

'I'm awake.'

'Let's go downstairs.'

'We can't. Maman said.'

'Let's do it anyway. I think Mikko is Maman's boyfriend. Did you notice how much she laughed at everything he said?'

'Antoine is Maman's boyfriend.'

'No, she said he's not.'

'But he is,' I say. I want him to be. He's kind and he has lots of dogs. 'Maman hates Mikko. She was only pretending.' It's only when I say it out loud that I know that this is true.

'No, she loves him. Let's go spy on them – we'll see them kissing!' Josie smacks her lips and makes kissing sounds and we both laugh, but I'm afraid.

We stop on the landing and listen. The house is quiet. We creep slowly down the stairs, holding hands in the dark. We get closer to the library and now we can hear the flames crackling in the fireplace, Maman laughing softly, and some music. When we get to the sitting room, we can see into the library, and we see Maman taking the wine glass from the man and putting it on the table. She holds her hand strangely in front of his mouth for a moment, then she gets on top of him and kisses his mouth. Josie was right. We stuff our hands into our mouths and sneak slowly back out of the room and up the stairs. Back in the tent, we fall asleep holding hands.

Moving orange lights, strange clunking sounds. I'm confused and it takes me a bit of time to work out where I am. I'm in the tent and someone is nudging me. It's Josie. The night before comes back to me in little bits. The stories the man told, the adults laughing, us spying, Maman kissing him.

'Come on,' she says, her face glowing orange in the weird light.

She takes my hand and pulls me up and we go down the hallway into my room. It's dark, but because of the strange light coming from outside I can see us in the mirrored doors of the giant wardrobe. We look the same, in our long white nightdresses and with our long dark hair braided exactly the same.

When we get to the window, Josie turns back around quickly and presses her finger to her lips. Then she beckons for me to stand like she is standing, pressed up against the wall next to the window.

'We can see everything from here,' she says, and I stare out the window, but I can't be sure what I'm seeing.

Next to the barn opposite there's a giant fire burning. So that's where the moving orange light is coming from. It looks like an enormous bonfire or maybe even a small building burning. A shape is moving to one side of the fire, and at first I don't realize that it's a person. Then it stops and walks around the fire, towards us, and I see that it's not an 'it' but Maman. I look from the window to Josie, but she is staring at Maman outside, throwing water onto the flames from a square black can. She should be using a hose or something – I don't think she can put the fire out with that can. The flames aren't getting smaller at all, instead, every time she throws water at the fire, it bursts into even bigger flames, reaching for her.

'What's happening?' I whisper.

Josie shrugs.

After a long while, Maman gives up trying to put the fire out and stands with her back to us, watching it burn, massive flames eating into the black sky.

46

Elisa

It's late when we finally land at Torp after a bumpy return flight. My mind feels foggy and sore, like any kind of thinking could hurt me. Perhaps that isn't so strange, considering I have been up most of the night several nights in a row and have worked back to back for weeks. I no longer switch flight mode off on my phone the instant we touch down like I used to, my finger flicking the little button in my pocket while we were still screeching down the runway, engines loudly reversing. I need a few more moments of quiet before I have to speak with anyone. It's a long time since I expected news of Lucia every minute of every day. I've learned to expect nothing but this unbearable blank silence.

I open the aircraft door once the plane has come to a standstill at Gate 24, but as the electric stairs are lowered to the ground I catch sight of a familiar face, and then another. It's Gaute Svendsen and Kristine Hermansen, the first two police officers Fredrik and I met at Sandefjord station that awful October night. We haven't seen them in months. Lucia's case is now mostly handled by Kripos in Oslo, as well as Scotland Yard and Interpol. Svendsen and Hermansen are sitting in an airport shuttle car at the bottom of the stairs, and behind them sits Haakon Kjeller and Fredrik, whose face is pale and blank.

This is it. She's dead.

'Excuse me,' I whisper to my colleague and I race down the stairs.

'Elisa, sorry to turn up like this,' says Kristine Hermansen. 'Please don't be too alarmed. There's been an important development—'

'Have you found her?' My voice rings out, shrill, above the plane's cooling engines.

'Not yet,' says Gaute as the shuttle car heads for the end of the terminal building. We're bundled into another car, a big black police BMW with opaque windows. It sets off before the doors are even fully shut, and we're ushered through a checkpoint at the edge of the airport area I wasn't even aware existed.

'We received an anonymous tipoff yesterday evening about an address in the Ardennes in eastern Belgium. The caller said that Lucia was there. Belgian police were on it immediately, and it turned out the house belongs to a man called Feodor Batz, who is known to police for several previous offenses. Among other things, he's had convictions for trafficking and is a member of the Vicodius network, which, as you know, also has links to Mikko Eilaanen and Heiki Vilkainen. The gendarmes searched the house early this morning. Batz was arrested and is now in custody in Liège.'

'And Lucia?' I screech, panting. They have to tell me,

before I pass out with anxiety. 'Where's Lucia?' I stare frantically at Fredrik, who's not said a word yet but is gripping my hand fiercely. 'What was this man arrested for?'

'It would seem Lucia was held at this house.'

'Oh my God.' I can hardly get the words out, my heart is thumping so hard. 'How do you know? Where is she now?'

'Elisa…' Kjeller speaks deliberately slowly, as though he's talking to a child. 'There's something you need to know. We've found forensic evidence of Lucia at the house. We're going to be sharing this information at a press conference today at 8.30, and I suspect there will be a media frenzy at this new development. But I want you to know that—'

'Wait!' I interrupt. 'What do you mean by "forensic evidence"?'

'Bloodstains were found. We've just had the results back and they match Lucia's DNA. We've also found DNA traces that match Mikko Eilaanen.'

'Now, it's very important, Mrs Blix,' interjects Kristine Hermansen, 'that you remain focused on a positive outcome here.'

I open my mouth to speak, but nothing happens. It feels as though my organs are shutting down, my vision is fading, my heart is withering in my chest. She's dead, is what they're saying. 'No,' I whisper. 'Oh God. Please… No.'

'Elisa,' says Gaute, 'the bloodstains are undergoing full screening at present and we should know more very soon. From what the Belgian force said, we have the impression that it was an insignificant amount of blood, so it is absolutely not indicative of… of… anything at this time. There was significantly more forensic material from Eilaanen, and a preliminary theory we'll be looking into is that he was killed by Batz and that Lucia has been moved to a new location, possibly by Heiki Vilkainen, who is believed to have been in the Ardennes region recently. It could well be that the caller was trying to make it look like Lucia is dead because they know we're onto them.'

47

Selma

She groggily opens her eyes but doesn't immediately recognize her surroundings. She's been so used to waking on the sofa, still holding a PlayStation console, or on her bed on top of the covers, Medusa's back pressed against her face. A shaft of light is shining straight in her face through a gap in the curtain. She sits up and the last ten days come back to her in flashes: her father driving her back from Oslo to her childhood home, here, in Drammen; hours spent aimlessly scrolling through Instagram and sleeping. She feels faintly annoyed with her father for meddling in her life like this, but she also knows that it isn't a great life she's been living since she was let go from *Dagsposten*.

She can smell coffee from the kitchen and her stomach growls. She picks Medusa up off the bed and carries her down the corridor.

'Morning.' Her father looks up from where he sits reading a newspaper, several others scattered on the table around him.

'Hi,' she says, flicking the switch on the kettle.

'What are you doing today then?' asks her father.

'Going back up to bed.'

He nods absentmindedly, his eyes scanning the front pages. 'Selma, have you seen the news?'

'No? I just woke up, Dad.'

'There seems to be a major development in the Lucia Blix case.'

'What?' Selma reaches across her father and picks up *VG*. Lucia is there, her familiar face smiling sweetly from the front page: 'Lucia Blix Very Likely DEAD, Says Crime Professor' reads the headline. She grabs *Dagsposten*, which also has Lucia on the front page. 'Lucia Blix's BLOOD Found in Belgian "Hell-Hole"'; and *Aftenposten* – 'Man Arrested in Belgium for Possible Connection to Lucia Blix'.

She pulls her phone from her pocket and scrolls through some other news sites. The Blix case dominates all the headlines.

Eilaanen Believed Dead, Lucia Blix Unaccounted For

Vicodius Network Busted in Belgium!

Caller Said Lucia Blix Has Been KILLED

Lucia: Did She DIE Here?

Blix Parents Faced with Tragic New Evidence

Selma's heart picks up its pace as she scans through several articles. The blood found in Belgium has been established as Lucia's and Mikko Eilaanen's, though police won't divulge whether it's recent. The police confirm that the ground-breaking discovery was made after a house raid in the early hours of yesterday, following a tipoff from an anonymous source.

Selma wonders what Elisa and Fredrik Blix are doing in this exact moment, how they can even begin to deal with this terrible new information. 'We'll never give up hope,' says a spokesperson for the Blix couple, according to NRK.no.

She feels a pulsating excitement building in her gut, mixed with a cold dread. First the blood; will it be a body next?

Back in her bedroom, she opens her laptop and scrolls through the most recent articles. Two months ago Scotland Yard began to assist the Norwegian police in the investigation as they have amassed potentially relevant material in the ongoing search for Madeleine McCann, Operation Grange. Nothing has come of this to date. Hans Gundersen spoke at a press conference on 7 March, updating Norwegian and international media on the case. 'It is our continued belief that Lucia Blix remains alive,' he said. 'We are currently following several new leads in cooperation with Scotland Yard.'

On 19 October, six months ago, on the one-year anniversary of Lucia's abduction, Elisa and Fredrik Blix gave a short interview to NRK, the national broadcasting corporation. Selma pores over the images of the bereaved parents, who look as though they've aged ten years, not one, since Lucia was taken. Fredrik holds a previously unseen picture of Lucia in his hands, a private photo of the little girl standing in front of a fireplace, wearing a stripy pink woolen suit, the kind Norwegian children wear underneath their snowsuits, a half-eaten raisin bun clutched in her fist. Her face is glowing with health, youth and exertion – she looks as though she's just come in from skiing.

Selma watches the interview clip over and over: the mother looking imploringly into the camera, saying, 'Please... Please... Please...', the little girl smiling innocently at the camera. Then something happens – something Selma has both consciously and unconsciously avoided for a long time. It's as though she is able to step into the photograph with the little girl. She can hear the crackle of the firewood burning in the hearth behind the child, she can feel its warmth against the back of her thighs. She can see the outline of the person taking the picture, their face obliterated by the bright burst of the flash. She can smell the sausages cooking on the stove in the primitive galley kitchen next door and taste the aftertaste of cardamom and yeast from the raisin bun in Lucia's hand. She can see the little boy, Lyder, spinning around on the floor over by the rocking chair in pursuit of a toy train, one yellow-socked foot caught in the corner of the photo. For a long while, Selma moves around the scene in her mind. When she opens her eyes again, she feels weak and depleted like she always does after expending so much energy on building these mental images. But she also feels the stirrings of something in her gut: a desire to return to her life, and to work. To the Blix case.

In the afternoon, Selma is sitting at the kitchen table fully dressed when her father returns from work. She's even put mascara and eyeliner on, and her father does an exaggerated double-take when he sees her. He looks impressed, then alarmed, remembering that his only child is basically a deadbeat now.

'Selma... what's going on? You look... like yourself again.'

'I was wondering if you could drive me to the station. I'd like to go back to Oslo.'

'But… why? I thought you were going to stay for another few days?'

'I've realized that you were right, Dad. I need to get my life back on track. I'm going to start boxing again. And see if I can get going with some freelance stuff.'

'Well, that's great news!' Alf's face is glowing with pride and excitement, and Selma feels moved, realizing how worried he must have been for her. 'Do you have anything in mind, writing-wise?'

'Yes. I want to return to the Blix case.'

'Oh.' His expression instantly darkens at the mention of the Blix case. Selma knows he blames that case for her breakdown following her departure from *Dagsposten*.

'I want to look at it from a different angle. From the inside.'

'From the inside.'

'Yes.'

'I'm not sure that's such a great idea, Selma. That case… I don't think they'll ever solve it. She's dead, poor kid. It seems pretty obvious.'

'How is that obvious?'

'They found her blood, Selma.'

'That doesn't make her dead. The fact is, someone knows something. And that person phoned in a tipoff to the police, which is interesting on so many levels. Why tell the police that she was killed in Belgium? And why now? That person wanted the police to know that Lucia was there. And that Eilaanen is dead.'

'Possibly. Sounds like the Vicodius network has an inside leak.'

'Sounds like a decoy to me. Like pointing out one thing

to divert attention from something else that's happening, perhaps fairly obviously.'

'Selma, that's all speculation...'

'Someone knows something. And they're talking. We just need to listen.'

'But she's been gone, what, eighteen months now? Think about what that kid will have been through...' Her father shakes his head sadly.

'We don't know anything about that, Dad. It's all speculation. And even if you're right, do you think that little girl will have given up on herself, on hope?'

'Well, maybe not, but—'

'The survival instinct is stronger than anything else. She'll be hoping and believing still, I'm sure of it, no matter what. That little girl is strong.'

'How do you know?'

'I just do. I can see it in her eyes.'

Her father nods thoughtfully. He knows how perceptive and sensitive his daughter is, and when she senses something about someone, she is generally spot on. 'I guess I'm just worried about you, Selma. That case almost broke you...'

'Yes, well, it won't break me again because *I'm* going to break *it* – wide open.'

'Very well, Sherlock. Come on, then, get your stuff and I'll drop you back into town. I have to go to IKEA anyways – your crazy cat has chewed my shoe rack to splinters.'

48

Jacqueline

It was a risky thing to do, most likely the single riskiest thing she's done since bringing Lulu-Rose home. It's been nearly forty-eight hours now, and Jacqueline is returning from one of her clandestine trips to a distant and anonymous internet café. She was desperate to find out whether her plan has worked. She's driving home slowly, careful as always not to rouse the suspicions of any gendarmes patrolling the A61 between Toulouse and the Mediterranean, and as she drives she goes through everything yet again in her mind, combing back through every moment from two days ago to make sure she didn't commit a single mistake.

It had taken her most of the morning to clean up the site of the fire and get rid of anything else that might be incriminating. She'd finally left Le Tachoué after lunch, reassuring the girls she'd be back by bedtime, leaving popcorn and ice cream and strict instructions not to step outside the farmhouse under any circumstances.

On the outskirts of Carcassonne she stopped at a

roadside bric-a-brac shop with a Vodafone sign blinking in the dusty air and picked up a new SIM card. She paid in cash, handing two crisp twenty-euro bills to the young man behind the counter, who didn't even glance at her. If he had, he wouldn't have made any connection to Jacqueline Thibault, even if there had been a recent photograph of her on the front covers of every newspaper in France – which, of course, there was not. Just to be safe, she'd disguised herself for the outing; her hair was styled in a sleek caramel-blonde bob, her naturally thin nose had been discreetly sculpted thicker and slightly crooked with silicone mold, and her eyes were a light, believable hazel, courtesy of FreshLook colored contacts. There couldn't be any way of chasing the SIM card back to her.

She got back in the car and drove for a long time, circling Carcassonne on the peripheral motorway before heading north into the hills of the Montagne Noire, following signs for Les Quatre Châteaux de Lastours. After several minutes of being on the main road without meeting another car, she turned down a random small road and followed it until she came to a junction. To the right, the road headed into a dense forest and she turned off again, driving slowly in the now dim light. After a short while, she pulled over at a deserted picnic area with a clear view of the road in both directions.

She inserted the new SIM card into a second-hand iPhone she'd bought several months earlier from a guy in Foix via the Leboncoin free ads website. She took several deep breaths and practiced keeping the tremble out of her voice before she dialed the mainline number for the Norwegian police force. A woman on the switchboard picked up, her voice unhurried and calm. Jacqueline knew that this conversation would be recorded and endlessly reproduced.

'Police. How can I help you?'

'I would like to give some important information,' Jacqueline said, in perfect English.

'Which department can I put you through to?'

'I just want to say that there is a house in Sainte-Ode, in the Ardennes, in Belgium, past the camping, on Rue des Vieilles Écoles, at the edge of the forest. Lucia Blix was killed there.'

Jacqueline pressed 'End call', her heart drumming against the seat belt. She closed her eyes. No way back now.

She got out of the car and placed the phone on the ground before reversing over it several times. She then picked up the pieces and dropped them into a Ziploc bag, which she threw from the window into a rocky ravine as the road climbed high above the Vallée de l'Orbiel.

Now, forty-eight hours later, she has reassured herself that the authorities have followed up on her tipoff in just the way she'd hoped. All the major news sites she scanned at the internet café are speculating about the Belgian house.

As she pulls up in front of Le Tachoué, Jacqueline can make out the outlines of the girls behind the linen curtains in Josiane's room. Moments later, they hurl themselves into her arms as she steps into the hallway.

'*Salut, les filles!*' She laughs, all the nervous excitement of the last few days evaporating.

Watching Josie and Lulu-Rose giggle and bounce around like attention-starved puppies, she's reminded exactly why she had to do what she did. Getting rid of Mikko wasn't easy in the end, and calling in the tipoff was certainly nerve-wracking, but Jacqueline will defend her gentle life at Le Tachoué with her girls to her very last breath. Now they can hopefully put the past to rest forever, while the police turn the Ardennes inside out looking for Mikko Eilaanen and Lucia Blix's body.

'Come here, *chérie*,' she whispers, and pulls Lulu-Rose close. She closes her eyes and breathes in the little girl's scent – clean cotton, fresh air, lavender soap, popcorn.

49

Lucia

When the sun's out, it's like summer. All the birds sing and we hear them so clearly here. Maman says it's because we're away from the noise of cars and trains and planes. Today Josie and me are going up to the woods and Maman has packed a picnic basket for us with chunks of ham and fresh baguette from Marie-Elodie's bread van – on weekends she leaves baguettes at the gates at the end of the track leading to Le Tachoué.

We pick wildflowers and play hide-and-seek and then we go down to the river. More snow has melted in the mountains because it's getting warmer every day and the river is wild, splashing our feet when we dangle them from the wooden bridge.

'We're lucky,' I say.

'Yeah,' says Josie.

We're sitting so close together that our arms touch, and we've taken our jackets off and tied them around our waists, even though Maman said, 'Don't take your jackets off – I promise you, you'll get sick.'

'Where do you think the man is now?' I ask.

'Maybe he's gone back to Belgium,' says Josie.

'Or maybe the yellow house.'

'Yeah. Or maybe he's still here.'

'Here? At Le Tachoué?' I ask, my voice trembling at the thought of the man still being here, hiding somewhere in the huge house. It could be true, he could be in the attic like I was in Arden, and Maman could be bringing him toast and sweets and wine.

'Yeah. His car burned, so how could he have left?'

'What do you mean his car burned?'

'The big fire Maman was trying to put out. It was his car burning.'

I think about this and maybe a little part of me already knew that. It could be he was still in it when it burned because I found a watch in the black dust a few days later and showed it to Maman and she snatched it out of my hand. I didn't know that it was his watch and I forgot about it.

'But Maman said he left in the night.'

'Yeah. But maybe he didn't.'

I stand up, holding the handrail on the wooden bridge. I swallow many times, as if there's a chunk of baguette in my throat. Sunlight is streaming through the branches, making the rushing river look like diamonds are floating on it downstream. I turn back to Josie, who is still sitting, trailing a long, thin branch in the water.

'Let's never talk about him again,' I say.

She nods.

50

Elisa

They still can't find her. It's the middle of the night and I've been on my phone for hours, googling and scrolling through article after article about missing children. I've been on Google Earth, too, zooming in on the house in the Belgian Ardennes where my daughter has been. Where her blood seeped into the floorboards and settled in a brownish spray on the untreated pine walls. The house is surrounded by forests. If you google 'Lucia Blix Belgium', which I unfortunately did, you get a series of images of the Belgian police excavation team looking for 'evidence' in the vast forests surrounding the village of Sainte-Ode. They have forensic suits and diggers and dogs and they move around silently among the trees, looking for any signs of upheaval or disturbance.

And yet, the strangest thing has happened since they found those traces of Lucia in Belgium: instead of feeling less hopeful that she'll be found alive, I feel more strongly that she will. I can feel her again, clearly, even more clearly than right at the beginning, and I know in my heart that she is out there, alive.

This is partly because of the testimony of Feodor Batz, whose house it is. Batz is adamant that Lucia was held there for only a few days right after she was taken, and that she was then moved to another location, which he doesn't know anything about, by Mikko Eilaanen. He maintains that Eilaanen was working solo for a private client.

According to Batz, Eilaanen very recently returned to the house in Belgium – alone. He says Eilaanen had a fight there with Heiki Vilkainen, got injured and left. The police don't trust Batz to tell the truth: he's had numerous previous convictions, and he's a known pedophile. Just looking at his mugshot, you can tell this is a particularly unsavory individual. He looks frail, like a man twice his age, with a halo of unruly red curls and a leering, intense smile. He looks completely insane, and my skin crawls to think that Lucia has ever met this man. But I believe his testimony even if the police don't. I have to.

Another thing that makes me certain that Lucia is alive is the strange conversation I had with Fredrik.

'Do you believe in karma?' I asked him, late in the night, as we sat on a hard maroon couch at the police station, looking out at the black water of Sandefjord's inner harbor, just waiting for more news. News that never came.

'Karma,' he said, tasting the word, seeming open to this conversation now.

'Yes.'

'As in, you do something and then the universe punishes you for that particular deed?'

'Yes.'

'I think that would require a pretty magical view of the world. I believe that we're of much less significance than we think. I believe the world just churns on and on and on and doesn't care if we do good or bad things.'

'So you think we can do really bad things and not be punished for it?'

'Well, yes,' said Fredrik, his eyes glinting as he began to fully engage in the conversation. 'It happens all the time. Bad things happen to good people. Good things happen to bad people.'

'So what's the point of being good?'

'Who said there is a point in being good?'

'Well, we're certainly raised to be good – or else! Aren't we?'

'You said it. We're raised to be good. Conditioned. Why does it naturally follow that the universe wants us to be good, or even cares? It just makes for a more peaceful life on earth if most people are mostly good.'

'Children are good. Lucia is good. She doesn't deserve this. Even if I'm not good. Even if—'

'Elisa, nobody is good or bad – those are relative terms. Nobody *deserves* anything, good or bad. Wherever Lucia is, her circumstances are not determined by anything other than the will of whoever has her. And we still have every reason to hope for Lucia's safe return. We must never lose sight of that. Or hope.'

I've been driving myself crazy with thoughts of punishment, and it feels freeing to think that the universe ultimately doesn't care about the mishaps and little cruelties of each tiny speck of a human. Even the very large mishaps and the very large cruelties. Could it be that no matter what, I don't deserve this? That this has just happened for reasons unknown, and the best I can do is focus my energy on hoping for her safe return?

Wherever Lucia is, her circumstances are not determined by anything other than the will of whoever has her.

I get up off the sofa and go upstairs. It's 2.11 a.m. and a brisk wind is blowing outside, smacking a branch against the window on the landing. I step into our bedroom, listening to the rhythmic purr of my sleeping husband's breath. I lie down beside him, draping my arm across his chest.

'Baby,' I whisper, more forcefully than I'd intended, my breath sweeping across his face.

He opens his eyes a crack. He sees me staring at him, my face pressed close to his, and he withdraws a little, alarmed.

'What is it? Honey, it's the middle of the night...'

'Do you remember that time we took Lucia to that playground in Vigelandsparken when I was pregnant with Lyder and she disappeared for a minute or so? And we ran around screaming her name? And all along, she was just sitting still inside one of those little huts?'

'Umm, yeah, I think so.'

'I can still remember how I felt when I spotted her. The relief. Holding her so close, she pushed me away.'

'Honey...'

'I need her, Fredrik. I can't live like this.'

'Shhh,' he whispers.

'Do you think we will get her back?' I ask.

I feel him grow rigid and alert. 'Of course,' he says, stroking my hair.

I pull back and look at him, properly, in the eyes. 'Do you really? Do you genuinely believe that Lucia will come home?'

He nods, but his eyes say *no* before they drop away from my searching gaze.

For a brief moment, I hate him. I hate him for not believing. Once, I promised to love this man forever. But there are limits to everything, even love, and we both know it. Hope, too.

I go downstairs when I'm sure Fredrik is asleep. In the kitchen I pour myself some water. I pour it back out before taking a sip and refill the glass with the remaining quarter bottle of Shiraz on the counter instead. My phone vibrates on the table. It's late; Fredrik must have woken up and found me gone, texting me to ask where I am. I sip at the wine for a long while, drawing in its smoky, peppery scent. I'm in no rush. The nights are mine, and I'm used to these lonely hours now.

I pick up the phone and see that I've received an email, from a Selma Eriksen.

From: Selmaeriksen@gmail.com

To: Elisa.J.Blix@nordicwings.com

Subject: Lucia Blix

Dear Mr and Mrs Blix,

I am a freelance journalist (previously in-house at *Dagsposten*) and I have been working on the abduction of Lucia since the beginning. I am currently looking at approaching your daughter's case from a slightly different angle of inquiry, especially in light of the recent developments. I was hoping you'd be willing to meet with me and discuss this. I really want to help – I remain very hopeful she will be found and returned home. Lucia's is the case I just can't let go.

Best wishes,

Selma Eriksen

I replace the phone face down on the counter. At the beginning, I used to get fifty enquiries like that every day. At least. But no one seems to want to get in touch with me directly anymore. The newspapers still write about her, though not very often – it's not like Lucia is on the front pages every day. At least, she wasn't, until they found the blood. I was never sure if all the exposure was a good thing or not; on the one hand, I thought it might increase the chances of Lucia being recognized somewhere by someone, but at the same time I knew that her recognizability would make her more of a liability and could put her in even more danger.

I feel so alone. So, so alone. The thought of going back upstairs and lying down beside Fredrik is suffocating. Another night in that room, staring at the grey blinds and the occasional roaming shadows from cars outside sliding across the wall, listening to the drone of his light snores. I let myself play a little game sometimes. I imagine that I live in this house with another man. Lucia and Lyder are here, sleeping. Everything is exactly how it should have been, except it's the other man, and for that reason everything is also different. In my fantasy, I lie down in bed, snuggling up to his strong back, slipping my hands around his waist, and he takes my hand and holds it against his heart. I never get back up again.

I pick up my phone and respond to the journalist. Why not meet with her, if she thinks she can bring something new to the table? I google her and she looks like she's barely seventeen, with a certain hungriness about her. I like that. I'd find that infinitely preferable to speaking with some of her more seasoned colleagues, who have seen it all one too many times and are riddled with cynicism. What we need is hope.

51

Jacqueline

She fights an intense craving to check the news. She pours another glass of wine, stares out the window at the night. There is no internet access at Le Tachoué, just like she wanted, but in this moment she would have appreciated a faint 4G signal at the very least.

For the past couple of weeks, Jacqueline has kept an even closer eye on the news than usual. She couldn't have anticipated the explosive effect her tipoff would have – she hadn't known about the bloodstains from Lucia in Sainte-Ode. Sometimes she feels a twinge of sympathy for Elisa Blix, but this is easily dispelled, considering the circumstances. Still, they are both mothers, and Jacqueline knows better than anyone what it means to have your child taken away from you.

She checks the time again: 8.40 p.m. He's never late, but he's late now. Every night for weeks now, Antoine has arrived at Le Tachoué in the evening. In the morning, he leaves before she goes to wake the girls, slipping from bed quietly in the weakening darkness, and she misses the feel of his strong body pressed against hers before he has even left the room. She hasn't yet wanted to have a conversation with the girls about what this new development might mean, but she senses that they know about it anyway; Antoine told her that Lulu-Rose waved at him from the window as he turned the car around in the courtyard one morning. Jacqueline deserves this unexpected happiness, she knows that.

The girls are in bed, Boulette has settled in her crate in the kitchen, and Jacqueline waits impatiently, sipping from a glass of delicious Madiran, smoothing her hair down and glancing once again at the dark nothingness outside the window. A storm swept across the region last week, pulling trees up by the roots and flooding the farms in the valley. Their little river broke its banks, pulling at the bluebells and daffodils on the side of the path as if it was a ferocious waterway that could actually take you somewhere, and Josiane and Lulu-Rose missed a day of school because of a landslide on the road near Encourtiech. The weather has been volatile ever since, with sudden bursts of torrential rain and ominous dark clouds hanging low over the mountains. This evening the rain has started up again – maybe that's why Antoine has been held up.

Showers hurtle loudly against the ancient lead windows and she doesn't hear him knocking, but Boulette erupts into hysterical excitement. And then he is there, wrapping her in his arms, kissing her hard, running his wet hands through her hair and across the warm skin at the base of her skull. He tastes of herbs and mint, and she pulls away, burying her face in his neck, the stubble on his throat rubbing against her cheek. His left hand is inside her blouse, pinching her nipple gently, and she slips her hand into the back of his underwear, running it across his buttocks, pulling him even closer.

Upstairs, he is inside her before they have had a chance to remove all their clothing: Antoine kneeling in front of Jacqueline on the bed, his trousers bunching around one foot, her bra pulled down but still fastened. She's barely conscious of the girls being just down the hallway and clamps her teeth down into the edge of the duvet to stop her urgent cries from growing even louder. He slows down for a while, pulling her carefully up to him, so that she is sitting at the very edge of the bed, her arms around his neck, her ankles touching below his buttocks, her nipples hard and dark in the dim light.

She stops him with a gentle hand and for a long moment they look at each other, in both awe and fear. *What could you do to me?* thinks Jacqueline. After all, nothing could be more dangerous to the heart than love. In this moment, she feels it, the very beginnings of it, when it can still be killed by a single word or a wrong look, and it is terrifying to her that the possibility exists that someone could make her feel something again. She breaks his gaze, needing to be in control. She moves down his body, feeling his fierce energy beneath her fingertips as she strokes his warm skin. She takes him in her mouth, feeling a thrill deep in her stomach at his low moans.

A powerful volley of rain crashes against the old shutters and the howling of the wind doesn't sound far off the storms of the previous week. Jacqueline comes back up and positions herself across Antoine, but in this moment it's all wrong: it's no longer the present, it's the night Mikko returned to Le Tachoué. The man beneath her is no longer a gentle, handsome Pyrenean man but an Estonian criminal who knew too much. The vision tears at her, like a sharp shard from a nightmare.

Antoine's strong body, relaxed and trusting beneath her, becomes Mikko's. Antoine's head is thrown back, his mouth open in pleasure, but his face becomes Mikko's face as he succumbed to the sedative, a thin line of drool emerging from his bottom lip, meandering into coarse stubble. Antoine, sensing she has grown still, takes control by pulling her down towards him, closing his hand around her neck. He pushes his tongue deep into her mouth, building a feverish rhythm, but to Jacqueline his hands are the hands of the dead man around her neck and she can't help but unleash a wild cry. Antoine must have assumed it's a cry of passion because he increases his pace, but she pushes him off hard and scrambles from the bed.

Somewhere in the house, Boulette is yelping. Jacqueline locks herself in the bathroom and splashes cold water on her face, her knees trembling violently. Her loose hair becomes drenched and she ties it back, revealing several red marks from Antoine's fiery lovemaking on her neck. There are marks on her chest, too, and on the insides of her thighs. She liked it. She liked how his lovemaking felt as if it was both worship and punishment.

She meets her own icy blue gaze in the mirror. She's tried to evade the memory of Mikko and what she did to him, but she realizes now that prison doesn't have to be a physical place. *These are the eyes of a murderer*, she thinks, knowing that this will forever be true of her.

52

Selma

Selma starts up again, going harder this time, sharpening her mind with each heavy blow to the punchbag. Sometimes, isolating individual thoughts in her mind feels entirely impossible – it's as though she's forced to think all the thoughts one might have in a day at once. Other times, she's able to channel a state of mind where things are not only crystal clear but where she can discern connections between seemingly unrelated information. This is what makes her a good reporter, and also what occasionally gets her into trouble. A gift, her mother used to say. But Selma knows it's a gift that can also be a curse.

Her heart is thundering in her chest, but she doesn't stop until she has to, bending forward and letting big drops of sweat fall onto the mat. She is thinking about the Blix case, like she's been doing most of her waking hours since she returned to Oslo. She doesn't buy the theory that Lucia has been murdered. It's one of the strangest cases she's ever come across, and she still can't get past the elaborate nature of the abduction. Why rent a house on Airbnb and engage a mysterious woman when they could have just snatched their victim off the street? And why take her from Sandefjord to Mölleryd to Sainte-Ode to somewhere else if the goal was to kill her?

She's more convinced by the thesis that someone either within the Vicodius network or who enlisted their help spied on the Blix family on Facebook or Instagram – Elisa Blix had been a prolific user of both, frequently posing photographs of her son and daughter, both of whom were particularly good-looking children. If this were the case, the motive could be familial rather than sexual or murderous. Lucia Blix might have been taken to fill a childless void, which may increase the chances of the perpetrator being a woman. She might have been sold to a wealthy family, perhaps in the Middle East or Asia, where she could be being kept in a gilded cage. Even so, Selma can't stop wondering how it's possible to conceal, for months and years, a child whose photographs have been widely circulated, without someone alerting the authorities. How? Unless she's being held somewhere virtually undetectable.

In the shower, Selma stands facing the wall, letting streams of slightly too hot water run off her body. She closes her eyes and tries to think about the mundane tasks she has to perform this morning before meeting with the Blix parents this afternoon: feed Medusa, start looking at her tax return, which is due in just over a week, write a thank you card to her Aunt Margot, who gave her money for her birthday earlier in the month. Her thoughts revert to Lucia Blix. How many times has she stared at that sweet, smiling face, imploring the little girl to somehow make her whereabouts known? Her muscles ache as she lifts her arms to refasten her necklace, which once belonged to her mother. She runs her fingertips absentmindedly across the cool moonstone as it rests in the little hollow where her ribs meet, below her breasts. *Your decision-making place*, her mother used to call it. *That's where your gut feeling sits. Your hunch.* She smiles. What began as a strange, murky idea is growing clearer and clearer in her mind. Now she knows what to ask Fredrik and Elisa Blix.

It's not yet 7 a.m., and outside it's cold and clear. She smiles to herself at what the day holds. Olav had hardly been able to believe it when she messaged him saying she was going to be meeting with Fredrik and Elisa. It feels good to be back in touch with him again after so many months of self-imposed silence. She begins to walk fast down Torshovgata, bracing her thin body against the wind, her mind spinning with images of the missing little girl and her possible whereabouts.

He is a lot like Selma's mental image of him, but his wife is not. Fredrik Blix has the easy, good-natured disposition of a kid, thinks Selma – he just doesn't seem to carry that seriousness or tiredness most adults do, especially men working demanding jobs. He is an attractive man but in an unremarkable way, and he seems nervous and bewildered. He reminds her a little of Olav – a typical Norwegian who feels more at home running in the forest or skiing across barren plains than in a fancy hotel lobby, which is where they've agreed to meet. Though Selma walked past the Hotel Continental almost daily for years when she worked in central Oslo, she never went inside. Her eyes travel from

Fredrik Blix to the sophisticated muted gilt of the interior and then back to Elisa Blix, who is sitting next to her husband, though at a noticeable distance from him.

Elisa is different from what Selma expected, based on her social media profiles and her interactions with the press. In the year and a half since Lucia was taken, she's lost a lot of weight, lending her the appearance of a weary, hungry animal. Her eyes are intense and searching of Selma's, and there's something unsettling about the way she is constantly fidgeting – shuffling her feet, rubbing her thin red fingers, running a hand through her newly short bob. When Lucia first disappeared, Elisa came across as a golden girl: rich-girl pretty, with straight white teeth, glossy hair and the subtle tan of someone who holidays when they please. Now she looks like that woman's less privileged older sister.

'Thank you for meeting with me,' Selma says, conscious of speaking slowly and clearly. When she gets too excited or nervous, all her words tend to come at once.

Elisa nods quickly and looks at Selma with suppressed impatience, as if she might at any moment throw her hands up in exasperation and ask her to get to the point. 'You said in your email that you had some thoughts that might shed new light on what happened to Lucia?'

'Yes. They are just thoughts at this stage, but I wanted to meet with you and see if you think I could be of any help at all. I want to help.'

Fredrik and Elisa exchange a glance. Everyone wants to help, and yet nobody has been able to. *Until now*, thinks Selma, and envisions the moment when Lucia Blix is back in her parents' loving arms.

'Did you say it's *Dagsposten* you work for? Until the,

uh, recent developments in Belgium, they hadn't written anything about Lucia's case in a long while, not even when that girl was found in Poland in January.' Fredrik pauses and fixes Selma with his deep blue eyes. She sees then that he too has a tougher side that his happy-go-lucky persona doesn't immediately reveal.

The girl Fredrik is referring to is ten-year-old Yanka Miloszewa, who was found half naked and running on bare feet down the side of a dual carriageway in eastern Poland at the beginning of January. She spoke in a foreign language, thought to be Scandinavian by the elderly couple who stopped their car, bundled her into blankets on the back seat and called the police. They saw the girl's matted blonde hair, filthy scraps of clothing and dark, frightened eyes and remembered Lucia Blix, whose face had been plastered on signposts and billboards and across the national newspapers. As it turned out, Yanka was the child of a Polish mother and an abusive Swedish-Iranian father and had been held inside the family home near Lublin for over two years. Her mother has still not been found.

'I used to work for *Dagsposten*. I'm freelance now.'

'Have you worked on other missing child cases?' Elisa asks, eyes sharp on Selma.

'I worked a lot on Lucia's case when I was still at *Dagsposten*, and at the time we were, of course, comparing your daughter's case with some of the others. Madeleine. Therese. Those two in particular, due to the similarities.'

Lucia's mother drops her gaze to her red, peeling hands and Selma imagines she's probably prone to compulsive behaviors, like constantly washing or rubbing her hands. She knows the signs because she used to do the same thing herself. It's Elisa's sore hands and jitteriness that triggers the first real feelings of empathy in Selma. She can see why this woman has been called 'strangely controlled' and 'unusually cold', but meeting her in person it's pretty clear that these are strategies to manage the chaos beneath the surface. What is each moment of each day like for this woman? How does she feel, catching her own gaze in the mirror as she brushes her teeth? Does she get a single moment of peace when she's eating, sleeping, peeing, walking down the street?

'Lucia's case has always been special to me,' Selma says, quietly now. Then she surprises herself. 'I lost my mother when I was seven. And... it almost broke me. It has defined my life. So I find it unbearable to think of another little girl like me being without her parents. I've not been able to stop thinking about Lucia. And to me, there's something not right about the investigation. Still now.'

'What do you mean?' asks Elisa, her eyes softer and bright with tears.

'They just seem so set on the network theory, as if they're almost disregarding any suggestion that the motive behind Lucia's abduction could be much more complex.'

'I think they have explored most avenues, Selma,' Fredrik says, not unkindly. 'And I hope they continue to do so.'

'What are your thoughts?' asks Elisa.

'Well, take the Belgian situation. Someone calls in a tipoff saying Lucia died in Belgium. Why would they say that? To make the police raid that house and arrest Batz. But why? And why now?'

'I've been wondering the same thing,' says Elisa. 'Why now, and who is the person who wants Batz arrested?'

'Exactly. And I believe Batz when he says he had nothing

to do with the abduction except for letting Mikko use the house in transit,' says Selma.

Elisa nods excitedly. 'I believe him too. I don't think he has anything to gain by lying about it.'

'Well, if he's... if he's done something to her, then he does have something to gain,' says Fredrik.

'He hasn't,' whispers Elisa, and Selma sees then how fragile the mother's hope is.

Selma nods. 'I believe that someone is trying to make it look like a murder in order to ensure that there's less focus on or speculation about other scenarios. And I believe that the reason they're doing this now is because they feel threatened somehow. Lucia may no longer be certain as to who she really is at this point – a vulnerable nine-year-old is extremely susceptible to manipulation. Her kidnappers have managed to avoid being caught for a long while and perhaps they've got bolder and have been taking her out and about and perhaps someone's recognized her. Or they could have been threatened by someone – Batz, for example. And that's extremely concerning: a nervous kidnapper will be much more dangerous than one who believes they're safe.'

'Right,' says Fredrik.

'Can I ask you a question?' asks Selma.

Fredrik glances at Elisa, but Elisa's gaze doesn't move from Selma's. 'Of course.'

'If, for a moment, we entertain the possibility that Lucia was taken to order by someone, what do you think their motive might be?'

'I guess... I guess... because they might have seen her on the internet.'

'But there are millions of children on the internet. Why her?'

'Because... I don't know. I'm not sure I understand the question.'

'What I'm asking is, just supposing that someone wanted Lucia, and very specifically her, what could that person's motive be? Entirely hypothetically, of course.'

'To punish me,' Elisa says softly, and looks immediately stricken, like she wants to take it back.

She glances at her husband, who, at the exact same moment, says, 'For revenge.'

'Revenge for what?' asks Elisa, eyes quick and hard on her husband.

'Punish you for what?' asks Fredrik.

Selma watches them carefully.

'I'm sorry, but what you're asking doesn't make any sense,' says Elisa, her face flushed. 'What I meant was that if I try to imagine why someone might take someone else's child, the only reason I can think of is that they might be doing it to punish someone.'

'And is there anyone that could hate you so much, with or without reason, that they could have taken your daughter?'

Fredrik makes a show of seeming completely bewildered, as though Selma is speaking a foreign language. Elisa looks angry – a vein has appeared at the side of her temple and Selma can tell she is clenching her teeth, trying to regain her composure. She releases a little incredulous laugh, as if to signal how utterly ridiculous Selma's question is.

'Of course not,' she says.

'Well, Mrs Blix, lots of people *do* hate other people. You said it yourself – punishment is the motive that comes to mind. Revenge is one of the most common motives for crime.'

Elisa has managed to regain some composure and to Selma it seems as though she is consciously summoning a meek, hurt look. There is something about this woman that doesn't feel quite genuine, and Selma realizes she felt more for her when she seemed angry – at least that felt real. She pictures Elisa with Medusa – would she run her hands down the cat's back and would the cat lean into her touch, flattening her ears and purring, or would she arch her back and skulk away?

'I'm afraid your question has thrown me a little. I can't think of anyone who would hate me or have such negative feelings towards me that they would consider taking my child. I actually think that's a really crazy suggestion.'

'The thing is, someone might hate you intensely without your knowledge. They might have watched you for years.'

'But why?'

'Only you can answer that.'

'Look,' says Fredrik, 'the police have thoroughly investigated the possibility of personal motives. They are highly competent and they're continuing to spend a great deal of time, money and expertise on our daughter's case, so I really can't think that we'll suddenly stumble across something new at this point.'

'Highly competent, but they still can't find her,' Selma says, her eyes not leaving Fredrik's.

'I'm not sure I entirely understand why you wanted to meet with us?' he says.

'My view is that this is, without a doubt, personal, and that whoever has Lucia has targeted her specifically to get at one or both of you. I also think that the Vicodius network was just used for transporting her and that if the police could find the woman who took her, they'd get much closer to the perpetrator.'

'The police believe that woman is dead,' says Elisa.

'Maybe. But you don't.'

'No.'

'You seem very certain about that. But the police seem equally certain that Silwia Truja was the same woman who you met with.'

'She wasn't.' Elisa shakes her head with conviction. 'I've said that all along. The woman I met was extremely sophisticated. She was also a native Norwegian speaker. And I feel like she really was the mother of the little girl – there was that unmistakable bond between a mother and her child there.'

'Okay, so I believe you. I don't think someone like Truja, who was a known heroin addict with a long criminal record, could have convincingly posed as a Norwegian mother to the point where someone like you wasn't even remotely suspicious. I just don't think it's possible.'

'I... Right. Thank you,' says Elisa. 'Nobody else seems to believe me.'

'I definitely believe you. Now, let's take this further: if the woman posing as Line wasn't Silwia Truja, what could have motivated her, a sophisticated and presumably fairly privileged mother from Norway, someone who sounds a lot like yourself, in fact, to participate in the kidnapping of a young child?'

The question hangs in the air between them, the Blix couple looking stunned and uncomfortable. Selma notices that Elisa Blix is digging the nail of her index finger into the side of her thumb incredibly hard. The skin whitens, then pierces. Dark droplets of blood appear. Elisa sees Selma looking at her and withdraws her hand behind her back.

Selma stands up, and Elisa and Fredrik exchange a surprised look.

'Okay,' she says. 'I guess we're done here. I hope, with all my heart, that Lucia is found and returned to you. Don't hesitate to contact me again if you come up with the answer to that question.'

She turns around and walks away from the Blixes, sensing their shock at her sudden departure. She goes through the revolving door and into the throng of people rushing to Nationaltheatret Station – it's rush hour and the cold but bright day has given way to a gloomy, foggy early evening. She walks away from the crowds, down towards the harbor at Aker Brygge. She finds an empty bench and sits staring at the black water streaked with orange from the streetlights behind her on the promenade. Her mind feels entirely uncluttered and calm. Something happened there, with Fredrik and Elisa. People can act as controlled as they want, but they can never completely control their non-verbal reactions. And Selma saw it there, in Elisa Blix's eyes: a jolt of doubt, a flash of dread – unmistakable.

53

Elisa

I need to think. On the train home, Fredrik won't stop talking. Unusual – my husband isn't particularly chatty. He keeps going over the meeting with the journalist, saying how she seemed odd and a little rude. I nod and stare out the window at a milky white fog settling upon the western outskirts of Oslo until the train disappears into a tunnel. I *need* to think. I feel his eyes on me, but I keep mine firmly on the view, even though there's nothing to look at but the sweep of the wall lights rushing past. I run my index finger over the bloody groove I made on the side of my thumb; it had stopped bleeding but starts again with a gentle prod. I feel the blood prickle out before wiping my finger discreetly on my dark jeans.

We walk home in heavy silence, through downtown Sandefjord, along the harborfront, past the shipyard and then up the long hill. It's cold and windy. It's Friday and Lyder has been picked up from school by Fredrik's parents, who'll take him to their cabin in Kviteseid until Sunday. In the past year this has become a routine – every other weekend Vigdis and

Karl take Lyder to the cabin, which is a welcome break for him as well as us.

When Lyder is around, Fredrik and I try to keep things as normal as possible. We eat together as a family most days, we help with homework, we put Lyder to bed at a reasonable time. To an outsider, we probably seem ordinary. Whole. Happy, even. But on the weekends, when Lyder is away in Kviteseid building snowmen, drinking cocoa and being doted on, Fredrik and I give in to our despair and powerlessness.

We spend hours on our laptops, staring at maps of the roads to Mölleryd or Sainte-Ode, or reading through the investigation material, or scrolling through the chat forums on the internet to see what people are saying about 'the Blix Case'. This, of course, is dangerous, because just like I suspected at the beginning, people say horrible, cruel things – about us, and about how they pray that Lucia was killed quickly because the alternative would surely be much, much worse. But no matter how hurtful and distressing the comments, I carry on reading in the hope that somehow, somewhere, some random person might stumble across a theory that leads to us finding Lucia. I can't live with the possibility that the answer might be out there, on one of those forums, and I missed it. In the evenings we sit in front of the TV, watching old American sitcoms and drinking bourbon on the rocks until we can no longer decipher the empty jokes or string a sentence together. We usually fall asleep like that, on opposite sides of the huge sofa, closing our eyes against the spinning room, the canned laughter the last thing we hear.

'What a stupid question to ask,' Fredrik says, again, as

he disables the alarm and hangs his jacket on a peg in the hallway.

I know he wants to continue this conversation, but I can't face it. I need to think, and I need to be alone. What if Selma Eriksen is right to insinuate that what's happened to us could be some twisted act of revenge? I stare at my husband, at his mild, faintly lined face and his big blue eyes that make him look as innocent as a child.

'Is it really such a stupid question?' I ask, and he narrows his eyes before relaxing his face back into its usual blank, slightly bewildered expression. In this moment, I hate him. Even though he's done nothing wrong, I hate him for his meekness, his idiotic look of perplexity.

'What do you mean?'

'Every single theory and line of investigation to date has led nowhere. None of it makes any sense. At least she asked a question that does make some kind of sense. Would it really be so stupid to look into possible personal motives?'

'But, Elisa, it's not like they haven't done that already.'

'Maybe they didn't look deep enough. Maybe *we* didn't. I've been trying to say that to you.'

'What are you saying? That someone hates us so much they could have taken Lucia?'

'I don't know!'

I do, of course, know that this could be the case. And yet I thought it was impossible. I've trusted the police and their main line of inquiry, even when a small voice in my head has said that it simply seemed too random. Because what are the odds that of all the children in this unremarkable suburb it was Elisa Blix's child that was taken in an abduction so seamless it was as though she'd vanished into thin air? What are the odds?

And yet, through all of my sleepless nights since 19 October 2017, I've concluded that what has happened to our family must be because of karma. A terrible, cruel punishment – brutal justice exercised in the most fundamentally painful of ways. Sometimes the punishment really does not fit the crime. And sometimes it does, however much it hurts to admit it. I've been thinking about these things in a cosmic way, but what if it wasn't cosmic or magical like Fredrik said, but rather willfully plotted by someone to bring me to some kind of twisted justice?

'You tell me, Elisa! Does anybody really hate you?'

He practically spits the words out and I back off to get away from the hot blast of his breath on my face, but he grabs my wrist and yanks it hard.

'Are you totally crazy? What's got into you, Fredrik? Jesus!'

'I said, have you given anyone reason to hate you!'

I shake my head, but Fredrik's eyes are hard on me. I sink to the tiled floor of the hallway and expect him to gather me in his arms and kiss my hair the way he usually would, but he backs away from me, then rushes up the stairs.

I scrub every surface in the kitchen, moving the sponge around in a circular motion, counting. Four times to the right, six to the left. Repeat. It gives me something to think about. The bleach in the cleaning product has seeped into the open wound on my thumb and the stinging pain feels almost good, as if some of what is held inside me is finally physically tangible.

My wrist, too, hurts from Fredrik's forceful grip. He's never grabbed me like that before or caused me pain. But my husband is no longer himself; how could he be? He might look more or less the same, but he's a different man underneath his skin.

Since that October evening eighteen months ago, I am no longer myself either. I am simply not the same person. The journalist, Selma, asked us if we could imagine anyone hating us, if a person exists out there who could hate us so much that they'd go to great lengths to take our daughter from us. I sit down with my back to the dishwasher, which is humming as it runs. I look out at the dark, empty dining room that leads into the lounge, also empty. Once, this house was messy and busy with the constant activity of young children. Lucia tottered around here as a toddler, holding on to these same cabinets for support as she took her first steps. Lucia ate breakfast at that table every morning. She would have, at some point, touched most if not all of the objects in this room. I run my hand along the cabinet next to the dishwasher, seeing the baby Lucia once was in my mind's eye, clutching this brass doorknob in a soft, chubby fist. What would be worse – if she was taken randomly like the police believe, or if she was taken very specifically by someone who hates us? Someone who hates *me*. Deep down, I know that if this is the result of someone's intense hatred, then it is more likely to be me they're after.

My mind churns with the possibilities this scenario suggests. Someone watching us – for years perhaps. Planning. Someone studying every detail of my family's routine.

Waiting. Someone who hates us. Me. Someone who would do anything, absolutely anything, to get revenge. Someone who knew that when the day came, there would be absolutely nothing I could do to stop them.

I feel the past stirring in me, as if time were running on a loop and I will now be forced to go back there. There are things that if I said them would cost me everything I have left. Fredrik, Lyder, this home, my job, perhaps even my life. Any chance of getting Lucia back. But could it be, if Lucia was taken for revenge, that speaking up could prove to be the only way to find her? And we *have* to find her. I have always said I would give up anything, even my own life, to find my child. But would I? Would I really?

54

Selma

She's there when they open, like every day this week. She hardly slept, and though it's just gone 5 a.m., Selma is alert and focused. She kicks off her sneakers and hangs her jacket in the changing room before going through to the gym. She warms up quickly, doing some stretches to soothe her aching triceps and some running on the spot, before launching a violent attack on the punchbag. With every hard, precise thud her jittery nervousness begins to fade. She feels like a bear emerging into the warm, fragrant spring air, shaky with hunger after months in hibernation.

She was awake most of the night. She kept seeing Fredrik and Elisa Blix in her mind: their sharply different body language; Fredrik's exaggerated surprise at her question, Elisa's focused attempt to show no reaction; and the strange thing Elisa did to her hand. To Selma she looked like a human pressure cooker, a person who might at any moment explode into bursts of burning air.

When she's finished pummeling the punchbag, Selma sits for a long while in the changing room, just stabilizing her breathing. She takes her phone out, scrolling through the news, clicking on any mention of Lucia Blix, but the media channels are just regurgitating old material now in anticipation of another breakthrough. *A body – that's what they are after*, thinks Selma. She finds Elisa Blix in her contacts and decides to give her just the smallest of prods.

Hi Elisa, I have some new thoughts I'd like to discuss with you. Perhaps we could meet again? All best, Selma Eriksen

She walks down Ullevålsveien towards the city center, deciding to stop in at a Deli de Luca for a double caramel spiced latte – her first in well over a year, since her regular fixes when she was working at *Dagsposten*. It's while she's waiting for her order that she glances at her phone. She's not like many of her generation, who seem to be glued to their screens, checking for likes and messages throughout the day. Even now, she doesn't feel the urge to constantly check her phone; chances are, Elisa Blix will take her time getting back to her, and it's not as if there's anything else important going on. Selma doesn't have a boyfriend, or a lot of friends. She likes to keep all Facebook notifications turned off. She doesn't need the distraction of a vibrating signal to let her know that Trine Jørgensen with whom she played the trumpet in third grade just got engaged to a man Selma will never meet and has no interest in, or that Petter Franzen went running with his Irish setter and posted seven pictures of it.

'One new message,' says her phone. From Elisa Blix, sent two hours ago.

Hi Selma, I'm afraid Fredrik and I feel that it's best to speak to the press only on the instruction of the police and to remain focused on the direction of the ongoing investigation. With best wishes, Elisa Blix

Selma feels a hot surge of disappointment and anger at Elisa's message. She would love to know what has transpired since she sat across from Elisa and saw the unmistakable flash of dread in her eyes. What is she afraid of?

She takes her coffee and steps back onto the busy street, where a blue tram hurtles past. She turns her face towards the sun emerging briefly from a dense mass of grey clouds. Is Elisa worried that an investigation into potential revenge motives might implicate her somehow? Selma supposes that her question could be seen as suspicious towards Elisa, implying that she must have done something to inspire such hatred.

She can't face returning home to while away the rest of the day indoors with Medusa, watching patches of sunlight on the wooden floor, lost in her own head. It's such a beautiful spring day, the first after what's felt like an endless spell of rainstorms. She walks aimlessly in the direction of Stortinget, the Norwegian Parliament. She heads down Lille Grensen and looks up at the big glass windows of *Dagsposten*'s offices. When she worked there, she used to sometimes walk past on a weekend, gazing up and counting down to Monday morning, the buzzy excitement of the editorial office and Olav waving at her through the glass wall. Now, she can't wait for the look on Olav's face when she tells him about the developments with the Blix couple. Or perhaps she'll keep it to herself for a while longer, until she uncovers something properly juicy.

In front of Stortinget, Selma stops and takes in the scene around her. Throngs of shoppers are milling around on Karl Johans gate, a couple of homeless men are sitting on a bench surrounded by bags full of returnable plastic bottles, and the sun has disappeared again, leaving a gloomy sky. A plane turns in a wide circle high above and Selma wishes she was on it, going somewhere far away. An idea occurs to her, and she pulls her phone out again.

No worries, Elisa. I've explored a little further and have some very interesting ideas about potential revenge motives. I'll pass them directly on to the police to assist with the investigation. All best, Selma

She has walked less than halfway down Karl Johan in the direction of the royal palace when her phone begins to vibrate in her pocket. She doesn't need to pull it out to know who's calling. For a brief moment it stops, and then it starts up again. She smiles to herself, trying to keep calm, relishing the excited flutter in her stomach. She puts the phone on flight mode, then strolls around the royal palace's public gardens, drawing the scent of freshly sprung bluebells deep into her lungs, marveling at the vivid bursts of green on the birch trees. In less than a fortnight, on 17 May, Norway will celebrate Independence Day, and the entire country will become one big street party. Children will wear their *bunads*, the ornate regional folk costumes revered by her countrymen, and they'll file onto the square in front of the palace, holding Norwegian flags and singing the national song to the royal family, who will stand on the palace balcony, waving to the crowds.

Lucia Blix would have been one of them. Could it be that she's being held somewhere where she can hear and perhaps observe festivities like 17 May, reminding her of what it was like to be a normal child? Again, Selma has a strong sense that Lucia could be hidden not in a basement or attic but somewhere altogether more clever, right underneath everyone's noses. And the answer, Selma is increasingly convinced, lies with the parents.

She begins to walk again, and for a long while she wanders around the city, lost in thought, around cozy Briskeby, over to the Vigeland sculpture park, which is busy with tourists and rollerblading kids, and then later among the swanky shops of Bogstadveien. It feels good to be out among people, even if she doesn't have much of a plan. She sits for a moment on a bench outside a coffee shop, considering what to do next. There might be an interesting talk on at the Literature House – it's not too late to become the kind of person who might unselfconsciously turn up to such a thing alone – but she decides against it. She's getting hungry and can't afford to throw away any more money in kiosks and cafés today. She walks up Pilestredet, before cutting across towards St Hanshaugen where she'd bought her little flat five years previously, with the money left to her after her mother's death.

The irritation she felt when Elisa declined to meet with her has been lifted by the long walk and the little game she played on a hunch. Perhaps it was cruel, to make Elisa nervous by implying she has some kind of information, but it might be the only way she can get Elisa to talk. There's something guilty about her – Selma can sense it. She doesn't for a moment doubt that Elisa is a loving mother or that she's suffering deeply at the loss of her daughter, but that dread in her eyes, at the Hotel Continental... To Selma, Elisa is unquestionably a woman living in fear.

She lets herself into her apartment, gives Medusa a couple of long, firm strokes, then pulls out her Mac.

'Elisa Blix,' she types in, not for the first time.

55

Elisa

All of yesterday, I felt as though I was about to throw up. And all night, I've tossed and turned, one crazy thought after another chasing around my tired mind. There is no reason for that girl to make me nervous. She can send vaguely threatening messages all she wants – the fact remains, she knows nothing, and that is what I need to remember. Nothing at all. She's a strange girl, Fredrik was right about that much. Attractive, but in such an unpolished and goofy way, it is as though she has never looked in a mirror. She has beautiful, long light brown hair which she gathers in a low ponytail beneath her ear to one side of her head. Her face is entirely bare, but fresh with youth. I wonder if Fredrik found her attractive.

Passing on my thoughts in aid of the investigation, she said. Why would her thoughts matter at all to the investigators? She's all talk and no substance. She needs to go and use her hunches on other people's affairs.

But… what if she really is right and someone has watched us for years, biding their time, readying themselves to take the most precious gift we've ever had away from us. Who would it be? My mind returns to Karoline Meister, the weirdo who tried to steal my husband on Facebook. Could she have had something to do with it? The police dismissed the idea that the mysterious micro-cheat woman from the internet could have anything at all to do with the case, just like they insisted that 'Line' was actually Silwia Truja.

Karo-Line. What if Karoline was really Line – someone whose sole purpose was to punish Fredrik or me? Or what if Karoline really was just a random loony on the internet, and Line was someone else entirely, who stole Lucia for another purpose. Revenge? Again, why? It always comes back to why. There are things in my past that would have inspired hatred. Wild hatred, even. But they are sealed off entirely, buried so deep I have managed, over the years, to trust that they will remain buried forever.

56

Jacqueline

In the morning when she wakes, Antoine is still there, sitting at the foot of the bed, watching her. His torso is bare and he has wrapped a white towel around his waist. His shoulder-length hair is wet and slicked back, little beads of water gathering at the tips before dropping onto his chest. Jacqueline smiles sleepily and turns towards him, letting the thin sheet slip off her body. Antoine doesn't return her smile but runs a finger lightly across her ankle bone. She knows this look; he is searching for words. Antoine is a man of few words, but when he does speak, his words are measured, and she knows he cares about ensuring they come out the way he intended.

'What time is it?' she asks, trying to gage from the bright light coming in through the slats in the shutters.

'Nearly eight.'

'You've usually left by now,' she says. 'It's nice that you're still here.'

'I thought perhaps we should talk.'

'Okay,' she says, and though she sensed he would say

something to that effect, she is gripped by anxiety and premonition.

'Last night, Jacqueline – do you feel able to talk to me about what happened?'

'What do you mean?'

'When we were in bed. And you suddenly... seemed very distressed. I was worried that I'd hurt you.'

They come back to her, the dreadful, insistent memories of the night before. The frightening coldness in her gaze when she met her own eyes in the mirror.

'Look, Antoine, I think you need to leave. I'm sorry... I need some space.'

She turns to the wall, fixing her eyes on the uneven surface of the stonework. Antoine shifts behind her, then she feels his hand pressing gently against her shoulder blades. She shifts away from his touch, willing him to leave, and after a long while he does.

The memories do not.

Mikko's face that night was shadowed with exhaustion. No wonder. She could only imagine what his life must have been like on the run for the past eighteen months as one of the most wanted men in Europe.

'Here,' she'd said, placing another glass of wine in front of him, once the girls were in bed.

'Oh no,' Mikko said. 'I'll need to be off again tonight.'

'Tonight? But... but you've only just arrived. It's so stormy out there.'

'Yes, well, I can always stop for a bit in a layby if I need to.'

'Oh,' she said, her mind racing. She'd hoped to get him to fall asleep first.

'We need to go through the payment. Better now than later.'

'Mikko, really, I must insist. Please stay. Just one night.' She wasn't going to let him leave again, no matter what. At first, it hadn't occurred to her, that it could come to this. If only he hadn't returned to Le Tachoué, she wouldn't have been in this position.

She consciously parted her lips a little and narrowed her eyes in the way she knew worked every time with men like Mikko. She took him in: his smooth, glinting head, his meaty, tattooed hands, his surprisingly long black eyelashes. He smiled at her, and it was a genuine smile; if she hadn't known what kind of man he was, she might have thought he was quite nice.

'Very well,' he said, his eyes sliding slowly down her body.

She buried her pronounced left canine into her bottom lip and smiled back. Would the sleeping girls hear anything from upstairs?

He passed out even sooner than she'd thought he would, tongue dropping out of a soft mouth, eyes receding back in his skull, big arms flung out on the sofa. He hadn't managed to stay awake long enough to lay a single finger on her, thanks to the drops of sedative.

She stood a while watching him sleep. For a moment, she wondered again if this was necessary – could she just let him go and trust that he'd return to his life of crime without a fuss? From what she'd gathered, Mikko was not a dangerous man compared to many – he seemed to be the brawn rather than the brains, and she imagined his criminal record would be full of break-ins and minor drug offenses rather than violence or murder. He'd done everything she wanted, without asking too many questions. He seemed like a simple man. The kind of man who, if you feed him and fuck him, would remain mellow for the most part. But Jacqueline had too much to lose now. Everything, in fact.

She thought again of the girls sleeping upstairs, of their innocence, their wonderful new lives just beginning in this most gentle and beautiful of places. She had to protect them – at any cost.

She took a couple of steps towards the sofa, positioned herself across the unconscious man and looked at his face one last time. Then she pressed a pillow hard against his mouth and nose. He twitched, but only a little. Still, it took a long while.

57

Selma

It's early evening already and Selma's searches still haven't brought up anything much. 'We have little choice but to go on strike, considering the current roster system,' reads an old quote in *Sandefjords Blad* from senior cabin manager Elisa Blix. Selma googles Elisa's junior school, which was mentioned on her Facebook page, and after scrolling through page after page of its gallery archives, she finds a picture of Elisa with two other girls, holding hockey sticks and grinning widely in front of the newly opened ice rink in Lillehammer. The photo is dated 1993, so it would likely have been built before the 1994 Olympics. Selma does the math – that would make Elisa nine years old in the photo, more or less the same age as Lucia now. Underneath the photo it says: 'Ida Helén Hansen, Maja Sørensen and Elisa Samuelsen are extremely excited about the opening of Lillehammer Storhall this weekend.' Elisa Samuelsen – her maiden name.

Selma enters the name into Google and sifts through the results. She tries 'Elisa Samuelsen Lillehammer' and there are several hits. One is from a horse-riding club, listing the trophy winners of summer 1995. Elisa Samuelsen is mentioned in three categories. 'Horses' writes Selma in the Word document she's opened to take notes. Another hit is from Jehovas Vitner Lillehammer – the local church of Jehovah. 'The Samuelsen Family Collected 7,400 Kroner in the Annual Door-to-Door Action Against Poverty in the Ukraine', reads the headline, accompanied by a photograph of the Samuelsen family. It shows a stern-looking mother with close-cropped curls and something reminiscent of Elisa in her alert, intense expression, and a tall, wiry man. There are also two little girls, the oldest of whom is vaguely recognizable as Elisa, and a much younger boy, perched on the mother's hip.

'Jehovah's Witnesses' writes Selma, and underlines it. She spends a while reading about their practices and history in Norway. Google tells her that there are 167 active Jehovah's Witness congregations in Norway, with over eleven thousand so-called 'street preachers', congregation members who go from door to door preaching their beliefs. What would Elisa's early life have been like?

Selma is easily distractible, and while this can sometimes be an issue, more often it leads to her learning a great deal about various subjects, people and places – surprisingly useful for a journalist. She googles the horse-riding center, poring over the images of horses carrying people in a long line up a mountain path, a narrow, dark valley with a meandering silvery river far beneath them. She moves on with 'Samuelsen Lillehammer' and several more hits appear. She opens one that reads 'Georg Samuelsen succeeds his father Iver at Lillehammer shoe factory', and the accompanying photo is definitely of the same man as the man in the Jehovah's Witness article about charity. Selma goes to 1881.no, the address directory, but there are no results for Georg Samuelsen Lillehammer. She vaguely notices her stomach growling and realizes she hasn't eaten all day. It's seven thirty already, but she can't face the effort of getting up, opening the almost empty refrigerator, thinking about what she can eat and then preparing it, so she returns to the screen and ignores her hunger pangs.

She sorts the hits on Georg Samuelsen into 'most recent' instead of 'most relevant'. The top result is an obituary in *Aftenposten* from 2012: Elisa's father is dead. Selma clicks on it and spends several frustrating moments logging in to the *Aftenposten* portal in order to gain full access to the online paper. When she finally opens the obituary, she is struck by confusion.

> Georg Samuelsen, born 11 December 1951, died peacefully at home in Lillehammer surrounded by his wife and children on 17 March 2012 after a long period of illness. He is safe in the arms of Jehovah and shall be fondly remembered on Earth.
> Kari Samuelsen, wife
> Thorvald Samuelsen, son
> Elin Samuelsen, daughter
> Nathalie, Emma and Lucas, grandchildren

Selma's heart begins to beat faster in her chest, though she must have misunderstood. Perhaps Georg and Kari were an aunt and uncle and not her parents – why else would Elisa not be included in the obituary? She returns to the first article and scans the photo caption, and there it is, clear as day: 'Georg and Kari Samuelsen, who raised a substantial amount of money for charity, alongside their children Elisa (11), Elin (8) and Thorvald (3).' What does this mean? What could it mean, besides Elisa Blix being estranged from her family? Selma returns to 1881 and types in 'Kari Samuelsen Lillehammer'. Only one hit, registered to Hellebergstien 62, Lillehammer. Selma writes the address down in the Word document, alongside *estranged??*.

After a long while, Selma gets up and stretches her legs. The hunger has faded and though it's late, she feels wide awake and alert, like she might have some kind of revelation if she manages to stay focused. Medusa drops off the windowsill and comes over to where Selma stands looking out at the night, weaving her soft, supple body around Selma's ankles in a number eight pattern.

'You weird little furball,' says Selma and picks the cat up. She realizes the apartment is completely dark – it is now past ten and Selma has been sitting on her bed with the laptop for hours, trying to construct an image of Elisa Blix in her mind. A small-town girl, Elisa grew up the oldest child in a seemingly devout Christian family and went on to become a flight attendant living in a different part of Norway. Interesting, though not that unusual. And yet, Selma has a vague feeling that there is something more to Elisa. Like an itch, it plays on her mind as she walks around the apartment, turning on the lights, still holding Medusa under her arm. Presuming she really is estranged from her family, there must be a reason for this. A daughter isn't left out of her father's obituary without reason. Georg Samuelsen died in 2012, and in the seven years that have passed since, it's possible that Elisa has reconnected with her family, but, either way, Selma wants to know.

She prepares a mug of Rett i Koppen instant tomato soup, thinking intently as she stirs the granules through the boiling water. What if Elisa did something in her youth that led to her family disowning her and this ultimately has something to do with Lucia's abduction? But what could the seemingly wholesome, sporty and attractive Elisa Blix have done to merit such punishments? Lost in swirling thoughts, Selma takes a big glug of the steaming soup, burning the inside of her mouth. She slams the mug down and soup splashes onto the white surface of the IKEA table.

'Fuck,' she hisses, running her sore tongue against the back of her teeth. She gets a wet cloth and is about to wipe up the spilled soup when she realizes that it resembles bloodstains. *Bloodstains, spilled blood, blood money, blood vengeance...* She leaves the spilled soup and returns to the bed and opens up her laptop. For several moments, she pores over the familiar images of Elisa Blix. Selma once stared at these photos asking herself *Why you?* and *Who are you?*, but now the question buzzing through her mind is *What have you done?*

58

Elisa

My head feels so leaden, I can't separate my thoughts or make any sense of anything. Maybe this is what it's like when you start losing cognitive functions and you have to make do with the grainy bits that remain. My mind is a labyrinth and every time I think I'm getting somewhere, I slam into a wall. Even more than my mind, it's my heart that aches. To work out why Lucia's gone, I have to examine the past. I need to figure out if it's vengeance, not karma, that's landed us here. I have to go back, all the way back, even if it hurts like hell. Even if it feels impossible. I have to do it for Lucia.

My heart is beating so hard, it feels like Fredrik might hear it.

'I'm going for a drive,' I say.

'But it's past midnight!'

'I need to think.'

'Honey, what's going on?'

'I said I need to think, Fredrik. You heard what the

journalist said. I'm trying to literally turn my past history inside out...'

'We've talked about this. What she suggested is crazy. We know for a fact that it's the network that took Lucia—'

'But *why*, Fredrik? I have to know why!' I'm shouting, and my words hang in the air between us. He rubs the bridge of his nose. I turn around and leave the room, slamming the door behind me.

I get in the car and drive aimlessly around the neighborhood for a while, looking out at houses much like my own through a heavy wash of rain. Inside, people who have everything are sleeping peacefully, like I once did. I let the car roll down the hill to the closed pizza restaurant and the supermarket next to it and sit a while in the parking lot, my tears falling as fast as the rain, trying to clear my thoughts. I know now for sure that I will do anything, anything at all, to get my child back.

I start the car again and head onto the empty road to the Vesterøya peninsula. I pass the international school by the water, where I used to dream of sending Lucia. She'd grow up into a confident, multilingual, sporty girl with lots of friends, or so I thought. Now I dream of her being alive; that's my only ambition for her. I pass Asnes but refuse a glance up at the big house on the rocky promontory, the last place I saw my daughter, doing cartwheels, laughing until she ran out of breath.

I drive on until the road comes to an end at the nature trail. I switch off the engine and sit a while looking at the rain-lashed sea through a web of tree branches. In my mind, *he* is there, clear as day, like I knew he would be if only I'd let myself go to him. I replay the moments that are seared into my heart, the ones I shut away in a little box, never to be brought out into the light. I bring them out now. The way he cradled my face in his hands, his thumbs digging into the grooves underneath my jaw. The way his eyes implored me. 'Forever,' he said. '*Forever.*' Could he have lied to me? No, it's not possible. And yet, anything at all is possible.

My thoughts keep returning to the past, brushing across painful memories like a hand moving fast through a flame. The two events are entirely separate; there is nothing at all to connect them. Nothing. The only way that what happened to Lucia could in any way be connected to what happened in Lillehammer is if my love has betrayed me.

Just the thought of it makes my insides harden. A chill chases up my spine. I need to know. I start the car's engine and the fog lights slice into the darkness surrounding me.

59

Lucia

'*Bonjour*,' says Maman, holding my hand gently between both her hands.

'*Bonjour*,' I say, and smile. She is holding Boulette on her lap and Boulette sticks her tongue out, trying to make it stretch far enough to lick my face.

'Are you ready?' asks Maman. I nod and get up and we go into Josie's room.

'*Bonjour*,' says Maman. It's still dark in the mornings when we get up at six, so we light the candles to go downstairs.

'Today is a very special day,' says Maman, placing the bread rolls on our plates while I fill our glasses with apple juice. 'It's Daddy's birthday.'

'In heaven,' says Josie.

'Yes.' And her eyes fill with tears like they always do when she thinks about Daddy. 'Let's take a moment to think about Daddy, okay?'

I don't remember anything about my daddy, only the pappa in The Other Family, and Maman knows this. *Your heart remembers*, she always says, *even when your head cannot.*

Josie and I close our eyes and I try to picture Daddy. I've seen so many pictures, so I know what he looks like, but I can't really see him in my head if I don't have a picture in front of me. I know that he was handsome and very kind and strong enough to lift me high on one arm and Josie on the other.

In the car to school, Josie asks a question I've been thinking about too.

'When is Antoine coming back?'

'I don't know that he is coming back,' says Maman. 'He just helped Boulette get settled and she's getting big now, so there's no real need for him to come back anymore.'

'But he's your boyfriend,' says Josie, and I want to laugh because I know it's true, but maybe Maman doesn't know that we know that.

'Of course he's not my boyfriend.'

'But he stays at our house in the night.'

'Enough, Josiane. Look, he's a friend, in a way. But I don't think we'll be spending any more time together. If I ever do get a boyfriend, I'll be sure to let you know, okay?' She looks at us in the mirror and from the look in her eyes I can tell this conversation is over. 'Tonight we're going to celebrate Daddy.'

It's Friday and our first lesson is *les arts plastiques*, my favorite. I love art. We can make things with scrap bits of paper from Monsieur Duchêne's enormous crate of supplies. He pretends like the crate is a bank safe and that the only way to get stuff out of it is by saying the magic word.

'*Le mot magique*,' he'll say, bending down to our height, and cupping his ear.

And we whisper, 'Fandango.' I don't know why, but it always makes us laugh.

Today, I sit next to Noémie, and Monsieur Duchêne says we can make whatever we want for the first half hour.

'I'm going to make a spaceship from Q-tips,' says Gabin, but what he really means is that he will stick them up his nose, because that's what he does every week.

'No Q-tips for you,' says Monsieur Duchêne.

I decide to make a card for Daddy and I choose three sheets of cardboard: one blue, one green and one gold.

'It's my daddy's birthday,' I say to Noémie.

'Your daddy's dead,' she says.

'Yeah, but it's still his birthday.'

'No, it's not.'

'Yeah it is.'

'Not if he's dead. Birthday is the day you became alive, so they only count when you're alive.'

'*Mesdemoiselles*,' says Monsieur Duchêne, 'stop the chattering, please.'

I feel angry and my hand shakes when I try to cut the cardboard pieces so they fit on top of each other. I'm going to glue them together and cut out bits so it looks like a 3D picture. I've seen cards like that before. I look up and stare at Noémie, but she is painting an ugly flower, her tongue stuck out like a dog's. She notices me looking and stares back.

'Besides, I have two daddies,' I say. 'And my other daddy's birthday is at Christmas, like Jesus, and he's still alive.'

'Lulu-Rose! Quiet!'

I carry on cutting the cardboard, concentrating really

hard to stop my hand from shaking, and when I look up again after a long time, Josie is staring at me, her face strange and maybe sad.

When the bell rings, I stand up quickly and hurry to get out of the room, but as I reach the door, Monsieur Duchêne says, 'Lulu-Rose, would you wait a minute.'

Again, I feel Josie looking at me, but I don't look back. When all the other kids have left the room, Monsieur Duchêne points to a chair in the front row.

'Lulu-Rose, we've talked about talking in class before.'

'Yes.'

'Don't worry about today. Class hadn't really started yet, so it's okay. But I wondered about what you said to Noémie about having two daddies.

Next to Monsieur Duchêne's head, on the wall, is a blob of purple paint, probably from when Gabin tried to turn on the light switch next to it. I stare at it and keep my face completely blank, like a doll's.

'I was joking,' I say and give him a smile.

'Joking?'

'Yes.'

'I thought it was funny to pretend like Jesus is my other daddy.'

'But that's not what you said. You said my other daddy's birthday is at Christmas, *like* Jesus.'

'Oh. I was joking anyway.'

Monsieur Duchêne, who is almost always joking, looks serious and strokes the side of his face with his hand. 'Is everything okay at home, Lulu-Rose?'

'Yes,' I say. This is The Truth.

'Look. I know that, uh, you and Josiane lost your father

some years ago. It is very difficult, sometimes, to understand why you feel sad about something. Sometimes it's easier to make it into a joke. Do you see what I mean?'

'Yes.'

'Perhaps it might be good for you and Josiane to have someone to speak to about it.'

'We speak to Maman. We can speak to Maman about anything in the world.'

'Sometimes it can be very useful to speak to someone outside of your own family, someone who doesn't themselves have feelings about what has happened. Do you understand?'

I nod.

'I think it might be a good idea if I recommend this to your mother.'

'No!' I say, but it comes out like a shout. 'I mean, *I* can tell her that. You don't have to. It's best if you don't. She might get very sad. I will tell her.'

'That's not your job to worry about, Lulu-Rose.'

'Please, Monsieur, please don't tell her.'

Monsieur Duchêne nods, but he is still frowning, then he taps his watch and looks at the door, and I rush into the empty hallway, my heart banging in my chest like I've just been running.

In the car on the way home, Maman talks about how we are going to celebrate Daddy's birthday. Josie and me will bake him a cake, and we'll set his place at the table. He would have been forty today if he hadn't been killed. *Murdered,*

Maman calls it, which is a special kind of dead because it's someone's fault.

I go to the barn and feed Samba. Her pink lips nibble hungrily at my gloves, making me laugh, but when I come back inside the house, Maman's face is different from a few minutes ago. She looks very angry. I look around the kitchen for Josie and Boulette, but they're not here.

'How could you?' says Maman. I don't get a chance to say anything because Maman keeps talking. Or shouting, actually. 'Lulu-Rose, do you even understand how serious this is? Do you? You might have ruined everything! Everything! How could you?'

'I haven't—' I begin, but suddenly my throat feels blocked and I can't talk and my eyes begin to cry. Usually, if I cry, Maman gets sad too, and she tries to help me see that there's nothing to cry about. *Don't cry, my heart*, she says. *Mon coeur.* Now she just stands there, very close to me, her face in front of my face. Josie must have told her what I said to Noémie, even if she promised – no – swore, that she never, ever would.

'How do you think I feel when I receive a call from your school saying you've been telling your *entire class* that you have two daddies and only one of them has died?'

'I didn't—'

'Yes, you did. Don't you dare lie to me. We tell The Truth in this house, don't we?'

'Yes.' Maman always talks about The Truth and how we must always tell it. But sometimes I tell it and she says it's not The Truth. Like now.

'So how could you?'

'I think I forgot.'

'Forgot? Lulu-Rose, we have spoken about this, so many times! We can't forget! Remember? We can never forget! Because if we do, then what?'

'Bad things happen.'

'How bad?'

'Very bad.'

'How bad, Lulu-Rose?' She is still shouting, and my eyes are still crying.

'The little boy in The Other Family will die and Josie will die and I will go to the bad man's attic.'

'So why did you say something so stupid?'

'I'm sorry, Maman.'

'Sorry isn't enough! Go upstairs! I don't want to see you until tomorrow.'

'What about Daddy's birthday? And his cake?'

'You don't deserve a daddy like him after what you've said. Go! Just get out of my sight!'

In my bedroom I scream and hit the wall and I don't care if Maman hears me. I sit on my bed and punch the pillow as hard as I can and I imagine it's the bad man's face and the man with the attic house and Maman, even. When I get so tired I can't hit anymore, I take out the special paper I keep inside my math notebook, because nobody looks in it. I don't lie, I tell The Truth. On the paper I write down everything I know is The Truth. I write: 'I have two daddies and only one of them is dead.'

I wake in the night and Maman is sitting on my bed. She isn't holding my hand and she isn't saying *bonjour*, which is what she says every morning. I am afraid and I don't want to open my eyes. I pretend to turn in my sleep, smacking my lips and making tired sounds and then I turn towards the wall. I open my eyes and for a very, very long time I lie still, waiting for her to leave. It takes so long, I almost think she already has and I didn't notice her leaving, but then the weight shifts off the bed and she leans in to kiss me, its sound loud in my ear, like a slap.

60

Selma

'Murders Lillehammer', types Selma, sifting slowly through the results. In 2009, a man in his twenties was murdered by a woman in Lillehammer. The woman is still serving time for the crime. Selma pastes the link into her Word document. There were no murders in the county between 1992 and 2005, when an eighty-six-year-old woman was killed by her own son. Selma considers it unlikely that Elisa was involved in a murder, but could she have witnessed something that placed her in a precarious position? Or could she have been involved with another kind of crime, financial or sexual? She googles 'rape Lillehammer' and is taken aback by the hits that appear. In 2005 alone, three violent rapes were reported, and all the victims were women in their late teens or early twenties – seemingly random victims and of a similar age to Elisa at the time. In a town the size of Lillehammer, she would have likely known, or known of, at least one of them. In both 2004 and 2006 there were two rapes, of which two were linked to the town's 'drugs environment'.

She googles 'Lillehammer drugs-related crimes' and, again, many articles pop up. One, titled 'Notorious Drugs Gangs Unstoppable in Lillehammer?', outlines the town's persistent problems with 'teenage drugs culture' and affiliated crimes. According to NRK, the state broadcasting corporation, crime in Lillehammer is relatively rare, but some particularly brutal gangs operate drug-related networks, and most other crime is traced back to these environments. In the Word document, Selma writes 'Could Elisa have been involved in the drugs culture and for that reason have been disinherited by her pious parents?'

She suddenly feels overwhelmingly tired and just wants to drift off to sleep, Medusa's little body held close to her own, one hand clutching the smooth, warm moonstone. Still, she can't shake the feeling that she is missing a connection or some obvious fact that might link Lucia Blix's abduction to something in her mother's past. She blinks hard, trying to rid her eyes of the inevitable dryness after so many hours in front of the screen. She types 'fatal accidents Lillehammer' and skims through the long list. A seven-year-old boy was killed when he tripped and fell into the road in 2002; the male driver was absolved of all liability in this tragic accident. Two girls aged nineteen died on impact when their car hit a truck near the Fåvang exit on the E18 in 2008. A young man was sentenced to three years in prison for reckless driving that caused the death of an eighty-two-year-old pedestrian in 2010. A man and his two-year-old daughter died after being struck by a car in January 2012 on Birkebeinervegen on the outskirts of Lillehammer; the driver was under the influence and tried to flee and is currently in prison serving an unprecedented twelve-year sentence. Selma feels a dull ache in her stomach at the awful reading – so many lives, particularly young lives, cut short in a split second.

She clicks on the article about the little boy, and a photograph appears. A sweet, unremarkable boy with an unruly mop of blonde hair and a gap between his teeth. Petter Mikkelsrud, was his name. Petter – dead, aged seven. His parents are inconsolable after the incomprehensible accident, reads the article. She returns to the feed and clicks on the piece about the father and daughter. The man had been sledding in the woods on the eastern fringes of Lillehammer with his wife and two daughters when a car came hurtling around a bend in the road, slamming into the family. The father died on impact, his child in the ambulance on the way to hospital. The other little girl sustained non-life-threatening injuries, and the mother was unharmed. Selma tries to picture that poor woman, how she must have howled, her screams cutting the freezing January air, hollering through the bare winter forests. How does one survive something like that? She presses the 'Back' button, but as she does it, she notices the article below the one she had just read. Its headline is 'Drunk Driver of Birkebeinervegen Tragedy Launches Appeal from Tollebu Prison After 7 Years Inside' and the article is dated just two days ago. *Jesus*, thinks Selma. *Asshole. Driving under the influence and killing an innocent child and her father.* She can't think of anything more selfish.

She closes her Mac and lies on the bed for a while, tickling Medusa's tummy, making her purr loudly, closing her eyes. There's no point doing any more research tonight: it's almost midnight and her head is spinning. Tomorrow she'll go through all her notes and investigate each point further.

After cleaning her teeth, she gets into bed and closes her eyes, expecting the strong pull of sleep immediately carrying her away. Instead, the thoughts just keep coming, one leading to the next, as though they are being fired at her.

61

Elisa

I come downstairs just before eight. Fredrik is standing by the refrigerator, drinking milk straight from the carton. Once, I would have told him off, but those days are long gone. We avoid each other's eyes, and I welcome the loud screech of the milk foamer on the espresso machine.

'I'm leaving in a minute,' I say, pouring the milk into a takeaway coffee mug then adding three shots of espresso.

'Where are you going?'

'Stepping in for a colleague. Trude. Rome and back. The return is into Oslo Airport, so I might crash at the staff hotel.'

'Wait, I don't understand. Elisa, we need to talk.'

'You know, I had a great drive last night and I got some proper thinking done. You're absolutely right,' I continue, keeping my voice light and even, 'we mustn't drive ourselves crazy with what-if scenarios. We need to let the police do their jobs.'

'Umm,' says Fredrik, staring at me as though trying to glean the subtext from my expression.

'She's alive, honey. We just need to keep hope alive. She's coming home – I know that.' I make myself smile at my husband, and he smiles back, relieved.

Turning away from him, I briefly think about all the little lies and untruths and omissions that pass between a husband and a wife over the course of a marriage. All the little betrayals. And the big ones. For some reason, Karoline Meister pops into my head, her last words to Fredrik as clear in my mind as though they'd been spoken out loud. *Enjoy your little life while you still have it, asshole.*

Once I'm outside the house, I allow my cool control to crumble again. My heart is racing and tears run down my cheeks, dripping off my chin and onto my light jeans. I drive faster than I should, taking the E18 to Oslo, then the E6 through the web of tunnels leading out of the capital to the east. Soon I will know if I've been betrayed.

'I would give my life to undo what has happened,' he wrote. 'Forgive me.' When I first read his letter, just weeks after Lucia was taken, I couldn't process it at all. I crushed it into a dense ball in my hand and made myself forget about it. I was in no state to be thinking about *him*. But why did he ask for forgiveness? 'What have you done?' I whisper out loud, steeling myself for what's coming.

I drive fast on the E6 but hit heavy traffic near Oslo Airport; there's been an accident. I find it hard to sit still as the car crawls along the tarmac past police tape, my fingers drumming nervously on the wheel. I follow the trajectory of a jet on its final approach, and it occurs to me that in this moment no one in the world knows where I am. I am obviously not headed to Rome.

My thoughts still feel jumbled and chaotic, like I can't

quite grasp the sequence of steps I have to take to fix this mess.

This could all be in my head. Karo-Line and karma and the notion that the past is suddenly coming for me – it's not real. *It isn't real, Elisa.* Remorse, yes. Shame, yes. Heartbreaking regret, every moment of every day. But that is all it is, and it could well be playing tricks with my mind.

The traffic starts moving again and I urge the car back to ninety, tears streaming down my face. Most likely, I've got this all wrong. I just need to be sure.

62

Selma

The train ride, which should have taken three hours, is delayed due to an accident near Oslo Airport. Selma is not a patient person at the best of times, but she feels especially restless today because what she's doing is unorthodox, even for her. She taps her fingers to an imaginary beat against her jeans-clad thigh and stares at a big patch of dirty, leftover snow in a field. A large jet drops out of the low-hanging charcoal clouds, wobbling visibly in the wind as it lowers itself towards the runway. Its tailfin is green and bears the gold-feather logo of Nordic Wings. Selma wonders if Elisa Blix could be on it, leaning her head back against the jump seat, perhaps counting down the final approach in her head.

She avoids the eye of the man sitting across from her. She's noticed him staring at her and she can't think of anything less appealing than making stilted small talk with a stranger on a train. She pulls her phone out and decides to do some more research on Lillehammer. The town is located on the shores of Mjøsa, Norway's largest lake. Selma vaguely recalls a school trip when she must have still been in primary school, where they went on an old steam ship on Mjøsa. Scrolling down, she comes across a photograph of the same ship, *Skibladner*, and smiles to herself. The man sitting across from her must have thought the smile was intended for him, because when she randomly glances up at him, he is beaming at her, and she immediately drops her eyes back to the screen. The town has a population of just 26,000, so it's significantly smaller than Drammen, where she grew up, but it's substantially better known, not only as one of Norway's oldest ski resorts but also on account of its outdoor museum of traditional homes, Maihaugen, which is among the most important in Europe, apparently. Lillehammer also has a 'well-preserved and historically important center with charming wooden buildings', according to its tourist office. The perfect destination for a day trip, thinks Selma as the train starts up again.

The town is indeed quaint, Selma decides as she walks out of Lillehammer station and up a quiet main road that peters out into a totally silent suburban avenue. It's also unremarkable. The few people she sees look healthy and relaxed, as though they've wandered down into the town from the surrounding mountains. Nothing on their faces speaks of the tragedies, secrets and sorrows that Selma knows simmer and burn underneath the surface. Like everywhere else, Lillehammer harbors unresolved cases and as-yet undiscovered criminals. She might pass someone on the street who knows Elisa Blix, she thinks. It's quite likely, in fact, considering Lillehammer's modest size. She might pass someone who's committed murder. She might even pass someone who knows exactly where Lucia Blix is, someone who could solve the case by making a single phone call but chooses not to.

She comes to a large Meny food shop and stops for a Coke Zero and a ham and cheese baguette. She's not so much hungry as nervous. She eats propped against a rain-soaked bench, drawing her jacket tight around herself – it's significantly colder here than it was in Oslo. From where she's standing, she can see a part of the big ski area on the hillside across the lake, and she can make out a snow scooter heading up to the crest of the hill, though she knows that the resort closed for the season the previous weekend.

Kari Samuelsen lives just behind Meny in an unremarkable red bungalow on a cul-de-sac of similar houses. Selma stands for a brief moment looking down the empty street before she walks up to the front door, imagining Elisa as a child, playing on this same street with her brother and sister. Her heart thuds as she presses the doorbell, setting off a shrill chime inside the house. There's no sign of anyone being at home, though an old Volvo is parked in front of the garage. Then a movement catches Selma's eye – the slightest twitch of a net curtain in the window to the left of the door. She acts as though she hasn't noticed but angles herself slightly towards the window, making her expression friendly and open so that whoever is behind it can see her clearly and will hopefully understand that she means no harm.

Nothing happens, so she rings the bell again. 'Kari?' she shouts at the closed door. 'I'm Selma.'

She has already turned to leave when she hears the sound of the door unlocking. It opens a crack and Selma can make out a hand holding a metal door chain on the inside.

'Hi,' she says. 'I was hoping we could talk. I've come all the way from Oslo to speak with you.'

'What do you want?' The woman's voice is flat and without any trace of emotion.

'Could I please come in?' She's bracing herself for the woman to say no, but the hand fumbles with the security chain and then the door is opened.

The woman in front of her is relatively young, in her mid-fifties most likely, but appears much older with her stern grey halo of curls and scrubbed, raw-looking face. Glancing at her hands, which are also very red and flaky in patches, Selma realizes she has some kind of skin condition. She's wearing an old-fashioned pale green housedress and orthopedic slip-on leather sandals. Over the top she's wearing an apron smeared with what appears to be tomato sauce. Her eyes are dark, like Elisa's, and hooded with heavy eyelids, not unlike Selma's. Her lips are thin and clamped shut. She stands with her arms crossed and waits for Selma to speak.

'I'm working on an article...' begins Selma, but as soon as she says 'article' the woman's expression grows even more forbidding and she begins to close the door.

'No, Mrs Samuelsen, please – wait. This isn't what you think. I just want to help find Lucia Blix. Please let me speak to you.'

'No,' she hisses.

'Why not?'

'I don't even know the girl. And I won't have my family's dirty laundry aired in your amoral press stories. My husband would turn in his grave, Jehovah bless him.' She crosses herself quickly.

Selma notices that Kari's gaze is drawn to something behind her. She glances around and sees a man and a woman emerge from the house next door, hands raised in a little wave.

'Can we talk about why your oldest daughter is estranged from your family?' asks Selma, almost loud enough for the neighbors to hear.

Kari Samuelsen looks as though she's been slapped in the face, precisely the reaction Selma had been hoping for. A large, strong hand reaches out and grabs Selma's wrist.

'Yes, come in, my dear,' says Kari in a strange singsong voice. She waves at the neighbors, her eyes shooting daggers at Selma, and closes the door behind them.

Selma finds herself in a sparse, unfussy hallway. There are two pairs of sensible brown leather shoes tucked away underneath a wooden chair, a hook with several sets of keys on it, and an old-fashioned landline phone mounted to the wall. She imagines Kari Samuelsen sitting on the chair, her thick fingers stabbing at the dial. Does she ever pick up the phone wanting to call Elisa?

'What do you want?' asks Kari, her voice barely concealing a furious tremble.

'I'm sorry for showing up unannounced, but I wanted to speak with you because I am trying to look at the abduction of your granddaughter in a slightly different way. I know you'll be extremely familiar with the case, but—'

'I am not familiar with the case,' says Kari Samuelsen, nodding briefly after Selma has slipped off her Adidas Superstars next to the chair. She turns around and walks into the next room, which is a clean, plain, pinewood kitchen. It has a table and two chairs, but there's nothing on the table, not even a little flower or a saltshaker. Looking around, Selma notes there aren't any ornaments or decorations on the walls either. It's as though the woman is allergic to personal expression in her home.

Kari Samuelsen indicates to one of the chairs and sits down on the other, pulling it forward so that they are strangely close to one another, their knees almost touching. Selma suddenly feels overwhelmed and uncomfortable, as though all of her bravado in coming here and ringing Elisa's mother's doorbell has instantly evaporated.

'Let me tell you something,' says Kari, fixing Selma with her unusually dark eyes, which are like little buttons sewn onto the face of a teddy bear, too close together. 'You have some serious nerve, just turning up here like this. You're young, I get it, you're hungry for a scoop, but there are laws in this country – anti-harassment laws. Though I don't expect you've heard of such a thing?'

'I just thought…'

'You thought what? That because Elisa Blix is my daughter, I'd want to talk to you?'

'Look, I know that Elisa is estranged from the Samuelsen family, and—'

'How do you know this?'

'Elisa told me herself.' Selma is good at thinking on her feet, and a white lie never hurt anybody.

'Oh, is that right? Did she tell you that I have never met her youngest child? Did she tell you that that little girl means no more to me than any other little girl snatched off the street? Did she tell you that she comes from a family that not only believes but *knows* that God's will is just, always just, and only ever just?' Selma's mouth has dropped open in shock at the tirade, and she feels real sympathy for Elisa having grown up with this woman as her mother. *Better to have no mother*, she thinks, though this thought is followed by a hot flush of shame.

'I'm sorry... I don't think I quite understand.'

'Some people question God's will when they should perhaps take a long hard look in the mirror.'

'What... what do you mean?'

'Why don't you ask your friend Elisa. Ask her what she did to her own father, who did nothing but love and cherish her.' Kari practically spits her daughter's name out. 'Now, I'd like you to leave.'

'But... but whatever Elisa did, surely you don't mean that a little girl deserved to be abducted?'

'I'm not talking about the child. I'm talking about adults of dubious morals getting what they deserve.'

Kari has stood up and is staring at Selma, waiting for her to do the same. Selma gets up slowly and follows Kari back towards the entrance hall.

'Don't you think Elisa deserves your support, no matter how immoral you judge her to be? She's going through a lot, and she is your daughter, after all.'

Kari stares at her, an astonished expression temporarily making her coarse features bland. Then she begins to laugh. A horrible, mocking laugh that brings on a coughing fit.

Selma's fingers fumble with her shoelaces as she tries to block out the disgusting guttural noises. The woman's ruddy, angry face will haunt her for a long while yet, she's sure of that. But as she stands back up to leave, she's stunned to see that Kari is crying now, her face twisted in a grimace, her eyes blurred with tears. Selma opens her mouth to ask again, but decides against it. Nothing about this visit has gone as she hoped, and all she wants is to be back outside, away from this odd, plain house and the mean woman. She opens the door and inhales the rush of fresh, cold air deep into her lungs. She turns back around on the doorstep to say sorry, or goodbye, but the door is slammed shut in her face.

Selma was right about Kari Samuelsen's face haunting her. She walks fast to the station, though her train back to Oslo doesn't leave for another two hours, and she keeps picturing the woman's livid red cheeks and the wildness of her expression when she spoke of God's will and how it is always just. What did she even mean by that? That Lucia being taken was some kind of divine justice or payback for whatever lifestyle Elisa had chosen in the face of her parents' violent opposition? Could it be that Selma was on the right track with the idea that Elisa might have been involved somehow with Lillehammer's drug gangs? Either way, she feels another surge of sympathy for Elisa; it must have been hard, growing up in that quiet, hostile house. She feels bad, too, about having asked Elisa whether it was possible that someone hated her – how was she to know that she had a mother like that. No wonder Elisa looked hurt at the question. Selma had no idea that women like Kari Samuelsen still existed in Norway in 2019.

She looks around, trying to decide what to do until her train leaves. She could walk around for a while, getting a feel for the place. The weather has improved since the dreary drizzly cold of this morning – and the sky is now mostly blue with patches of wispy white cloud. She heads down the pedestrianized main street, slowing down to look into the windows of the familiar chain stores: Nille, G-Sport, Cubus, Peppes Pizza. She sits down on a bench, eats a chocolate-chip cookie from 7-Eleven and watches people meandering slowly past. Everything seems less rushed here than in Oslo. There are groups of gangly teenage girls, skinny legs in Bik Bok tights, phones clutched in their hands, chewing gum and chattering loudly. There are old people, walking leisurely along. There are families, lots of families: normal-looking, unremarkable mothers and fathers, with big boys and small girls and big girls and little boys.

Selma's thoughts return to the strange meeting with Elisa's mother. It never ceases to amaze her how different families can be from how they seem. Growing up, Selma always felt different, growing up with a single dad and as an only child. She might as well have had 'odd' written on her forehead, judging by the way the other kids treated her in school. She craved a 'normal' family – a mother and a father, siblings and maybe a little dog. 'A *real* family,' she used to say to her father in her teens, if she wanted to really hurt him. She feels ashamed, thinking about it now. She knows now that there are no normal families and that every family is as real as the next, no matter the constellation. And she knows that it is most definitely possible to grow up in a family with a mother, a father and a couple of siblings and have crazy, disturbing things happen behind closed doors. The question is, what happened behind the Blix family's doors?

A chill has crept into Selma's bones; she needs to keep moving before her teeth start chattering. She walks back down towards the station, stopping to take a picture on her

phone of the iconic Olympic rings painted on the ground
– Lillehammer is fiercely proud of hosting the Winter
Olympics in 1994, the single biggest event Norway has ever
seen. She catches a glimpse of the lake further down the hill
from the station and decides to walk down for a look – she
still has more than an hour until the train.

There's a large park beside the lakeshore, as well as a
beach promenade. *It must be nice here in summer*, thinks
Selma. She passes a garage with an unseasonal sign reading
'Cheapest Winter Tire Change in Lillehammer', and a
garden center. Everything feels so intensely normal – people
driving places without urgency, people buying dinner in the
shops, people walking home with their kids after school
– and yet, this town, like every other town, is marred by
tragedy. Selma thinks about the two nineteen-year-olds
she read about, killed when they drove into the truck by
the Fåvang exit. What were they doing in the last seconds
before impact? Selma has a mental image of them laughing,
moving their shoulders in sync in a little dance to loud music
blasting from the stereo, chunks of chewing gum shuffled
around their mouths so they could sing the lyrics. Young
hands loosely holding the steering wheel, wrists clogged
with bangles and hair ties and ribbons. Foot too eager on
the gas, the truck too close, the hand on the wheel a fraction
too slow, the sound of metal splintering too loud, too loud.

Selma glances up at Lillehammer High-Security Prison,
sitting high above the town on a hill. *Funny that they decided
to give prisoners the best views in town*, she thinks. She
remembers the man appealing his case for killing the father
and daughter. 'An unprecedented twelve-year sentence', the
article said. She pulls up Google on her phone and types in

'Lillehammer father and daughter killed by driver under the influence'. There are several hundred hits, and she clicks on one from February 2012, from *VG*.

Marcus Meling has been identified as the driver of the vehicle that plunged into a family in Lillehammer on the evening of 27 January, killing a thirty-three-year-old man and a two-year-old girl.

Meling is pleading guilty to manslaughter and driving under the influence, as well as attempting to avoid law enforcement. His hearing is at Lillehammer Court tomorrow.

Meling is known to many as the multimillionaire founder and CEO of tech firm iNovo and is a resident of Oslo. Little is known of Meling's victims as their identities have yet to be released.

Meling was significantly over the limit when he was arrested.

Selma returns to Google and types in 'Marcus Meling'. She is about to scroll through the results when her phone starts ringing.

63

Elisa

Everything happened because I fell in love. So very deeply in love. It hit me like a tornado, a white heat, this instant surrender to a stranger. It grew into me, became a part of my insides. It was outshone only by my children. Still, it burns in me. And every day I am reminded that women like me don't deserve men like Fredrik. Women like me don't deserve a son like Lyder and a daughter like Lucia.

I indicate and exit the E6, and Lillehammer comes into view ahead. I opt for the smaller district road that bypasses my hometown; there's no need to save five minutes if I can avoid the place altogether. Seven years and three months, that's how long it's been. At least today is bright, the scent of thawed snow and last year's decay drifting down from the mountains that tower over the road as it meanders into the hills east of Lillehammer. I roll down my window and stop for a moment in a layby, looking down at Lillehammer in the valley, the windows of the houses reflecting the sharp sunlight like pebbles in a rock pool.

Down there somewhere is my mother. My sister and

brother, too. Nieces and a nephew I've never met. Further on, the road I'm on peters out into a long gravel track, and at its end is Tollebu Prison.

I drive through a little copse where vast patches of bluebells carpet the forest floor, then a series of buildings become visible in front of me. There's a large main house which looks more like a mountain hotel than a correctional facility and a series of smaller buildings set around it in a semicircle.

I close my eyes for a long moment. I try to still my racing heart. I take a few deep breaths and gently rub the still sore scab on my thumb. I read somewhere that rubbing the spot between your thumb and your index finger sends calming signals to the brain and makes you feel like someone is taking care of you. I think about when Lucia was a baby, how I used to stare at her for hours. Her sleeping face with all its odd little expressions, her tiny clenched fists, the wispy white hair covering her pink skull, her sheer beauty – I was awestruck by her. She was just pure love. I wanted to do right by her. And doing right by Lucia, and then Lyder, meant growing up. It meant getting real and getting serious. It meant watching my heart splinter into shards.

64

Marcus

After two years he was moved from Lillehammer High-Security Prison to Tollebu. Many freedoms were returned to him, such as the right to speak on the phone whenever and with whomever he pleases, though any conversation may be listened to. He is allowed visitors any time during visiting hours. No one ever comes. In addition to being allowed to go to the timber yard twice a week to work, he's also permitted once a month to run errands in Lillehammer, accompanied by two plainclothes guides. On these occasions, Marcus wanders down the streets, stopping every so often for a leisurely look in a shop window or to pop into a 7-Eleven for a bacon hot dog with chili sauce. At the beginning, he worried about these outings, and specifically the risk of being seen by the woman whose life he had destroyed. Back then, he wouldn't have known her if he passed her on the street – she'd never spoken to the press and had remained anonymous – but she would have known him. His identity was splashed across the media after he pleaded guilty to manslaughter.

How terrible it would be for her, he thought, if she happened to walk into a shop only to come face to face with him. He mentioned his fears to one of his guides once, but the guide told him he had nothing to worry about because the victims' next of kin were always informed before every such excursion. It then occurred to him that instead of making every effort to avoid him, she might roam the streets of the little town until she found him, perhaps browsing the aisles at H&M like a normal guy on a Saturday afternoon shopping spree, and drive a knife into him. Marcus imagines that's what he'd want to do, if the tables were turned.

Then, the widow came to see him at Tollebu.

Now, Marcus gets up from the desk and stands a while by the window. It's a brilliant spring day and the forest beckons him with its vibrant new life after the long winter. He can evoke its smell even though the window is closed: moss, water, wildflowers.

There's a knock at the door.

'Hi, Marcus,' says Pål, one of the guides. 'There's no cause for alarm. It's just, you have a visitor.'

'A visitor?'

'Yes. She's in reception.'

Pål winks at him, but Marcus frowns as he kicks off his slippers and pushes his feet into his trainers. He doesn't get visitors. In fact, this is only the second time in all the years he's been at Tollebu. *She*, Pål said. Could it be...? *No*, he tells himself, *that would be impossible*. But still, a sliver of hope stirs within him.

65

Selma

'Hey there, Selma,' says Olav. 'Just returning your call.'
She turns her back to the wind and cups the
mouthpiece. 'Hey. You'll never guess where I am.'

'Locked in Fredrik and Elisa Blix's basement?'

'Ha ha, very funny.'

'Sorry, that was wrong.'

'On so many levels.'

'So, where are you? And what have you got?'

'I just met with Elisa Blix's mother.'

'Ah. And?'

'Get this, Olav – Elisa is estranged from her entire family.
They are strict Jehovah's Witnesses and she hasn't been in
touch with them since before 2012, when her father died.'

'Hm. How come?'

'I don't know why. The mother is the most bizarre
woman. Seriously, I've never met anyone like her. I got a
really bad feeling.'

'What kind of bad feeling, Selma?'

'Well, she didn't seem at all affected by the fact that

her own granddaughter has been kidnapped, presumed murdered, by a trafficking network. That in itself is pretty damn weird.'

'Yep. Weird.'

'I mean, she even said that Lucia meant no more to her than any other randomly abducted child.'

'Hm.'

'She also insinuated that Elisa isn't as squeaky clean as she seems.'

'In what way?'

'Not sure. She shut the door in my face – literally. But there is something there, I can feel it. She's been involved in something bad enough to cost her her relationship with her parents, and I'm convinced it's linked to Lucia's disappearance.'

'Have you seen the news?'

'Just quickly scrolled through. Why?'

'Nothing major, but Scotland Yard mentioned Lucia's case earlier today, saying there's no evidence she died in Sainte-Ode other than the blood traces and the tipoff, and that it's important to remain open to all possible scenarios. So, you keep digging, Eriksen. It's not going to hurt, either way.'

'Okay. I'm hoping Elisa will talk to me again. It didn't go that well last time – maybe I pushed her too far.'

'Knowing you, I'm sure she'll talk to you. The question is whether you're barking up the wrong tree. Time will tell.'

'I don't think I am.'

'So, Selma, you mentioned you were going to bring me some other juicy stuff, too. What have you got? Or have things been a little, uh, one-track?' Olav laughs, though not meanly. Selma has always seen him as a bit of an older brother figure.

She's started walking back up towards the train station and just as she's about to go through the pedestrian tunnel under the tracks, she glances up at Lillehammer High-Security Prison. 'Actually, there is a case I'm looking into. You might be interested. Have you heard of Marcus Meling?'

'No, I don't think so. Why?'

'He's the founder of iNovo. You know them? Made it big in app development a decade ago.'

'Ah. Yeah.'

'He's been in prison for years, serving a long sentence for double manslaughter.'

'Okay...?'

'He's just launched an appeal. I thought I might try to look into his case.'

'Why?'

'There's something weird about it.'

'Weird how?'

'Well, first of all, he was way over the limit and hit a family out sledding, killing the father and one of the children.'

'Jesus Christ.'

'Yeah. So far, so awful, right? What I find weird about it, though, is that Meling had no previous convictions, no known substance addictions and no reason to be in Lillehammer. He lived in Oslo and was a multimillionaire and philanthropist with everything to lose. So why would he be by himself in a random town far from home, driving too fast on icy roads, under the influence? It makes no sense.'

'Yeah, that is weird.'

'He got twelve years, which is the longest sentence being served for manslaughter in Norway. He refused to divulge his reasons for being there on that road and he refused to cooperate with the investigation, which is why he got such a long sentence.'

'All right, well, have a poke around and keep me posted.'

Selma presses 'End call' and walks across the parking lot to the station, where her train is scheduled to leave in ten minutes. At the other end of the lot is First Hotel Breiseth, a charming Jugendstil building with little towers flanking its sides. What if she were to stay in town and probe a little further? Medusa has enough food and water in her bowls and most likely won't care if Selma returns today or not. She could spend the evening on her laptop doing some more research and tomorrow she could try to get Kari Samuelsen to speak to her again, or perhaps Elisa's sister, Elin. She can get in touch with Marcus Meling's prison officers, and perhaps she can interview him, too. It would be like a little holiday.

Selma goes into the hotel and stands a moment admiring the giant chandelier that hovers low over the reception area like a spaceship about to land on a newly discovered planet. She feels a deep thrill in the pit of her stomach to be here, in Lillehammer, alone.

66

Elisa

The drive takes over five hours and when I finally pull up in front of our house, it's almost ten. The light is off in our bedroom upstairs. I don't know how I can do what I have to do – wash my face and clean my teeth and lie down next to my husband. But I don't want to lose even more of this life; I want to piece it back together, and I will pay almost any price for it. I want it to be Fredrik and me and Lucia and Lyder again, and forever. It worked on so many levels, and no family is perfect.

There's a light tap on the car window. Fredrik must have heard me pull up and now he's standing outside in the tatty grey T-shirt and stripy pajama bottoms he sleeps in. In spite of everything that happened today, I feel a rush of affection for him and step into his embrace.

'How was Rome?' he asks.

'Oh, you know Rome. It was fine. Airport life, huh?'

'What was the weather like?'

I pull back slowly and look at Fredrik, keeping a neutral expression, trying to gage whether he is innocently interested in the Roman weather or if he is suspicious of something. My heart is thundering wildly in my chest.

'It was normal Rome weather. Slightly overcast, mild.'

He nods and turns to walk back inside the house. Before he goes upstairs, he says, 'Don't forget that we have a meeting with Kripos in Oslo on Friday.'

A lot needs to happen between now and then.

Fredrik goes up to bed, tense and exhausted, and the night is mine. Before he went up, I smiled at him, rubbed his arm. He blinked, perplexed, like this morning. It's as if he doesn't quite trust my words or my actions. I wonder if he thinks I will divorce him eventually. But what I want is the exact opposite. I want my child back and I want to live in this house with my family. In the years after I had Lyder everything went to hell, but I got used to pretending, and it got easier and easier until it became real: I was a happily married wife and mother of two.

Now, in the early hours, my head is beginning to clear. I sit down to do some research. I need to get all the facts straight before I speak to Fredrik and the police. The only way to get my life back is to face the past. I just need to tweak it a little.

67

Lucia

It's a Wednesday and that means we come home from school on a bus before lunch. It drops us off at the bottom of the hill and Monsieur Chabanne waves at us and then Maman picks us up from there. But today she doesn't come.

'She'll be here soon,' says Josie and I nod.

We wait and a few cars drive past. We wait some more, but it's cold and we get tired of the little word games we play.

'Want to play Funky Lady?' asks Josie, but I shake my head.

I think about the other night when Maman came to my bedroom. Even after she left, I couldn't sleep and when I was sure she wouldn't come back I got out of bed and stood by the window looking out. I remembered the first night at Le Tachoué and the way Maman held me close when I screamed. I was afraid then because I didn't know The Truth. But what if The Truth isn't The Truth for real? Adults aren't allowed to lie, but sometimes they do it anyway.

'She isn't coming,' says Josie.

'We could walk,' I say.

Josie looks afraid and probably so do I because it's very far to get home. If we follow the road, we'll get to a row of stone houses, but only two of them are lived in by people. In one of them lives François, a shepherd. We only meet him when we play down at the bottom of Le Tachoué, by the river, because his property begins on the other bank and we aren't allowed to cross the river. After François' stone house we'll have to walk up the track for a long time, and then there's a very small road full of mud and potholes which leads to our house.

'We could go through the woods,' I say. It's a better idea, because it's shorter.

Josie stares at me like it's a crazy thing to do, but she follows when I start to walk. The nice thing about having a twin sister is that there is always someone to play with and someone who helps you. Many other children go home after school and then they're on their own. That doesn't happen to me because me and Josie are always together. It wasn't always like that, but now I don't remember it that well anymore. I remember The Other People, but it's like Josie must have been there too, because I can't totally remember not having her. I know she wasn't, but maybe when I lived with The Other People I remembered deep down that I'm a twin even if I'd forgotten many things. Twins are special and can feel things other people can't feel.

Anyway, I can't remember it all now. Josie went to live with Other People too because Maman had to live in a hospital for a long time. Her heart was sick. It's because of what happened to our dad. He was killed and we were almost killed too, that's why Josie has a big scar on her cheek, and it's why my head hurts sometimes and I can't remember stuff, like all the French verbs. It was so hard for Maman that she had to go to the hospital to learn how to be happy again. When she came back out, Josie came back to her, but The Other People wouldn't give me back because they pretended I was theirs. So Maman had to take me.

It's The Truth.

It's very difficult walking up the hill inside the woods. It's warm now, but it isn't that long since big storms came and knocked trees over and made floods. We have to climb over trunks and brambles and lots of sticks piled on top of each other, and by the time we reach the river and the bottom of our fields, we are so tired we can't talk at all. Josie's foot slips on one of the stepping stones we use to cross the river and she hits her knee on a sharp rock. She's wet and bleeding and she's crying loudly. I tie a strap from my backpack around her leg with one of my socks underneath it to stop the blood. We keep walking, slowly, and I hope that soon we'll be able to see the house.

'Why didn't Maman come?' Josie cries loudly. 'What if she's dead, dead like Daddy?'

What if she *is* dead? I picture Maman on the stone floor of the hallway, dead, with lots of blood splattered around her. Or on the sofa, still and beautiful like Sleeping Beauty. If Maman died, what would happen to us? We wouldn't have anybody. Only each other and Boulette. Or... or maybe me and Josie could go and live with The Other People in that house and we'd have Lyder as a little brother and the mamma who wore a uniform with shiny gold buttons, and we'd have a daddy too.

'Why are *you* crying?' asks Josie.

'Because your knee hurts.'

This makes her laugh and cry at the same time. We rest on a tree stub and eat our snack, which today is some sliced apple and a yogurt.

'Let's take that shortcut,' I say.

'We can't,' says Josie. 'Maman says we aren't allowed.'

'But it's shorter. Come on!'

There's a path that cuts across the field that belongs to François and reaches Le Tachoué from the back. I've seen it from the bottom of the garden when I take Samba there to play. After François' top field the path goes straight through a very thick bit of forest and after that you're at Le Tachoué. We've never been in that part of the forest because Maman says we can't and that it's easy to get lost there, but we've walked around it on the outside, and it isn't very big, so I think we'll be okay.

We have to walk slowly because Josie's knee is still bleeding; it's gone through the sock and is running down the side of her leg like a muddy red-brown stream. We hold hands and go into the forest. It's true what Maman said – the forest is very thick here. The trees stand so close together that we have to squeeze past some of them to get through. Our feet catch on thick roots and we keep tripping over twigs and fallen branches, so it takes a long time to move forward. It's kind of exciting to be here among trees we don't know. In the forest at the top of the hill, where we usually play, we know all of the trees now, and I think I could find my way through it in the dark. But here everything is new. After a bit, the trees get more spaced out and I think we must be near our garden. Instead, the forest opens up like a kind of room and we're in a little clearing. It's like a bubble of air in the middle of all the trees.

Josie and I look at each other and step into the center of it.

'Woah,' she says.

'Yeah,' I say. 'Woah.'

She laughs, even though her leg must still hurt, and I laugh too. Now that we've discovered this place, we'll have to come back here to play. We just won't tell Maman.

We turn to leave, carrying on in the same direction we were going, when I notice something strange on the ground. It's a big stone, on its own, held snug by wild lavender, heather and moss. The stone looks like it's been brought there from somewhere else because it's clean and square. On it, letters have been carved and painted gold.

It says:

Rose Olve Thibault

21.01.2010 – 27.01.2012

'Come on,' says Josie. 'I'm scared.'

I'm scared too, because the stone is the kind of stone they give to dead people. We turn around and run and run.

68

Jacqueline

She hadn't planned on going all the way to Toulouse. After dropping the girls at school, she had intended to go to one of her usual haunts, Cybercafé Roc in Saint-Gaudens. But on the way there, driving through Salies-du-Salat, she felt an overwhelming sadness as she passed the turnoff to Antoine's street. She glanced down the Rue des Bains in the hope of catching a glimpse of him or his car, but the road was deserted, still glinting with the morning's rain. Potholes had filled with murky water and the asphalt had split in the recent storms, long cracks running along the tarmac. At the end of Antoine's road fields rolled out into the distance, swelling into hills, then mountains. In spite of her somber mood, Jacqueline had felt overwhelmed by the sheer beauty of it all and drew in the crisp air through her open window, denying herself the sight of Antoine's house in the rearview mirror as she turned the corner.

Four nights have passed since she last saw him, and she's spent each one of them lying motionless in bed, not even attempting sleep, her thoughts racing with frightening, intense images. On her mind have been Mikko, Nicolai, Antoine, her mother, Lulu-Rose, Mikko again, the future… Things seemed to be going well until Mikko came back, and then there was Lulu-Rose's strange behavior at school, and now her plans have suddenly become soured and hazy.

As she comes up to the big roundabout at Saint-Martory, a dull ache spreads through her stomach at the thought of the Cybercafé Roc's depressing mock-kitsch velour chairs, watery coffee, and shifty, leering customers who never hide their ogling. On a whim, she turns right for Toulouse instead of left for Saint-Gaudens.

The sun is reaching its zenith in the deep blue sky and she pulls down the eye shield and drops her speed as the industrial fringes of Toulouse give way to the more densely populated suburbs. She leaves behind the maze of flyovers circling the city, driving down unremarkable tree-lined boulevards with rundown apartment blocks and modest street-corner restaurants, their owners setting plastic tables and chairs out on the sidewalk for the lunch trade. Soon, the river appears in silver glimpses between the houses, which by now are the characteristic rose-hued buildings of the city center. The languid, shining Garonne slithers beneath the Pont Neuf as Jacqueline crosses the bridge in slow-moving traffic. She parks on the square behind the magnificent Basilique Saint-Sernin and stops to take a picture. She'll show it to the girls; it's a fine example of both Gothic and Renaissance architecture. She smiles at the thought of Lulu-Rose and Josiane peering seriously at her picture, leaning the phone against the saltshaker on the kitchen table, attempting to copy the intricate structure in their notebooks. They are both so eager to learn, and so eager to please her.

Jacqueline walks around the Place Saint-Sernin, considering a coffee in one of the sidewalk cafés, but decides against it – she feels restless and knows the caffeine would make it worse. She walks down the Rue du Taur towards Rue des Lois, where she's found an internet café on Google, stopping to peer at a nice pair of shoes and an original handbag in the display windows of a couple of the many charming independent shops. Tall brick houses stand across from each other, sheltering the narrow pedestrian street from the midday sun, which doesn't yet reach street level but makes the upper stories glow a golden pink.

'La Ville Rose'... Once, Toulouse, the Pink City, was her favorite place. Pink used to be her favorite color, too. Her favorite wine was rosé with a lump of ice, and of all the flowers she favored the rose, with its tightly held petals, distinctive pure scent and undeniable beauty. She named her child Rose for those reasons. She mostly avoids Toulouse now; she can't bear all the rose connotations, which are everywhere. Besides, she's embraced the quiet life at Le Tachoué and wouldn't risk taking the children to a big city. She's in no doubt that it's best for them to stay at home, where they know what to expect and who they are.

The internet place is much nicer than any of the others she's been to; it's a laundromat with an attached café. The other patrons are cool students with oiled beards and hipster jeans, eating smashed avocado on sourdough while their socks and pants spin in the washers next door. Jacqueline smiles at a couple of tattooed girls sipping kombucha while she edges past them to a free computer in the corner by the wall. What must they think of her, this much older, slightly tired-looking woman, hanging out in a place like this? Perhaps they think she's so old that she's only just figured out the internet and is contemplating whether or not to acquire her own computer. She smiles at the thought and orders an almond turmeric latte. Her low spirits begin to lift – it feels good, in this moment, to sit among young people in a big city, ordering things they would never have heard of in the remote huddled stone villages of the Pyrénes Ariégeoises.

It feels good, too, to have a moment's uncomplicated anonymity. Nobody here is watching her or seems particularly interested in her, unlike the villagers of Rivèrenert and Encourtiech, who never pass up a chance to engage in conversation. Still, she wouldn't change her life with the girls at Le Tachoué for the world. Coming home was the right thing to do, she knows that with every cell in her body. In fact, it was the realization of what Le Tachoué would enable her to pull off that made her decide to bring Lulu-Rose home in the first place. If she hadn't had access to a remote mountain farm with no near neighbors, how would she ever have set about creating such a life for Lulu-Rose? She would have had to keep her hidden somewhere, and the child would have suffered as a result. She pictures a moldy cellar somewhere, the child growing pale and ill, stumbling around in a confined space – what a contrast to the wild freedom the girls enjoy at Le Tachoué.

At Le Tachoué there is no phone signal, no landline and no internet. Their nearest neighbors, Monsieur Chabot and his three sons, who run an eco-farm four kilometers away as the crow flies, installed broadband last year and approached Jacqueline at the Carrefour in Saint-Girons to ask if she would like them to extend it around the crest of the hill to

Le Tachoué. But the kindly old man got his answer from the horrified look on Jacqueline's face.

She gets lonely sometimes at Le Tachoué, when the girls are in bed and the storms howl and chase frozen rain down the mountainsides, or in the summers, when the evenings are warm and violet, throbbing with life. She feels entirely alone with her thoughts then. In such moments, it would be nice to be able to do some mindless surfing, watch Netflix, get the news in real time instead of caught in snatches several days later, engage in some flirtatious chats, perhaps. Still, she doesn't want the girls to grow up with the pressures of social media or the potentially terrible influences on the internet. More than that, she doesn't want to be traceable in any way.

At the beginning, it was hard to live mostly cut off from the web, because in the years leading up to Lulu-Rose coming home, Jacqueline used the internet as much as, if not more than, most people. It was on the internet that she found the information she needed. How would she have been able to establish contact with Fredrik Blix had it not been for an attractive Facebook profile picture and a friend request? But now she's become used to her long, slow evenings spent catching up on reading; her grandparents' library is well stocked and Jacqueline has become an avid reader for the first time in her life. It keeps her mind off the things that still haven't been fixed, that can never be fixed, and puts her suffering in context, setting it against what humans have endured throughout the ages, immortalized in fiction. It makes her feel connected to humanity, to the world, and to her own grief, which she thinks of as vast, dark rooms inside her, never to be opened, like the room at the far end of the first floor at Le Tachoué that overlooks the meadows at the back of the house and the forest beyond.

She types 'Fredrik Blix' into Google. Even though it's been five years now, the images of Fredrik still unsettle and repulse Jacqueline. She underestimated him; she thought he'd be easier to win over. She made some big mistakes there – she used her own photos on the profile and had numerous video chats with him. She was lucky he didn't try and track her down or get the police involved – she'd be known to them then, her picture would be on file, and she'd never have got away with bringing Lulu-Rose to Le Tachoué. The whole mess of the Fredrik affair still bothers her sometimes, but back then she was still reeling and out of control. Had she approached him later, when she was emotionally and mentally in a better place to make a sound plan, it might have been a different story. Still, it worked out for the best.

She studies a recent photo of Fredrik, taken by a press photographer outside the house he shares with Elisa and their son. He is holding a hand up, seemingly to illustrate a point, or perhaps to stop the photographer from taking the picture. If her first plan had actually worked, he might have been her husband by now.

Jacqueline scours the various Norwegian newspapers for updates on the Blix case, but there is nothing new, only more farfetched speculation as to where Lucia's body might be buried. *Good*, she thinks, finishing the turmeric latte and gazing out the tall windows at the beautiful golden light so particular to Toulouse. She does something she mostly manages to resist: she googles 'Elisa Blix'. And then she is faced with her – the woman she hates more than anything in the world. They never subside, the waves of hatred Jacqueline feels when she looks at Elisa Blix. She scans the first row of pictures, which range from smiley private photos sourced from Instagram and Facebook, to a self-confident professional headshot of Elisa in her Nordic Wings uniform, to more recent press photos. In the latter, Elisa's effortless good-looks have become ravaged and tortured, her hair matted, her eyes circled by puffy purple patches. She deserves all that pain and despair, Jacqueline thinks. And more.

Jacqueline gets up slowly; her stomach feels weak and hollow after looking at the photographs of Elisa, and her expression must betray this onslaught of emotion – the girls she passed on the way in stare at her, mouths unselfconsciously open, coffee cups suspended in mid-air. She walks out of the café and back to the car, oblivious to the warming sun, which has now reached the pedestrian street, bathing it in a beautiful light. She thinks about Elisa, unable to let go of the images of her face, particularly the most recent photographs. Jacqueline has won, like she knew she would.

Back at the beginning, when she was still at the psychiatric hospital, Jacqueline had considered killing the little girl. It would have been the obvious thing to do – poetic in its simplicity. Still, Jacqueline could not reconcile herself to the brutal reality of actually doing it or getting someone to do it for her. It wasn't the punishment that worried her; it was the fact that the child was entirely innocent. She hadn't thought herself capable of murder – though she knows different now. Instead, she decided that the best way to get Elisa was by taking Fredrik from her, the way Elisa had taken Nicolai. When that didn't work out, she became increasingly unhinged. Looking back at herself during that time, newly released from the psychiatric institution, stunned from months of hallucinations and heavy medication, desperately yearning for Nicolai and the girls, rejected by Fredrik, Jacqueline feels deep sympathy for herself. She was well within her rights to do what she did.

She could have left it with the sordid attempt at an affair, all those late nights taking her clothes off in front of Fredrik on video calls. She was furious with him for not having the balls to move their relationship forward and into real life after everything she'd put herself through. It felt unbearable that Elisa still had everything while she had nothing. It sent her mad. She knows that now. Dangerously mad. But then on one of the many occasions when she followed Fredrik and his family, a much better plan came to her. A plan that would change everything and restore some balance.

It was a drab evening in late fall and Fredrik and Elisa had taken their children to see *Frozen* at Hjertnes Cinema in Sandefjord. Jacqueline followed at a safe distance, and while the Blixes were at the movies, she sat across from the main entrance, in the library's window seats, drinking whiskey and honey out of a thermos. The thing that surprised her about following them was how easy it was. It simply didn't occur to them – as it doesn't to most people – that they might be being trailed, because why would they be? Eventually the family emerged on a strong current of parents and chattering children, many of them around her own girls' age. Lyder was perched on his father's shoulders and Elisa looked sullen and a little distant, which made Jacqueline hate her even more. There she stood, in the center of her perfect family, seeming like she'd rather be somewhere else. They started heading for the car park, but then Lucia briefly turned back to look at something, pulling at her mother's hand. Elisa wasn't paying attention, she was talking animatedly to Fredrik, but Jacqueline followed Lucia's gaze to a stray red balloon rising through the freezing grey air. The little girl stared at it, transfixed, and Jacqueline stared at the little girl, because, in that moment, something in her shifted. There was something painfully familiar about the slope of Lucia's chin and the low, dark eyebrows. *You'd be easy to love*, she thought to herself.

That night, in bed in her anonymous hotel room near Sandefjord train station, Jacqueline's conviction grew and grew until she could think of nothing else. This would allow her to punish both Fredrik and Elisa in the worst possible way, and without harming the child. In fact it would be an act of kindness, saving Lucia from growing up with parents like that. It was easy to justify after that.

She drives home slowly from Toulouse, mind awash with thoughts of those early days following her disastrous attempt on Fredrik. She was still insane, then, she knows that now. But who wouldn't have been driven to madness, or death even? She glances at the clock – almost 2 p.m., so she still has plenty of time before the girls finish school at four thirty. She feels herself relaxing as she reaches the outskirts of Saint-Girons, and the steep hills that are also visible from Le Tachoué come into sight in the distance. It was coming home to this place that saved her. That, and getting her girls back.

The girls... She suddenly realizes that it's Wednesday and the girls finish at 1 p.m. and will have been waiting at the bus drop-off at the bottom of the slopes of Lucasso since 1.45 p.m. She will be much too late to pick them up. She pictures them, waiting, perplexed, at the remote bus stop, peering at the empty road, fear rising in their throats. She is always there for them – how could she have let this happen? She swears under her breath and drives fast around the periphery of Saint-Girons before dropping south onto the D33 towards Rivèrenert.

When she eventually reaches the bus drop, it's empty. She stops for a moment, as though the girls might suddenly materialize, her heart hammering. They must have started to walk. Up ahead, the road becomes steep and twisty – they won't have got far. She glances up into the densely forested ravines. They wouldn't have dared take the shortcut through the steep woods, would they?

She takes each turn of the road carefully, mindful not to rip around them in case Josie and Lulu-Rose are just around the bend. She fights away thoughts of them having been struck by a car and lying immobile and broken on the tarmac, black blood seeping into the concrete. Further and further she drives, up into the hills, and she is almost at the track to Le Tachoué now, but there's still no sign of the girls. It's impossible – they wouldn't have got this far after being dropped off at 1.45, even if they ran. Maybe the bus was late, maybe they're just being dropped off now and she's going in the wrong direction... *Get it together*, she tells herself, taking deep breaths and exiting the main road onto their private dirt road.

Even though she has a four-wheel drive, the car struggles

with the mud on the final steep track up to Le Tachoué. As she passes through the gate at the top of the track, the side of the main house comes into view in its lush hollow. There's a small white car parked in front of the farmhouse and the heavy oak double-door is wide open. Her heart lurches and she stamps down hard on the gas pedal, tearing down the narrow driveway.

As she screeches to a standstill, Antoine steps out of the front door, followed by Josiane, Lulu-Rose and Boulette. Jacqueline stares at them, blinking away the anxious tears blurring her eyes, then crouches down to pull the girls into a close hug. She is still holding them when she glances up at Antoine, meaning to send him a look of gratitude for having clearly turned up at exactly the right time; he must have spotted them walking along the road and picked them up. His expression is strange – tender and troubled at the same time. But he's here. He came back.

69

Lucia

I wake because someone sits down on my bed. It's Maman. She used to come into my room often in the night, crying quietly and just looking at me but I pretended to sleep. She stopped doing it when Antoine started to stay with us in the night. I pretend to be asleep now, too, turning over and opening my eyes just a tiny bit so I can make out Maman's shape.

'Rose,' she whispers. 'Rose.'

I could let her know that I'm awake, but I feel afraid and I'm not sure why. It's weird, Maman whispering the name on the stone we found and not 'Lulu-Rose', like she normally does. But Antoine told us not to say anything about that, so I just lie still, pretending to be asleep.

We ran as fast as we could away from the clearing after we found the dead-person grave this afternoon. We ran until we tasted blood. We ran so fast, we tore our clothes. We came through the woods into the bottom of the garden and rushed up to the house and then around the front to the main door.

'Look!' panted Josie. She couldn't talk properly because of running. A little white car was coming down the driveway.

'It's Antoine,' I said, my voice weird too.

'Hi, ladies,' said Antoine. He must have noticed that our faces were scared because he said, 'Hey, what's the matter? You look like you've seen a ghost.'

Josie and I looked at each other.

'Maman didn't come to get us,' I said.

'Oh. Okay. That's strange. Let me call her.' He took his phone out of his pocket and stared at it. Then he frowned and waved it around – phones don't work at Le Tachoué, Maman said.

'Something bad happened,' said Josiane. 'We found something bad in the woods.'

'What do you mean, "bad"?' he asked, his kind face worried. He sat down so he was our height and took one of my hands and one of Josie's.

'Josie...' I said, trying to warn her. I didn't think we should tell Antoine what we'd seen. I didn't know why, but I knew it was a secret.

Josie didn't listen. 'Come on, we'll show you,' she said, and she pulled Antoine by the hand, so Boulette and I followed them back down into the garden. 'Ow,' says Josie, stopping to show Antoine her bruised, bloody knee. Blood still seeping through the sock bandage.

'Jeez, how did you do that?' he asked.

'I fell,' she said. Antoine bent down and picked Josiane up and put her on his shoulders.

We kept walking into the woods. We didn't speak, not until we reached the clearing.

'There,' said Josie, pointing at the stone with the name on it.

Antoine lowers her to the ground and stands a long moment staring at the stone. Then he said, 'I don't think you should tell your mother about this.'

'Why not?' asked Josie.

'Because it might make her really sad,' he said.

'How do you know she doesn't know about it?' I said.

He rubbed the hairs on his cheek and kept on staring at the stone. 'Has she ever mentioned it to you?'

We shook our heads.

'No? Then I think it's best to not say anything.'

I didn't want to look at Josie, but we were standing very close together and I could feel her nodding. I nodded too. Then we came back home with Antoine.

Maman is running her fingertips across my eyebrows, then my bottom lip. It's ticklish and I'm trying really hard not to sneeze because then she'll know I'm awake.

'I just wanted to bring you home, Rose.'

I keep my eyes shut and leave my mouth a little bit open.

'No,' she whispers. *No, no, no.* I feel tears drop from Maman's eye onto the side of my face and they slide into my ear and I want to scream and run away from Le Tachoué, from Maman, and from Josie and Boulette even, all the way down into the valley where the river runs and I would follow it down the steep slopes to where there are other houses, screaming all the way.

70

Jacqueline

'I missed you,' says Antoine, his eyes warm and lively in the flickering light from the flames in the hearth.

Everything is okay again, in this moment. The girls are sleeping peacefully, Antoine is there, a large glass of red in his hand, the evening stretching out in front of them.

'I missed you, too,' she says. 'What made you come back?'

'I thought I saw your car this morning,' he says. 'I was out running in the fields with Safina, and I could have sworn I saw your car. I hoped it was yours, that you would turn down my street, that you'd come looking for me. But the car just kept driving. It made me realize that we can't just sit around waiting for the other person to make the move, because they might not. So here I am.'

Jacqueline doesn't tell him that it was indeed her car he saw, when she passed through Salies-du-Salat on her way to Toulouse. She just nods. 'I'm glad you came.'

'You know, I've been thinking about how much I love talking to you. It's always so easy but also exciting between us. I hope you don't mind me saying that.'

'Why would I mind?' she says, giving him a big smile, picking an imaginary speck of dust from his sweater. 'I feel the same way.'

'I was also thinking about how little I actually know about you, even though we've spent quite a lot of time together.'

Jacqueline feels the faint stirrings of alarm in her stomach. He seemed a little different earlier, when she arrived home in a panic about the girls – guarded, perhaps. Or maybe he was just nervous. She focuses on keeping her smile warm and steady, narrowing her eyes slightly – she wants him to think about sex rather than how little he actually knows about her.

'Well, you can ask me anything you want,' she says. 'Anything at all,' she adds suggestively, running her hand up the inside of Antoine's thigh, feeling the warmth of his skin through his jeans.

He doesn't take up the sexual reference; instead, he meets her gaze unwaveringly, his expression serious. 'Okay,' he says, swallowing, making his Adam's apple quiver on his throat. 'How long were you married?'

'Uh, eleven years. Almost twelve.'

'So you were married a while before you had Lulu-Rose and Josiane?'

'Yes. Why?'

'I just wondered. And did you want more kids?'

'Well, we tried for quite some time to have kids in the first place, and it didn't happen. In the end we had IVF, several rounds, which gave us the twins. I didn't want to go through all that again, and we had the girls, so…'

'I see.'

'Anything else you want to know?' she says, making sure she comes across entirely relaxed and calm, as though it really is okay to ask her anything at all. She playfully nudges him with her fingertips, then leans in close for a kiss. He relaxes into it, opening his mouth to allow her probing tongue, and she moves closer still, twisting the longish hair at the back of his neck around her index finger. After a while he breaks away.

'Do you keep in touch with your husband's family?' he says. 'Since he died, I mean. And what about your family? Are they close to the girls?'

Jacqueline feels a sharp stab of irritation but makes herself chuckle softly and take the wine glass from Antoine's hand. She closes the gap between them and kisses him more insistently this time. She places his right hand inside her blouse, straight onto her naked breast, and uses her own hand to rub at the bulge in his trousers.

'Listen, Antoine, you can ask me anything you want, and we can talk about absolutely everything together. My life is an open book. But first… first you need to make love to me.' She smiles at him again, watching him melt, before pulling him all the way down on top of her and closing her legs around his back.

When she wakes in the night, she untangles herself from his embrace. His skin feels hot and sticky. She stands a while watching him sleep, wishing he would rouse some emotion other than weariness in her, but he doesn't – not anymore.

71

Marcus

'You seem preoccupied,' says Niels, Tollebu's therapist-in-residence.

Twice a week Marcus sits in this chair, speaking about whatever pops into his head. It's little surprise to him that most of these sessions are dominated by long silences. He's good at silence. 'Not really,' he says.

Niels watches him closely but doesn't push further. He just waits for Marcus to speak again. Marcus doesn't feel like he has anything he wants to talk about today, but he also doesn't want Niels to think he's refusing to speak simply to be contrary.

'I guess I haven't been sleeping very well.'

'Do you have any thoughts about why that could be?'

'No.'

'I saw in your log that you had a visitor yesterday.'

'I don't want to talk about that.' He doesn't want to think about it either: how age and sorrow have sharpened her, like a diamond whose beauty is intensified by its edges.

'You don't have to.'

'I know.'

Marcus likes Niels and has over the years had many enjoyable conversations with him, and with the prison chaplain, especially on philosophical rather than personal matters. Today he doesn't want his thoughts and feelings prodded by a professional. He feels like a wild animal whose every contact with other humans will inevitably result in wounds; he has an overwhelming need to withdraw for self-protection.

'Our time's up, I'm afraid,' says Niels, glancing at the clock.

Marcus walks quickly back down the corridor, past the recreation room and the canteen to his room in the left-hand wing. He rounds the corner to see a guide approaching him from the opposite direction.

'Hey there, Marcus,' the young man says, raising his hand in a fist pump, as though they are buddies.

Marcus swallows back his irritation, touches his fist against the guide's and attempts a smile.

'I've been looking for you. You've got another pretty lady waiting for you in the visitors' lounge. Two in a week, not bad, eh?'

72

Selma

Her first impression of Marcus Meling is that he is preoccupied and tired. He's a good-looking man, someone who, in a different setting, might be considered very handsome indeed, and with a certain easy charm. Separated from the trimmings Selma knows he would have had access to in his previous life – money, power, tailored suits – the effect is more subdued, but his natural charisma shines through. He is tall and broad-shouldered, with sandy blonde hair and dark green eyes flecked with hazel. He has a strong nose and a healthy complexion with olive undertones, unusual in Norwegian men.

'I'm not sure I understand why you wanted to speak with me,' he says as he settles into a lime-green armchair in the meeting room they were shown into.

'I came across your case, and as a freelance journalist I'm always on the search for interesting stories that merit media attention.'

'Okay... Well, shoot.'

'I'm currently working on an article about remorse. I'm talking to people who carry a heavy burden of guilt, and the focus of my piece will be how to live with something like that.' It's not a piece she's planned as yet, but as she speaks, Selma realizes she might well be interested in writing it.

'Right.' Marcus looks stricken, and for a moment Selma worries he'll stand up and walk back out of the room.

'Would it be okay to ask you a few questions along those lines?'

'I... I haven't really spoken about what happened before. To the media, I mean.'

'You might find it cathartic, especially now that you've appealed for an early release. It's a chance to say something in your own words.'

'I'm sorry,' he says, his eyes darkening, his mouth set in a tight line. 'I don't think it's fair that I should say anything, considering. I don't want anyone who was affected by what happened to randomly come across *my* version of events. You can imagine how it would look – me asking for forgiveness and sympathy in a national newspaper.'

'What *are* your thoughts on forgiveness?'

Marcus shifts in his chair and looks seriously at Selma, considering the question. He must spend his life running over that same subject.

'I suppose I think of everything in life as weight placed on scales. It's our job to make sure more weight is placed on the good end of the scales. So if you've done something terrible, then it's your responsibility to somehow restore the balance by adding good to the world. If that makes sense.'

Selma nods. 'And how do you attempt to restore that balance?' she asks, softly, sensing he'll shut down and bolt if she oversteps in her approach.

'By repenting. By giving something back. When I went on trial, I sold my apartment in Oslo and donated the proceeds to the air ambulance. I also sold most of the shares in my company and donated the money to a charity supporting children with life-altering traffic injuries. Stuff like that. In the greater picture, it isn't much, I know, but I want to do what I can. I'd like to make a real difference in the lives of children, or at least one child, someday.'

'I wish you luck,' Selma says gently. She empathizes with the man – as far as careless drunken child killers go, he seems a highly unlikely candidate. 'If you do decide you'd like to talk some more, feel free to drop me a line. You could be off the record, or anonymous, if you prefer.'

She hands him one of her newly printed fancy business cards, then stands up. She's already slipped her arms back into her jacket sleeves when he speaks again.

'It was all my fault. If it wasn't for me, none of it would have happened. One episode of real madness in all my life and then... this. The repercussions... It's the repercussions I think about the most. Forgiveness is almost beside the point. It's like I dropped a meteor into a shallow lake, obliterating everything around its shores. Wave after wave of tragedy, all caused by me. You know, the widow – the bereaved mother – came to see me here. She may well have been expecting me to ask for her forgiveness, but I didn't because I knew it wouldn't be possible.'

Tears are falling from Marcus's eyes now, but he makes no attempt to wipe them away. Selma holds his gaze, willing him to keep talking. He doesn't, so she sits back down, slipping her leather jacket back off her shoulders.

'Why were you out there on Birkebeinervegen that night, Marcus?'

He cradles his head in his hands, his shoulders quivering with silent sobs.

Selma feels a strong urge to get up and place her hand on his shoulder.

'I was going to kill myself,' he whispers, after a long while. 'I was every cliché you could imagine back then. Before. I had everything. Every *thing*. But every single thing in the world adds up to a big fat fucking nothing if you don't have anything else. I'd turned thirty a few years earlier and it was tough coming to terms with not having any of the elements I'd thought I would have in my life by then. A wife and kids. Friends. It was my own fault for not having pursued them. I only cared about money and success. I was always on a plane – I must have been one of SAS's biggest clients. I didn't even know how to use my own washing machine, even though technically I'd lived in my apartment for eight years. I had no idea what it might feel like to come home to someone you loved. And then I met someone who brought all that into my life. It hit me like a freight train. When it ended, I wasn't able to be rational about it.'

'Why did it end?'

Marcus shudders and looks up at Selma with a blank stare as though he'd completely forgotten she was there. 'I'm sorry,' he says. 'I think we'd better round off there. You won't write about any of this, will you?'

'Not without your permission, no.'

He nods, his face spent and vulnerable, like a young boy's.

She stands up again, but Marcus doesn't move.

'Did you work on the Lucia Blix case, by the way?' he asks, tilting Selma's business card to catch the overhead light. 'I think I recognize your name.'

'I did, yes.'

'What do you think happened to her?'

'It's anybody's guess at this point. I don't think she's dead, though. Never have. But it's such a strange and complex case – it's never made any sense.'

'I think you're right about her not being dead,' says Marcus.

'Why do you say that?'

'It wouldn't make any sense to kill her.'

'Surely that depends on why she was taken. Presumably it might make sense to kill her if she was taken for sexual abuse or child trafficking.'

'I don't think that's why she was taken,' says Marcus.

'Why not?'

'Just a feeling I have.'

'You seem interested in this case.'

'Isn't everyone?'

'Not necessarily.'

'It's an extremely high-profile case. Not many like it in Norway. I guess most people would like to see it solved and the child returned to her mother.'

There is something strange about how Marcus refers to Lucia's 'mother' and not 'her mother *and* father' or 'her family'.

'Do you know her?' A long shot, but in Selma's experience those are the ones that bring the greatest rewards. Caught off guard, people tend to spill the beans.

'Who?'

'Lucia Blix's mother. Elisa. I'm sure you're aware she's from here. It's a small town.'

'It was my first time here when the accident happened.'

'No previous ties to Lillehammer?'

'No.'

'So why *were* you here? Why were you driving around that particular area in this particular town when you were planning to take your life? Why here, Marcus?'

He is wringing his hands now and his eyes are brimming with fresh tears. He stands up fast, knocking one of his big knees against the low walnut coffee table between them.

'Goodbye,' he says and lets himself out of the meeting room.

On the train back to Oslo, Selma's thoughts bounce back and forth. She feels profoundly affected by the meeting with Marcus Meling. She had expected an arrogant, uncaring person, an unsavory character with whom it would be impossible to empathize, not a humble, broken man intent on doing good.

She stares out the window at the grey blur of Lillehammer's outskirts rushing by. Down there, Elisa lived her early life. Marcus went there to die. Kari Samuelsen goes about her daily life there, pretending she has two children, not three. And down there is also a woman whose world was devastated by Marcus Meling's decision to drink and drive that night. Who is she and what is her life like now? If Selma decides to pursue Marcus's story, she would be interested in speaking to the widow. It would make for a powerful article, she imagines: interviews with the victim and perpetrator side by side, speaking of forgiveness, guilt and repentance. Snatches of the conversation with Marcus return to her. *The widow came to see me*, he said. He didn't ask her for forgiveness. Did he say what they'd talked about? *I was every cliché... I was always on a plane... Then I met someone who brought all that into my life.*

Selma opens her browser on her phone as a strange unrest begins to grow in her chest, making a bigger and bigger space for itself. She goes to iNovo.no, the website for the company Marcus founded. She's been to the site before, trying to get a sense of what kind of services the company provided, and she remembers seeing a section about conferences. She clicks on it and a picture gallery opens of various international conferences attended by iNovo in the years between 2004, when the company was founded, and 2012, when Marcus was jailed. He was always on a plane. *I must have been one of SAS's biggest clients.* Miami, Amsterdam, Berlin, Palma de Mallorca, Malaga, Reykjavik, Bordeaux, Geneva, Helsinki, all of them just in the last quarter of 2010. She clicks on 2011, and in January alone there are pictures of Marcus presenting at conferences in Amsterdam, Paris, Stockholm and Bucharest. There's a pattern here, and for a brief moment a tangled web becomes impossibly clear, like the tight knots of a spine under the X-ray.

'Jesus Christ,' whispers Selma. She opens the Instagram app and types in @elisablix. How many times has she scrolled through Elisa's account before? Too many to count, and she knows most of the nine hundred posts by heart, especially the many, many of her children. There are others too, selfies of Elisa, shots out of airplane windows, and various pictures of places Elisa has gone for work. She scrolls back, all the way down to the beginning of Elisa's feed, to when Lyder hadn't yet been born and Lucia was a gorgeous chubby toddler. Elisa traveled then, too, posting frequently.

In January 2011 Elisa Blix posted seven times on Instagram. Selma's hand begins to shake as she opens the first post, a selfie with the tip of the Eiffel Tower positioned behind her to resemble a goofy hat. The next picture was taken the day after, by someone else, and shows Elisa at the top of an aircraft's steps, in her SAS uniform, smiling widely, her signature scarlet lipstick a bright contrast to the bleak sky and white plane behind her. There's a picture of Lucia in the bath, her face haloed by soap bubbles. '#lulubaby #norwegianmamma #loveofmylife' read the hashtags. There's a picture of Elisa's bare legs, taken from above, stretched out on what looks like a hotel bed, and captioned '#bucharestbabe #businessandpleasure #radissonblu'. There's a picture of a lavish sushi display, with no caption or location identifier. The next is a deliberately blurry selfie of Elisa laughing on what looks like a bridge, a frozen river vaguely visible behind her. 'My favorite town,' reads the caption, followed by: '#amsterdam #ohmyheart #planelife #crew #luckyme #somegirlshaveallthefun'.

Selma's heart is beating so fast, she has to place a hand on her chest. She closes her eyes and for a moment she feels utterly calm and clear-headed. She realizes the train is approaching a station and she decides to get off it – she needs to take a chance on a wild hunch here. She stands up slowly, her hand still inside her sweater on top of her heart, and walks down the aisle and off the train. She rushes to the end of the platform and then up and over the rickety metal pedestrian bridge over the tracks. On the opposite platform she buys a single ticket back to Lillehammer, her fingers stumbling several times on the ticket machine screen. Her card payment has only just been approved when the red train that will take her back up the Gudbrand Valley appears, the sun shimmering in its bright red paint.

73

Selma

Marcus looks agitated and confused. She knows she's lucky he's agreed to speak with her again, especially as she's back at Tollebu with just thirty minutes to spare before the end of visiting hours. Hopefully that will be all she needs.

'What do you want from me?' he asks, his face partially hidden behind a steaming cup of coffee.

'Thank you for seeing me again. Something occurred to me after our conversation earlier today.'

'Okay.'

'I was wondering if you could tell me about when the widow came to see you.'

'No,' he says, his voice cold. But then he softens it. 'Look, I'm sorry, I don't see what good that would do. I shouldn't have talked to you in the first place.' He gets up, placing the paper coffee cup on the table.

'You know, the most important forgiveness is the forgiveness you grant yourself.'

'What?'

'It would be okay to forgive yourself, Marcus,' she says.

He sinks slowly back into his chair, staring emptily into the air. 'It's not possible,' he whispers.

'It is.'

'You don't understand.'

'What if I do?'

'You can't. Everything... everything is my fault.' He begins to cry again, tilting his head back to keep the tears from falling, but they overflow down the sides of his face.

'Forgive yourself, Marcus. Even if nobody else does.'

'A two-year-old died. And a father, a man probably much better than me. A little girl has been taken. And it's all my fault.'

Selma's hands grow slick with sweat and she is aware of holding her breath, willing Marcus to continue. When he doesn't, she softly nudges him.

'What do you mean, "a little girl has been taken"?'

'Lucia Blix.'

'How could that possibly be to do with you?'

'When the widow, Jacqueline Thibault, came here, it wasn't an apology she was after.'

'What was she after?'

'She wanted a confession.'

'What kind of confession?'

'She wanted the whole truth about what happened that night. She... she saw stuff that was disregarded in the investigation. She was made to seem crazy. She lost everything. One kid dead, the other taken into state custody after she attempted suicide and had a psychotic breakdown.'

'Jesus.'

'You can perhaps imagine what it was like to sit across from this woman begging me for answers.'

'And what did you tell her?'

'The truth.'

74

Elisa

I take the stairs slowly and stand a while on the landing outside our bedroom. The door is ajar, and the orange light from the streetlamps is filtering in through the blinds; it's just gone 4 a.m. I can hear Fredrik's soft, even breath. I step into the room and sit down on the edge of the bed. I place a hand on his bicep, and he jerks awake.

'What is it?' he asks, searching my eyes.

I must be a real sight – I've been up all night, tears are slipping down my face in unstoppable streams, my hands are shaking. The tears are real – of course they are. In my hand I'm holding my phone and on the phone is a picture of Line.

'Is this her? Is this "Karoline"?' I whisper, holding my iPhone out to him, close to his face.

He blinks, and sits up fast.

'Jesus Christ,' he says, studying the woman's face. 'How did you—'

'Is it her?'

'Yes.'

'Jesus. We need to speak to the police.'

'But how did you... how did you find her?'

'It was never you she was after, Fredrik. It was me. It was me, all along.' I'm crying harder now, and my husband is watching me, motionless and serious.

'But why?' I swallow hard. I need to get this entirely right. Then maybe, just maybe, Lucia can come home.

'Because I took her husband.'

75

Elisa

It's late morning by the time Fredrik and I have finished. He reacted more or less as I knew he would. At first with anger, lashing out and breaking things, making me cower even though I know he'd never hurt me. He picked up the bedside lamp and smashed it against the wall until only metal splinters remained. I sat and watched silently, waiting for him to calm down. When eventually he did, we talked and cried and sat for long moments in silence, staring at each other, at the floor, at the dented wall.

'I guess when Nicolai and Rose died, she felt she had nothing to lose. And she irrationally held me responsible for her life unraveling. Poor woman – she's obviously genuinely insane.'

'The whole thing seems completely unbelievable to me... I mean, the lengths she's gone to for revenge...' says Fredrik.

'We need to call the police.'

'Yeah,' says Fredrik. 'Just... Jesus Christ, I don't know if all this makes it more or less likely that Lucia's alive. I just hope—'

'Shhh,' I whisper, pressing my fingers to his lips. 'Shall I call Gaute or do you want to?'

'You do it.'

My hand begins to shake violently so I place the phone down on the table and turn away from Fredrik. I can feel his eyes on me.

'What is it?'

'Nothing.'

'Elisa? What's going on?'

'Nothing is going on, for fuck's sake. I'm going to call Gaute now. Okay? But... I need to get some air. Today's really taken it out of me.'

'Out of *you*? How do you think *I* feel?'

'Look, let's not do this. The only thing that matters right now is that we get her back.'

Fredrik nods thoughtfully and I go out into the hallway and shove my feet into the nearest pair of sneakers I see.

'There's something I need to know,' Fredrik calls, louder than normal, as he comes towards me. 'Elisa, stop. Look at me.'

I glance up from where I'm fiddling with my laces.

'I want you to look me in the eye and tell me that she's mine. Is Lucia mine?'

He stands blocking the front door. I try to duck underneath his outstretched arm, but he grabs me, hard, and pushes me up against the full-length mirror.

'Answer me, goddammit. Is she mine?'

I nod, at first hesitantly, then properly, but I must have hesitated for a second too long because Fredrik steps back and stares at me with a disgusted expression.

'Yes,' I whisper.

'I don't fucking believe you.'

As I turn and make for the door, I trip over one of Lyder's studded football boots in the cramped hallway and fall to the ground, hitting the side of my face against a metal umbrella stand. It feels as though my cheekbone has been pulverized and like I've been blinded in my left eye.

'Jesus, Elisa,' shouts Fredrik as I stumble from the house and woozily run towards the car.

I lock the doors and sit in the driver's seat, sobbing, clutching my face and wiping at the blood running from my nostril. Fredrik has followed me and is trying to open the car door, hammering on the window and crying. The neighbors must be watching in horror – they'll think he did this to me. I start the car and drive off, holding the wheel with one hand. I glance in the rearview and see my husband still standing in our driveway, his hands thrown up in surrender, his white shirt streaked with blood.

I pull over in a layby and get out my phone. It's time.

76

Elisa

'Okay, let's start from the beginning,' says Gaute Svendsen, his handsome face bewildered and sympathetic.

When I arrived at the police station, Kristine Hermansen was there and she gasped when she saw me. She took me into the women's changing rooms and ran a warm, damp cloth across my cheekbone and down the side of my nose.

'We need to take you to the emergency room,' she said.

'Not yet,' I said. 'This is very urgent.'

So, here I am, in an interrogation room at Sandefjord police station with Gaute and Kristine. Haakon Kjeller and Jens Stenersen from Kripos are listening in to my testimony via video link.

'Okay,' I say, and take a deep breath. 'The name of the woman who took Lucia is Jacqueline Olve Thibault. I've never met her before she took Lucia. I believe she is half French and that she lives in Lillehammer.'

'Are you certain about this?' asks Haakon Kjeller from the screen.

'One hundred per cent.'

'We're putting the intel guys on Thibault immediately. We should get a profile up shortly.'

'Continue, Elisa, from the beginning, please,' says Jens Stenersen.

I take a sip of the water on the table in front of me, but even forming my lips around the rim of the glass hurts, waves of pain spreading out from my fractured nose.

'I have to start from very early on in my life to give enough context, but I'll try to keep the less relevant details short—'

'We'll decide on the relevance, Elisa, so just tell us everything you can remember, completely uncensored.' Again, it is Haakon Kjeller who speaks, and even through the screen his sharp eyes unnerve me.

'I grew up in Lillehammer, in a very strict Jehovah's Witness family. I basically hated my entire childhood. Always different, always excluded. As a teenager I became very rebellious. I refused to participate in family activities and started secretly meeting boys, things like that. I drank and did some drugs. Fairly normal stuff, but not in my family. My parents were exasperated and though my father was kind, my mother used to beat me. It was a shitty way to grow up, frankly.

'Then, at sixteen, I got pregnant. I was terrified and didn't know what to do. I told the school nurse, who told my parents. Jehovah's Witnesses don't believe in abortion and my parents were so ashamed of me, I actually worried they might kill me. The father was an older kid I smoked pot with and I refused to reveal his identity. My parents decided to send me to a Christian institution on the west coast where I would be "dealt with". I pretended to agree, but just before I was due to travel there, the school nurse helped me to Oslo, where I had an abortion. I pretended that I'd lost the pregnancy, but my mother never really forgave me.

'I became obsessed with winning her affection back – in spite of everything, she was my mother, and I loved her. My father always did what he could to please her, and he, too, was very devout. I guess I thought they didn't know better and that they'd done what they thought was right. The summer I was seventeen, they insisted I go to a Jehovah's Witness camp in Larvik. That was where I met my husband. He's from a Jehovah family too, but much more moderate than mine, and they left the church around ten years ago. It wasn't love, exactly, but I liked Fredrik very much. I still do.'

Kristine Hermansen stares at my bloodied face and raises an eyebrow. She didn't seem to believe me when I explained that I fell over. I bet she's heard that one too many times before.

'I realized quickly that Fredrik could be the ticket to winning my parents back. A squeaky-clean Jehovah boy wanting to marry me – it was a done deal. And it worked. My mother especially adored Fredrik and our relationship began to repair itself. Behind the scenes, though, things were different. We were both so young, only twenty when we married. And people don't really change, do they? I didn't suddenly become a calm, content wifey in a little house in a little town. I felt trapped and resentful.

'We had Lucia, and it got even worse. And then I fell in love. You could say it was for the first time, and it caught me entirely off guard. It rocked the foundations of everything

I thought I knew about myself and about marriage and family. It was passionate and incredible and painful in equal measure.'

'Who was this man?' asks Gaute.

'Nicolai Olve Thibault, the husband of Jacqueline Olve Thibault,' I say. 'That's why she must have taken Lucia.'

'What I find impossible to understand is how you could not have mentioned this previously? It's been eighteen months! Your daughter could be dead. If you knew all along who was likely to have taken her, how the hell could you have not said something?' An angry vein is pulsating at Haakon Kjeller's temple, but I force myself to maintain eye contact with him.

'His wife never knew. He swore to me that she never knew. I believed that. And then he died. It meant that no one knew about us except me, so I just didn't think it could be related in any way.'

'Why now? Why did you suddenly think it could be her?'

'I did briefly think of it back when Fredrik confessed about his Facebook fling. I almost said something then. But then Lucia was caught on CCTV with Eilaanen and the body turned up in Sweden and it seemed certain that she was in the hands of the Vicodius network. So it made no sense for me to make everything even worse by admitting that I'd had an affair, which only myself and one other person knew about. And that person was already long dead.'

'But why now, Elisa?'

'A journalist got in touch. She asked me some very pointed questions about revenge. And the only person I could think of who might truly hate me was Nicolai's widow. So I started to seriously wonder whether there was any way she could have found out – and she must have done. How, I don't know. Maybe he betrayed me, even though I never, ever thought he would.'

I burst into tears again and just let myself cry silently. *I'll never say anything, no matter what. Never.* Those were his words. *I'll love you forever, Elisa.*

A heavy silence momentarily settles on the room, thickening the air.

'We should have some info on Thibault shortly,' says Kjeller. 'Let's dial back in fifteen.'

The screen goes black.

'I was devastated by Nico's death. I still am. It ruined my life,' I say softly, wiping at the tears still streaming down my face. This, at least, is true.

'I can't believe this,' says Gaute. 'That all along it was this woman. The wife of the man you had a relationship with. To go to such extraordinary lengths to punish you for having had an affair with her late husband. To take your child out of revenge…'

I nod and wonder if they feel sorry for me now, or if they are full of judgment and condemnation. Either way, it feels good to have told them everything. Well, almost everything. For a moment I wish that Fredrik was here, but I needed to do this on my own. Besides, I'm not ready to face my husband again yet. I don't know that I ever will be.

77

Elisa

'We're going to need a very careful strategy here,' says Stenersen, rubbing his fleshy chin and staring hard into the camera. 'Later today we'll issue a wanted call – nationwide, and across Europe. We'll keep all images out of the press to start with; this woman could be dangerous if she knows that we're onto her. Our priority is to track her location and establish Lucia's whereabouts. From what we gather, Thibault sold her apartment in Lillehammer in 2014 and her daughter Josiane has never been enrolled in school in Norway. We believe that she's left the country and that very possibly she built a life somewhere else with the intention of taking Lucia there. We're going to verify the information you've provided, Elisa, and we'll need you to supply us with as much supporting evidence as possible. Where were you on the night Nicolai Olve and his daughter were killed?'

'At home in Sandefjord.'

The three men watch me intently, Stenersen writing something on his notepad.

'Did Nicolai, over the course of your relationship, discuss his wife with you at all? Do you remember anything about her that might be relevant – anything at all?'

'He told me she was French, though I believe she grew up in Norway.' It's incredible, the things one can learn from Google, when one knows where to look.

Stenersen writes something else on his pad.

'We'll look into whether she might have taken Lucia to France.'

'What I fear the most is that she has killed Lucia for revenge. Or had her killed by Mikko Eilaanen or Batz? Or...' *Or...* I stop.

'Or perhaps she took Lucia as a way of trying to replace her own child, the girl that died,' says Stenersen. 'Rose.'

Rose. A sweet, solid name. And yet, to me, her name feels like a dagger.

'That seems really farfetched,' I say.

'Well, this is a woman who's lost a child, so she might have a very compromised sense of reality. It's something we see over and over. Most female abductors have, in fact, lost a child and are seeking to replace them. Given that Thibault is the mother of twins of a similar age to Lucia, she may have access to things that would make it easier for her to do something like this.'

'Like... like what?' I ask.

'Like two birth certificates.'

I'm suddenly reminded of something I read in a newspaper many years ago, about how there's an ancient Native American practice in which, in the event of a person accidentally causing a child's death, that person then has to hand over his or her own child to the bereaved family.

ALEX DAHL

'I'm wondering whether this woman might have even more complex reasons for wanting to take Lucia,' he continues, and I nod, but I can feel the hairs on the back of my neck prickle and rise as he speaks. 'Avenging marital infidelity by kidnapping a child seems very extreme.'

'Well, she's clearly crazy. You said it – that she might have a, uh, compromised sense of reality.'

'She may have been under the impression that Lucia could be her husband's biological child.'

'Oh,' I say. 'No, I don't think it's likely she would have assumed that. Also, for the record, she's not.'

'Are you absolutely certain that's not possible? You said yourself that you were in an ongoing relationship with Nicolai Olve at the time of his death.'

'I already had Lucia when I met Nicolai.'

Kjeller and Stenersen exchange a glance.

I've thought this out thoroughly, but I need to get all the facts entirely right. I swallow and make sure my eyes don't waver when I look at Gaute Svendsen. He nods thoughtfully.

'We would like to firmly establish Lucia's paternity, given these highly unusual circumstances. So, with your permission, we'll be seeking to run those tests today.'

Fine with me. I nod.

'We'll break for a while now,' says Haakon Kjeller. 'I'd like to reconvene later this afternoon, to go over some more details with you, so if you could stay at the police station until then, please. We'll be asking your husband to attend as well.'

78

Selma

When she finishes speaking, there's a long pause on the other end.

'Selma, I don't know,' says Olav finally. 'This all sounds utterly crazy.'

'Indeed.'

'I mean, are you sure?'

'One hundred per cent.'

'You couldn't make this stuff up. To think that they've been playing a total charade with the police, and the media, it's just—'

'I think it's more complicated than that.'

'Why would she keep this secret though?'

'I don't know. There must be more to it.'

'How soon can you be here?'

'I'm on my way in now. The train just passed Stange.'

'If you're right, this is going to be the biggest story, possibly ever—'

'I'm right, Olav. Trust me.'

'Jesus Christ.'

Selma pictures him spinning slowly around on his orange office chair, chewing absentmindedly at the white wire from his headphones. He'll be digesting everything she said, fighting disbelief.

'Hold on a sec,' he says, lapsing into silence.

Selma stares impatiently out the window, at the grey fields sliding past.

'I just had a message from my guy at Kripos.'

'And?'

'The police are about to announce an unscheduled press conference at six. The rumor on the street is that they've uncovered the identity of the woman who took Lucia Blix.'

Selma becomes aware of the train slowing down and approaching a station. Her mind is crowded with a mass of conflicting thoughts, making her wince, stopping her words from coming.

She removes her phone from her ear to see whether any new messages have come in. Elisa Blix still hasn't answered. Is she finally going to tell the truth?

79

Jacqueline

It's early evening and the girls are sitting side by side in silence at the kitchen table, not playing with Kimmi or Boulette, just watching Jacqueline stirring the pots. It makes her angry that they're not chattering away like they usually do; instead, they just sit there, grave and silent. For eighteen months now, Jacqueline has made this home the center of the universe for the girls, for herself, for their many beloved pets. She has made sure she is always there for Josiane and Lulu-Rose, no matter what. She is mother, teacher, friend, everything. She couldn't have done any more; she is perfect. The perfect mother. She had believed that it was possible to create a perfect life if you just tried hard enough – she'd had to believe that. For several days, the girls have been sullen and unresponsive, and she can't help but feel angry with them.

Jacqueline has a headache. She feels trapped. She wants to be like she imagines her own mother: alone and anonymous in Paris, sipping coffee at a different pavement café every morning, reading in bed until late into the night, moving like a shadow on the periphery of other people's lives. Jacqueline wishes she could just call her and tell her everything.

'Do you want to come with me to Saint-Girons?' she asks the girls. She feels the need to leave the farm and be among other people. To stand on a street corner and feel people moving past her without particularly noticing her presence. To browse the aisles at Carrefour, weighing one brand of soup up against another, like any random customer.

The girls both shake their heads. Again, they make her irrationally angry. Don't they understand that this is all for them? Will they ever be able to grasp the extent of Jacqueline's sacrifice? She hastily spoons the aubergine and lamb stew into bowls and places them on the table in front of the girls.

'Well, I'm going to Carrefour,' she says.

She drives faster than usual; the sky is deepening into a drab slate-grey and she wants to be back before it's totally dark. Antoine is supposed to come at nine, and she imagines the evening ahead, once the girls are in bed. The wine, the laughter, the easy conversation, the sex. Can life stay like this – a peaceful life in a treasured place with a kind, attractive man like Antoine by her side? The thought no longer fills Jacqueline with excitement but with vicious dread. On the approach to Saint-Girons, she pulls over in a layby. She sits for a moment, her head in her hands, trying to make sense of her confusing emotions and spinning head. She stares at the blue-and-red flashing lights of Carrefour in the distance; they remind her of the ambulance lights sweeping across the bodies of her family.

The last time she held Rose in her arms, she was screaming her name, shaking her, staring into the tiny child's wide-open, unseeing eyes. On the ground next to her was Nicolai, clearly already gone – his eyes were glassy, and dark blood had spread out on the snow around his head. Also on the ground was Josiane, face down, whimpering. Did Jacqueline pick her up? She must have. She must have carried her babies, stumbling on the ice, screaming, towards the sweep of blue lights from the ambulances rushing up the hillside towards them. She must have carried them like she had when they were newborns, one on each arm, close to her body.

She doesn't remember any of it, except Rose's face and the halo of blood around Nicolai. She remembers the bright lights of the car that hit them and how they were briefly switched off – it was dark, completely dark, as she scrambled across the ground towards her husband and daughters. Then the lights came on again and the car tore off, disappearing around the next bend, heading away from Lillehammer. She heard wailing – her own, Josiane's, and also the uncontrollable, anguished sobs of the person who'd emerged from the car and run into the forest before it drove away. Jacqueline can still hear those sounds in her mind. But nobody has ever believed her. Not the police, and not the doctors or the nurses at the psychiatric hospital.

She wipes at her tears and turns the key in the ignition, but her foot feels leaden on the brake, like she simply can't drive the car. She switches the engine off again and allows herself to give in to the despair. She rubs at the soft space between her breasts – it's hurting – and tries to take deep breaths, though the air won't go deep enough. She leans her head against the window, staring absentmindedly at the blue-and-red lights from Carrefour, blurred through her tears, giving herself time to regain her composure. Then she'll just go home. She takes out her phone and switches on cellular data. She usually keeps it off – it's meant for emergencies only, and she knows how easily she could be traced by it, should someone grow suspicious of her.

She opens the browser and goes to *Dagsposten*, expecting to see the usual underwhelming newsfeed from one of the safest countries in the world: man attacked by kitten, metros delayed in Oslo due to signal failure, married politician apologizes for sending intimate pictures to seventeen-year-old boy. They calm her, sometimes, these snippets from life in Norway.

She does a double-take when she sees the headline:

BLIX CASE: Emergency Press Conference, LIVE Now

She clicks on the link and watches a live-streamed video of a uniformed police officer speaking. His name is Tim Bruun, according to the name at the bottom of the screen, and he is the head of the missing persons department at Kripos.

'We can confirm a major breakthrough in the Lucia Blix abduction case. We have a female suspect, who is closely affiliated with the Blix couple, currently under investigation by Norwegian police, assisted by Scotland Yard. We remain hopeful that Lucia Blix will be recovered alive. We ask that the general public, in Norway and across Europe, remain vigilant and observant. Please do not hesitate to contact the police if you have any information or suspicions about the whereabouts of Lucia Blix.'

Jacqueline closes the tab and opens a new one. She goes

to Aftenposten.no and here too the Blix case dominates the headlines. 'Deranged Woman Hunted by Interpol', reads one. 'Women Who Kill Children – a Character Study', reads another.

She messages Antoine, saying she feels unwell and unfortunately needs to cancel. Turning the car around and heading back in the direction she'd come, Jacqueline feels strangely calm. It must be a rush of adrenaline keeping her alert and focused. Could someone have tipped off the police? But who? Or perhaps they're still looking for someone else. She needs to work out where to go from here. She thinks of Mikko again, how it wasn't that difficult to get rid of him when she realized how dangerous he was. She feels a cool shiver of guilt. But she only did what she had to. And she will do what she has to again.

When she gets back to Le Tachoué, Antoine's car is in the driveway. He's more than an hour early. She messaged him to cancel – did he not get her text? She feels a rush of irritation. How can she make him go away? She can't go ahead with their evening together now, not after what she's just discovered. 'A female suspect', the detective said. 'A Deranged Woman', read the *Daily Mail* headline.

The front door opens and Antoine emerges, smiling, but his eyes look distant. At his feet, Boulette and Safina are hopping around joyfully.

'Let me help you with the bags,' he says.

'What bags?'

'The girls said you'd gone to Carrefour?'

'Oh. Yes. Yes, I was going there, but when I got to the valley, I started to feel bad. Yes. I have a really bad headache. I messaged you – didn't you get my text?'

'Come here,' he says, and pulls her into his arms, kissing the top of her head.

It feels good, to be held by Antoine, but it's too late now, it's all too late. 'I think it might be best if you went home. I'm feeling quite under the weather and I just want to put the kids to bed and get an early night.'

'I'll help you,' he says.

'No, Antoine, really, it's okay. Why don't we make some plans for this weekend instead?' She says it knowing that this weekend she will no longer be here.

'No, I want to help you,' he says, and she senses a strange determination in his voice.

He takes her hand and leads her into the house, which feels vast and cold. At the top of the stairs stand the girls, looking down into the atrium stairwell. She smiles at them, but they don't smile back, though Josie raises her hand in a wave. Then they turn around and disappear down the hallway, most likely into the tent in Josiane's room, where they spend so much of their time talking and drawing.

Jacqueline turns to face Antoine, swallowing hard, thinking of ways to get rid of him, but there is something about the way he looks at her which sends a chill through the pit of her stomach.

80

Selma

She watches the press conference on her phone, her hand shaking with rage and disbelief. Her whole life, Selma's been told she's too black and white, that she isn't able to see the nuances or shades of grey, but as far as she's concerned, there is nothing grey about lying to the police and the entire world. Selma feels as though she's attempting to solve a puzzle that's growing clearer and clearer with each piece found and placed in context, but she still can't make out what the final picture is meant to be. Could it be that she's got it all wrong and that Elisa is speaking the truth now?

Back in her Oslo apartment, she opens her Mac and finds a photograph of Elisa Blix back when she was all groomed and pretty. Back when she had everything. *You're lying*, Selma thinks, *but why? You want them all to believe that this was some kind of twisted four-way affair.* She scrutinizes Elisa's carefree smile and those dark, unreadable eyes. *There you are, on TV, crying about Nicolai Olve Thibault, speaking so convincingly of an epic love story tragically lost, fishing for sympathy, even now. But you never even met him, did you, Elisa?*

She returns to the folder into which she's pasted pictures of Elisa and Fredrik Blix, Lyder and Lucia, Marcus Meling, Mikko Eilaanen, Feodor Batz, Heiki Vilkainen, Jacqueline and Nicolai Olve Thibault. She studies each face in turn. And then, finally, she sees it, the missing piece, as clear as day. Again, all Selma will have to do now is wait.

81

Lucia

I wake in the night and Antoine is in my bedroom. He is sitting by the side of my bed and nudging my arm gently. I sit up and I feel afraid. It reminds me of when the man took me to the house with the attic room in Arden and I woke in the night and the man who looked like Ronald McDonald was in my room laughing at me while I slept.

'Lulu-Rose,' he whispers. 'Wake up, sweetie.'

I open my eyes so he knows I'm awake, and my mouth, too, so he knows I can scream. But he puts his finger on his lips and I don't scream because I don't think he's going to hurt me.

'Can you sit up a little bit more?' he asks, and I sit up all the way in the bed, leaning back against the pillow.

'I'm going to take a picture of you, okay?'

'Why?'

He's about to say something, but then he suddenly looks behind him, at the open door and the dark corridor. He presses his finger to his lips again and then he takes his phone out and takes a picture of me. The flash makes my eyes hurt and I rub at them.

'I need to ask you something,' he whispers, and from the way he speaks I think it's an important question.

He fumbles with his phone and in the light from the screen his eyes look scared. I don't know why he's afraid, and I want to ask, but I'm afraid, too, now. He turns the screen over and what he shows me makes me want to scream, but I don't. It's a picture of me when I lived with The Other People. I remember the day it was taken. It was at the school I went to then, Korsvik School, and I was wearing a purple velvet dress with pink flowers and my hair was yellow. I look small but happy. I was laughing at the man taking the pictures because he made a lot of funny faces.

'Is this you?' says Antoine.

I can't speak. He shows me another picture, this time of me and Lyder and Mamma and Pappa at Christmas. Me and Lyder are sitting on the floor in front of the Christmas tree holding big presents and smiling. I didn't know The Truth back then. I start to cry because I'd forgotten The Lady's, no, Mamma's face a little bit, and when I look at it now I remember so many things. She has a mole on the side of her forehead, and I'd forgotten about that. She used to draw little shapes in the palm of my hand when I was really little. Her teeth are really round and quite small and my new teeth that have come out not long ago are like hers.

'Is this you?' Antoine asks again. I nod and try not to cry with sounds, but he pulls me close and hugs me, whispering, '*Mon Dieu*,' and then '*Putain*,' which is actually a very bad word.

'Tell me your real name,' he says, holding me at arm's length and staring at my face.

'Lucia Blix,' I whisper, but just then Maman comes rushing into the room.

82

Elisa

Sitting here, it's like I'm having an out-of-body experience. Every part of me is on the highest alert and it feels as though my nervous system has been rewired on the outside of my body. A chair scraped back sounds like tires squealing. The tap-tap of the police receptionist's keyboard sounds like automatic gunfire. My phone ringing sounds like a child screaming for help. I pick it up off the table in front of me, but it's Fredrik, so I put it back, face down.

I've been made to sit out here in the waiting area for hours, ever since the end of the press conference. Fredrik still hasn't arrived, but I couldn't care less where he is. Gaute Svendsen came past earlier, asking if I wanted a couple of slices of pepperoni pizza from the staff canteen, but I just stared at him and he looked away before skulking off back down the corridor.

My phone rings again and I jump painfully. Probably Fredrik again, but I turn it over and see that it's Selma Eriksen.

'Hello?'

'Hi, Elisa, how are you doing?'

'Okay, I guess. Considering the circumstances. They're trying to locate Jacqueline now.'

'I can't imagine how such a massive breakthrough must feel. I'm crossing everything for Lucia, and for you.'

'Thank you. I guess it was partly thanks to you, really. If you hadn't pushed the possible revenge motive, I probably wouldn't have made the connection.'

'Did you tell them everything?'

'Yes,' I say. This is true, I told them everything they need to find Jacqueline and Lucia.

'I can't imagine how hard this must be for you. Waiting.'

'And hoping,' I add, my voice cracking. I'm so tired. The one thing that helps, right now, is to imagine an invisible thread between myself and my child, a thread that is shortening every moment until I get her back.

83

Lucia

Maman is shouting and she grabs Antoine by the shoulders and drags him backwards, away from me. I'm shouting, too, but mostly crying because I am sadder and more afraid than I have been in all my life. Maman is saying very bad words like '*putain*' and '*connard*' and I know what they mean because sometimes Gabin says words like that to the other boys and then he has to sit in Monsieur Arché's office all afternoon.

Antoine takes Maman by the wrists and makes her sit down on the bed. He says, 'Listen to me, Jac. Listen. *Écoute! Écoute! Écoute!*' She is screaming and I am screaming too. Antoine reaches out for me for a moment, but Maman leaps up off the bed and claws at his face. I don't know how it even happens, because it's as if my legs decide and not my head, but I run from the room and down the stairs and outside into the night and across the courtyard.

The night is black but with many big stars and they are so close it's like I could pick them like cherries from a tree. I run through the cow gate and up the hill, cutting my feet on sharp stones in the mud, and it's just like the first day when I came here, but I keep going until I reach the edge of the forest. I choose a tree almost at the edge, one with very wide and bushy branches low down so it's hard to see up into it. I climb up and sit across a thick branch very high up. It's cold and I'm wearing only my nightdress, the one with my name stitched across my chest. 'Lulu-Rose', it says. But maybe that isn't my name. Maybe The Truth was A Lie. I don't want to ever come down.

I count to one hundred three times, first in Norwegian, then in French. I start to do it in English, but that's much harder, so I only get to number eleven, and then I hear some strange sounds. I stand up carefully on the branch, holding on to the trunk, and then I can make out the shape of Le Tachoué in the moonlight, far down the hill. Someone is crying and shouting my name – I think it's Josiane. I hear a second voice too, and it sounds like Maman. Then it's quiet for a long time before I hear the sound of a car starting. I can just about make out the shape of it moving up the driveway.

I hear a strange sound and realize it's actually my own breath going whoosh, whoosh, like waves on the beach. I clutch the trunk and stare at the car disappearing at the top of the driveway, and then at the empty house. Then I notice something unusual. Le Tachoué is shining very bright, like a yellow star in the night, but the light isn't coming from inside the house like I thought – it's flames, big flames, twisting out from the windows and licking at the roof. It doesn't take long for the whole house to be burning, and the smell of smoke fills the air, even up here in the woods.

84

Jacqueline

It's the first thing her hand touches upon as she scrambles to get out of Lulu-Rose's room, away from him, fumbling to feel her way down the dark corridor, Antoine in close pursuit. A tall wrought-iron candelabra, hanging on the stone wall, never used. It is easily wrenched loose from its mooring and Jacqueline swings around just as Antoine catches up with her, his hands trying to grab her. She smashes the candelabra full force into the side of his head before he has a chance to realize what's happening, and he crumples to the ground, making a strange high-pitched spluttering sound, before falling silent.

Her heart is racing, but she feels strangely calm, like all her senses are sharpened. It's as if she can hear the moths in the attic flapping their wings, as if she can see in the dark, Antoine's beautiful face struck motionless but his eyes staring at her, as if she can taste his blood in her mouth.

A noise separates itself from the silence. It's a wild cry and Jacqueline realizes it's coming from Josiane's room. Josie is in her tent, curled up against the far canvas wall, her

419

knees drawn up, her eyes squeezed shut, her hands clamped around her ears. 'No, no, no!' she's screaming between sobs, and when Jacqueline reaches out to touch her, the little girl's eyes open and she stares at her mother as though she's never seen her before.

'Come on,' says Jacqueline.

'No,' says Josiane. 'No, no, no!'

Jacqueline half drags, half carries Josiane from the tent and out into the hallway, angling her away from Antoine's body, though she'll probably see him anyway because a bright shaft of moonlight is streaming in through the ancient lead windows at the top of the stairwell, bathing everything in its yellow light.

Jacqueline rushes towards the stairs, holding Josie like a baby. Lulu-Rose could have reached the stone houses of the hamlet further down the valley from Le Tachoué by now, if she ran fast enough. Or she could be up any one of a thousand trees in the forest, shivering and holding her breath as Jacqueline and Josiane search for her, most likely unsuccessfully. Or she could be hiding somewhere in the vast house, in which case Jacqueline will never forgive herself. But either way, Jacqueline is out of time. Antoine knew. But how? He might have alerted the authorities already, and even if he hadn't, intending to confront her first, she simply can't risk it. She has no choice but to leave Lulu-Rose behind.

She carries Josie outside and places her trembling little body in the front passenger seat.

'Don't move,' she says, forcing the terrified girl to meet her eyes, but Josie starts to scream Lulu-Rose's name. Jacqueline closes the car door and locks it from the outside, but Josie keeps screaming hysterically. She will forget all this – she's so young. They will start a new life somewhere, they will build a home together once again, and that will be possible because Jacqueline and Josiane are each other's home – she knows that now and should have known it all along. It was enough.

She tears across the courtyard into the barn and switches on the lights. She can hear Samba bleating through the thin partition wall separating the animal pen from the main barn. She grabs a can of gasoline from the many lined up on the shelf to the side of the door, then rushes back outside. As soon as she is through the front door, she begins to splash the gasoline up the stone walls and the wooden beams, down the length of the corridor leading to the kitchen, into the vast, dark rooms lining it. She runs up the stairs, pouring gasoline as she goes, and when she reaches the end of the landing by Lucia's room, she hurls the rest of the liquid towards Antoine's immobile shape by the wall. As she turns to leave, she hears a faint bubbling sound coming from him, like the sound a fish still alive in the fish counter might make, struggling for a few last breaths. Some squeaking, too, like he is trying to speak.

She retches at the smell of gasoline and pushes her fist hard against her gut – it's as though her insides will fall out otherwise. For the last time, she walks slowly down the sweeping wooden staircase built by her great-grandfather. At the bottom of the stairs, she stands entirely still for a long moment, feeling Le Tachoué vibrate with memories around her. Then she brings out the long matches from her pocket and strikes one after the other, throwing them like flaming arrows into the corners of the room. The hallway flares up and bursts into flames.

85

Elisa

They are all looking at me when I sit back in the chair.
'Thank you for your patience,' says Haakon Kjeller.
'We've had the team look into the information you provided.
We've also called another press conference in the next hour
in the hope of receiving crucial feedback from the general
public. In the meantime, the team is working intently on
sorting through the initial responses from police across
Europe – the photographs of Jacqueline Olve Thibault have
been sent out across the line. We're continuing to keep them
out of the press at present.'

I nod.

'As you can imagine, we have quite a few questions for
you.'

I nod again. 'I understand,' I say.

'We've run the DNA sample given by your husband
against Lucia's DNA sample on file.'

'Oh,' I say.

'The test suggests with a probability of one to 750,000

that Lucia is the biological child of Fredrik Blix,' says Jens Stenersen.

I look up at the ceiling, trying to contain the tears pooling in my eyes. It's not like I needed a fucking DNA test to know that. Fredrik is there in Lucia's expressions and gestures, in the sharpening or softening of her facial feature as she's grown, in her long, thin fingers, in her dimpled smile.

'However, we've had another tipoff we consider highly reliable, which compromises your previous account. I'm going to give you a chance to tell the truth this time or the consequences may turn out very serious, both for you and for Lucia.'

I need to stick with the story I've already told them. It's watertight. It gives them everything they need to find my child while preserving my own relative innocence. I open my mouth to repeat what I've already told them, but in my head, gruesome images rush at me, silencing me. A little girl, just a baby. Rose. Her father, Nico. The man I love. Jacqueline, screaming in the night. I close my eyes.

My thoughts are interrupted by a hand on my shoulder, shaking me gently. I look up. I'm still here, still in the interrogation room. The police officers are still staring at me. I see Kjeller on the screen; his lips are moving.

'What?' I whisper.

'Get ready,' he says. 'It looks like the team over in France have found something.'

86

Lucia

The flames stretch up high into the sky and they make everything light, even though it's night-time, so I can see big clouds of smoke rolling up the hillsides. I shimmy down the tree, but my hands are so cold I can't grip the trunk properly and I fall the last bit. Everything hurts – my eyes, my lungs, my legs, my heart. I run back down the hill and all the while I'm thinking about the night when Maman tried to put out the big fire in the courtyard. It really was Mikko's car that was burning. I also think about back when I didn't know The Truth and refused to talk and didn't want to be at Le Tachoué and didn't want a twin sister and thought that Mikko or Maman might kill me. Before I became happy here.

I can feel the heat from the fire when I reach the courtyard. The right side of the house is completely on fire, and so is upstairs. I hear a weird noise and it sounds like barking and then I remember Safina and Boulette in their crates in the kitchen. The left side of the house isn't on fire yet, only a little bit, so I open the back door and then the sounds from the dogs get really loud. They're yelping and howling because they think they're going to die. I scream 'Antoine!', but he doesn't answer. He must have gone in the car with Maman and Josie. There's a lot of smoke, it comes out into the courtyard. I hold my breath and crawl on my hands and knees into the kitchen and when I get to the cages over by the door to the pantry I undo the clasps on the cages and Safina and Boulette run out, barking like mad. I can't hold my breath for much longer and the air is hot, like it's on fire too, so I rush back outside into the cold.

The dogs are going crazy and they push their bodies against me, needing me to pet them. I'm so cold and alone; all I have is them now. I run across the courtyard away from the house and open the door to the barn because the barn isn't on fire. Samba is in her pen, stomping around, ears twitching. I let myself and the dogs into the pen and that's fine because they know each other and love each other like friends. I sit down in the damp hay and I'm shivering so much. Samba, Safina and Boulette notice how cold I am, because animals can feel many things, sometimes more than humans can, so they snuggle up really close to me to make me warm. I'm so tired and even though my eyes are still crying and my heart is hurting, I fall asleep.

When I wake up, it doesn't feel like I've been asleep for very long, but the air's all smoky and Boulette and Safina are barking and tearing around Samba's pen. I try to get up but everything hurts and I can hear a strange noise slowly coming closer, like wailing.

87

Selma

Her anxiety levels are through the roof when the plane takes off; it is already late and the sky is a murky, dense charcoal. They only just made the last connecting flight from Oslo to Toulouse via Amsterdam, landing at midnight. She presses her face against the window, watching the lights on the ground grow increasingly distant until they disappear. It will be hours until they get there, hours without news, hours in which anything could happen. The last they heard was that Jacqueline Olve Thibault is thought to have been living near the Spanish border at a vast, distant mountain farm, passing Lucia Blix off as her dead daughter, Rose. Selma thinks of the vision she had of the missing child all those months ago, cradled in a mother's arms, just not *her* mother's arms.

'You okay?' asks Olav.

'Yeah. Just can't stop thinking about it. We could land to the news that they've found her dead, after all.'

'Or that they've found her alive.'

'I guess.'

'You know, there are some things I just don't get. Who tipped off police saying she'd been killed in Belgium?' asks Olav.

'Jacqueline herself, I imagine.'

'And where is Eilaanen?'

'I bet he's dead, like Batz says. Vilkainen, too.'

'Why, though?'

'Because he knew where Lucia really was. No way Jacqueline could take that risk.'

'What, you think she killed him?'

'Definitely.'

'What about the blood stains in Bastogne?'

'Either she got Batz or Vilkainen to kill him there, or it was planted to divert everyone.'

For a long while, Olav and Selma sit in a tense silence, Selma staring out at a full moon casting the layer of clouds in a metallic sheen, Olav playing a game on his phone. As soon as the plane touches down at Schiphol, they switch their phones off flight mode.

'From Jens at Kripos,' says Olav. 'They've raided the farmstead where she is believed to be held. Apparently it's burning.'

88

Lucia

I saved the animals and then the animals saved me. The flames from the farmhouse blew across the narrowest part of the courtyard and the barn's roof caught fire. The dogs barked, so I woke up, and when I went outside there was a whole line of firetrucks coming down the driveway. It looked like one of the scenes Lyder used to build with his Lego.

A man gave me water and wrapped me in a metallic blanket like a silver cape. Then a helicopter came and took me from Le Tachoué, but it wouldn't take Safina, Boulette and Samba, even when I cried, so I need to know where they are now and who is looking after them. A nurse is sitting by the side of my bed. Every time I look at her, she smiles. A policeman is standing by the door and I want him to go away because he has a strict face like my head teacher, Monsieur Arché, and he has a gun in his belt which makes me feel afraid.

'Where's my dog?'

The nurse jumps when I speak. 'Oh, I will find out for you, *chérie*. I am sure your dog is fine.'

'Can you find out about my goat, too?'

The nurse smiles and nods. She has a thick red braid and at first when I opened my eyes I couldn't make out that it was her hair because my eyes sting still. Lots of smoke got in them and I have to rinse them with salty water for two weeks.

'They'll be here soon,' she says and checks the levels on the water that goes into my arm.

'Who?' I ask, but just then there's a knock on the door.

The policeman steps aside and a man and a woman come into the room. Behind them is a little boy and some other people, some of them in police uniforms. The woman and the man are both crying and the woman carefully picks up my hand. The woman is my mother and the man is my father and the little boy is Lyder. Lyder is carrying Minky Mouse. My eyes are crying because I wanted to see them again so much, but I didn't think I ever could.

'Lucia,' they say, over and over, and it feels so good to hear my name. My name is Lucia Blix.

'Can I have yellow hair again?' I whisper, and everyone laughs.

Mamma says, 'You can have everything back, my angel. Everything.'

89

Marcus

He picks up today's issue of *Dagsposten*, the iconic image of Lucia Blix back in her mother's arms on the cover. He runs his fingers gently down the outline of her face – over her eyes clamped shut, her smile, the tears streaming from her eyes.

'Lucia Blix Recovered Alive at Remote French Farm', reads the headline, by Selma Eriksen. Marcus reads her words one more time, his eyes twitching with exhaustion – he's hardly slept in two days.

Toulouse: On the morning of 12 May, Lucia Blix of Sandefjord, who had been missing since 19 October 2017, was finally reunited with her mother and father, Elisa and Fredrik Blix, at the Centre Hospitalier Universitaire de Toulouse. The child had been airlifted to the University Hospital in the early hours after being discovered alive in a burning barn by the fire brigade of Saint-Girons at a remote farmstead near Rivèrenert in the French Pyrenees. She is currently receiving medical treatment for smoke inhalation and shock, but is otherwise in good health and spirits.

Lucia Blix has been at the center of one of the world's most baffling abduction cases since disappearing from a playdate at a schoolfriend's house in Sandefjord nineteen months ago. The Blix case has attracted enormous media attention, both in Norway and beyond, but remained unresolved until 12 May. Lucia Blix was initially thought to have suffered the fate of thousands of other children stolen from their families and trafficked by professional networks for sexual exploitation.

Mikulasz Vrcesk Eilaanen (41), an Estonian national with known connections to trafficking networks operating on the dark web, was involved in the early stages of the Blix abduction, but is no longer thought to have been central. The decomposed remains of Eilaanen have been recovered in the wreckage of a burned-out vehicle at Ferme du Tachoué, the farm owned by Jacqueline Olve Thibault. A second body, identified as Mr Antoine Berrier (29), of Salies-du-Salat, Haute-Garonne, was also recovered. Mr Berrier is thought to have been gravely injured before the fire but died of smoke inhalation as the flames ravaged the farmstead in the early hours of 12 May. His involvement in the abduction of Lucia Blix remains unclear.

It was Mr Berrier who tipped off the police in Saint-Girons in the hours before his death by sending them a photograph of Lucia Blix, who was living as part of the Olve Thibault family under the false name Lulu-Rose Thibault. It is thought that the kidnap of Lucia Blix was orchestrated by Jacqueline Olve Thibault, who lost her husband as well as one of her two daughters in a tragic hit-and-run in Lillehammer in 2012. The driver of the vehicle that killed Olve Thibault's family members, Marcus Meling, is currently serving a twelve-year prison sentence for manslaughter. Elisa Blix is thought to have had a long-standing extramarital affair with Nicolai Olve Thibault in the years before his death, further complicating this extraordinary and tragic story. Police are investigating revenge motives for Mrs Blix's relationship with Mr Olve Thibault.

As a result of several years' meticulous planning, Jacqueline Olve Thibault was able to slip under the radar after taking Lucia by using false identities, most likely provided by Mikko Eilaanen. She was able to assimilate Lucia Blix into the local community by using the birth certificates of her own daughters who were twins, and passing Lucia off as the twin that died in the accident. Neighbors and villagers in this remote corner of south-western France did not raise the alarm or become suspicious as Mrs Olve Thibault settled in the area, as she had previously spent significant amounts of time there with her husband and the two little girls. Mrs Olve Thibault is thought to have enlisted the help of Eilaanen to take Lucia from her family in Norway, and to have murdered him when Lucia was safely deposited in the Ariège, and he was no longer needed.

Lucia Blix was intensively taught French before becoming a pupil at the École Lambert in Saint-Girons from September 2018, where no one grew suspicious of her real identity. Jacqueline Olve Thibault explained to the school that her daughters' French was imperfect due to the years the family had previously spent living in Norway. By the time Lucia's true identity was uncovered, the child is thought to have acquired near native level fluency in French.

In the aftermath of the accident that killed Nicolai and Rose Olve Thibault, Mrs Olve Thibault spent a significant amount of time in a closed psychiatric ward at Lillehammer Hospital. She is thought to have been suffering from psychotic hallucinations and to have been acutely suicidal at the time.

Josiane Olve Thibault was placed into emergency foster care at the time but was returned to her mother in the fall of 2013. They are then thought to have spent a year living in Lillehammer, before living in the French Pyrenees under the radar of local official authorities until shortly before the abduction of Lucia Blix.

On Wednesday, senior features journalist Selma Eriksen will explore several previously unknown aspects of this extraordinary case with Elisa Blix, in a first world-exclusive interview, live on television. (Dagsposten Live TV, 7.45 p.m.)

The search for Mrs Olve Thibault and her surviving daughter, Josiane Olve Thibault, remains active and urgent. Members of the public are advised to exercise caution if they observe Mrs Olve Thibault or come into contact with her, as she is believed to be highly dangerous if confronted.

Marcus kicks his shoes off and lies down on the bed. He stares up at the ceiling and tries to imagine Lucia Blix in this moment. She's alive and Elisa got her back. As so many times before, he tries to picture himself as Elisa's husband and father of her children, but tonight, his imagination draws a blank. Instead, he sees little Lucia. Tonight she'll sleep, breathing in the familiar air of her old bedroom, her subconscious taking in the sounds she once knew – the crickets chirping in the fields opposite the house, the occasional rumbling jet approaching Torp Airport, her parents' voices drifting upstairs, the muffled thuds as her brother turns in his bed next door.

His timer goes off. It's 7.45 and he wouldn't miss this for anything. Marcus places the newspaper on the floor next to the bed and switches on the TV, and instantly, Elisa's close-up face fills the screen. The shout line at the bottom of the screen reads: 'The Entire Truth – Elisa Blix in conversation with Selma Eriksen'.

I love you, is Marcus's first, overwhelming thought as he takes her in, transfixed by Elisa's beauty. Then, listening to her speak – *You fucking liar*.

90

Selma

It's the first time Selma has done a live television interview. Her mouth feels dry and strange and her palms are slick with sweat. She fights the urge to fidget, to rub her hands on her smart navy pinstripe trousers, or to clutch her necklace, its little stone smooth and soothing in the palm of her hand. It calms her to think of Olav standing in the dark wings to the side of the podium, rooting for her.

Elisa sits down across from her, nodding at her in greeting, though doesn't meet Selma's eye. She looks different than before – the color is back in her cheeks and there's a sparkle in her eyes. Selma wonders where Lucia is in this moment, whether she might be somewhere in the broadcast building with Fredrik, waiting for Elisa to finish this interview. Or whether she's at home, watching cartoons next to her brother, her family home surrounding her like a perfect cocoon.

For several long moments, Selma and Elisa sit awkwardly in silence, until the TV crew count down from *five until live*.

'Thank you for watching Dagsposten Live TV this

435

evening, and with us in the studio today we have Elisa Blix, mother of Lucia Blix. Lucia was returned to her family in Sandefjord after eighteen months, after being taken by Jacqueline Olve Thibault, who sought revenge for Elisa's relationship with her late husband, Nicolai, in an abduction case that has shocked not only the country, but the world.' She pauses for a moment for dramatic effect, then smiles gently at Elisa, whose face is calm and composed. 'Elisa, thank you so much for coming here today.'

'Thank you for having me, Selma.'

'I imagine all of Norway want to know how Lucia is?'

'She's good. Fantastic, really. It's been an easier transition home than I would have dared hope for.' Elisa's eyes shimmer with emotion.

'Will you tell us a little bit about the last week, since you returned from France?'

'Well, we've just been at home together, really. The grandparents have been with us. Lucia has spent a lot of time in her room, playing with her brother, surrounded by her toys, that kind of thing.'

'I can't imagine the word relief would even begin to describe what you must be feeling?'

'No, it doesn't.' They smile at each other, genuinely, like friends. Selma feels a wave of nervous excitement at the thought of the direction this interview is going to take. But first, a warm-up.

'What were the first few moments with Lucia like, Elisa?'

'They were the best moments of my life.' Elisa's voice is thick, and she stops for a moment to compose herself. 'She... she could have died in that barn. We are so lucky she was found in time. She was in a hospital bed when I first saw her. Her hair had been dyed dark brown. She's grown so much and her milk teeth have fallen out, so she looked quite different. But at the same time, she was exactly the same. Her essence was unchanged, if that makes sense.'

'It does. It must feel incredible, that Lucia's ordeal has not only come to a happy end, but that she appears to not have been harmed during the time she was away from your family.'

'Of course. But she's still suffered. I can't imagine what she must have felt. It's still too early, but with time, I hope to get a complete picture of what happened to her in France. Lucia will be given all the support and help possible to cope with the aftermath of what Jacqueline Thibault did to her.'

'Thibault is still on the run with her daughter, Josiane. How do you feel about that?' Selma notices Elisa tense up at the mention of Jacqueline Olve Thibault.

'I hope she is caught and brought to justice.'

'And yet, I suppose people aren't always brought to justice. Some people get away with their crimes.' Selma pauses for a long moment, her eyes on Elisa, who stares back unflinchingly. *She's good*, thinks Selma. 'A lot has been written about the turning point, when you realized that the abduction of Lucia was likely to be a revenge crime.'

'Yes.'

'Can you say something about that?'

'Well, it was partly thanks to you, Selma. You asked me very directly, whether there was anyone out there who could truly hate me and have a personal motive. The only person I could think of was Thibault, but I just didn't think it was possible. Nicolai died many years ago, and I was certain that nobody other than the two of us knew of our relationship.'

'Do you feel able to set the record straight about this relationship?'

'It is a very personal matter. But I will say that I was very much in love with him, and that I am truly sorry for the effect my actions have had on my family.'

'Do you feel guilty?'

'Of course.' Elisa looks miserable now, and big tears roll from her perfectly made up eyes down her face, but she makes no effort to wipe them away. 'If I hadn't done what I did, Lucia would never have been taken.'

'It just seems very extreme, for this woman to have taken your child as revenge for your affair with her husband.'

'Yes. Which is also why it didn't occur to me. It's so extreme. Then again, I think it is beyond doubt that this poor woman is clinically insane.'

'Do you think she could have had other reasons for taking Lucia, in addition to your affair with Nicolai?'

'Such as what?' Selma senses it again, a certain steeliness beneath Elisa's surface.

'I don't know.' Selma doesn't immediately proceed with another question, merely sits across from Elisa, waiting. Elisa shows no signs of nerves or discomfort. Selma continues. 'There was something else I wanted to ask before we round off. It's been said that Lucia's paternity was questioned by police during the investigation, but that a DNA test proved your husband Fredrik to be her father—'

'Obviously.'

'Well, I suppose due to the admission of the affair it was an avenue the police needed to explore—'

'Look. I am not prepared to answer any more questions

about Lucia's paternity. It has been established, and is fully irrelevant to the outcome of the case.'

'What about Lyder, though?'

'Excuse me?'

'Has Lyder's paternity been formally established?' A thick vein pulsates at Elisa's temple and a sarcastic little smile plays on her lips.

'Are we done here?' asks Elisa and stands up. 'My child has been found. I've told the truth. Now, let's wrap this up.'

'Not the whole truth, though.' The cameras are still rolling. Elisa is still standing, staring at Selma, who remains calmly seated. 'Lyder is Marcus Meling's son, isn't he?'

Elisa lets a little theatrical little laugh out. 'You've lost me now, Selma?'

'Marcus Meling, the man serving time for the murder of Nicolai and Rose Thibault. In fact, you never even met Nicolai, did you? But you were in the car when it crashed into them. And then you ran away without even trying to help the victims, including a dying toddler. I've been trying to figure out your motive for lying. Like, why would you say you'd had a relationship with Nicolai, when really it was Marcus? You needed everyone to believe that Jacqueline Thibault had reason to hate you, but you didn't want to admit what you were actually involved in. But I get it now, it's because you had Lyder with him. You knew he'd keep quiet. Lyder is Marcus's.' The relief at speaking the words out loud feels so physical, Selma almost wants to giggle.

'Like hell he is.' Elisa is visibly trembling with fury, or

shock, or grief. Is she going to bolt into the dark wings, tearing the microphone off, throwing it at the stunned producers and cameramen? She rubs at a little patch of skin on her hand, and Selma thinks it's a strange thing to do.

She makes her voice low and soothing, as though she were speaking to a very young child

'Sit down, Elisa. Talk to me.' And then, to Selma's surprise, Elisa sits back down, and begins to talk.

91

Elisa

I should walk out. I should unclip the microphone from my silk shirt and fling it to the ground. I should insist on a lawyer. I have my child, and my life back. Everything is perfect and I'm not going to let this little bitch ruin it. And yet. That life is an illusion now, an empty glasshouse. All I can see is the truth. And I realize that the only way I can be free is to tell it.

'I met Marcus on a plane,' I begin, my voice quivering. I take a few deep breaths, then close my eyes, and I can't help a small smile at the thought of him, at the beginning.

'Several planes, actually; over and over. Looking out for him whenever I stood at the plane door greeting boarding passengers became a welcome diversion from the daily slog of work after I'd had Lucia. I'd see him at least monthly, always at the front of business class in the aisle seat of row one. He'd stare at me. One evening our flight back from Munich was canceled due to a technical fault and all passengers and crew were put up at the Radisson Hotel; it felt inevitable that we met at the bar. That we ended up in bed. That we started seeing each other whenever possible. I fell so deeply in love with him that it felt like I'd been set on fire. I couldn't think straight, or at all, even.'

'How long did the affair go on for?' asks Selma.

'Just over two years.'

'What happened on 27 January 2012?'

'I'd gone to my parents' house in Lillehammer. In the weeks leading up to that day, things had gotten more serious between Marcus and me. I'd started to seriously think about ending my marriage, and how to do that. What held me back was Lucia, and the thought of how my parents, especially my mother, would react. It was my marriage to Fredrik that had finally mended our relationship, so I dreaded having to tell them it was all over. At the same time, I knew, deep down, that the way I felt about Marcus was the real deal.

'Everything was further complicated by the fact that I had just discovered I was pregnant again, and according to my calculations it was highly unlikely the baby was Fredrik's, though not entirely impossible. That Friday, 27 January, I'd gone home to my parents to tell them I would be leaving Fredrik and starting a new life and family with Marcus. Fredrik and I would have to work out a custody arrangement for Lucia, and I figured that because she was so little, she'd grow up not remembering her father and me together. Besides, other people seemed to manage to create new, happy family constellations, why shouldn't we? I wanted to live my one and only life in the kind of intense love I had with Marcus. I wanted it so much.'

I can't stop the tears here, because in spite of everything – all the terrible, terrible things that have happened – I still want that so much, however irrationally, and I will never have it.

'Please continue, Elisa,' says Selma, handing me a tissue from the table between us. I snivel miserably, bringing the terrible events of that night back.

'As it turned out, my parents had news of their own that day. My father had been diagnosed with terminal bowel cancer and wasn't expected to survive the year. I remember his sunken, pale face. He took my hands in his own and said "As long as we stand strong together as a family, we can beat anything." When they told me that, it wasn't like I could respond by saying that I'd fallen pregnant by my lover and was going to leave my marriage. It just wasn't possible. Marcus was due to come up to Lillehammer later that evening, and the plan had been that I would tell my parents and then he would pick me up and we would spend the night at a rented cabin north of Lillehammer, like we'd done many times previously. I messaged him, telling him not to come, explaining the situation. I told him that I loved him and that everything would work out okay, I just needed to focus on my father for a while. He didn't react rationally at all: he phoned me repeatedly and sent lots of irate texts. I couldn't deal with it on top of the situation with my father. I remember feeling completely out of it, like I was about to black out.

'Hours later, I was upstairs, in the bedroom I'd spent my whole childhood in, sobbing on the bed, when the doorbell rang. I heard voices from downstairs, at first courteous and subdued, then agitated, and a man's voice broke through the commotion, screaming my name at the top of his lungs. The next few minutes are a blur. I remember my mother charging at me, clawing at my face, and Marcus holding her back. My father's face was waxy and perplexed; he just stood there staring at us. It was the last time I ever saw him.

'I remember regaining my composure outside on the street, standing next to Marcus on the front steps, the door slammed in our faces, the harsh cold biting at us. I had no choice but to get in the car with him, and it wasn't until we'd driven for a few minutes that I realized he was drunk.

'He kept misjudging the speed and clamping down suddenly on the brakes. I kept asking to be let out. He was crying and muttering to himself. I was terrified. He said if he couldn't have me then nobody would. He said that soon this would all be over and we'd be together forever. He was driving so fast, the trees by the roadside were a black blur. I pleaded with him, begged him to stop. I tried to reason with him, saying of course we could still go to the cabin, of course I would leave Fredrik in light of what just happened at my parents', of course the only possible way to live was together. But he just drove faster. It was icy outside, and I could smell the alcohol on his breath in the overheated car.

'We came up to a bend in the road, we were going too fast to make the turn, and I screamed as the car skidded into the middle. Both Marcus and I pulled at the steering wheel to straighten up, but the car slammed into something, I thought we'd hit the curb protectors by the ditch. For the briefest moment a man's face flashed before my eyes. There was a series of thuds. The car slid to a standstill across both lanes. Marcus was shouting and saying something, but my mind was completely blank. I couldn't understand what he was saying or where I was – everything was just one big hazy white blur. I turned around and saw the outline of someone on the ground. I saw someone else stumbling towards us, and I could hear her screams through the closed windows of the car.'

I stop for a moment, take another sip of water. The room

is so quiet, it's as though I'm in there by myself. I can't look at Selma.

'Then Marcus was holding the sides of my face, staring into my eyes, shouting at me. *Get out! Get out! Just run.* He said it was his car, and nobody would ever know I was in it, he would never tell. He told me he loved me. That our baby needed me. He just kept telling me to run.

'So I did. I stumbled from the car, and as I turned back, Marcus sped off. In the light from a distant streetlamp I saw a woman limping towards me, her face all twisted and bloody, holding two dead children. At least, they both looked dead. "Help me," she whispered. I turned and ran into the forest and I just kept running, through the snow, tripping over rocks and tree roots. I didn't stop running until I reached the main road. And by then I could hear loads of ambulance and police sirens, and not long after came the chop of rotor blades and then I saw an air ambulance lifting up from somewhere in the forest.'

I keep my eyes on my folded hands in my lap. Selma's stunned silence is palpable.

'At home, late that night, I sat by Lucia's bed and watched her sleep, my mind haunted by images of another mother limping towards me, carrying a dead child in each arm. I sobbed and sobbed, stroking my baby's velvety palms in circles and whispering promises into her ear. I swore on my life that I would never look back and that I would never let anything get in the way of my family ever again. I swore that I would protect her from all the evil things in world. But I didn't, did I? I failed. I failed on every level. I told myself the past would stay buried, but maybe I always knew, deep down, that it would come back and take from me what was owed.'

92

Selma

Lisbeth stands up and gives her a huge hug as she walks through the door at *Dagsposten*. Olav, too, steps forward and hugs her. 'Look at you, Sherlock,' he says, mischievously. 'Reporter extraordinaire. But then again, we knew that already.'

They smile at each other and then Olav and Lisbeth, together with several other members of staff, lead Selma into the staff room where a marzipan cake, her favorite, has been placed in the middle of the table. Lisbeth pours sparkling apple and pear Mozell into plastic champagne glasses and they raise them in a toast.

'To Selma,' says Olav, his eyes warm. 'Our star!'

Late that evening, Selma walks home. It's a warm spring night and the sun is still burning on the horizon, though it is past nine. Karl Johans gate is buzzing with young people walking in the direction of downtown, carrying shopping bags and laughing, or sitting at one of the many sidewalk cafés. Selma smiles to herself and feels suddenly, overpoweringly, young and energetic. Life seems full of possibilities again, like she can go anywhere and do anything; like happiness is something more than an obscure impossibility.

In her apartment, Selma picks Medusa off the windowsill and stands a while, stroking the old cat and looking out at Oslo in the fading pink light.

She places the cat back down on the floor and goes to stand in front of the bathroom mirror. It's a warm night and Selma steps out of her clothes. She looks at herself, stripped down to her underwear, the moonstone resting in the little hollow where her ribs meet, below her breasts. *Your decision-making place*, her mother used to call it. *That's where your gut feeling sits. Your hunch.* Selma smiles at her reflection, then feels goofy but keeps doing it anyway, because she is seeing it, now, how much she resembles her mother. It's like standing opposite a young Ingrid and seeing her smile back at her. This makes Selma cry, but they aren't sad tears this time. They are tears of relief, and hope, and gratitude.

Epilogue

Jacqueline

By the time the sun breaks over the peaks of the Alt Pirineu National Park, shining its sharp rays onto the hillsides of Le Tachoué and its burned-down farmstead, Jacqueline and Josiane are already south of Barcelona, heading down the AP7. Josiane is knocked out in the passenger seat in a deep sleep, aided by a sedative, her mouth slack. Jacqueline stays in the slow lane, mindful not to attract the attention of the many *gendarmes* and *guardia civil* she's passed along the way. In her purse are the false identity documents Mikko Eilaanen provided her with. She will board the ferry from Alicante to Algiers this afternoon as Marilena Albert from Nancy, along with her daughter, Thérèse Albert.

As they rumble on down the Spanish motorways, the sharp morning light growing hazy and mellow as the day gathers pace, Jacqueline's mind slips back to the past, to the first few years after the accident. In early 2013 she was finally discharged from the psychiatric hospital where she'd been incarcerated since the accident. She'd been on suicide watch and had been given lithium to curb what the doctors described as hallucinations. But Jacqueline knew them for what they were: real memories. What she was seeing, over and over, as lifelike as her own reflection in the mirror, was a vision of Elisa's face the split second before the car ploughed into Jacqueline's family and obliterated it. It may have been the briefest of glimpses, but it was enough to sear Elisa's face into Jacqueline's memory.

In those early days after the accident, when she would lie awake for days on end until they held her down and medicated her, she talked constantly out loud to the woman in her mind. 'I saw you,' she would say. 'I saw you. And you saw me, you must have done, coming towards you with my bleeding, silent babies. But you ran away. You left me there, alone, with all that death. But I know your face. Your face is burnt into my brain. And I'm going to find you. Somehow, someday I will find you, no matter what.'

Marcus Meling had accepted his punishment without question, even though he was given the strictest sentence ever for manslaughter in Norway. Jacqueline hated him with a white-hot rage, but at least he was behind bars and genuinely tormented by guilt. That much was obvious to her when she went to see him. It was guilt that had made him break down and admit to her that she was right, that he hadn't been alone in the car. And it was Elisa she truly wanted to punish – for running away and continuing her seemingly perfect life as though nothing had happened, as though Jacqueline's husband and child were less important than a speck of dirt caught underneath her shoe.

Over time, Jacqueline became increasingly obsessed with Elisa Blix and her family. Jacqueline's own precious daughter, Josiane, was returned to her in the fall of 2013 and soon blossomed into a confident and contented child despite what had happened to her. But, still, all Jacqueline could see was Elisa Blix. She was determined to take everything from her. Everything.

But now it's Jacqueline who's in danger of losing it all, again. She has already sacrificed Le Tachoué and all the irreplaceable memories it holds. If she is caught now, she will lose Josiane too. Her darling daughter. All that she has. All that she really needs. She glances anxiously in the rearview mirror, alert to every flashing light, however distant. It wasn't supposed to come to this. She was supposed to be at home in this moment, at Le Tachoué, where she grew up and where her children should have grown up.

She sees Lucia in her mind, running wild and free through the fields at Le Tachoué, long dark hair flying in the wind, her laughter echoing down the valley. She sees the blurred silhouette of her, high up in her favorite tree, her giggles cascading to the ground like falling leaves. She sees her in the garden overlooking the snow-clad mountains, dancing around herself, Boulette and Samba barking and bleating, wagging tails and stomping feet, the little girl singing and laughing. *I love you, Lulu-Rose*, thinks Jacqueline. *All I wanted was to love you.*

Whatever happens next, this new life will necessarily be one of flight and secrets and borrowed time. But at least, for now, she is free.

Acknowledgements

A novel is a hugely collaborative undertaking, both on a professional and a personal level. Writing *Playdate* was a real joy – it reminded me of all the countless reasons why I love my job and wanted to be a writer. Still, there were moments of sheer panic and exasperation – no wonder, really, when you have a full cast of demanding characters in your head, chattering away and plotting vengeance across timelines and countries. I am lucky to have a solid support system around me for those times.

A huge thank you, as always, to my enthusiastic, encouraging agent extraordinaire, Laura Longrigg – I lucked out big time with you! Thank you also to the whole team at MBA Literary Agents, your work is deeply appreciated. A big thank you is due to Louisa Pritchard, whose hard work and enthusiasm is very much appreciated. Thank you also to Jill Marsal of Marsal Lyons Literary Agents, for everything you do for me in the United States.

To Madeleine O'Shea, my editor at Head of Zeus – thank you, merci, tusen takk – it is such a joy to work with you. I always look forward to our meetings and hearing your thoughts, and your insights have benefitted *Playdate* immensely. I'd also like to thank the whole team at Head of Zeus, I love working with all of you, and you make every occasion feel like a party.

Thank you to Lucy Ridout for your concise and hugely constructive insights into *Playdate*. A thank you is also due Eirik Husby Sæther, a Norwegian police investigator and fellow crime writer who was kind enough to talk me through police procedures in the event of a child abduction in Norway. I was also fortunate enough to receive unique and useful advice from Lillehammer native Kristin Marøy Stockman, so thank you. To my office colleagues at K19 Sandefjord – thank you for tolerating a highly reclusive writer, though my presence was mostly ghost-like, I enjoyed being surrounded by you all while writing *Playdate*.

I am fortunate to have acquired a nurturing and interesting community of writers over the years, including novelists across the world, and my much-loved writing group in Bath – thank you to each and every one of you.

Thank you to Tricia Wastvedt, for friendship, for sanity, for everything – I thank my lucky stars for you. Thank you to Kristina Takashina, for our wonderful and nurturing long-standing friendship. A big thank you is also due Rhonda Guttulsrod – for all the laughter, and for handling the tears with equal constancy – what a gift our friendship is. To Elisabeth Sandnes, Elisabeth Hersoug, Trine Bretteville, Sinéad McClafferty L'Orange, Olivia Foster, Krisha Leer, Renate Mjelde, Katrine Bjerke Mathisen, Richard and Elizabeth Bailey, and Barbara Jaques- thank you for being there.

Thank you also to Lisa Lawrence, for not pretending to have all the answers, and for the (very big) difference you make.

To the Norwegian School of London – thank you for

nurturing my littles in the best way so I could spend my days in a parallel universe creating this book.

Music is hugely important to me in the writing process, I simply do not write without it. *Playdate* was written to two songs on repeat, and these two will forever be the *Playdate* songs for me – so thank you to Moha La Squale for 'Ma Belle' and to Lana Del Rey for 'Venice Bitch'.

Finally, to my family – thank you for putting up with me and for enabling me to pursue a life as a writer. Oscar and Anastasia and Louison – thank you for tolerating your scatterbrained mother, and I hope you know that everything I ever do is for you – I love you. To my mother, Marianne, for all your help and support over the years, I would not have been able to do any of this without it – thank you. And thank you to Judy and Chris Hadfield, the best in-laws. Last but not least – thank you to Laura for adulting, for partnership, for home, and most of all for love.

About the Author

ALEX DAHL is a half-American, half-Norwegian author. Born in Oslo, she studied Russian and German linguistics with international studies, then went on to complete an MA in creative writing at Bath Spa University and an MSc in business management at Bath University.

A committed Francophile, Alex loves to travel, and has so far lived in Moscow, Paris, Stuttgart, Sandefjord, Switzerland, Bath and London. Her first thriller, *The Boy at the Door*, was shortlisted for the CWA Debut Dagger.